Kingdom Alliance

Robert Stanek

Ruin Mist Chronicles

This is a work of fiction. All the characters, names, places and events portrayed in this book are either products of the author's imagination or are used fictitiously. Any resemblance to any actual locale, person or event is entirely coincidental.

Ruin Mist: Kingdom Alliance

Reagent Press
Published by Virtual Press, Inc.

Cover design & illustration by Robert Stanek
ISBN 1-57545-070-4

Also by Robert Stanek

Ruin Mist Chronicles
Book One: Keeper Martin's Tale
Book Two: Elf Queen's Quest
Book Three: Kingdom Alliance
Book Four: Fields of Honor
Book Five: Mark of the Dragon

Ruin Mist Heroes, Legends & Beyond
Magic Lands & Other Stories

Sovereign Rule
Stormjammers

Table of Contents

TABLE OF CONTENTS

TABLE OF CONTENTS

Praise for Ruin Mist &

Keeper Martin's Tale

"A gem waiting to be unearthed by millions of fans of fantasy!"

"Brilliant… an absolutely superior tale of fantasy for all tastes!"

"It's a creative, provoking, and above all, thoughtful story!"

"It's a wonderful metaphor for the dark (and light) odyssey of the mind."

"The fantasy world you have created is truly wonderful and rich. Your characters seem real and full of life."

The Reaches

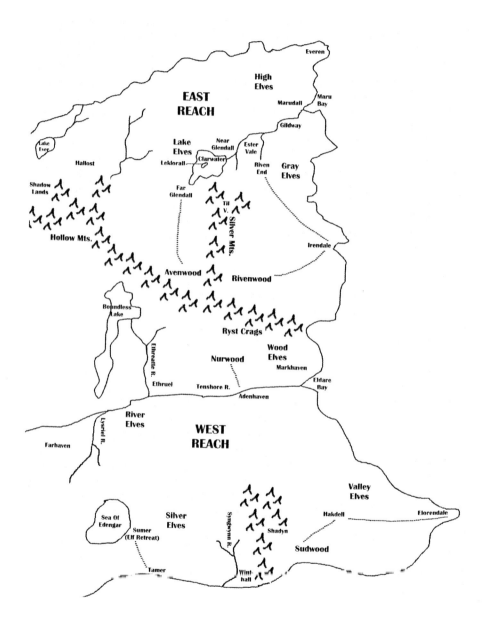

EAST REACH

High Elves

Everen

Marudall

Maru Bay

Gildway

Lake Elves

Near Glendall

Ester Vale

Gray Elves

Leklorall

Clarwater

Riven End

Lake Ever

Hallost

Shadow Lands

Far Glendall

Til. V.

Silver Mts.

Hollow Mts.

Irendale

Avenwood

Rivenwood

Boundless Lake

Ryst Crags

Ethreatle R.

Nurwood

Wood Elves

Markhaven

Ethruel

Tenshore R.

Eldare Bay

Adenhaven

River Elves

Lysriel R.

WEST REACH

Farhaven

Valley Elves

Sea Of Edengar

Silver Elves

Sumer (Elf Retreat)

Hakdell

Florendale

Syngwynn R.

Shadyn

Sudwood

Tamer

Wint- hall

Great Kingdom

Under-Earth (Lands of Greye)

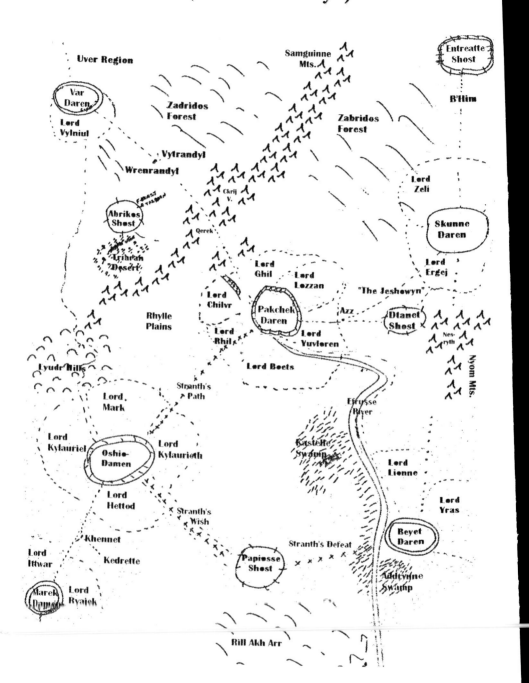

Chapter One:
Unto the Winds

Adrina shivered uncontrollably, and the more she shivered, the more she cried. She cried because she felt so desperately alone and because she felt utterly responsible for all that had happened. She, after all, had been the one who longed for change, and change had come in the form of a dark storm that threatened to sweep away everything she cared for and everything her family had worked so hard to maintain over these many past years.

As she looked on, the carriage master turned onto the main thoroughfare of the East–West Road and for a fleeting moment as the carriage mounted a small hill, she caught a last glimpse of the West Deep off in the distance. The waters, deep blue and ever tranquil, seemed to be calling out to her, "Don't leave. Stay."

She did long to stay but she couldn't have made and kept her promise to Rudden Klaiveson even if she had wanted. Her heart and thoughts were miles away, lost in secret thoughts of the elves Seth and Galan. And though Rudden and his family had opened their hearts to her, she could not open her heart to them. Klaive was not Imtal, and it was not, nor would it ever be, her home. She was confident of this as she was of no other thing.

Still, the past two weeks in Klaive hadn't been all bad, and she had Valam to thank for urging her to change her mind and temporarily postpone her return to Imtal. Just as the baron, baroness and their son had been, the people of Klaive had been kind to her. They came to the streets to greet her and Rudden whenever they left Klaive Keep. Gentlemen would remove their hats and bow. Ladies in the flowing dress of the day would offer flowers and children would chase after them laughing through the streets.

Adrina smiled, wiped tears from her eyes. She leaned her head out the window, turning to look back at Klaive, half expecting to see Rudden chasing the carriage and her entourage. But Rudden was nowhere to be seen along the long dusty road, and it was just as well for Adrina had broken his heart, though it had not been her intent.

She switched to the carriage seat opposite her and removed the cover from the painting the Baron had commissioned of her and Rudden. In the picture, Rudden had a broad smile and he held her hand. She remembered the warmth of his hands in hers and smiled. It had taken several days for the painter to complete his work and many long, quiet hours of standing and holding hands.

Her leaving Klaive without allowing the Baron to publicly announce the betrothal had been a betrayal of the unspoken promise her presence spoke of. She disgraced Rudden's family to be sure, but the thing she couldn't forget or forgive herself for was the hurt she caused Rudden. She could see the anguish and pain in his eyes clearly, even now, and unexpectedly, her heart and eyes mirrored that anguish and that pain, and it was the source of the emptiness she felt.

In her mind's eye, she saw her mother, Queen Alexandria, nodding, giving silent approval to the idea that swept in from the corners of her mind. She laughed, and the laughter was almost healing. She moved the curtains aside from the coachman's window, speaking quietly to the waiting attendant.

The coached turned. The riders in her entourage followed. She smiled.

***

"Ahoy, the Mouth of the World!" screamed the lookout.

The call was quickly relayed throughout the whole of the Scarlet Hawk, followed by a call of "Down the main sails! Oarsmen to the ready!" from the ship's captain.

Vilmos avoided the tangle of sailors amidships and raced to the bow. He and Xith had left the seaside town of Eragol the previous day and the Mouth of the World, a natural river cave that cut under the Rift Range near Jrenn, was their destination.

He swallowed a heart-sized lump in his throat when ahead in the distance he saw only ice-capped mountains on both sides of the river. As he looked on, a small dark space within the gray stone of the mountain seemed to grow and grow until the darkness was a thing that seemed would swallow the whole of the ship, and indeed it did, just as the captain called out, "Lanterns, fore and aft!"

Lanterns soon cast a dull glow into the darkness. No light reflected back to say that the rocks were close around them—or to say that anything was close around them for that matter. Everything seemed dead calm and just as the ship seemed to stand still in space and time, Vilmos heard the low thumping of the pacekeeper's drum. The oarsmen struck their oars. The Scarlet Hawk lurched forward. Soon the rowing became a smooth seesaw that hinted of movement and progress through the darkness.

"Vilmos, come away from the bow!" yelled Xith, "You don't want to be standing there."

Vilmos gripped the staff Xith had given him in Quashan'. "Is it always this dark here?"

"Sometimes darker," replied Xith, "Sometimes it is a place that resembles its namesake more so than any would like." Xith didn't give Vilmos a chance to reply as he led the boy below deck. "Gather your belongings quickly. We won't have much time once the ship is docked to get passage across the river to Jrenn."

Vilmos took to the task of packing without complaint. He wouldn't miss the Scarlet Hawk or the bucket that had been a constant companion during the journey. He knew he didn't have sea legs. Still, the voyage was his first and the open river was truly a remarkable place.

He and Xith had made many stops on their journey north to Eragol. He had seen Mir, Veter, Klaive, Heman and many sights in between. The shaman had been secretive of most of his activities and he was learning not to ask too many questions. Still his mind filled with questions—oh so many questions—and it seemed he would never get answers.

As he packed he thought about Efryadde, whose path Xith said he followed as a human mage in training. He knew of Efryadde from the Great Book, and what little he knew troubled him. The darkness had overtaken Efryadde, and in the end those he trusted most had betrayed him.

Calls went up from the crew as the Scarlet Hawk came to a full stop. He looked up from his task to find Xith regarding him. "To Jrenn and then to Solntse?" He asked.

Xith nodded and led the way to the top deck. "Stand close now, we have to move fast if we are to get across the river today."

As the two emerged from below, Vilmos' eyes lit with wonder at the sight of lanterns spreading out in every direction, revealing the outline of enormous docks and many ships in the port. He shouldered his bags and gripped his staff tightly. Lanterns overhead, suspended in the darkness by unseen ropes, lit their way along the docks.

All around them sailors, merchants and travelers hurried about their business. Everyone, Xith included, moved with a sense of purpose, seemingly oblivious to the fact that just beyond the shrouded yellow of the lanterns lay absolute darkness. Vilmos practically had to run to keep up with the shaman, and he did so with a sense of urgency because he didn't want to lose Xith in this crowd, in this place.

As they reached the long straight run that led to the innermost section of the docks, Vilmos stopped. Ahead of him, no more than a hundred paces away, was open water, and across the open water was a city in the center of the docks. This journey with Xith had opened his eyes to the wonders of the world, but none was as grand as the sight of the floating city ahead.

From this distance he could see the gentle swaying of the water as it rippled beneath the city, and, in the dark waters ahead, rowboats, whose paths were lit by a single lantern suspended from a tall pole aft, moved back and forth like carriages following unseen roads.

Xith hurried toward a line of rowboats at the end of one of the docks and Vilmos truly did have to run to catch up. For the sum of two coppers an oarsman took Xith and Vilmos to the inner docks of Jrenn.

The inner docks were very different from those used by the large sailing boats. They were low to the water and lined with tiny piers that made it easy to dock small boats, such as the rowboat they were in, anywhere along the floating circle of the city. The trick, however, was to find a section of pier that was unoccupied, and this turned out to be more of a problem than Vilmos imagined.

Xith solved the problem by giving the oarsman two more pieces of copper, immediately after which the oarsman docked and bid the two farewell.

***

"Until spring then," said Adrina turning back to the carriage.

Rudden smiled and kissed her hand before he let go. "Until spring."

She regarded Rudden, saying nothing more. Behind him, on the balcony overlooking the keep's courtyard, she saw the baron and baroness.

The baron stood still and there was a slight smile playing on the corners of his lips. The baroness's right hand was touched to her cheek and there was delight in her eyes. But it was Rudden that she was focusing on.

It was as if she was seeing him for the first time as the man he was and not as the man everyone else wanted her to see. He was tall with fair hair that showed his heritage and bright eyes that seemed to ask questions of her even now. He was the same man that had traveled all the way to Imtal just to meet her and then rushed to Quashan' to bring supplies to the beleaguered city after the battle Great Kingdom had nearly lost, but yet he wasn't. Things had changed and her heart had changed—and it had all happened in space of a few heartbeats.

She turned away. The attendant helped her into the coach, closing the door behind her. The coachman took his position. The Knight Brigade, Klaive Keep's most elite mounted horsemen, took to the saddle.

As the coach started out of the courtyard, she turned to look back. Rudden waved and she smiled more deeply. In her heart, she knew she had made the right decision. The journey from childhood to womanhood wasn't an easy one, but she would undertake it—it may lead her to a place quite unexpected.

Chapter Two:
The Long Road

Emel spurred Ebony Lightning on and the great black stallion charged across the open field with a speed that few other horses could match. As a ranking member of his father's company, he had more responsibilities than ever before in his life and none so important as the safekeeping of the elves who accompanied the battle-weary group of Kingdomers as they returned to Imtal.

He cursed low under his breath as he urged Ebony to even greater speeds, vowing to Great Father that he would find the truth of the matter before him no matter the cost. On the return trek, his father, Ansh Brodst, King's Knight Captain, had opted to take the faster, more dangerous route north. They took the Old Kingdom road through Moeck, skirting the Belyj Forest, Fraddylwicke Swamp and the Dead Sea, braving the Cliffs of D'Arndynne in rains that had swept far braver men into the sea and from this world.

But they braved and surpassed the deadly cliffs without mishap, and it was within the lands of Fraddylwicke that the trouble had occurred. At first, the onlookers had been curious, to be truthful, and so no one could have foreseen what was to come. Still, there was little excuse for failure and absolutely no excuse for forgetting one's ancestry.

Ancestry in a place such as Fraddylwicke was everything. For it was here, in lands as harsh and desolate as any found in the whole of the kingdoms, that the Blood Soldiers had been born and here that thousands upon thousands had died defending a stretch of land whose only value was in the boundaries that its borders represented.

Dnyarr the Greye, the last great Elven King, had laid siege to Fraddylwicke Castle two times during the Race Wars in his attempt to gain the southlands. The first siege lasted over one hundred years, which wasn't enough time for young elves to grow to maturity but lasted generations for the men who defended the fields with their blood and their lives. Yet, if such a thing was unimaginably horrible to endure for those who served, could one possibly imagine a thousand years of such existence, as was the case of the last great siege?

Or could one doubt without any certainty that after the final victory in the fields around Fraddylwicke that those who survived were no longer what they once were? So when the victorious sought to rule the lands of Man, it should have been no surprise that divided kingdoms united against them and their allies, pushing them back to the dark corners of the world and, ultimately, leaving them forgotten like the past from which they came.

Emel Brodstson never should have forgotten this and his father, Ansh Brodst, shouldn't have either. For the blood in their veins was that of those who Emel now eyed with a murderous rage as he chased them across the sodden field. Yet a distant kinship didn't stop his sword arm or cause him to slow Ebony's thunder as he ran down the last of the attackers.

By the time he returned to the company, the berserker rage in his blood had passed, but its short presence within had changed him in ways that he later would not be able to explain. In a way, it made him less human, less a man—but someone who could separate himself from his feelings and find only the burning rage within could never see this. It would only be apparent later, much later, to those who knew him before this pilot light of rage was ignited.

***

Vilmos awoke suddenly in the darkness, staring about the strangely shaped room as it shifted with the movement of the water beneath the floating city. He and Xith had not made it out of Jrenn the previous day and had rented a room at an inn instead. Now he was alone in the darkness and Xith was nowhere to be seen—*or was he?*

Vilmos stood and walked to the far corner of the room where there was an alcove. He moved quietly and carefully. It took a moment for his eyes to adjust to the brightness of the glowing orb the shaman held in his outstretched hands. He saw images flash by in the orb as if the shaman was looking for a thing he could not find.

The shaman's face, lit dully by the glow of the orb, reflected frustration, and he was muttering to himself. "Step aside; move about so that I may see."

Vilmos leaned on his haunches, taking the weight off his feet. The flash of images was hypnotic and as he looked on it was as if he was being drawn into the orb. Soon it seemed he was standing within the glow of the orb itself and the images of the world—vivid and real—were before him.

He took a deep breath, closed his eyes and waited. When he opened his eyes again, hoping that he would be standing in the room of the inn, he instead found that nothing had changed. Large as life images still played before his eyes—and even more strange, the images called to him.

Stunned panic set in. He forced himself to rip his eyes away from the hypnotic flash. It was then that he knew for sure he was indeed standing within the orb. His heart started racing. He twisted his head back and forth like a trapped animal. He was about to take a step backward, away from the flashing world, when a strong hand firmly clasped his right elbow.

He turned and saw Xith standing beside him.

"Don't move," said the shaman. "Dangerous, often lethal, to do so."

"Where are we?"

"You mean, where are you? I just followed as you were drawn into the orb. Doesn't happen often mind you, but it does happen. You were drawn into the orb for a reason."

"Is this a part of the training? You said the training was to begin."

"Vilmos, my boy, your education is never-ending and always ongoing." Xith laughed, a fleeting laugh. His expression became dark and serious. "Dnyarr's orb is one of the greatest powers in all the realms. I don't pretend to understand, understanding is beyond the likes of those of this world. I only know what I can do with it and what others before me have done with it."

Vilmos took a deep breath in an attempt to calm himself. "Why does it want me?"

"Why indeed," said Xith, "Why indeed. I should like to think it has something to do with our present course—"

Xith stopped abruptly as the glow of the orb around them disappeared and the scene before them exploded to life as never before. The two raced through a great forest, and as they raced onward the mountains in the distance grew ever closer.

Soon the air around them grew cold as snow-capped peaks raced beneath their feet. In the distance now, they could see a swarm of flying beasts in the sky.

"Dragons?" cried out Vilmos as they raced into the midst of a raging battle.

Xith didn't answer.

As they raced on, Vilmos saw two winged serpents locked in combat in the center of it all. They were larger and fiercer than any of the others around them. Their great wings beat at the air as their massive jaws locked one upon the other.

Just when Vilmos and Xith were about to crash into the fighting beasts, the two dragons turned as one and stared directly at the men before them. They spoke then in a language that was long gone from the world as everything around them began to fade away.

Reality came crashing in. The two were left standing in their rented room, staring at the glowing orb in Xith's outstretched hand. They didn't speak for the span of many heartbeats, the silence burning the images deeper into their minds.

***

The coach and the horsemen made fair progress along the East–West Road. By the end of the fourth day, the group reached the crossroads that would take them north to Ispeth, Mellack and then on to Imtal. Adrina was tired of the soft cushions of the coach. She longed for the leather of the saddle and wanted nothing more than to feel the open road all around her.

She passed the time thinking of Imtal and all that had happened since leaving home. In her mind, it seemed only yesterday that she was leaving Imtal with garrison soldiers all around her as they journeyed south to Alderan. But arrival in Alderan hadn't brought anything that they thought it would. Instead they discovered Alderan had been captured by King Jarom's soldiers and Quashan' was next as Jarom sought to capture the key cities that would give him control of the southlands.

In her mind it was clear that the elves, Seth and Galan, single-handedly changed the course of the Battle of Quashan'. Galan had helped guide her through the treachery of William's camp, and it was there that she had convinced William to quit the field, turning the tide in the Kingdom's favor. Seth had helped guide the scattered Kingdom forces defending the walls of Quashan', and it had been his superhuman speed and skill alone that had pushed back attackers more than once. Together the elves had communicated over the distance, using only the power of their minds, and giving the Kingdomers another advantage on the field.

No, Adrina had no doubt of their deeds. She only hoped her father, the king, had the good sense to listen to their words when they sought his support.

Outside the windows of the carriage she heard Landon, Chief Knight of Klaive Keep, call the group to a halt. The carriage kept moving, albeit at a slower pace, until she could see the doors of a clapboarded inn. The waiting attendant opened the carriage door.

The carriagemaster swept her from the carriage and hurried her to a room inside the inn that had already been prepared. She thanked the carriagemaster as he let himself out and bid her a good evening. All the pampering was going to her head. She had never been treated so well—in Imtal, attendants knew she loathed such foot to hand pampering—and she was never so miserable.

She longed for conversation. Open, honest conversation, angry, heated conversation, any conversation. She would have talked to anyone, if there were anyone to talk to. "Is this what true royalty is like?" she wondered aloud. "I'd rather be tarred and feathered."

"Be careful what you wish for," said a voice from the shadows.

Adrina turned, startled. She raised the flame on the oil lamp beside the bed to cast a brighter glow about the room.

She was frightened, but only barely so. In truth, returning to Imtal was more frightening.

Returning to Imtal meant opening many old wounds and

remembering things that she didn't want to remember. For years Imtal's walls had symbolized and housed her fears. The walls were the keepers of secrets she had worked hard to forget. But when she returned—and proved to herself that one could get beyond Imtal's walls—she would have to look beyond and within those walls.

So as she stared into the eyes of the one who sat waiting, she had the dark desire that she should never return to Imtal. And as the other smiled, deeply, darkly, she thought her wish would indeed come true.

***

Xith closed his palm about the orb and then released his grip on Vilmos' arm. He staggered backward, his strength clearly gone. It was only Vilmos' quick response that kept Xith from falling.

Vilmos helped Xith to a chair, took a seat opposite the shaman. "I'm frightened, Xith," he said quietly, "I just don't understand."

"As am I," said Xith, "More is at hand than I thought. To be sure, we must begin earlier than I planned and for that I am truly sorry."

Vilmos turned his great brown eyes in a wide circle about the room. "No, you aren't listening. I think I've made the wrong decision. I want to go home. I want to go home to Lillath now!"

"What?"

"Magic is evil! Why should I learn such a thing?"

"No Vilmos, you are very wrong. Magic is not evil."

"Magic destroys!"

"Magic can be evil if used in the wrong hands, so can all things. Money is the worst evil of all, but if used properly it can be used for good. You learn magic for the purpose of good and not evil. I would think you would have accepted this now, particularly after Quashan'."

"Magic tears things apart, it destroys! It destroys everything!"

"Don't be so hasty in your judgment!" Xith was almost angry; he had to calm himself before he continued. "Magic is only evil if the person using it is evil. Those of weak mind are easily overcome by the greed for power and too much power can be an evil thing. This is why you will learn to control the gifts you have been granted. This is why you must learn patience. Great power in unskilled hands is useless; great power in skilled hands can shape mountains."

Vilmos shook his head. He watched Xith but in the back of his mind he saw dragons battling in the sky. Somewhere in the dark corners of his mind he knew what it was that they fought over and it was this thing that terrified him. He shouted in a booming voice, "But he will return!"

"The dark one is a myth, a legend." Xith carefully shaped the truth. "He is not real. He is real only in our imaginations. The legend was created long before the Blood Wars… Maybe he existed at one time, long, long ago. I don't know for sure. No one does, but I do know he does not now exist. Now his existence is only through lore and myth, perpetuated by those who wish to control. They are the true evil; they are what we should fear. For it is they who manipulate such things to their own ends, using it to justify all that they do."

Xith continued, although Vilmos had stopped listening to the words. "During the time of the gathering they will try to destroy us to prevent the coming… Yet a few, a very select few, have used the myth for the good of all. They have turned it around. They use it to prepare us for what the future will bring and this is why we study the histories. We must learn from the past and when the time comes we must be ready so that we do not repeat it."

Xith rambled on, speaking words he should have never said to Vilmos, but for a reason unknown to him he spoke anyway. Vilmos half listened but couldn't shake the images from his mind. "But if magic is not evil, why is it forbidden? Why do the Priests of the Dark Flame destroy magic?"

Xith collected his thoughts. "It is to prevent the corruption the future will bring. You must learn to use your magic to its fullest. You must learn to master it before it masters you."

"What?" asked Vilmos not understanding as the images in his mind's eye faded, leaving him confused.

"*Remember*," said Xith using the dominating nature of the voice, "the fate of all the lands will one day rest in your hands. You must believe, Vilmos. Believe because you have to believe and because you want to believe. He does not exist. You must believe and remember only this. You must be ready for our journey to Under-Earth. Forget all else..."

Chapter Three:
An Unexpected Discovery

Vilmos and Xith departed Jrenn with a protected caravan bound for the Free City of Solntse. For days afterward, the unchanging sun beat down upon them. Xith's skin, unnaturally weathered and dark, proved to have better tolerance for this than Vilmos' fair skin, which was now burned by the sun and wind.

The sound of dozens of feet and hooves crunching the stones of Great Kingdom's High Road echoed in his ears. A steady gale coming out of the mountains to the north carried the dust of the Barrens across River Krasnyj. The handkerchief tied around his nose and mouth did little to keep out the dirt, and as he ran his hand across his cheek the gritty film made him long for a hot bath and clean clothes.

Sunset was near and more than anything he wanted to hear the caravan master call out the final stop of the day. The ten garrison soldiers that protected the caravan were the only ones on horseback. While two stayed at the fore of the caravan and two to the rear, the others clustered near the carriage ferrying a lady of some standing in the Kingdom. He caught glimpses of her pale face from time to time through the carriage's white lace curtains.

He was surprised when the city of Solntse came into view and even more surprised when the caravan reached the city before nightfall. As they passed under the walled city's outer gatehouse he watched the gatekeepers who stood watch, certain that at any moment they would unloose volleys from their readied crossbows. But once they were safely within the city's protective walls, his thoughts and attention turned to the grandeur of the streets and buildings spread out before him.

Xith held Vilmos by the scruff of the collar to ensure he watched where he was going while he was gawking, and gripped the collar tighter suddenly to pull him away from a brightly clad female who was beckoning for him to follow her. Xith sighed; Vilmos didn't know that this was where his journey to the destiny that awaited him would truly begin.

Several times he stepped around men who simply stopped dead in their tracks in front of him. Once he bumped into one, almost causing a ruckus, and Xith dragged him quickly away. Finally, Xith gave him an ultimatum, "Follow me and do only what I do. Or I'll leave you in the street to fend for yourself!"

Vilmos took the threat seriously and did exactly as Xith said. This allowed Xith to relinquish his firm grip on his collar.

They passed through the central portion of the city with its high, three-story structures reaching into the sky and then made their way to the city's southernmost sector. Most of the buildings in this area were saloons or 'rest houses' as Xith called them. The heavy smell of whiskey and perfume wafted out onto the street to assault their nostrils. Along with these odors came the sound of music and laughter, singing and even brawling, coming on a puff of air as patrons would enter or exit.

Vilmos would sneak a quick glance inside as doors swung inward or outward; the sites within often amazed him: men drinking tall tankards of ale or slugging down small glasses of this or that, Vilmos really couldn't tell what. Women sitting on men's laps or dancing happily.

A large crowd was gathered off one of the side streets they passed now. Shouts and the clashing of blades filtered to his attentive ears. His mind filled with glee and he tried to dart toward the fracas. He would have made it cleanly away too, if Xith didn't snatch at his collar, latching onto a clump of hair instead. With a shriek, Vilmos stopped.

"Don't stray," said Xith. "Perhaps tomorrow we can return."

"Tomorrow they will be gone. The square will be empty. I've never seen a *real* brawl." Vilmos looked dejected. His eyes grew sullen.

"I assure you that tomorrow they will be in that same courtyard from sunup until sunset. And that is not a brawl."

"But I would rather watch today—"

"Quiet!" said Xith.

The avenues they walked along gradually grew narrower and the saloons and shops became dingier and dirtier. Xith took on a slower, more aware gait as a feeling of unease filled his mind.

Vilmos noticed this, and instead of peering into the places he passed he clung close to Xith and watched his surroundings with wide, wary eyes. Unconsciously, he clinched his fists to the ready, not that he really knew how to use them, just that he felt more secure.

Xith stopped in front of a large, squat inn and motioned Vilmos to follow him inside. Vilmos cast his eyes up and down the building's rough outer face, looking hard at the shattered windows and the dilapidated shutters; the run-down place had definitely seen better days. "It isn't that bad on the inside," said Xith patting Vilmos on the back.

When Vilmos stepped inside, he knew he had been right. The interior *was* in as poor a shape as the exterior. At least the last place they had stayed in had been somewhat pleasant inside. Vilmos looked about unhappily.

"Don't worry," said Xith, "we'll stay here just long enough to get the additional supplies we need and that's all."

"Here?" stammered Vilmos in disbelief.

"Believe me there are worse places to stay and you'll find that the rooms are actually quite nice. Trust me."

Xith got them a room, which wasn't actually quite nice, but at least it was clean.

"See I told you to trust me," said Xith swatting Vilmos on the head. "Besides we can stay here cheaply and without drawing attention to ourselves."

"Why? Is there someone watching us?"

In the midst of formulating a list of all the things they would need for the journey ahead Xith didn't offer Vilmos an immediate response. After a time he said, "Stay here, I have to attend to a few things. I'll be back."

***

Several hours passed. Vilmos waited patiently. His thoughts wandered and a cataclysm of images swam before his eyes. He saw the days with Xith and how dramatically his life changed. He couldn't truly understand why this was all happening to him but he tried. Everything was moving so fast and the little boy inside him was crying out to go back home to see his mother and father, but another voice within told him he could never go home, would never go home again.

With eyes unfocused and thoughts jumping to and fro, he stared blankly at a wall. Eventually this inward reflection slowed and fell silent as he slipped into a light sleep. He awoke a short time later when Xith returned muttering loudly to himself. He caught pieces of what the shaman was saying and to him it sounded as if Xith was having an argument with himself about money and thieves.

"What's wrong?" he asked excitedly, cueing in on "thieves."

"Bloody street thievery I tell you. The prices here are worse than I've ever seen and it cannot bode well."

"Prices for what?"

"Horses among many other things." The bags Xith was carrying fell to the floor with a loud clank as he dropped them. He sat down, pulled off his boots, emptied their contents unceremoniously onto the floor, then lay back and closed his eyes, yawning mightily. "I tell you. In all my years I've never had to pay these prices. It's like the merchants can smell winter on the air and they know that soon afterward the supplies will dry up. In winter, I would expect to pay such prices, but not now—it is too early."

***

Later that evening Xith and Vilmos ventured out to the streets. The streets after dark looked more ominous to Vilmos. The people he passed, both male and female, appeared to be in somber moods, and were darkly clad with long flowing capes or large collared cloaks. Flickers of light and the outlines of people speaking in muffled voices loomed in the alleyways, but thankfully the dreadful portent was absent as they entered a nearby pub.

The atmosphere of the small pub was light and happy. Xith ordered gruel for two and they sat waiting. Vilmos watched the patrons come and go. He studied the clothes they wore and the weapons they carried, yet his main interest was in catching pieces of what they were talking about as they passed.

As he ate gruel and black bread, his attention remained on a man who sat in the corner, his back to the wall, opposite the most beautiful woman he had ever seen. The man, obviously a fighter of some sort, wore a roughly hewn chainmail shirt with heavy leather underings and an odd branks.

From time to time, he could see the man's hands, which were covered in a mailed half-glove that left the thumbs and forefingers exposed. Taking inventory of the man's weaponry as he had the others, he had seen the great sword slung crossways over the man's back—even now he could glimpse the jeweled hilt—and an auxiliary blade of considerably smaller size sheathed in his belt.

Of the woman, he could only see the long, black hair and sometimes he'd catch a glimpse her face. She had come in separately from the man and all eyes in the place had been cast upon her as she crossed the room, but when she sat down with the broad-backed warrior everyone returned to their own business—everyone except him. He couldn't look away.

A hue of somber amber, the dress the woman wore was elegant. The dress had lace at the top that swelled around ample breasts and flowed down her arms in an open and obviously revealing fashion that caused him to blush and avert his eyes until she passed in front of him. She possessed no weapons, save for her intoxicating, cold gray eyes, which were down turned.

He watched the two as they sat still, neither uttering a word. The man from time to time would grind his teeth against the iron bit in his mouth or twist his mailed fist into the table. The woman sat still, her head turned away, as if she was suspended in time. He pitied them, though he did not know why.

As the pub's owner delivered a second round of gruel and black bread, he turned his eyes away from the couple but, as the fish to the lure, his gaze returned shortly afterward and he stared openly as he ate. He wondered what the couple's story could be and when finally he could no longer hold his tongue in check, he asked, "Those two. Is it odd or is it just me?"

Xith didn't have to look to see whom Vilmos was talking about; he knew. "The warrior is an indentured man and the woman is of the street. You should concern yourself with other things."

Vilmos didn't think that, though. He saw another story, especially in the man's eyes.

***

The meal finished, the drink consumed, Xith and Vilmos returned to their rented room. Vilmos was quiet for a long time, content to sit on the edge of the bed and stare at the wall. This puzzled Xith, as he hadn't seen Vilmos like this before and he didn't know what could be wrong. He asked several times what was wrong, but Vilmos didn't respond.

"Are you sick?" asked Xith, "You haven't said a word since we ate. Usually you are teaming with a hundred different questions." Xith paused to collect his thoughts. "*Forget* about the two. We can't do anything for them."

The subtle directing of the voice stimulated Vilmos' subconscious. Again, Xith knew of a secret yearning.

"But why?" said Vilmos, "What could make someone so miserable? I could see pain on both their faces."

"He is a debtor. Once caught in the cycle, it can never be broken." Knowing something else was wrong, Xith fixed Vilmos with a discerning eye. Vilmos was referring to more than what he was talking about. He was also talking about himself, though he was not fully aware of this. "Tell me what is really bothering you, Vilmos?"

Vilmos shook his head. He heard Xith, but in the back of his mind he saw the warrior poised with the great blade at the ready. Vilmos called to the warrior but the warrior ignored him and walked away.

Chapter Four:
Return to Imtal

The walls of Imtal were ahead in the distance but this didn't improve Emel's demeanor. He was frustrated, angry and tired. When the garrison troops left Imtal they had numbered in the thousands. Now, those that returned—the survivors—numbered in the hundreds. How did one explain such a thing to the King? How did one explain such utter failure, followed by more failure? How did one explain losing the only good things to come of the Battle of Quashan'?

Emel did not envy his father this day. Ansh Brodst was sure to be stripped of his title as King's Knight Captain and the land grant that had gone with it. Emel himself, promoted in the field to Fourth Captain, Imtal Garrison, doubted the promotion would stand.

No, those returning would surely be cast out of the city and sent to the wild outposts: High Road, Serant, Reassae or worse: the territory outposts from which few ever returned.

Emel hung his head in shame as they passed within the protective gates of the city. He wished this day would end and didn't see how things could get any worse.

Fortunately, it was well into the evening and no one turned out to greet the returning soldiers. Even the heralds upon the walls had the good sense not to call out to mark the return.

The clatter of hooves and boots echoed along Imtal's cobbled streets for some time as the group slowly made their way toward the central district. Soon Emel could see torches lighting the way to the parade plaza within High King's Square. Even in the darkness, he could see the faces of the soldiers around him. Their expressions, once sad and grim, turned upward. Smiles replaced tears and, sometimes, tears of joy replaced frowns. It was good to be home regardless of the circumstance, and he knew this as well.

Just as the relief at being home faded, the group reached High King's Square. There, a miraculous sight awaited them. The square, save the central parade route, was filled to overflowing with Imtal's citizens, and the streets beyond the square were filled as well. The lines of people went on as far as he could see.

A sense of purpose returned to the group's actions. Soldiers walked with their heads up, digging their boots into the stones as they marched. Riders sat true in the saddle, reigns in one hand, the other hand up in greeting.

Emel maneuvered Ebony within the ranks until he rode beside his father. He reached out and clasped his father's arm, grinning broadly. "It's a homecoming I never thought I'd see!"

"And I as well," said Ansh Brodst, "But this night isn't over."

Impulsively Emel looked over his shoulder at the carriage behind his father. "Two dead elves won't please his majesty, that is for sure."

"Dying, not dead. Keeper Martin and Father Jacob are doing their best to see that the elves at least survive the journey to its end. After that, who can say."

"Dying, not dead," corrected Emel.

"I will release the company until the first day of the new moon so that they may be with their families. What is unspoken is that officers are not granted this leave."

"Yes of course father, I understand this."

"Your duty will be to work with the other captains to restructure the garrison and put these battle experienced soldiers into positions that best serve the Kingdom. Such experience is valuable, and it will be expected of you to make tough decisions in the name of the crown.

"Each of the fallen will need to be put to rest in the eyes of their families. You will take your share of the black sheets. You will get no special favors, you understand?"

Emel slowed Ebony's pace as the group prepared to stop. "I understand completely."

"No Emel, you don't understand," said Ansh Brodst as he raised a hand to command the group to a halt. "You earned the rank of captain in the field. Now you must earn the respect of those who know nothing and care not of your deeds. Don't take this lightly, or you will meet your end with your belly gutted in an empty field."

***

Except for the unexpected encounter in her room at the inn, Adrina's return to Imtal was uneventful. The Klaive Keep Knight's escorted her to Imtal, through the city streets, and conveyed her and her belongings directly to the palace proper. Most of the city was still deep in mourning the lost and the fallen, so her return was completely overlooked. Even her father, the king, did not turn out to welcome her home, and now she paced nervously in her room as she waited for the evening meal and a chance to speak with her father.

She was agitated because two of the knights refused to leave her side. "Rudden Klaiveson bade us to protect with our lives until your return to Klaive in the spring," they said when she urged them to go with the others, "And we gave a blood oath as such that cannot be broken by any command. Only death will cause us to leave your side."

She was also agitated because she couldn't find anyone with information on the elves. Emel was gone. Father Jacob wasn't in his quarters. Keeper Martin wasn't available: he was in council with her father. No one else she asked knew anything about the elves—not even the cooks, who always knew the scuttlebutt of the day.

The only good thing to come of her return home was a bath. A long hot bath that Myrial drew for her and she soaked in for what seemed hours.

Myrial was in Adrina's chambers now readying the wood for the evening fire. From time to time, Adrina could see the servant girl watching as she paced. Most of the time, Myrial's attention was on the wood that she stacked carefully.

"I think it's going to be cold tonight," said Adrina. "What do you think?"

Surprised at the direct question, Myrial dropped the wood she was carrying and then hurried about the floor picking it up. Adrina touched the girl's arm to stop her flitting about. At first, Myrial squirmed away as if Adrina's fingers burned into her skin, but soon she calmed.

"I think it is going to be cold tonight," repeated Adrina, "Don't you?"

"We played together as girls," whispered Myrial, "I remember Queen Alexandria holding my hand and yours. We'd walk through the gardens until we got to a new section and then she'd set to planting and we'd pretend to do the same. I was a fool in childhood to think we could be friends—I was a fool as a girl to think that by serving you well you would return my family honor. But you don't even remember who I am, let alone my name. So yes, yes I think it will be cold tonight, but you will not feel the chill of it—only I."

The words stung Adrina. She had blocked out just about everything from her childhood—everything around and before *that* day, the day she couldn't before bring herself to remember. She had walled off that day and with it, most everyone around her. "Your name is Myrial," said Adrina, "And I remember. I remember now, but I don't want to. How I wish I could forget again, to be numb is better than to remember."

"No," said Myrial, "Not if you remember the way I do."

"What do you mean? I remember and I cry."

"I remember and I laugh," said Myrial. "How could you do otherwise? She loved you so. You were her world, her everything. So how could you remember and not laugh? We had grand times in the gardens, in the halls, in the bathing pool, right here in this very room. The room that was hers before she left us."

Adrina was about to scream "US! WHAT DO YOU MEAN?" But she bit her tongue and said nothing. She would not take away Myrial's one joy: there was no joy in drudgery so there must be some joy somewhere.

"Do you remember," said Myrial with a laugh, "the day you got bit on the nose by a bee? Oh it was a grand and silly day. You and I were screaming, running around the garden, screaming and running, shouting, 'The bees, the bees!'

"Alexandria laughed and laughed as Izzy chased us: round and round in circles. Izzy was trying to put a salve on your nose and to calm us. But only Alexandria was able to catch and calm us. She caught us both in a great big embrace and we rolled with her on the ground to Izzy's dismay."

Adrina laughed a soft girlish laugh then as she remembered and saw with Myrial's eyes. She threw her arms around Myrial and cried, saying, "Where were you when my insides were being torn apart?"

"I was here," said Myrial, "right here. I was always right here, but you, you never left that day, and you only remembered what happened later… It is good to have you back Adrina, very good."

Adrina wiped tears from her eyes and regained her composure. "I should think that you will address me properly from now on. Do you understand?"

As if suddenly remembering her place, Myrial's smile faded. She curtsied and started to pick up the firewood that lay on the floor at her feet.

Adrina put a hand on the girl's shoulder. "No I mean, you should call me, Dri."

"Dri," said Myrial smiling as if remembering fondly. "I didn't think you remembered?"

"I did and I am sorry," said Adrina, "Can you ever forgive me?"

"If it is your wish, then it is so."

"No, I mean really and truly in your heart and not because it is your place but because it is what you want to do."

Myrial was silent for moment. "Dri, I don't think I can just yet. You hurt me, you really hurt me, and I came to know much more about *my* place than you can ever know. I sleep in the dirt many nights because there is no straw. I eat if there is food, when there is food. I do the tasks as the housemaster asks of me, even if those tasks take what little dignity I have left."

"What do you mean? What are you saying?"

"My family served yours for generations and in times past we earned some status. When that status was lost, we paid ten-fold for every favor we ever got. So now I do whatever I have to and I survive because I am a survivor. I won't give in or give up as easily as you."

Adrina was speechless for a moment. "My mother was my world. I could never understand why it happened and so I could never forget. I am passed the why now, and in time I think I will be able to accept it and perhaps to remember those days as you do. I will try, if you will try to forgive me. I should think there will be many changes around here from now on and starting with the dismissal of the housemaster!"

"Don't," said Myrial, "You'll only stir up a hornet's nest and then, and then…"

"And then what?" demanded Adrina.

"And then you'll go off and forget and I'll be left in a worse place, a place I won't be able to let myself go back to."

Adrina's expression became determined. She took Myrial's hand and led her from the room. Myrial tried to speak but Adrina wouldn't let her. Once they were in the lower level of the palace, she said, "Show me to the housemaster's room."

"Don't," said Myrial.

"Or what? Last time I checked, I was Princess Adrina and my father was King."

Myrial pointed out the housemaster's room. Adrina knocked on the door but didn't wait for an answer before trying to enter. When she found the door locked and no answer forthcoming, she began shouting, "Guards! Guards!"

The two knights of Klaive Keep, only steps behind Adrina, were the first to respond. Their presence surprised Adrina for she had forgotten they were even there. "Bust down the door!" she told them, "Bust it down now!"

The two knights pressed their weight against the door two times before the door crashed inward. Adrina stepped around the fallen door, dragging Myrial behind her.

The housemaster's chamber was huge—and rivaled her own lavish living quarters. Adrina found the housemaster in one of the rear rooms, sitting on a fluffy couch with several attendants catering to his whims. The knights of Klaive Keep were right behind her and behind them were many palace guards.

Adrina glared at the startled housemaster. "Housemistress!" she called out shrilly.

"House*master*, Your Highness. Assure you, I didn't know you'd returned. If I had, everything would've been in order. Promise you, if you tell what's wrong, I can fix it."

Adrina turned to Myrial. "Housemistress, what is this man doing in your quarters? I gave you express orders before I left that you are to run the household. If you cannot see fit to replace this man, I will send him to the gallows so that you have no excuse!"

The housemaster jumped to his feet, screaming, "The gallows? Why whatever for? Assure you I can train, I can train—"

"Myrial," said Adrina.

"Yes, Myrial," said the housemaster, "I'll be out of these quarters immediately and I'll train her. I want nothing of these quarters or this office, I assure you."

"Then you shall not mind being Myrial's man servant?"

The housemaster swallowed a gigantic lump in his throat. "It shall be an honor to serve," he said bowing deeply, his eyes betraying his anger.

Adrina turned to one of the guardsmen. "You, what is your name?"

"G-G-Garette. Garette Timmer."

"Swordmaster Timmer's son?"

The guardsman nodded.

"You are dismissed of all duties, save one. Your duty is to Housemistress Myrial. You are to see that no harm befalls her— ever. No order save mine or Myrial's shall you heed. It is my wish and my will. Send your captain to me if there is any disagreement."

Chapter Five:
The Competitions

Vilmos awoke. He looked around the room, not surprised to find he was alone. A cold breakfast was on the table next to the window.

He brushed sleep from his eyes, finding no cheer in the new day or the bright sunshine. As he scooped tasteless spoonfuls of thick, pasty gruel into his mouth, allowing it to slide across his tongue and down his throat without chewing, he stared out the window. A blank expression was on his face, and for a long while, as he thought about the shaman, the city below cried out to him. It was his to explore if he dared—the whole of the largest city in all the lands, the whole of the Free City of Solntse, was his.

The early-day sun shining through the window brought out sudden bravery. It seemed as if the sun was inviting him to come outdoors. Suddenly he was no longer content to sit indoors and wait idly, and so he hurriedly gulped down the last of the cold gruel.

**

After stepping out onto the dusty street, Vilmos veered left, ambling around several long blocks before deciding which direction to proceed in. Passing some of the dingier establishments he recalled from the previous day, he quickened his pace, content to continue straight for a time. At the next intersection he paused, unsure whether to turn left, right or proceed.

"Lost, boy?" called out a gruff voice.

Vilmos rolled his eyes upward, taking in the tall figure in a single, gradual panning glance. "N-no, not really."

"That's not much of a response," said the man, laughing.

Vilmos backed away warily. His eyes never straying from the long blade sheathed at the other's side. "I have to go now."

"Wait! Perhaps, I can help you find the place you're looking for."

"There is a square near here. I must have passed it. Good day to you, sir."

"Perhaps we're going to the same place. Describe the market you're looking for and maybe I can help."

Vilmos wanted to run but didn't. "It's not a market. I'll find it. No need to worry." Vilmos ran from the outstretched hand.

"You wouldn't be looking for the competitions, would you?"

Vilmos' eyes lit up as if the man had just offered him a piece of candy. "Maybe. Maybe I am; maybe I'm not."

"Not too sure of anything are you? Do you have a name, boy?"

Vilmos thought about the question; he didn't see any harm in answering it—*or did he?* "V-Vil... Vil... Vil-am. My name is Vilam, and yours?"

"Don't worry, your secret is safe with me," said the man, grinning as he tugged at the stubble on his chin. "I'm not supposed to be here either. Maybe we can both do the thing we're not supposed to be doing together. This is no place for a boy such as yourself to be about—and if you plan to go to the competitions, you had best take my hand."

Vilmos stepped into the street.

"If you're going to the competitions that is the wrong way. I'll guide you—for a price."

"For a price?" asked Vilmos, confident he had finally discovered the man's ploy.

"For you, my friend, a one-time fee: good for all time. All I would ask is—" Vilmos took another step away. He had no money and didn't know what the man would do if he refused the offer. "All I ask is a simple thing. You needn't be afraid of me. For, you see, when I said I'm not supposed to be here either, I was referring to…" The man switched to a low, whispering tone. "…viewing the competitions."

The man switched back to a fuller speech. "Allow me to introduce myself. Bladesman S'tryil, a ridesman by trade, a bladesman by necessity. But please don't call me by my name, as I said, I am not supposed to be here either. So, I will call you… Vilam… Is that correct?" Vilmos nodded. "You can call me, Greer. Do we have a deal?"

Vilmos nodded agreement again.

"You drive a hard bargain, Vilam. Come this way and you'd better walk beside me. As I said before, this is no place for a boy to be alone—" Vilmos glared at the man. "—If I were going to rob you. I'd've done that a long time ago. I wouldn't've even bothered talking to a boy. I'd've just grabbed you by the ankles. Just like this…"

The bladesman made a lunging motion with his right hand, reaching low and then flipping his gripped hand up. Vilmos flinched, imagining himself dangling upside down, both ankles gripped firmly by one burly hand.

"I'd've held you upside down until all the coinage dropped from your pockets. But you don't have anything in your pockets do you, Vilam?"

"Vilmos. My name is Vilmos."

"Vilmos is it?" S'tryil offered Vilmos his hand to seal their pact. "Well I shall stick with Vilam. Is that all right?"

Vilmos nodded. The two continued down the block, across the next, then turned right.

"Is this your first time at the competition?" asked S'tryil, not waiting for a response before continuing, "You see that long, high building there with the balcony? That's City Garrison Central Post. That's where the competitions take place every year. Now, if you can find that one building, for no other looks like it, you're there. And look, here we are."

Surprised, Vilmos looked away from his companion's face. The first bouts of the morning were already under way and a fair-sized crowd was gathered. Vilmos pushed his way into the circle beside the man he would call Greer. He reminded himself of this fact.

"Here stand in front of me, but don't take a step forward. You see that circle there? Good, don't break it, and if someone comes lunging at you out of the circle, in the name of the Great Father, jump out of the way!"

"Who's going to attack me?"

"No one, as long as you stick close. I was talking about the combatants. If they start to get too close, back away or you're liable to get a sharp blade stuck right where you don't want it." S'tryil motioned graphically with his hands. "They've taken people away every day so far. They just don't want to move out of the way. So mind my warning... Move, and be quick about it!"

"How many days does this go on?" asked Vilmos excitedly, swaying his small body to the reactions of the warrior to his right, the one he favored. The two men struggled with great battle swords, the kind Vilmos had seen yesterday.

"Weeks, until the final competitors are chosen," said S'tryil. Vilmos jumped back as the competitors battling in the circle came close. "And then those chosen will go on to train for many more weeks. There is a special grudge this year... Do you see the man seated up on the high balcony? He is Lord Geoffrey."

"Is he dead?" One of the fighters had just fallen.

The first match ended. The victor returned his great sword to the long scabbard strapped crossways upon his back, dipping the blade skillfully and quickly over his right shoulder with a casual, fluid motion that made the blade seem unencumbering. Then the victor raised both arms high over his head, waiting for the next challenger to enter the circle. The man on the balcony, the one Greer had called a lord, stood. A voice boomed out across the courtyard.

"Shalimar takes the first match. Who would challenge?"

A hush came over the crowd as the waiting began.

Vilmos pressed close to Greer and whispered, "Why is no one moving?"

"Stand still and silent!" hissed the bladesman.

Lord Geoffrey spoke again, "There is no challenger? Are there none worthy?"

"What's wrong?" asked Vilmos, "Why has the fight stopped? Is it over already? Did we miss it all?"

S'tryil snapped a hand to Vilmos' mouth. "Be still!"

"You there!" A hand pointed and all eyes followed its path. "Do you take the challenge?"

S'tryil swallowed hard. "No, my lord," he said in the gruff voice again, "I was just quieting my... 'm son. Please forgive me, my lord."

All eyes turned back to the balcony as Geoffrey continued, "Then I declare, Shalimar the—"

"Hold on," cried out a man from the crowd, hastily appending "My Lord."

The man, clad in light mail, entered the ring, removing the chain shirt as he did so. The next bout began, and with its commencement S'tryil removed the restraining hand.

"During relief you must say nothing," said the bladesman. "That man there is one of the best in the whole of the Free City. I may bout him one day, though not today."

"I am sorry," said Vilmos, "I didn't know. Why do you know so much about the competition? I thought you said you have never been here."

"Well that's not quite accurate; I said I'm not supposed to be here. I didn't say I've never been here."

The two combatants faced off. The winner of the first bout was clearly tired but this did not slow his attacks. A relentless, heavy arm drove the challenger to the far side of the circle, nearly chasing him beyond the line: a disqualifying step for the challenger.

"Do you see now why no one wanted to compete with this one?" asked S'tryil.

Vilmos nodded. He understood.

"He will be chosen if no others challenge him after this bout. He will join the others on the balcony..." Vilmos' eyes followed the gesturing hand up to the balcony. "I've seen him win five battles in one day. He is good, really good. Today should be his last day. Do you see the weariness in his eyes? He is fatigued. He will not last much longer, especially if there is another challenge, but I don't expect there to be."

Vilmos asked, "How do you know?"

"We'll have to wait." The bladesman smiled. "But only a true fool would enter the ring with so weary and fierce a competitor. Instead of quick victory, such a challenger more often than not ends up being carted away to the death house. They say, if you corner a snake and don't expect it to strike—to kill—you are to blame and not the snake."

"Those three?" Vilmos pointed to the men who stood behind the seated lord. "Did they go through the same... the same...?" Vilmos was unsure what word to use.

"Yes, they did. Do you see the man standing in the middle? The broadest one?"

"Yes."

"He's the lord's son—"

"Then he was assured a spot."

"I wish that were the case," said S'tryil, "I wish that were the case." After pausing momentarily to regard the sure victor in the contest, he continued. "The test of steel lasted six days for that one, a record I do believe. Many believe the same as you, and every year he teaches them the meaning of the word defeat. No, he is by far my biggest concern."

Vilmos was silent for a time. The match ended. The one called Shalimar won again; the challenger was carried out. Vilmos pursued no questions about the defeated man. He waited quietly, eyeing the dark, red stain that marred the hard dirt only a few steps away.

A new challenge never came. Vilmos saw glee in the jaded face that marched from the courtyard.

A ruckus erupted from the crowd amidst shouts of applause. Two men were shaking a stout, fat man and behind them another pair faced off about to brawl.

"Stand close!" shouted the bladesman.

Unsure whether to remain silent or speak again, Vilmos clung close to S'tryil. "What is wrong?" he whispered.

"This always happens. Someone doesn't want to pay their marker—and this happens. He'll pay or he'll suffer the consequences... Don't worry, the contest will continue. It always does." S'tryil turned his eyes back on the vacated circle. Vilmos did likewise. "One more," whispered the bladesman, not meaning for Vilmos to hear him.

"What do you mean? What one more?"

"Well, let's just say that the matches after next are the ones I came to see."

Vilmos, not knowing when to stop, asked, "What is that supposed to mean?"

"Don't worry, the next combatant is very skilled. So skilled in fact I'm confident he'll go on with the others, but that'll be days from now," said S'tryil. "There, you see the one stepping back into the circle? He is Shchander: quick and sharp. His attack is his best skill, not very good on the defense."

"Do you know all the fighters?"

"Quick, aren't you?" said the bladesman, "In a way, yes, I do." He was starting to like to the inquisitive youngster.

"If he's not very good defending, how come you think he will be the victor?"

S'tryil grinned. "You're smart aren't you? Watch the way he jabs. He'll get two to three thrusts for every one of his competitor's. I guarantee you. That's why he'll win. He never tires; it's amazing. The sad thing is that most of the would-be challengers know it. No, they're waiting for the next. The strongest have been holding back. They want a taste of the best, especially after his lordship's defeat in Imtal last winter. They figure he's getting old. Gray, if you know what I mean. Me, I don't think so. He's been the best for a decade now and, the Father willing, I think he'll make a comeback this year."

Vilmos nodded, which was a sign for the bladesman to keep mumbling on and on. It was strange that he told a boy things that he would not tell any other.

"Beat by a captain of the palace guard. Can you imagine the

thoughts that flooded his mind in that moment of defeat? ... Now if you want to see a real test, a combat to the death, there is such a test of steel."

"I think the boy has heard enough!" boomed a voice that Vilmos instantly recognized. He knew he was in trouble, though he didn't know how much.

"I beg your pardon," said S'tryil, "Do you know this man, Vilam?"

Vilmos replied, "Yes," at the same time Xith asked, "Vil-am?" Then Vilmos quickly said, "Thank you, Greer, for allowing me to stand under your protection. I must go now."

***

Xith and Vilmos hurriedly returned to their rented room to gather their supplies and pack what few belongings they had. Vilmos' only real possession, the staff Xith had given him, was his most prized, and he carried it downstairs with the last of the supplies. Then he packed the goods into the saddlebags and stood by the horses.

Xith came out of the inn a few minutes later, but instead of mounting a horse as Vilmos expected, the shaman touched a leathery hand to Vilmos' bare arm and said "Stay here. I have one last task to perform. If I don't return by twilight, leave the city. Go south; take the horses and supplies with you. Follow the Kingdom road. I will find you when I can."

Chapter Six:
A Fitful Transition

The sun shining on the tall, wide window across from Adrina created an orange glow on the glass panes and lit up the room with a spray of golden rays. She drew out a lengthy yawn; the day was growing heavy on her and for a few fleeting moments she thought of Isador, the nanny who had raised her and brought her to womanhood.

A light rapping came to the door, and as it opened a moment later she recognized the familiar form of Keeper Martin. Her face lit up when she saw the old keeper and the sad thoughts vanished. She turned away from the window. "The elves?" she asked.

Martin averted his eyes from hers. "Beautiful sunset, 'tis a shame if we don't take a moment now and again to wonder of it."

"The elves?" repeated Adrina. Martin moved to the window beside Adrina. Across the room, Myrial placed wood in the fire and Adrina turned to regard the girl. "Myrial?" she called out. "Don't you have better things to do than to see to the wood in my fire? And where is Garette?"

Myrial tidied the hearth stack and then started to rebuild the fire. "His captain wishes words with you, my princess. Do not be harsh with Guardsman Garette. He knows not which path to follow."

"I'll see to it," said Adrina. She turned back to Keeper Martin, "Keeper, certainly you've come to talk with me about something?"

The keeper scratched at the gray in his beard as if he could scratch out the salt in the salt-and-pepper color. "I've been doing a great deal of research on the elves since my return. Our lore library in Keep Council has the best records, but many of the records are incomplete and the oldest records burned in the great fire. A lecture in the Great Book speaks of the healing powers of the elves and I wonder at the truth of it. You were there when elf Galan took the arrow out of my side."

"I believe Keeper," said Adrina, "The correct designation is Brother: Brother Galan."

"Most unnatural to name a woman brother," said Martin. "I suppose I shall get used to it, but in the meantime I have other issues to deal with." He paused as if thinking deeply. "What can you tell me of that incident, the arrow, for I remember little. It was as if I was in another place and I felt no pain."

"I was repulsed and attracted by the goings on," said Adrina, shivering as she remembered. "It was as if the skin around the wound and Galan's hand suddenly became fluid as she reached into your side. When her hand came out, she held the shaft of the arrow, and there was no blood as I expected. But what does this have to do with what has happened?"

"Everything and nothing," said Keeper Martin, again looking away. "I wonder if they've perhaps separated themselves from what has happened and they need now to find their way back. Elf Seth is the one who seems to be the strongest. Galan's light is fading and we think she won't last to this day's end. We've tried everything— I've tried everything I know to do."

"I'm sorry, Keeper Martin, I don't think I saw or know anything that would help. At the end, there was a pink-yellow light and I had to turn away from it. When I turned back, the wound was—" Adrina stopped speaking abruptly, then continued. "With Father Jacob, I heard it. That could be it."

"Go on," urged Keeper Martin.

"In my mind I heard it and I saw his face. At first I thought it was Prince William that I saw, but it wasn't. It was Seth. He called out to me and that is what brought Father Jacob and I to the coast." She put a hand to her mouth suddenly remembering something else. "That is what the Lady spoke of."

"The Lady? I'm not following you, child."

"The Lady of the Forest, the Lady of the Night. I have met her twice now: once on the way to Alderan, once on the return from Klaive. It makes sense now, it all makes sense."

"Slow down Adrina so that I may follow. What of this Lady? Can you tell me more?"

"No," said Adrina as she hurried away, pulling Keeper Martin behind her. "Seth is the link and the key. Don't you see?"

***

Xith paused briefly, seemingly to check the air. He eyed the sky, staring out across the horizon from north to south. Apparently satisfied, he urged his mare onward and Vilmos did likewise.

As the light of a new day gathered behind them, the horses were allowed a brief reprieve. The area of rocky crags and jagged, peaked hills they were in seemed familiar to Vilmos. Xith pointed out that they were still in the hill country separating Great Kingdom from the Borderlands, and from the vantage point atop one of the jagged hills they had come to they could see most of the unofficial boundary that the hills formed.

It was there atop the jagged hill that Vilmos heard Xith speak the words *"Eh tera mir dolzh formus tan!"* in rapid sequence and there that Vilmos felt the tremendous raw power of the untamed lands unleashed. A moment later, he and Xith were in the icy bounds of the between—that place between worlds where the souls of the dead lingered before they passed beyond this life. That place without dimension that a mage could use to transition between realms.

The icy cold and darkness of the between melted away to become something else, and in this place there was no moon or stars, only boundless lines of fire cutting into the ebony of the heavens. At Vilmos' feet lay a dirt road and ahead beyond a crossroads was a forest of dark trees. The dark trees, glowing with an eerie radiance, called to Vilmos, and in that instant he knew he was in Under-Earth.

***

Adrina was fast asleep soon after her head touched her pillow. When she heard Isador enter and push back the curtains, it seemed she had just gone to sleep. She wondered if the old nanny was daft and she opened her eyes only after long hesitation, astonished to find it was already morning—late into the morning by the show of the sun.

"Good morning, princess," said Isador cheerfully, though she didn't feel cheerful today. "Remember, today I leave for South Province and I'll be departing shortly." Isador didn't really want to leave so soon, but winter promised to come early and she had so much to do before then. Her house had not been occupied for some time, and it stood much as she had left it decades ago. Oh, the house had its caretaker, appointed by the king. In fact, many caretakers had come and gone over the years, but the house had not weathered well under the well-meaning hands. She had much to do before winter snows covered the roads. "But not a moment before

I'm sure you've eaten a good breakfast. You haven't been eating well these last several days."

"*Days?*"

"Yes, days."

"I just went to bed. The last thing I remember is Father Jacob walking me back and I just went to bed when you came in." Troubled and trying hard to think, to remember, Adrina recalled only blackness. "What do you mean? You are leaving me, Izzy? You can't leave. I won't let you go."

The nickname flooded the nanny with happy memories but the memories also brought tears. "You rest and eat, dear. We'll worry about all that later. I had a long talk with Father Jacob this morning. He is concerned about you, do you know that?"

Adrina shrugged.

"Now stay in bed, I'll return shortly with your breakfast," said Isador in her motherly tone. "I'm truly sorry Adrina, but South Province can wait no longer for my return." It wasn't the truth. The truth was that Adrina had grown up, Andrew would have no more children, and she was no longer needed.

Hearing the ring of wonder and promise in Isador's voice as she said the name of her home region of South Province reminded Adrina of her older brother, Valam. Knowing that her place was in Imtal and Isador's was now elsewhere, Adrina said nothing.

***

Isador returned, carting a tray piled high with food, smelling of delicious and mouth-watering aromas. Servants followed in the nanny's wake, fluttering about the chamber, dusting and cleaning. Myrial watched from the far corner of the room until they finished and then, like the other servants, she wordlessly departed. She did smile though, and at the door she spun around to show off a new dress.

Isador settled the tray in the middle of the bed, tucked a cloth napkin into Adrina's blouse. "You eat now. If there's one thing I'll do before leaving today, it's ensure you've eaten. I've left orders with Myrial as to your care—should you need it."

"What do you think of Myrial?" asked Adrina before she realized that Isador was talking about leaving this very day. "And you are leaving today? Can it not wait?"

"So many questions mean that you are recovering. It was a dangerous thing you did and you should be ashamed of yourself, causing so much worry over silly elves."

"Silly?"

"Silly," said Isador. "Elves and humans do not mix and should not mix. It is a simple law of the land. They should keep their affairs to themselves and keep out of ours, I say."

"You don't mean that really, do you, Izzy?"

"I mean it. I mean every word of it. Mark my words, nothing good will come of this. Queen Alexandria would have chased them out of Imtal and back to the West Deep where they belong."

"I am not my mother. Nor are you my keeper!" Adrina was angry and hurt by Izzy's words.

"Just as I thought," said the nanny taking a step back. "How long now? How long has it been?"

"How long has what been?"

"You know what I'm talking about, and you just forget those silly notions. Elves and humans do not mix. You are sworn to Rudden Klaiveson and I'm going to ensure you have the grandest wedding ever seen in a thousand years!"

***

Breakfast finished, Adrina took Isador's hand. Isador had practically been her mother these past several years and it saddened her deeply to think of the nanny's departure, perhaps the reason she had pushed the thought from her mind.

Adrina helped Isador pack the remainder of her belongings and the two walked quietly to the waiting coach. Dourly, she gave the old nanny one last hug, tears in her eyes, as the bags were being loaded. She would miss Isador very much.

"Good-bye, Izzy," she whispered.

"Don't worry princess, I will keep in touch. I promise. You are old enough to take care of yourself now. You don't need me holding you back any longer. I must return to my home and settle a score with the years and you must go on to lead your own life." Isador stepped into the carriage. "I must go, princess," said Isador with a heavy heart, "It has been so long since I last visited my home. You are welcome to visit any time you like. A visit in the spring would be grand!"

"Grand indeed," whispered Adrina, hiding her tears.

Neither said any more after that. There wasn't much else to say. They embraced—the great wrapping, smothering embrace of close kin. Adrina held the embrace for several long heartbeats for fear of letting go. Then Isador signaled the driver to proceed.

Adrina watched the black back of the coach pull away, wheels spinning, spinning. She was sad, but happy in a way. It was time for Isador to return home.

Adrina waved until the coach disappeared from the courtyard, still seeing those four high wheels spinning.

As she turned from the courtyard, she found her father standing not far removed from where she had said her good-bye. His shoulders drawn back taunt, his eyes wide and sullen. Adrina knew in that instant that her father, the king, would miss Isador as well. Adrina smiled, embraced her father warmly, then took his hand and mounted the long alabaster stair that flowed upward to the entrance of the central audience hall.

෧〇ෆ Kingdom Alliance ෧〇ෆ

Father Tenuus, the palace's only in resident priest, stood rigid at the top of the stair, doing his best imitation of the stone warriors that embellished the upper deck. His gaze fixed on Adrina as she and her father passed. She had been skipping evening meals and missing his invocatory prayers, and while he wanted to talk to her about this, he remained silent and statue-like as the two passed.

Father and daughter parted in the hall. Adrina walked more quickly now while Andrew continued at a sedate pace toward his chambers. Adrina pictured her father the way she had seen him once not long ago, in his bed robe and slippers shuffling to his private audience chambers—that was the night Keeper Martin arrived unexpectedly, followed by Father Jacob. Her thoughts quickly became lost and tangled again as she reminisced about the days that followed.

Upon reaching her room, Adrina changed out of the colorful housedress Isador preferred and into drab riding clothes. Though she never made it to the stables, she wandered the halls content. Eventually, she found herself standing before a familiar door, which she quietly opened. Inside, the warrior elf, Seth, lay near death, but she was confident death would not claim him now.

***

Storm clouds that the early morning had hinted of still loomed in the east, slowly progressing westward with the passing of the day, but it was not clouds that marred the sky and made the day seem drab. It was the dust; and the folded cloth wrapped around his face did little to help matters either.

The dust blew into Vilmos' eyes and made it painfully difficult to stay alert as Xith had asked, and it obscured what could have been a clear day—if you could call a blood-red sky with eerie yellow clouds in the distance a clear day. Everything that grew along their path was stunted from the lack of light the eternal dust storms created. Strange blue grasses, bunched up in large, thick clumps, made the horses falter. The wind carried with it the occasional tumbleweed, which, in addition to the unbearable dust, harassed them. Ahead in the distance grew scattered groves of trees, which also appeared to be of the same unhealthy variety of plants as the grasses.

Progress across the windswept land was slow and it was nearly an hour before they wound their way to the first stand of trees, which, as they passed between, struck Vilmos as oddities. The stunted trees had knotted trunks, thick at the base with sudden spurts of thin and thick in between their wide outreaching arches, and at the very tips of these wide outreaching boughs were sickly yellow-green leaves.

For a time, it seemed they jumped between the stunted clusters of trees, playing leapfrog with the dead land, then for a long time afterward it seemed the dead land swallowed them.

A large grove, formed from several smaller groves that many long years of persistent growth had matured, was ahead. In the center of this large grove was a small clearing formed from the odd felling of the largest tree that had for a millennium served as the centerpiece of the grove, but now lay wasted, oddly smitten by the same elements that spawned its growth.

"Can we stop here for a minute and catch our breath?" asked Vilmos wearily, pulling the mask down as he did so.

"Only for a moment," replied Xith, "Even though we're out of the open, it is best to be a mobile target."

"Target for what?" began Vilmos, just as several somethings dropped out of the trees around them.

Humanoid, or at least human-like, the creatures had tough, scaly, green skin, clawed hands and feet. Vilmos covered his nose with his hand as he breathed in their putrid stench. His stomach churned and it was all he could do to keep for throwing up. Vilmos held his breath, begged at the air for mercy, did the only thing he knew he could, hoping it would be enough.

Chapter Seven:
The Awakening

"Promise you'll stay?" Adrina asked Keeper Martin, "If he wakes, I want to be the first to know of it. I am sure he will know how to help Galan."

Keeper Martin walked Adrina to the door. "Go now. I'll take care of him."

Adrina watched Martin close the door and then took a walk to clear her mind. After a time she found herself in the kitchen, where despite the cooks and the scullions who were in the middle of preparing the evening meal, she made herself a snack and then wandered out to the far terrace to watch the sunset.

As she walked, she looked about dourly for Father Tenuus. She whispered to herself, "Yes Father Tenuus, I am going to miss the evening meal, but I will say my prayers just the same. You can count on it."

She expected to find the balcony vacant when she reached it and was surprised to find her father. He was sitting alone: no aides or pages, not even Chancellor Yi who was always at his side, were present. She knew her father well enough to know that he was best left alone, for he was surely remembering her mother and the great waves of sadness within him could swallow her just as they had many times before. Quietly she turned and walked away, so as not disturb him. She understood the need for recalling the past from time to time, and held the hope that one day her father would come to an understanding with the pain of loss just as she was starting to.

Shortly after she backtracked across the garden and circled her way up the western tower, she found herself watching the sunset from one of its uppermost stonework windows. From where she was perched, she could turn and look below to see the balcony and her father.

The changing colors of the setting sun sinking below the horizon dazzled her eye and captivated her heart for a time, and it wasn't until the sun faded completely from sight and darkness enshrouded her that she turned to look down at the balcony again. It was also then that she felt the presence of someone standing behind her, lurking unseen in the growing shadows.

She smiled as she turned to see the outline of a man in armor standing stout against the stonework of the tower wall, knowing instantly it was Emel. He motioned her to follow as he moved to the door across from her and out onto the upper bulwarks. She heard the clanging of his heavy armor and the banging of his heavy stave as it struck the broad stones of the floor. And, slowly, she followed.

The stave, the symbol of the watchman, was a thickly carved piece of hard wood about five feet in length, finely sharpened at one end and blunt on the other. The watchman tapped the stave onto the resonant stone floor as he walked to let those on the opposing walls know he was there, and when he heard the returning taps, he knew his fellows were also still present. They walked at a stately pace and when in step built up a rhythm that circled around the four walls, always starting from the east in the morning and during the day where the sun arose, and from the west in the evening and at night where the sun set. The ritual was an old one from times past.

Adrina grabbed Emel's hand, held it for a moment. "Wait," she said.

"You know I can't."

"But you don't have to do this anymore, you are a garrison captain."

"I can't," said Emel, pulling away. His staff rapped the ground as he marched, partially drowning out her words. "I must earn my men's respect through diligence and attention to detail. I am not my father."

"Nor should any expect you to be," said Adrina quickly. She reached out to touch his hand. "Only for a moment," she begged, throwing her words softly to him in an attempt to lull him into listening to her.

Emel smiled and walked away. He called back to her, "Follow me and we can talk."

Adrina ran to catch up. Emel's staff rapping the floor annoyed her and caused her sentences to come out broken as she attempted to talk between each tap. "Can you... stop... that infernal... noise... for a second."

"You know I can't!" said Emel.

Adrina stormed away, running back to the stairs and out of sight before Emel could respond. He had been avoiding her since the return to Imtal and that cut into her heart more than anything.

***

Adrina sat beside Seth, dabbing a wet cloth to his forehead. She heard his question, but didn't know how to answer him. She didn't know if he could understand her thoughts as she could his. She felt responsible for the attack upon Seth and Galan. She, like the others, had underestimated the fear with which Kingdomers and Southerners alike regarded the two.

The company had barely left Quashan' when it happened. The attack came in the middle of the night as they made their way north. The poison in the darts was the same poison that took King Charles. That they could fight its deadly affects this long was surprising. That Seth was winning against the poison and gaining strength every day was clear.

Seth probed Adrina's mind for the words that eluded his memory, using her tongue, the Kingdom tongue. *Do you know where Galan is? Does she yet live?* But even as he asked, the answer came.

"Your companion lives, but we know not for how long. It is a miracle she has lasted this long. She is very weak but she has great will to live. She must be holding onto the last ounce of her life. Father Jacob is doing all he can to save her. I am truly sorry. I pray for her and you each night."

Seth knew Adrina's words to be true. He would not release the last thread of Galan's life. Defying the laws of natural order and the laws of the Brotherhood, he held it firmly in his grip and vowed he would never let it go. He reached out with his mind to Adrina now, again in the language of her people. *You must take me to her!* This time the words came easier and he did not stumble over each. His memory grew clearer.

"No, you must rest for a while yet, then I will take you to her. You must understand..." Adrina paused and her words turned to sobs of regret, "I am sorry. We have tried everything. We didn't think you'd live. But I hoped and prayed you would, and you have..."

I have rested too long. You must take me to her! I haven't the time to explain to you why, you just must!

The words thrust upon her mind like a hammer, Adrina winced

from the sudden pain. She closed her eyes for a moment in a failed attempt to fight back the sting. Weariness swam through her body, fatigue sought to carry her into sleep, sleep she wouldn't allow. "Not just yet," said Adrina. She heard the urgency of his plea, but held firm. "Father Jacob is with her and so are many other priests. You can see her tomorrow."

Seth's short attempt at resistance ended as he collapsed back into the bed; he had made it to a seated position and no farther. Adrina leveled a spoonful of warm soup upon him, which he promptly refused. The soup didn't look appealing and it smelled rather odd.

Adrina raised a finger and waved it. "If you don't eat, you will not regain your strength!" She thought she sounded rather like Isador, and perhaps she did.

Seth was about to argue that he wasn't hungry, but he decided to the contrary. He would eat first to appease her, and then he would argue his point. The broth did taste good despite its odor, different from what he was used to, yet very good.

Adrina emptied spoonful after spoonful into his mouth, satisfied to see him eat and happy he appeared to be recovering. Her thoughts wandered after she watched sleep overcome him again. The power of his voice, the voice that could reach inside her mind and seemingly touch her very soul, brought to her wonderment.

***

After Seth slipped back into a deep sleep, Adrina left his room, closing the door carefully behind her. Outside the door, the two Klaive Knights waited. She had forbidden them to enter.

"Don't you ever tire?" she snapped as the knights took up positions at her side. "Why don't you return to Klaive and do so quickly!"

She stormed away down the hall, going at a pace that she knew caused her protectors to labor under their armor.

As she turned a corner, heading into the old section of the palace, she entered a dark corridor. Ahead in the hallway stood a figure shrouded by the shadowy gloom.

The knights swept past Adrina protectively as a safeguard—a safeguard that saved Adrina's life. An instant later, she heard the swish of arrows and one of the knights fell momentarily, but he was quickly on his feet.

"Long live Oshywon!" shouted the attackers as they swept in from all sides.

The Klaive Knights boxed Adrina in and circled her protectively.

One of the attackers approached out of the darkness, saying, "We will not harm her. This is a kidnapping and not a killing. Had we wanted her Highness dead, it would already be so. Lay down your weapons and you will return to your families."

The Klaive Knights' response was the clash of steel on steel. The two moved with speeds that surprised Adrina—the only others she had seen who were so quick were Seth and Galan. But where the elves had skill of feet and limb, the Klaive Knights had skill with a blade, and when a single blade wasn't enough to hold off the press of attackers, the knights switched to two-weapon combat, taking their great swords in their right hand while using a long dagger in their left.

Adrina began shouting frantically as the attack went on. "Guards! Guards!" But there was no response and no one came to her aid. She could see the leader of the attackers smiling as he clutched something in his hand—something magical or mystical Adrina presumed.

Adrina decided then to be daring. The two knights circling her had auxiliary blades at their backs—blades that were made for throwing. She watched, timing her move carefully, grabbing a blade in each hand and then throwing the blades quickly.

One of the blades raced by the leader's head as he bobbed out of the way but the second blade—the one the leader hadn't seen or expected—hit its mark. The leader's eyes went wide and wild as he staggered and then collapsed.

The attackers fell back, dragging their fallen comrades with them. As Adrina looked on speechless, the attackers slipped into the shadows of the night. She sank to her knees, trembling.

She wondered at herself, wondering what it was that she had become. In her mind there was no doubt she had killed the leader, if only by luck. Was she a killer now? Was she now no better than those that attacked her? Could she look at herself in the mirror and not see that face—the face that saw death and the eyes that mirrored it?

Suddenly, there were hands around her arms and she struggled: biting, scratching, screaming—wild.

"It's me, Adrina," said a voice.

"Emel?"

"Yes, I'm here now."

"The Knights of Klaive, where are they? Did they chase after the attackers?"

Emel didn't say anything for a moment, then he said, "No, they are here." He helped her to her feet she was still trembling. "Don't look back. They rest well. To die in service and to know that you've saved the one you've sworn to protect is the ultimate honor and sacrifice."

"They're dead?" whispered Adrina, sinking to her knees as she suddenly went numb. "What have I done? I gave no kindness and was rude at every turn. How I wish I could turn back time and make it all right."

Emel kept Adrina walking: moving away. The palace was alive with the sounds of guardsmen and garrison soldiers scouring the grounds. "No kindness was asked or expected; it is the way of it. You cannot make things right—no more than you can turn back time."

"Did they have families?" Adrina asked through great sobs.

"You know, it's a good thing I was walking Garette's watch. My relief had just come, I was just finishing when I saw you racing down the corridor. I followed only moments later, and it was a good thing—a good thing indeed. I don't understand why you didn't scream out. There were guards all around."

"But I did scream, I screamed and no one heard." Adrina scowled. "Did they have families?"

"That's impossible. I didn't hear anything—but I saw it."

"The bauble—the leader had some trinket in his hand. He was holding it and smiling when I screamed. He may have dropped it when he fell."

"What are you saying?"

"We must go back! Grab that torch! We must search—it was round and—" Adrina stopped abruptly, turned around, and then ran back in the direction they had come from. "—it glowed. Yes, it glowed. I remember now! The Lady told me of a link and a key—and a box without sound. I didn't understand before but I do now. I was the link for Seth that brought him back and the box without sound must be—"

Emel caught up to Adrina and grabbed her about the arms. "Adrina, you're babbling. Something must have happened to you. We should go see Father Jacob, perhaps there's a tonic he can give you."

"No, you don't understand! I see it all now—I understand it all now, or at least I think I do."

Emel slapped Adrina across the face, his hand hitting harder than he wished. "Tyr had two daughters, Aryanna and Aprylle, and a wife, Kautlin. Etry's wife, Ontyv, was with child, their first. If you want to do something, see to them. They were brave men." Adrina pulled away from Emel and at the last, he added, "Come back to me, my princess. I think madness has beset you." —and madness and rage were things Emel was coming to understand all too well.

Chapter Eight:
Phantoms of the Past

Vilmos ran for what seemed hours—if not days. Out of the corner of his eye he saw a glimmer of white fangs. The next instant he smacked into the ground in pain. Xith glared at the creature perched on Vilmos' chest, about to rake his head from his shoulders. A blue-white flame shot out from the shaman's hand, striking the creature full force, engulfing it in flames.

Vilmos tossed the screeching beast off him. It slumped to the ground and did not move again. Feeling helpless, Vilmos looked worriedly to Xith, his body frozen to the ground, his mind not allowing him to move. He could only see the faces and watch. A tingling sensation surged through his arm, perhaps the letting of warm blood across cool skin.

"Come on Vilmos, snap to it!" yelled Xith as he dispatched another of the creatures. He called out with more words, but frantic howls snatched them from the air.

A creature dropped down beside Vilmos. Its eyes moved to the ground where its companion lay and it lunged. Instinctively, Vilmos threw up his shield, barely in time as the creature's claw struck the barrier and glanced off.

The raising of the shield was as the turning of a switch that brought awareness to Vilmos. He searched for Xith, only to find the shaman was gone. Three creatures circled him, watching his every move, waiting for the right instant to pounce.

In alarm Vilmos cried out, but no answer came. He was afraid. Something might have happened to Xith, though he didn't know what or how. He watched the beasts carefully as they came for him one by one, shivering increasingly with each successful reflection.

"Xith!" he shouted with all the strength of his voice.

No answer came.

"Xith, are you hurt?"

Again, nothing.

Fear built within Vilmos, if Xith was dead so was he. He couldn't possibly survive where the shaman had failed.

More of the creatures came. They surrounded him. Gradually they crept forward. Their stench overwhelmed his senses—it was the putrid odor of rotting flesh. "Xith? You can't be dead!" shouted Vilmos, "You're the only real friend I've ever had! Come back! Please!"

As if in response, a knifelike claw broke through his magic shield, ripping into his shoulder and then his side. The pain was excruciating, filling him with anger and fear. His thoughts turned to Xith. Suddenly he could feel the anguish Xith must have felt at the end.

"For this you shall die!" he shouted.

A flame sparked from outstretched hands, striking one of the beasts dead in the chest, and in a burst of flame the creature died. Surprised at the power that surged in him, he shouted, a wicked smile touching his lips. He released the power within again. Two attackers fell.

He whirled around to face the last of the attackers. He didn't know how but he detected terror in their expressions as they started to flee. "You shall not run away from me foul creatures!" he said with a loud booming voice as flames bright and deadly sprang forth from outstretched hands. "I have arrived!"

The creatures' last sounds were agonized cries of pure pain. He almost pitied them but that thought didn't last long.

***

"Adrina, stop!" yelled Emel, "This is madness! Talk to me!"

"It's here! I know it's here—it has to be!" Adrina grabbed Emel before he grabbed her. "Trust me like you did once before—trust me!"

Emel stopped protesting and helped Adrina search. The ground was bloody, but the bodies of the fallen knights had already been taken away. The pursuit through the palace continued—near and far shouts could be heard but there were no sounds of skirmish. "What does it look like?"

"Round, I think—silvery. It glowed."

"Glowed?"

"Yes, glowed! He held it in his hand. I think he was rubbing it or squeezing it. He might have been whispering something too—I'm not too sure. Everything happened so fast…"

Emel extinguished the torch he held and started extinguishing the other torches that now lit the area clearly. Adrina helped, shouting, "Yes, that's it!"

Soon the hallway was shrouded in darkness. Emel and Adrina waited as their eyes adjusted, then began to search again.

Emel talked as he searched. "You never told me about a second visit from the Lady."

"You never asked. You were too busy playing captain of the guard."

"Too busy? Too busy? What's that supposed to mean? Do you know we had to restructure the whole of Imtal Garrison? Three squadrons of trained soldiers are not easily replaced—and throughout it all, I and the other officers had to contend with the families of the fallen.

"After the first hundred or so the faces of the mourners become the same, but you can't let them be the same or you lose what little compassion you can continue to muster. It's not easy and it's not that anyone ever told you it would be easy. It's so effortless to lose yourself and there's no one there for you as you are there for others. So yes, I was busy playing—"

Adrina stopped searching and put a hand on Emel's arm. "I didn't know. I assumed—I assumed... I missed you on the return to Imtal. It wasn't the same. I wish I had been there for you. The attack on the elves wasn't your fault. You don't need to try to make everything right."

"Looks who's talking. Do you know what you've done, stirring up the household and appointing Garette Timmer as Myrial's protector? Swordmaster Timmer is furious and says his family is humiliated." Emel pulled away from Adrina's touch, his hand coming to rest on a thing most unnatural. He picked it up and wondered at the radiance of it.

"I don't always think before I act. You should know that by now Emel. Myrial *does* deserve to be housemistress though. She's always been there for me as you were—even when I was lost to the world around me. I will speak with Swordmaster Timmer. You'll see—"

"Is this what you saw?" cut in Emel. "Because I think it must be."

Adrina took the strange glowing orb in her hand. "It is," she said, "It is."

***

As the frenzy in his mind passed, Vilmos stood silent and still. He was shocked, simply amazed at what he had wrought for many long minutes. Tears rolled down his face and his words were drowned in sobs.

He sank to the ground; he was alone. Xith was gone without a trace—and he had become a monster, no better than those he had slain. The force of the raw energy flowing through him seemed a drug in his mind.

It took quite a while, but finally he rose to his feet and wiped away his tears. The wounds in his side and shoulder ached but luckily were not too deep.

His thoughts returned to concerns about Xith. He thought perhaps the creatures dragged Xith's body off to feast on. He began a search that took him well into the evening.

As night arrived deep and dark in the land, he set up camp in the grove. Although he wasn't really hungry, he ate all of what little rations he had. He made a bed among the boughs of the great fallen tree.

He was unaware of the tiny seedling nestled within the tangles of the shattered trunk and once proud roots, nor was he aware that it was the spirit of the great tree itself that told him to start the warding fire. He only knew that the horses were gone, Xith was gone, and he was desperately alone in a place that was completely foreign to him.

He knew little of Under-Earth, and what little he did know alarmed him. This was the place where the land called Rill Akh Arr existed, and within its shrouded forests lived the shape changing beasts of the night—the Wolmerrelle. He had faced the Wolmerrelle before in Vangar forest—before he had barely escaped with his life.

But thoughts of the Wolmerrelle weren't as frightening as

thoughts of Erravane, the leader of the Wolmerrelle. Erravane would want revenge and her revenge may not be that of death. As Xith had told him before, there were worse things than death. He believed this wholly and without question now.

Troubled sleep found him a short while later. The dreams playing out behind his eyes were of the past—a past that he had hoped was behind him but wasn't.

Chapter Nine:
Against the Odds

Brother Seth of the Red, corrected Seth to Adrina.

"Are you always there in my mind?" whispered Adrina in her thoughts.

Not always, but I am... I am sorry if it offends you...

"It does not offend," whispered Adrina in her thoughts.

You must take me to Galan!

The sense of urgency touched Adrina. She sensed the pain and she tried to explain that the council needed him first, but he refused. The vigor with which his emotions and thoughts hit her today surprised her. And upon reflection, she didn't think just taking him to see his companion could hurt anything. The council could wait a little longer.

"I know of councils," said Seth, "You are right, they can wait. I must attend to more urgent matters first, then I will surely sit before your illustrious council." *You could not keep me away...*

Adrina called out to the guards posted outside the door. They came bursting into the chamber, half prepared to do battle with the mysterious stranger and half prepared to vault away if there was indeed trouble.

You see, whispered Seth to Adrina alone, *where I come from all are friends and if someone were indeed your enemy, only then would you need such men...* He had searched Adrina's mind for the correct word for the two guardsmen, but the word guard didn't really seem fitting.

"Lower your weapons!" said Adrina, "Brother Seth and his companion are guests. They are not under house arrest."

The guards looked first to Adrina, then to the stranger. They would run from the room if she dismissed them. "We are truly sorry, Your Highness. We meant no affront."

"Give me assistance. We will take Brother Seth to his companion in the far wing."

"But... We are under orders to see that—"

Adrina cut the guardsman off, "Under whose orders?"

"Captain Brodst himself," replied both men at the same time.

"You heed a captain's order over mine? You are indeed fools!" shouted Adrina.

I'm all right, Seth sent to her mind alone, *I need no assistance.*

"Quiet!" said Adrina. She directed it to the guards, but it was perfectly timed with Seth's statement. "Guards," she said, "To his side! Take his arms and follow..."

Really... I can walk on my own...

"Really, indeed."

The guards cast her odd glances. They were more concerned for her than for the stranger, but they did as she requested.

The foursome traversed a long hall, descended a twisted stair, then proceeded along another lengthy hall. They came next to the open courtyard, and here Seth asked to pause, momentarily captured by the beauty of the open air, the sunshine, the brightly colored flowers of the garden. It seemed so long since he was this close to the earth and the forces of the Mother, and the touching hand of the Father flowed more readily to his prescient mind.

Release me, he thrust into the minds of the guardsmen, strength returning to his limbs.

The guards backed away warily. Again, they would have run if not for the cross look in Adrina's eye. They continued on.

Galan's bedchamber was filled with a collection of clergy led by Father Jacob. They were whispering an ancient prayer, a healing prayer, one of the most powerful they could tap. The priests were using Jacob as a focus through which their energies flowed.

So far they had made little progress. Galan's face was deathly pale and her heartbeat was barely perceptible. As Seth entered the chamber, the focusing stopped, the prayer stopped, and as one the priests looked up—Seth's powerful will acted like a magnet upon their minds. A voice entered their thoughts, shocking them into bewildered frenzy. *I am very grateful for your effort, but I am afraid only I can save her.*

"No," shouted Adrina in response, "You need to save your strength!"

The chamber was absent of sound for a time. Father Jacob understood Adrina's concerns and honored her opinion. He furrowed his brow, cleared his throat several times, then repeated Adrina's words but more tactfully. "Friend, save your strength. We will save your companion. The poison will work itself out, I promise."

Seth studied Jacob for a time before he offered a response. Jacob interested Seth. Jacob had called him "friend." Seth could feel a sense of power in this one, power of a different sort, not of will per say, more of intellect or wisdom. And Seth smiled in polite form.

She is beyond your help, said Seth in response to the anxiousness that flowed from the gathered priests. *Father Jacob, would you ask your fellows to leave?*

"Perhaps we can do this together," said Jacob, thinking, but not saying, that since they were all males it would be best to pool their healing powers. Jacob muttered curse under his breath and it brought a smile to Seth's lips. He wondered if Seth would understand the absence of the priestesses and know they held no malevolence.

I understand, said Seth into Jacob's mind, *my people too have their holy customs and if you would honor them, I must do this alone...*

Again Jacob's expression grew wide with amazement, perhaps there was indeed more here than he understood. "Please leave us..." began Father Jacob. "Brother Seth wishes time alone with his companion." He stood a moment, staring at Seth. He would have to find Keeper Martin immediately; they must find all they could in the histories. The Great Book told little about Seth's kind, but perhaps if they delved deep enough into the ancient texts they could glean more. He also had to inform the council. They could call a General Assembly soon. "Let's go now... Father Tenuus, are you coming?"

Father Tenuus nodded and followed Jacob from the room.

The room was empty now save for Adrina, Seth and Galan. Adrina stepped quietly away from Seth's side, glancing at the last moment into his eyes. She stopped, reached out and touched his cheek. She was the only one who saw the tears well up in his eyes and stream down his face, whether they were tears of joy at seeing his companion or tears of sadness she did not know. Sorrow filled her heart and as she departed the room, tears glistened down her cheeks.

Father Jacob waited for her in the hallway and she saw him hazily through her tears. "Father Jacob?" she sobbed.

"Yes, princess."

"Do you think he can save her?"

Jacob took her hand and walked with her down the corridor. "If there is one in this world who can, I believe it is him, child. Never have I felt the will of any as strong as the one I felt when he entered the room."

The tears dried up and Adrina paused to stare out over the garden as Seth had. Somehow to see bright sunshine and vibrant life made her feel better too. She kissed Jacob's hand in appreciation of his kindness, and as she did so Jacob blushed faint red. She knew he understood how she felt.

"He regained his strength quickly."

"This morning he awoke and ate well. By afternoon, it seemed most of his strength had returned, and now he seems to have almost fully recovered."

"Strong that one, I'll say. Come child, I will see that you sleep!" said Jacob, dragging Adrina along behind him, "You look so very tired, you must rest… Besides there is nothing we can do now save pray. We must pray long and hard."

Adrina didn't refuse. She knew Jacob wouldn't have believed her, and she wouldn't have been telling the truth, if she denied her exhaustion. Yet, as fate would have it, the two passed Chancellor Yi who was busily rushing past on his way to King Andrew's chambers. The council was awaiting the king's presence at the day's session, which he was late to again, but he was the king after all and therefore pardonable. Luckily for Adrina, Yi snatched Jacob away to the meeting and she was left on her own.

For a moment, Adrina considered Yi's face. His nose wasn't red any more and the dark circles were gone from under his eyes. Adrina broke her stride. She had heard no sniffles as he approached or after he had passed. A touch of mirth lit her face. Imtal palace had been dead before, gnawing away at them a piece at a time, the chancellor especially, but no more.

She considered following the two to the council chambers and sitting in on the session, but quickly let the idea pass. She would rather be alone for a while, and she almost walked to her room to lie down as she knew Jacob would have wanted her to do and as her body desired—but instead she crossed back to stare silently at the closed chamber door, listening intently for any sound that might escape from within.

After hours of waiting and pacing back and forth alone, stirring her mind with frenzied thoughts, Father Jacob returned from the council meeting. He was surprised and not surprised to find Adrina waiting there slumped against the wall, half asleep. He muttered under his breath that he should have taken her back to her room first and then gone to the meeting, but now it was too late.

He shrugged his shoulders in a gesture to show the futility of arguing with her, and then joined her. A strong force of will emanating from within the chamber told Jacob that Brother Seth was occupied in activities beyond anything he could comprehend. For many days, the priests had been changing off in the healing chant without success. It seemed they could do nothing to aid the dying one.

Only today they decided to try the impossible, to breach the realm of their powers and combine their wills. At the time Jacob thought it was the only solution—he was not so sure anymore.

All his thoughts of failure did not disappear so readily. He cursed the priestesses and their damnable rituals. An image of Jasmine, the High Priestess, flashed through his mind. During the days before winter, a priestess was not to be found in the whole of the Kingdom. Sealed away in sanctuary, carrying out private worship, which although Jacob knew and understood he did not fully condone. His thoughts lingered on the face a moment longer, then he turned to careful, reverent prayer—the prayer he promised before but had not had time yet to give.

Neither he nor Adrina said a word as they waited, slumped against the wall. Interrupting the silence seemed wrong. Despite the skirt she wore, Adrina sat on her haunches. The good father simply abided by leaning a heavy shoulder against the stonework of one of the hall's grand arches. Unconsciously between breaths one or the other would pause to listen, hoping for a sound or a sign, anything at all to cast away the fears.

***

Beyond the door, inside the room, Seth sat engrossed in meticulous calculation, ensuring every detail down to the last minuscule item. Once the others left, he raced to Galan's side and kissed her lightly on the cheek. His thoughts ran wild—the task that lay ahead, that which he must attempt, the sacrifice he must make, the denial he must send to the Father, all things he must consider.

Oh Galan, my Galan… What have I done?

He breathed in a deep breath to relax his mind and body, quickly pursuing it with another, waiting until his thoughts were absolutely clear before he delved into the long, tedious task ahead. The room, having served as a meditation chamber of sorts, would suit his purposes well.

Slowly, methodically, he spread unlit candles around the bed in a full circle, chanting a prayer long forgotten, lost to all save his people, the prayer's pious message designed to begin focusing his will as well as to gather his thoughts. Curiously, the candles served only as symbols of faith to the Father, each representing a material thing, thus to remind the Father of times past, times of great need.

Seth's labor began with channeling a single thought, allowing it to occupy his consciousness. He maintained the chant, fixing his will, refining it, until all else faded—the last candle gently put in its place completed the circle. Seth crossed to the head of the bed and kneeled, cross-legged. He increased the level of his mental chant, reaching out until it encompassed the entire chamber, yet not beyond. The sound of his silent words of thought was so intense that others of lesser will would have been driven out of the room.

He cast a wayward thought away from his mind and touched outward to the air, slowly lifting himself above the bed with a levitating force. He raised his hands, turning them palms up, fingers at first interlaced to channel the energy better.

Moving each finger now, separately in an independent flicker, he touched the candles each with a different spark of energy, forcing them to light in the same instant as one. A cleansing of his inner self allowed him to reflect his will inward while he waited for strength to build—the bright red-orange of the sun, the green, green pastures of open plains, the placid blue waters of a gentle lake and the serenity of life were his only thoughts.

The power of the world encircled him and he had only to reach out to grasp. He could shape this power, bend it to his desires, caress it with his touch. The will of nature, the will of the very air in which he floated, came to him and he focused, channeling ever so carefully while a pleasant calm passed over him. Suspended in time, touching its boundaries, he held the power of the world.

He called the wind.

A breeze, a warm soothing flutter, blew in a fine whisper, increasing until it was a gust, then a gale. He touched the forces of will he held in his beckoning hands; the wind became a raging torrent of swirling force. The candles blazed, burning with such intensity as the wind gathered strength that their heat brought beads of sweat to Seth's brow.

The peace of the earth surrounded and took him. It was time.

Seth cast his spirit to the place of Galan's moribund soul, the moaning wind becoming a deafening roar. The brightly burning flames became ten tiny suns. Seth leapt beyond.

Everything stopped, deadly silent. The air, no longer warm to the touch, but cool, cool enough to drive a shiver into one's heart.

Seth reached for the last unraveling strand, not knowing if his strength was enough to sustain it. He felt the will of the Father all around him.

The Father wanted to bring his daughter home, to end her suffering, to carry her away to a better place, but Seth was selfish and did not want to let her go.

He had held the last strand of her life too long to let it slip away. He held her spirit, success was so near. *Two must survive*, went the whisper in his mind.

Father, I implore you! Seth cried out, *My need is great! Please hear my call and listen to my words!*

His message fell as a wave smashing against the shore in the dead of night. Matching that of the land as it was rent and hopelessly twisted, his will became the soft grains of sand sucked out by the churning black waters.

Wallowing in darkness and turmoil, Seth collapsed to the floor at the head of the bed. His journey ended. Galan's journey ended.

Chapter Ten:
A Strangeness in the Air

Vilmos awoke. He was terrified—and for good reason. He was not alone. The grove was occupied by those that were not of this realm.

"Dark master, we heard your call upon the wind. The sign is in the east and the peoples of North and South gather. Is it time?"

Vilmos tried to back away but quickly found he was surrounded. "You are men? There are *men* in Under-Earth?"

"Less a man, less men, than once before. Come with us. We will accompany you on your journey and ensure your safety."

"I don't know where I am going. I'm lost. I lost my master."

"Lost your *master?*" The speaker started laughing—almost a cackle. "Lost your *way?*" He turned to his fellows, still laughing, and then he turned back to Vilmos. "Stranth was lost because of Kastelle and Adrynne, but you are never lost. This cannot be so. The tower awaits. Let us guide you."

Vilmos stared at the streaks of fire racing across the skies of Under-Earth. His longing was almost a plea for help but he didn't cry out aloud—only in his thoughts. He stood uneasily. The robed figures took a few steps away as if in reverence. "Will you hurt me?" he asked.

"Pain. There is always pain. Pain is all around us; it is within us and in the air we breathe. Pain is to pleasure as joy to sorrow. So what is hurt?"

"But you will help me find my way? And you will take me to wherever it is that I want to go?"

The hooded ones moved around Vilmos, circling and chanting. The one speaking never moved. He stood still.

Vilmos gathered his belongings—what little he had—still eyeing those around him. "Do you have a name?"

"Servants do not have names. They are best nameless."

"Do you have names?" said Vilmos indicating the group with his hands.

"Think of us as your shadows. Your will is ours. We will walk with you to the end of your path."

"I don't think the boy needs shadows!" said a voice in the distance.

Vilmos turned, as did the hooded ones. He saw a mass of silvery armor, a great clubbed weapon held in an outstretched, mailed fist. The armored warrior seemed to be as tall and large as the trunk of a tree.

Vilmos gulped as he looked down the length of the spiked club—a club that was nearly as long as he was tall. Vilmos backed away. The robed figures filled the space between him and the armored warrior.

"You are making a mistake," said the warrior. "Human meat just doesn't taste as good as it used to. I'm not going to eat you. That is a promise, but what of your fellows? What are their plans for you? Do you know?"

"They are friends. They have come to help me along my path. I will go with them if it is all the same to you."

"It *is not* all the same to me—I assure you! I have a great deal to do this day, so make your decision and be quick about it! You have a lot to learn if you are to get along here. Do you know what they will do to you when they find out you are not the one?"

"He is the one," hissed one of the hooded men. "The sign is in the east and he has come. We have come for him; he is ours. Leave us now or we will do what we must to protect that which is ours!"

"You will now?" The warrior swung the great club around his head. The hooded ones cowered away. "Are you so sure of yourselves?"

***

"Good morning, Myrial," said Adrina quietly as she stretched through a waking yawn. "What hour is it?"

"Late in the day my princess. You've had several would-be visitors already."

"News of the elves?"

"Not that anyone has said but I do believe you have a visitor waiting. He may have some news."

"He?" asked Adrina, sitting up, turning to the bedside.

"Quite handsome I must say. I do find him striking, but I think he has eyes for you."

"Myrial you play with me," said Adrina putting on her slippers and going to the mirror. "You know I'm betrothed to Rudden Klaiveson and it is as it should be. My father is pleased and will dower all the lands between Heman in the North and River Opyl in the South. There's a promise of a grand palace as well—but as to that I'll have to wait and see."

Myrial started combing Adrina's hair. "You care nothing of palaces and land holdings—I know this, so don't try to make me a fool. What does your heart tell you? That is the question you must answer."

Adrina stood and went behind the changing partition. Her

clothes had already been carefully laid out. "What of the household? How are you managing? I've heard good things from the cooks." There was a moment of silence and Adrina repeated, "I've heard good things from the cooks."

"I think the cooks are right," said a strong masculine voice.

"Emel is that you?" shouted Adrina. "Myrial? …Myrial, I'm not finished!"

"Yes, Emel. Don't worry I'll keep the appropriate distance. I don't want any rumors—but I couldn't wait any longer. I've been pacing the hall for more than an hour."

"Do you have news of the elves?" asked Adrina as she straightened the dress about her shoulders, emerged from behind the partition.

"No news of the elves." Emel glanced to the window, to Adrina. "I'm being sent to the Territories: Krepost'. It is my father's wish."

Adrina's face turned pale. "Is this a punishment of some sort—like High Road last summer? I'll speak to your father and to mine. This isn't right!"

"No Adrina don't," said Emel. "This is something I must do."

"Why?" cried Adrina, throwing her slippers at him. "Did you tell someone of the orb? Does this have to do with the attack? It wasn't your fault. Don't they know that?"

Emel turned away. "I was the ranking officer on watch. It was my fault regardless and I have accepted responsibility. Exile in the Territories is far less a punishment than the alternative. My shortsightedness nearly cost your life and the king—"

"My father? What does my father have to do with this? If he has any part in this, banishment has less to do with the attack and more to do with—"

"Your father has nothing to do with the orders. It is my father, but it is my obligation as well. I have brought shame and dishonor."

"Shame and dishonor?" shouted Adrina. "How could anyone have known of a secret attack? Did you show them the orb? It has powers that will prove your innocence—magical powers that create a ring of silence. I know this to be true, I was there."

Emel walked to the window. "Listen to yourself. Do you know how that sounds? No, I'd rather the alternative. It is my duty to go and I will go. I've just come to say goodbye."

"Goodbye with your back to me? Look me in the eye Emel and tell me you don't believe!"

Emel turned to face Adrina. "I don't believe. Nothing good will come of talk of the orb. I am sure of this as I am sure of no other thing. The Territories aren't so bad—I'll be Captain of Krepost' Guard! It'll be a grand adventure…"

"Adventure? No one comes back from the Territories—no one!"

Emel forced himself to smile. "Well maybe no one wants to come back. Maybe once they get there they find it's such a grand place that they just don't want to leave—maybe that's the *real* secret."

Adrina was quiet and just when she was about to speak Myrial entered. "Adrina?" Myrial called out. "Sorry to interrupt but the lady elf is asking for you. I told Keeper Martin I would come straight away."

"Galan? She's awake?"

"Yes—and eating!"

Adrina's face showed relief and surprise. She turned back to Emel. "Go!" Emel told her, "I leave tomorrow morning at first light. There's a supply caravan heading east and I'll travel with it beyond the Wall of the World."

Emel handed Adrina a small leather pouch. "Take this! I won't need it."

"The orb?" whispered Adrina.

"Maybe you'll have better luck with it than I," said Emel as he turned away and left Adrina's room.

Adrina wrapped her hand about the leather pouch and then grabbed Myrial by the arm, saying, "Let's go! I've waited days and weeks for this!"

***

Emel watched Adrina go; his heart went with her. "It is done," he whispered as he walked away in the opposite direction.

A figure in the shadows whispered, "You have done right; this is as it must be. You know what you must do next—don't delay any more than necessary. I'll wait outside the city, on the morrow."

"On the morrow," whispered Emel without looking at the speaker. He walked through the palace halls, leaving through the side entrance and making his way to the officer's quarters within the central keep. Although the old keep was a part of the palace structure, it was separated by courtyards and gardens.

Once inside the keep Emel passed his quarters without stopping. He went instead to his father's official station within the keep. "Captain Brodst," he said as he made his way through the outer door unannounced. "I've come to speak with you."

"So official," said his father, looking up from his papers. "Please come in and sit down."

"I'll stand if it's all the same," said Emel looking about the room. He leaned to the right and closed the inner office door. "I've come to speak with you on an urgent matter."

Ansh Brodst looked up from his papers again. "Requisitions, hate them," he said, "But what would we do without provisions and proper weaponry?"

"I've come to speak with you on an urgent matter," repeated Emel. Ansh Brodst put down the papers and the pen he had been using. "I've come to resign."

"Steadfast in this decision, are you? If that's your mind, I'm not the one to change it. You are making a mistake, of course. There's soldier's honor and duty, and then there's pride. If it's pride that's bringing this on then it *is* best that you resign. No room for arrogance, self-importance and conceit in our business."

Emel bit his tongue to keep from saying something he knew he'd regret. When pain cleared his thoughts, he replied, "No father, not pride. For me, you've made the favor of exception. Any other would have been banished—sent to the Territories or worse."

"Sit and lets discuss this—" It was an order not a request. Emel sat as his father spoke. "—Seventeen generations have served and to have the line broken now for such a thing? I think there's an easier way to accept responsibility—if there's a need for accountability and that should've been for me to decide. If this is about last spring, I think I—"

"This isn't about last spring. I didn't know what I was doing or thinking then, and the summer did clear my thoughts. I need distance or I may..." Emel's voice trailed off.

Ansh Brodst nodded solemnly in understanding. "Distance is sometimes a good thing. Take a leave of absence, surely one is deserved after all that has happened—" Again it was an order and not a request. "—it's settled then is it not?"

Emel persisted though he knew better. "Leave of absence? I may not return—I've a mind not to return."

"You'd have to ask yourself then if it was worth it—if *she* was worth it. I can tell you from experience that it is—and *isn't*. But you shouldn't forswear your future for a notion that can never be real. Where will you go on your leave?"

"The Territories," whispered Emel, his thoughts elsewhere. "I have some business in the Territories. I leave tomorrow at first light."

"With the supply caravan? That's a dangerous business. You'd be better off going alone or with a small company of guardsmen."

Emel stood. "Dangerous if one is a fool."

"Many men have been a fool then," said Ansh Brodst, standing as well. He clasped his son about the elbow. "Safe journey, may you find what it is you seek."

***

Vilmos awoke in a warm, soft bed. He peered around the room warily as a knock came to the door, soft and then hard, but he didn't move to answer it. After a couple more raps, he heard the rattling of something being set onto the floor, then the sound of footsteps as someone walked away. He waited cautiously for the footsteps to fall away and then he opened the door slightly. On the floor he found a tray containing a bowl of murky soup and a large chunk of black bread covered with some sort of jam or honey. Also on the tray was a pair of candles, with one lighted and placed into a wooden candleholder of sorts.

He eagerly picked up the tray and carried it back into the room. He placed the candlestick on the small table next to the bed and sat down, preparing to eat. To his delight, the soup was a wonderful combination of beef and vegetable, and the jam on the black bread was mouth-watering.

As he slurped the last bit of soup from the bowl and placed the bowl back onto the tray, he noticed something odd. A small object, a tiny wooden figure painted white with a crown adorning its head. Vilmos thought it odd, but without really thinking about it, he placed it on the table next to the candle.

A warm, full gut brought the yearning to sleep but the aching of his shoulder and side did not go away. It was then that he saw the bandages over his wounds and recalled the happenings of the previous day.

Some hours later the last rays of the setting sun filtering in through the window awoke him. He crossed to the window, pressing his face against the cool, cheerless glass, and stared out into the growing darkness. The sun slowly disappeared below the horizon.

Hours later, the glimmer of a dull, yellow light brought him to the window again. A large figure carrying a lantern completed crossing the narrow street below and disappeared into an adjacent building. A shadow of light could be seen through the opposite windows, meandering back and forth as the figure crossed to a staircase and faded from sight again, ascending into what must have been an attic, since the structure had only one apparent floor.

He mused momentarily about sneaking out of his room to check the surroundings. Deciding to do just that, he opened the door slowly, quickly realizing he was in an inn. The upstairs had an odd number of rooms: three rooms on either side of the hall marked 1 through 6, and another marked 7 at the far end.

He listened at each door along the sides of the hallway. Hearing no sounds of occupancy, he checked the door handles. The rooms were locked. The room at the end of the hall appeared similarly empty, though a faint light shone under the door. Interested, he stooped down to peek through the keyhole; unable to see anyone in the room, he put an ear to the door.

"May I help you?" said a burly voice from behind him. "You must want of something to be sneaking around in the dark. Is this the way you behave when you think you are alone?"

Vilmos jumped up, smacked his head on the door handle. He winced while rubbing the top of his head. "Sorry, I dropped something," he said, quickly adding as he turned around, "How did I get—"

His words cut short as he stared in horror at the abhorrence before him. The creature was well over six feet tall and so large-boned that it scarcely fit into the hall. Its skin was scaly with a yellow-green tinge.

He tried to run back down the hall, but he couldn't quite squeeze past the hulking figure fast enough. Caught by the scruff of his shirt, he struggled to break free.

"What's the matter, never seen a troant before? I'm not going to hurt you—I don't eat people. Human meat just doesn't taste as good as it used to."

The creature grinned, its teeth glistening yellow-brown in the torchlight, then shouted, "Boo!" and Vilmos nearly wet himself.

Vilmos fixed his face in a half smile, half scowl, but didn't manage a response.

"So my father was a troll and my mother a giant, big deal. It's not that unusual—and I'm only distantly related to wood trolls, so don't get any ideas about that either! I'm a swamp troll. Well half a swamp troll, the other half of me is—well, giant. I don't know what clan—there are six clans of giants you know: hill, stone, mountain, ice, fire and storm. Never got a chance to ask mom which clan it was—"

"How did I get here? Last I remember I was in the grove and there were these strange men and someone—*you?* That was you in the armor?"

The troant scratched at his chin. "My name is Edward. I am the innkeeper. You can call me Eddie—or Ed, which is even shorter—if you like. How come you didn't return my invitation?"

"What invitation?" Vilmos asked.

"I gave you white," said Edward. Vilmos still didn't know what Edward was talking about. "Haven't you ever played King's Mate before?"

Vilmos thought about it for a moment. "No. Is it fun?"

Edward put a hefty arm around Vilmos' shoulder. "Get the king piece I gave you and I'll teach you... It is more than fun!"

Chapter Eleven:
Galan's World

"How long have I slept?"

Adrina replied, "Since the day before yesterday."

"And Galan?"

"She started to recover almost immediately. She is growing stronger with each new day. She hasn't said very much and she would rarely leave your side. "

"I would speak with her."

"Rest and you will be up on the morrow. The council wishes to speak with you then."

"What is wrong with now?" Seth didn't see why he couldn't sit before the council now. The power of speech didn't tax his weakened condition; he could still think and thus talk.

Adrina thrust out a restraining hand. "They will wait! Tomorrow is a better day, you'll see."

Adrina soothed Seth until he drifted back to sleep, making him drink some broth along the course. She waited until he had passed into deep slumber before she left his side. As Galan now rested across from Seth, Adrina checked her next, surprised Seth's outburst hadn't awoken the lady elf.

Adrina's chambers were not far off and her aim was to steal several hours of much needed sleep, but she only made it as far as the hall before running into Keeper Q'yer. "How could you, keeper?" asked Adrina, knowing Keeper Q'yer's presence could mean only one thing: the council had come to the end of their patience.

"How could I what?"

"You know what I am talking about. We must wait."

"Princess, I must be frank with you, the council can wait no more. I see no reason to delay."

"Would you disturb a man on his deathbed?"

"He isn't dying."

"Does Father Jacob know you are here?" Adrina tempted the wrath of the man's office. A short time ago she wouldn't have had the nerve to put demands on a keeper, but things were different now.

"Under the circumstances I elected to come. Father Jacob knows I am here." The keeper attempted to move past Adrina. "I must see for myself. Now if you will allow me to pass."

"Another day couldn't hurt, could it? I'm sure Seth will be fully recovered. His companion should also be able to attend. You can have them both then."

Adrina followed Keeper Q'yer into Seth's room, and after a few minutes, back into the hall. She saw Father Jacob standing at the far end of the hall—a torch in its iron bracket cast an orange glow behind him. He raised a finger to her lips. She was not to say anything about his presence. "I will go to my father if need be. He will of course listen to reason."

The keeper eyed Adrina. "I am afraid that will do no good. See that the strangers are ready for council by midday tomorrow."

"Their names are Seth and Galan. Brother Seth and Brother

Galan... They are not strangers. They are friends."

"Don't be cross with me, I am only performing as told," said Keeper Q'yer as he walked away and was quickly lost in the shadows of the hall.

Adrina almost screamed another response, but a restraining hand stopped her short. "You've won, dear," said Father Jacob. "He said tomorrow. Take such victory and be at ease. You've done well."

***

Voices in the hall roused Galan to conscious thought. She opened her eyes and looked about the room, slowly taking in Seth's form in the bed across from her. Images of the world before her, however, paled in comparison to those captured in her mind's eye.

In her mind's eye she saw images from the dream—images of home. Leklorall, Kapital to those that dwelled there, was a city of grand canals and countless spiral towers—towers whose heights were matched only by those of the Silver Mountains looming at the southern edge of Lake Clarwater. Across the lake to the east she could see the outline of Near Glendall, and beyond was Ester Vale, the place of her birth.

She remembered sailing upon the Gildway as a child, sailing all the way to Riven End and back—it was the trade route of her father—but no journey held to her mind's eye like the journey to Near Glendall. That fall she had journeyed to Near Glendall and beyond: across the Clarwater and into the folds of the Elven Brotherhood. To be taken into the Brotherhood at such a late age was unusual and everyone she encountered reminded her of this—and they reminded her that to be taken into the Order of the Red was just as significant.

"Father," she whispered now as she had then, "I don't want to go. I don't want to disappear from life—it is not the journey I want. I would prefer to sail the Gildway to the ends of time. I'll take ship with Cagan. He is distant kin and will treat me fairly."

"The honor of it, my child. You must see, such sacrifice and service will bring status and title to our family—and to you. There is no greater achievement—it is the yearning of every father, every mother, for their children to earn such success."

"But I am unlike the others, father—the others were chosen at birth and I was chosen by chance."

"Queen Mother doesn't make mistakes and there was no chance in the matter, only fate. It is your fate and fortune."

"She entered my thoughts, father. I felt her in my mind, traveling my soul. I don't wish this."

"Soon their ways will be your ways and you will forget our ways—you will forget everything that you are now. That is the way of it."

Tears rolled down Galan's cheek. "No father, I will not forget where I came from. My past is who I am."

Aelondor took Galan's hand. "No my child, your future is who you are. Should we meet again you will not know me. It is the way of the Brotherhood. You must shed your past life and accept the new to become—and to become is everything."

"But I am not a child like the others, father. I won't forget—I won't let myself forget and I won't allow them to make me forget."

"Hush, my daughter," said Aelondor, taking Galan's hand and walking with her to the stairs leading from the docks. Upon reaching the stairs, he told her, "I can go no further. But I will return on the day you have achieved and with title, I and ours will walk the streets of Leklorall and take passage across her canals. It will be a grand day, and it is my fondest hope that I may see your face on that day."

Galan tried to speak but Aelondor touched a finger to her lips. "They wait at the top," he told her. "You will do well."

"Elf Galan?" called out Myrial, "I heard your voice from the hall. Who were you talking to? Can I help you?"

It took Galan a moment to return to the waking world. *Daydreams,* she whispered into Myrial's mind. *If the dream and desire are patent, you can journey to the past—and the past can often be a wondrous place when you don't wish to be in the here and the now.*

"My Lady Elf?" asked Myrial.

Call me, Galan. Brother Galan if it must be so.

"Princess Adrina is waiting to speak with you. She was here earlier but you had gone back to sleep. Perhaps you would like to walk with me? We could cross through the courtyards. A few moments of sun and fresh air may do you good. It is on the way to Adrina's quarters."

***

Adrina sat quietly, watching the changing colors of the day and absently moving the yellow orb back and forth in her hand. The balcony off her room was a quiet place where she could easily get away from the world.

Her thoughts were heavy. Emel left in the morning. She had hoped he would come speak to her one more time, but he hadn't. She would miss him but didn't envy him.

A journey to the wilds of the Territories didn't have the appeal that it once did, and the path was a long one. A path that would take Emel south to Ispeth, east to Hindell and Reassae before leading through the mountains and into the Territories.

Her thoughts floated, as if she rode with Emel. She was nearly asleep when the sound of someone clearing their throat roused her. "Yes?" she said absently, without turning.

"Sorry Your Highness, I don't mean to disturb you but Galan—"

"Galan?"

"Yes, she's here. She wishes to speak with you."

"Here?" Adrina placed her feet on the stones of the balcony, about to stand. "Please show her in."

I'm here, directed Galan, *I hope I'm not interrupting.*

"Not at all." Adrina turned to Myrial and grabbed the girl's hand. "Thank you, this is a wonderful surprise!"

Myrial smiled as she excused herself saying, "So much to take care of, I must be off. Your leave, Highness?"

Adrina nodded and turned back to Galan. "Please join me, sit. The air is surprisingly warm—it won't stay this way long mind you, so we had best enjoy it."

Winter is close indeed. I can feel it... You have been asking for me? Adrina regarded the silver-bronze of Galan's skin and the purple radiance of the eyes. *If you would prefer, I can...* Galan swept a hand along the contours of her body, leaving a trail of lightly tanned skin that matched Adrina's own.

"I don't prefer," said Adrina, "Your difference is your beauty." *Are you there in my mind, like Seth?* she whispered to herself.

"Your customs, I am sorry," said Galan aloud. "I will try to remember to keep to my own thoughts—and from yours."

"I don't find it offensive—"

"I didn't think you did but it does trouble you. Can I share a secret with you?" Adrina's expression brightened as if Galan was about to give her a gift. "I too once had the same thoughts as you. Voices in my head were most unnatural to me then."

"I thought all elves spoke thus. Is it not your way—" Adrina paused. "—the way of the Brotherhood?"

"The way of the Brotherhood, yes. The way of my people, no. Only someone who had never—"

"Seth," cut in Adrina, "Father Jacob told me of a conversation with Seth. Seth said—"

"Seth would not have remembered. He has never been among our people. Kapital is all he knows, yet its boundaries don't represent the boundaries of our lands—and it shouldn't be the only thing we know."

"Leklorall?" asked Adrina squeezing her hands together.

Galan's eyes showed surprise. "Who told you of Leklorall?"

"The capital of East Reach is Leklorall, just as the capital of West Reach is Elorendale," said Adrina matter-of-factly, fidgeting with her hands.

Galan stood—and for an instant Adrina could see fear and anger in Galan's eyes. *You can't know this! None of your kind has ever been to our lands and you have no records of our kind!*

"But of course we have records of the elves. Keeper Martin has many scrolls and tomes filled with your lore. He says that there were once more but they were lost in a great fire."

"You don't understand Princess Adrina," said Galan. "We *know* your history and your records—we wrote it, after all."

"Sit," said Adrina, "What do you mean?"

Galan, shocked at her own words—at their truth which she knew never to speak and wasn't even supposed to know—tried to stop herself from speaking but couldn't. "The Second Age—the histories recording the end of the Second Age were penned by Aven and Riven, half-elven. They were the original Lore Keepers as you call them. When the Elves of the Greye laid siege to the Kingdoms—the lands of Man—it was the Elves of the Reaches who came across the water to your aid."

"You speak lies!" shouted Adrina. "I have been made to study the histories all my life—and I know what occurred! The elves invaded our lands and though it took nearly two thousand years to drive them away, we succeeded!"

"Half truths, I assure you! Half truths!" Galan was shouting now and she was angry, and anger was not an emotion that came to her mind willingly—the Brotherhood had seen to that. Galan glared at Adrina—her thoughts racing. Adrina was still fidgeting with her hands and it was as Adrina's eyes became angry and wild that Galan saw the glowing orb Adrina held.

Galan snatched the orb away. Adrina tried to fight the elf off but was no match—and this was a good thing. The wildness in Adrina's eyes fell away the instant she released the orb.

Galan breathed deeply, calm, even breaths to steady her emotions. "Where did you get this? Do you know what this is? What this can do?"

Adrina was beyond speech as she collected her thoughts. Galan continued as she studied the orb, "This... This is Dnyarr's Orb—like the Gates of Uver the Orbs are forbidden. Where did you get this?"

"Dnyarr? Uver? I don't understand Galan. There was an attack and the one who led the attackers held this in his hand. It is magical, I believe. Somehow he used it to make a box of silence. I know this sounds of madness but—"

"Not madness, truth. Each of the Orbs has different properties, different powers—and different effects on those who hold them. They say the Orbs, like the Gates, are made of a magical substance once mined from the deepest, darkest reaches of the Samguinne—in Under-Earth."

Adrina touched her hands to Galan's shoulders. "I'm not of your world Galan. I don't understand. Where does it come from? Why is it here? What is it doing to us?"

"Dnyarr, Elf King of Greye, fashioned the orbs and the gates. The orbs are keys of sorts and the gates, doorways between realms. There are believed to be four orbs and seven gates—and Dnyarr hoped to use them to control the known realms. He gave three of the orbs to his sons: Daren, Damen and Shost, keeping one of the orbs for himself. The gates are scattered throughout the three realms.

"After the Great War, Dnyarr passed from the world of the knowing—not into death, as there is no true death from natural causes among the elves, but as it is said he lost the will to go on and so departed Under-Earth for the next life. His sons divided the Lands of Greye into three kingdoms, but as your people succumbed to a war of blood, so did Greye—a war where the three sons of Dnyarr fought to control Greye.

"As with the Kingdoms, the enemies of Greye saw the strife as an opportunity and so began the Rhylle/Armore wars. In the end Greye was left without its kings—and no king has ruled since. The people of Greye have been enemies of Rhylle and Armore since that time and it has kept their focus away from our realm, but the time of change is upon us again. And the Dark One, the one our people called Sathar, returns."

"Sathar? Who is Sathar and what does all this have to do with—"

"Not so much a who as a what. Sathar represents darkness. But to say that Sathar is darkness doesn't show an understanding of what Sathar is."

Adrina scrunched up her eyes and rubbed her temples. She wished Keeper Martin were here. He would understand what Galan was speaking of better than she. "Back to the orb. Can it really project a box of silence?"

Galan judged Adrina's expression without probing thoughts. "This is important to you?"

"More than you would ever know."

"Yes I believe so, particularly as Myrial has been standing in the far hall trying to hear our words—and though they've often been heated, she hasn't been able to hear anything. So yes, I think this orb has that power, among others. It is dangerous, though, to the untrained. You have seen how it can pervert thought and action."

"How do we turn it off?"

"Like this, I imagine," said Galan, putting the orb in the leather pouch Adrina had been holding after Galan snatched the orb away. She fought the urge to read Adrina's thoughts and emotions, hoping Adrina wouldn't be too hard on the good-intentioned Myrial. Her own good intentions had caused her to listen to many things that she shouldn't have been privy to.

"Myrial, come!" called out Adrina. Wide-eyed, Myrial entered Adrina's room and came out onto the balcony. "You've been standing in the hall, listening all this time?"

As a child caught stealing cookies, Myrial's eyes appealed to Adrina silently and her face turned red with embarrassment. "My thoughts are only of you. I ... I—"

"I know, I know," said Adrina. "Did you hear what we were speaking of?"

"I tried," said Myrial. "But I could hear nothing."

"Just as well, I don't fault you." Adrina raised an eyebrow and nodded to Galan. "Will you have dinner ordered and brought to us here?"

"Of course, dinner for two," said Myrial turning, about to hurry away.

"Dinner for *three*," said Adrina. "You will be joining us, yes?"

A smile lit Myrial's face. "If it is your wish, I would enjoy it immensely."

"No, it is *your* wish Myrial. Is it not Galan?"

Galan laughed.

"It is," whispered Myrial, turning to Galan. "Do you walk in my thoughts?"

Galan laughed. Adrina found she was unable to keep from laughing as well. Soon Myrial was laughing too. The laughter was cleansing for them all.

Chapter Twelve:
King's Mate

Vilmos hurriedly retrieved the tiny king piece from the table where he had placed it. Then he and Edward made their way to the stairs. Edward's large arm returned to Vilmos' shoulder as they did so, and, for an instant, Vilmos thought he would collapse under the tremendous weight.

The stairs creaked and moaned under Edward's weight as the two slowly descended to the first floor. The large open room below was pleasantly lit with candles hung from the ceiling in raised candelabra. On the center table, in a room filled with tables and chairs, was a large wooden board with small, hand-hewn squares etched into its surface and a number of tiny wooden playing pieces strewn haplessly about.

Edward ushered Vilmos into one of the chairs and turned the board to face them properly. "So you've never played before?" asked Edward checking Vilmos' eyes for honesty. Vilmos shook his head. "Well I'm going to teach you, so listen closely."

Vilmos leaned forward.

"Look carefully at the board. You will see it is seven columns wide and nine rows deep. There are... Hold on just a moment, I forgot something." Edward rose from the table, a slow and careful feat. He poured a draught from a large wooden keg, setting a frothy mug onto the counter momentarily as he tapped a second keg. He then filled a second mug and handed this to Vilmos. A healthy swig left thick foam around the innkeeper's lips, which when clean-licked roused a smile. "Go ahead try it! I just can't play without drink— and neither should you!"

Vilmos sniffed at the liquid in the mug. It had an unpleasantly strong odor. He raised the cup to his lips and stuck his tongue in for a taste. To his surprise, the drink held a sweet, tantalizing taste, somewhat like honey. "I's good!" he exclaimed.

"Why of course it is," said Edward. "Now listen closely to what I have to say… Where was I now?" Edward scratched at the thick scales on his forehead. "… Oh, yes. The board has seven raised areas. Five are in its center. These form an 'X'. The remaining two are in the center of the last row on each end."

Edward began to organize the pieces. He told Vilmos to put his king—the white king—on the board. The white king had an oversized, jeweled crown on its head and a sheathed sword in its right hand. As Vilmos did this, Edward placed his king—the black king—on the board. The black king wore a dark cape with a circlet of gold for a crown, and held a scepter in its left hand.

The next piece was a knight with a sword raised high into the air. This piece was the swordmaster and one occupied a square on either side of the king. Placed beside the swordmaster on the left was a priest and on the right a priestess. The priests held a long bone in their left hand and their right hand turned palm up contained three round pebbles. The priestesses held a ring of flowers.

As if bookends, two pieces representing Lore Keepers went into the end spaces of the last row. The Lore Keepers bore a great book before them as if it was a weapon—and there was no question in Vilmos' mind that the book was indeed a weapon in the right hands. He had seen his father, the village counselor, use the book to solve many issues—even heated disputes.

Into the next row Edward put five figures. "Fools," he whispered to Vilmos, as he placed the figures on the board in the first, second, forth, sixth and seventh columns, leaving an empty space in front of the swordmasters and explaining this by saying, "Swordmasters need extra space to maneuver, and fools understand this."

Intrigued by the game he had seen old men labor over for long hours, though they had never offered to show him how to play, Vilmos listened to Edward's every word intently. He paused only to drink as Edward did.

Finishing off his mug, Edward went to pour himself another, deciding after he had already filled it to pull the entire keg over next to him so that it would be within arm's reach. He also filled Vilmos' half-empty mug before he sat back down.

"Drink up Vilmos! I's good for you," said Edward laughing. "Are you ready to begin?"

Vilmos raised the mug to his lips and smiled, indicating a yes.

Edward continued, "All the pieces move differently. It is easiest to remember the moves this way... The king can only move one space at a time but in any direction. The swordmasters may move any number of spaces but must always be adjacent to the king. They revolve around him and rotate around his moves, moving always in direct lines. One must always be in a square touching the king, and the other may be adjacent to the king or the other swordmaster. So you see it is fairly tricky to move these three pieces around the board, particularly as you can only move one piece per turn. So you have to really plan your moves. Are you following me or did I lose you?"

Vilmos shrugged. He understood, somewhat. He would wait to play the game and hope he moved correctly.

As Edward wanted to clarify this point anyway, he went through a few practice moves with the black king and his swordmasters. He moved the left swordmaster forward one square, indicating that it was still adjacent to the black king, and then he moved the right swordmaster diagonally two squares until it rested before the other swordmaster. Edward indicated why this was a valid move. He then moved the king forward one square. He followed through a number of these simple maneuvers until it seemed Vilmos caught on.

"The priest and priestess move diagonally," Edward said, "in one direction only, any number of spaces on a given turn. Similarly, the keepers may move vertically or horizontally any number of spaces. The fools can only move one space at a time, either forward or backward. That's how they move...

"Now you must just remember this one last, very important rule. Only the king or the swordmasters may pass through the raised squares or stop on them..."

Vilmos watched as Edward pointed out the locations of the seven raised squares again.

"With one exception— if the king occupies the center raised square, any of the pieces of his color may cross the raised squares, but only for as long as he remains on that space." Edward stopped to take a heavy swig.

"You capture the pieces according to the direction that the piece you are using moves. Except for the fool, the fool only takes pieces that are diagonal to it. That is why he is called the fool, for he is the only piece that captures other pieces opposite from the way that he moves. The king cannot be captured until both his swordmasters are taken from him... So you must take the swordmasters first in order to capture the king and win… Do you understand?"

Vilmos thought about what Edward said, confused. In his mind, he moved the pieces around the board. He understood that part of the game, but not how to capture another person's piece. "But how can you capture the king and win if you have to take the swordmasters first?"

"Through sacrifice, Vilmos… Nothing good is gained without sacrifice."

All the pieces in place now, the game progressed, with Edward observing the defense while Vilmos gradually learned the intricacies. Vilmos was enjoying spending the evening in Edward's company. Edward's honest, open, goodhearted spirit was exactly what Vilmos needed to fill the empty spaces of his mind and heart.

After a short period of moving the pieces back and forth, neither gaining nor losing ground, Edward switched to an offensive posture and with great precision, not losing a piece, he stripped Vilmos of his five fools.

Amazed at how suddenly his pieces had been captured and taken away, for he thought he had been careful, Vilmos became inspired by the strategy involved in maneuvering the pieces. Before, he had been reluctant to attack, yet after Edward's wave, Vilmos was left with no other choice.

Seeking to recoup some of the losses, he ended up sacrificing his pieces instead. In an amazingly short time he was down to only three pieces, a single swordmaster, a priestess and his white king. A few moves later and the game was over. Edward's boisterous laughter filled the small inn, echoing long along its halls and through its many empty chambers.

✢✢✢

"Again?" asked Vilmos.

Edward took a long swig from his mug. "Again indeed!"

As Edward began to reset the board, Vilmos followed. "They are symbols, aren't they?" Vilmos asked. "I mean each piece represents something. Right?"

"More than that, I'm afraid." Edward winked at Vilmos. "The history of King's Mate is as long as time itself, or at least that is what I was told as a boy. I think that you'll understand it all one day—no, I'm sure you will."

Vilmos was quiet for a time as he placed the remaining pieces on the board. The white king he positioned last—and it was the one piece that intrigued him the most. The crown was too big for the king's head, and while the other king held a weapon—the scepter had a blade at either tip—the white king's weapon was sheathed and his hands were empty.

"First move is yours," said Edward. "When you are ready, of course."

Play began when Vilmos moved one of his fools, but Vilmos' thoughts were less on the game and more on other matters. "You brought me here. Didn't you, Edward?"

"I did. Would you rather I left you to the Followers? They'd not be showing you kindness right about now, I assure you. This realm is not yours—and you should be wary of everything you encounter in it."

"Even you, Edward?" Vilmos looked up from the board.

"Especially me," said Edward as he captured one of Vilmos' fools.

"I thought you were my friend. Do you know the shaman, Xith?"

"I do."

"And?" Edward took a deep swig from his mug and then made his next move but didn't answer. "And?" repeated Vilmos.

"I'll tell you one thing Vilmos, and you remember this clearly—

and you remember that I'm the one who told you." Edward sucked at the air nervously, emptied his mug in one great gulp. "You have no friends in this realm or any other—nor will you ever have any true friends. Those you count as friends will all betray you."

Vilmos blinked several times to be sure he was sitting with the same gentle giant that he had come to know in these past few hours. He found darkness and bitterness in Edward's words but strangely he wasn't upset or frightened by them. "Your truth?" asked Vilmos.

"It is my truth." Edward filled his mug and said nothing further.

Vilmos turned his attention to the game as well.

The two played late into the evening, with Vilmos losing many games and winning none. Eventually his skills and strategies improved though. By the evening's end he was providing ample challenge for the astute master of King's Mate.

Chapter Thirteen:
The High Council

"She is really quite remarkable," said Jacob, "This is the first time I really got to talk with her."

"Yes she is," said Adrina, "Who is that with her?"

"Father Francis. He is here for the council session. He wanted to help out."

Knowing the other's nature Adrina said, "More like he couldn't wait to see our guests."

Jacob smiled and nodded. The two talked for a time, turning from conversation about Seth and Galan to various other subjects, chief of which was the council meeting tomorrow. Adrina was attempting to wedge herself into a seat, and as she talked to Jacob she thought of ways to convince her father. She didn't want to miss anything that went on within those walls, and if she had it her way, she wouldn't.

Eventually Father Francis joined them in the hall. Adrina didn't know much about Francis, only what she had heard from others. She hated to pre-judge someone, but his reputation preceded him. He did appear to be as inquisitive as she had heard, but other than that, she couldn't confirm the other things. He seemed conservative and knowledgeable. Perhaps that was the reason Jacob had chosen Francis to accompany him today.

The three talked at length. Father Francis was curious about every detail Adrina could give him about Seth and Galan. He pondered her every word and she marveled at his great consideration. By the time the two priests departed, she had a totally different opinion of the pious Father Francis.

Adrina? came the whisper into her mind, the voice was pleasant and feminine. Before she realized whose voice it was, Adrina looked about the vacant hall. *Princess Adrina, are you listening?*

"Yes," said Adrina in kind with a whisper, although it was aloud and not a thought. "Can you hear me? I thought you were sleeping."

Not really. Come into the room. The door swung eerily open at Adrina's touch. Galan had been trying to sleep but many thoughts clouded her mind. Images of all sorts, pleasant and unpleasant. *I heard your voice from the hall. Have you been here long?*

"What is your home like?" asked Adrina, a thought she had considered but until now had been afraid to ask.

Galan answered with, *It is hard to explain. I do not know what to compare it with. I have not seen your world, your...* Galan borrowed the word from Adrina's mind. *Great Kingdom is unknown to me for the most part. I know only what I've seen in the South and now here in Imtal.*

Adrina frowned. She had hoped to learn more about the elves, anything at all would have helped—this frustration readily filtered to Galan. Adrina had given her and Seth so much. Galan wanted to repay that debt in part, a token of some sort.

"Tomorrow at noon, the council will meet," said Adrina, "They wish you and Seth to attend. Do you think you will be able?"

Don't worry so, Princess Adrina. This is the reason we came across the great sea. We must speak before your council. It is what we were destined to do.

ಐംಆ Kingdom Alliance ಐംಆ

You can prolong fate only so long, replied Galan, reading Adrina's innermost concerns. She almost asked Adrina about Seth, but she could feel his presence nearby now. Thoughts of Seth made her happy and she thought of home. In her mind she saw Queen Mother, the palace, and the beauty of her homeland. An idea came to her, she knew how to let Adrina see her world. *Adrina,* she began. *I have an idea... I want you to relax and open your mind to me. I want to show you something...*

Adrina didn't quite understand what Galan meant, but she did relax, and eventually Galan coaxed her into opening her mind. With warm, gentle feelings, Galan stroked Adrina's mind.

A warm breeze tantalized her skin and a picture began to form before her closed lids, fuzzy at first, then clearing. An enormous palace loomed in the window of her mind. She stood at its foot.

Beautiful, spiraling towers reached up into the heavens. She could reach out and touch them. Peace and happiness flowed and overwhelmed her. She was free, happy.

Abruptly the image blanked, the flow of emotions ebbed. "What's wrong?" Adrina asked, bewildered, blinking her eyes at the seeming sudden brightness. "What's wrong? Are you all right, you don't look so good."

Nothing, nothing, whispered Galan through tired eyes. She was glad her simple picture had brought Adrina joy. *I must rest a bit more, that's all.*

Adrina watched Galan drift back to sleep, soon her own eyes became heavy. As eyelids melted into place Adrina followed Galan into the land of dreams. The face before her eyes was Seth's, and it lay frozen in the window of her mind against a backdrop of spiraling towers.

***

"Galan, are you listening?" asked Adrina.

They find it very strange when we speak with our minds. Their customs are very different from our own.

I know, yet perhaps it is best if they think us different.

Perhaps not...

Adrina tilted her head back and dipped her long hair into the waters of the bathing pool. "Galan, what's wrong? Did I do something?"

Galan broke the link with Seth and focused on Adrina. While churning up the waters of the bathing pool, she said, *It is nothing. I'm a little confused that's all... Tell me more about this council of yours. What is it like?*

"The Great Council, the High Council, is made up of the ten wisest of the Kingdom. They are chosen for their skill at making decisions and positions—"

Sounds very much like our own council in the Eastern Reaches, said Galan, reading the thoughts before Adrina could put them fully into words and not meaning to cut the princess off. The hot water seeped into her body, soothing and invigorating.

All conversation ended as the two enjoyed the bath. Galan didn't restore the link with Seth, though he thrust thoughts into her mind two more times. Remembrance of the homeland that seemed so far away came to her, allowing her to think of little else.

When they finished, they found a pair of silken dresses where their discarded gowns had been, put there by the invisible hands of attendants. The same invisible hands that busily dried the princess then fitted one of the dresses.

I cannot wear such as this.

"I have given it to you, it is yours," said Adrina.

"I am sorry," began Galan, not realizing she spoke aloud. Her speech flowed with a broken pace, but other than that, it was Kingdom tongue with Kingdom accent—borrowed from Adrina's mind. "In my homeland… one of my office cannot wear such as this. My robe of office is a subdued shade of red. I am only the second, Brother Seth is the first."

Seth cut in, *You are not in your homeland, Brother Galan.*

"You must take it, the tailors made it especially for you. It is for the council meeting. I won't let you sit before our upper council in a house robe."

Seth, we are in a private conversation… Galan clipped the link forcefully, even though she had been the one to re-establish it.

You're still angry about our earlier conversation. Forget it, you owe me nothing. Nothing, remember that… We shall sit before the council and you are to do as told, threw in Seth, just before the link broke.

Adrina slipped the dress around Galan's shoulders before any further objections could be offered. The fit was perfect. Cool silk against her skin sent tingles through her body. She had never before worn silk.

"It is truly beautiful," she whispered, "Thank you!"

***

Seth, Galan and Adrina waited in the antechamber of the council hall. Adrina assured them the wait would only be a few minutes. Seth's mind flowed fluidly in and out of conscious thought while Adrina and Galan talked. He remembered sitting in the antechamber of another hall, far away.

Seth, called out Galan, *What do you think?* She hadn't considered that she would be interrupting his thoughts.

I'm going to probe their thoughts, Galan. I need to know their intentions before we go in. And I need to know if their— Seth touched Adrina's mind slightly, *—King Andrew is akin to our Queen Mother.*

You shouldn't, said Galan, *Adrina's thoughts are open and she won't mind the intrusion.*

Don't worry, they can't detect it, and besides, her thoughts are prejudiced.

King Andrew is her father.

Despite Galan's cautioning eye, Seth reached out to those within the hall, wandering in through the eyes of a broad-shouldered, broad-backed man seated upon a high-mounted chair. He gazed out through those eyes, regarding those that were gathered before him, seeing only the faces, nothing more. He heard their voices and followed their conversation, silently joining them.

"Out with it captain, have the rumors been confirmed or not?"

"No Keeper Martin, they have not." The captain grimaced.

"Get on with it man," demanded the black-robed priest.

"Father Tenuus please contain yourself," said King Andrew.

"You must excuse me, sire. I am not well. I think I have the chancellor's cold," replied the priest.

A raucous laughter erupted from the chamber, audible even behind the closed doors.

"Then we should proceed as planned, sire," said another priest, the white ribbons of his office decorating the dark sleeves of his robe.

"Yes, Father Jacob," said King Andrew, "I should think so." He turned to regard the captain then, "Send word to the garrison. Keep the patrols light but keep them steady. We do not want any more problems."

The captain's frown broadened as he waited for the king to finish.

"This should be a matter you handle yourself." King Andrew paused, regarding Captain Brodst. "Is there something wrong? Or should we find another who is more willing?"

"Sire, there is none more willing to serve than I... You have my word and my oath of honor," quickly returned the captain as his eyes darted about the room. There was a look of pain as if he had been stung. "Sire, I mean no disrespect but—"

"But what?" demanded Andrew.

"It is nothing, sire. By your leave, sire," said the captain excusing himself.

Silence followed. A set of doors opened. Seth saw a long, unhappy face stare back at the king from the doorway. The eyes were not quite angry, rather, openly displeased and the frown quickly shifted to a scowl.

The captain looked away. His footsteps echoed across the chamber once more and the doors were closed behind him.

"Father Tenuus?" said King Andrew. "You know what to do. Correct?"

"Yes sire," said the priest.

"Good, very good," said Andrew. "And father, ensure that the poor captain doesn't discover our little ploy. The celebrations will commence on the Seventh day and carry forward to the next. Imtal has not forgotten the deed!"

"Yes sire," said Father Tenuus smiling. He regarded the king, and in his eyes Seth saw a mix of admiration and adulation.

"Ensure the captain has an enjoyable time but have Swordmaster Timmer keep a close eye on him. We want him fit. Remember, no swordplay other than the trials. And Chancellor Yi?" The chancellor turned to regard the king. "What of your sources in the Free City, what do they tell you?"

Chancellor Yi looked about the chamber, seeming hesitant to speak.

"Out with it! What is the lay of it? Is it the same as we thought or not?"

"Yes sire, I believe it is," said Yi, a hint of submission in his voice.

"Good, send something special to our mutual benefactor in Solntse."

"I will at once sire," replied the venerable chancellor. "Is this the end of the previous business? Are we then on to those waiting?"

King Andrew nodded, sitting straighter in his chair as he looked about the room.

***

Suddenly the antechamber doors opened. Seth's mind jumped for an instant back to the High Council of East Reach. *I know what I must do, Queen Mother,* he whispered.

"His Royal Majesty, King Andrew, King of Great Kingdom, requests the presence Elf Seth and Elf Galan, friends of the realm."

Seth stood and took Galan by the hand. As he walked into the audience hall, he said in the polite form of his people, "I am Brother Seth of the humble Order of the Red."

"I am Brother Galan, also of the Order of the Red," added Galan.

Both spoke aloud.

"Welcome unto High Council of Great Kingdom! Please be seated," said Chancellor Yi. Father Jacob graciously indicated the two seats the elves were to occupy on one side of a large, triangular-shaped table.

Seth drank in the influence the hall held over the mind in one glance as he sat. The king and his advisors were seated on the longest side of the triangle. Others, like Seth and Galan, were seated on the short sides of the triangle, turned at an angle to each other and the king. The high vaulted ceiling, accented by each cutting rib with their intricate tierceron design. The table massed in the center of the hall, following each diagonal cross-section of the vaulting above, with three carefully placed groups of five chairs per side. The enormous oaken pews leading out in three concentric rows. All hinted at an unusual balance of power that Seth wished he understood.

ಶೂಂ Kingdom Alliance ಶೂಂ

The chamber emanated a subtle power all its own, perhaps it was the gathered knowledge of the men who sat within it or perhaps it was due to the design, Seth couldn't tell which, although both seemed very real possibilities to him, and here he felt at home. The hall reminded him of another place far away, that place, too, held a far-reaching power.

Keeper Martin spoke first. As head of the Lore Keepers, he spoke the words best that King Andrew wished expressed. "Brother Seth, we of the council of ten have many questions about you and your people, as we are sure you have of ours. The first question we must direct to you pertains to the purpose of your journey. What has brought you to our lands? Why have you come now?"

"I would gladly answer all your questions," said Seth closing his eyes, breathing in the profound air around him before he began again. "Once, long ago, our people, the Elves of the Reaches, came to your aid in your hour of need.

"The ancient evil has come to our lands now. We are under siege. If you do not help us this evil will spread to your lands—and it will spread until it dominates the world. For this is its goal. Even as I speak armies gather, the war begins, and such a war there hasn't been in generations of your kind."

Keeper Martin stood and turned to the king, speaking the king's will. "You speak of things of which we have no recollection. The Elves of Old are our enemy. We count you, Seth, and you, Galan, friends, only because of your actions in the South and because of the word of a friend who is unknown to this council."

"I have been granted the right to speak truth by my queen and to show truth. If you would allow me to do so, it will only take a moment of your time."

Chancellor Yi tapped his staff to indicate approval.

"Keeper Martin do you recall the Battle of Quashan' and the

injury you received during the battle?"

"But of course," said Martin. "The battle was turning against us and in the rush to get to Princess Adrina's company I took a wound—an arrow in the side. Elf Galan removed the arrow, and may have saved my life as well that day."

"On that day Galan did more than remove an arrow. She gave you a gift for safekeeping, for we were unsure that we would survive the day but Galan foresaw that you would—and that you would one day share the gift with this council. I would ask your permission to remove that gift from your person and share it."

"But I have no recollection of a gift and I carry nothing on my person."

"Exactly," said Seth, "The gift is within you, in the place made by the arrow."

Chancellor Yi tapped the floor to quell the growing murmurs but that didn't work to bring silence. Only King Andrew's raised hand brought silence.

If you will allow me, whispered Galan to Keeper Martin as she moved toward him. *I will reach my hand within you and remove the item. It will be painless—I assure you.*

As Galan began to reach within Martin's robes, the keeper put out his hand to the guards who were coming to his aid. "It is all right. There is nothing to fear. Galan means me no harm."

Please stand still, Keeper Martin, it will only be a moment. You shouldn't feel any pain. Galan's hand melted into Martin's side, and when she removed it she held a slender rod. She handed the rod to Seth.

Seth removed a thin casing from the rod. He began to unwrap the scroll within. "May I read this?" he asked. "You will find it—"

Chancellor Yi cut in, "Why have you waited until now to return to our lands, only in time of need? Why did you not tell this to those who found you? Wouldn't that have made more sense?"

Seth turned to the chancellor, reaching out with his hand and pointing a sinewy finger. "Chancellor, as a member of the High Council, you know why we left your lands and why we haven't returned. Your kind drove us away... in the Race Wars all was destroyed."

Wide-eyed the old chancellor sat back, leaning away from Seth's outstretched hand. He did not make further comment. Keeper Martin quickly stepped in, saying, "Brother Seth, please continue."

As with the chancellor, however, King Andrew didn't want Seth to speak. He stood purposefully, and when he did so all eyes in the room went to his. "We are in a time when the careful peace we have had these many past years has been broken, and we are working to repair the damage to prevent the collapse of the Kingdom Alliance." The silver of Seth's skin and the odd color of his eyes called to Andrew as he spoke. "Our new alliances with the South will ensure peace, and we have no desire to bring war to our door or to carry out war on a distant shore."

Seth switched from talking aloud to speaking with his mind. A whisper of his thoughts met each person sitting around the table, touching King Andrew last. Then Seth spoke aloud with purpose, "I waited for this moment when I could sit before your council and address it as an equal. I wanted to know the thoughts in your minds, your concerns and most importantly your reactions. This is why I waited. These words were meant for me to speak, and not from a sick bed."

To hold the others in check, Seth switched to thought, sending words and emotions, *But standing before you! War will come to your door and when it does it will be too late. You must act now! The Elves of the Reaches need your support, do not wait until it is too late.*

Directing his words to Andrew and others who he could see were confused, Father Jacob jumped into the conversation. "Do not be alarmed! As I have told you, Seth and Galan can speak with their minds."

Brother Seth speaks the truth. Please, you must help us! The voice that touched their thoughts was Galan's. *Let him speak from the scroll and all will be clear.*

Chancellor Yi thumped his staff. "Brother Seth when you speak of support, what type of support do you mean?"

"Ships, men, supplies! We need all you can spare and we need quick action beyond all other things!"

"We need to know more of your lands and your enemy. Speak to convince his majesty. In this instance, we, the council, are echoes of his will and serve only to raise questions and get answers."

The tide of the conversation flowed heavily back and forth, growing heated at times, stopping at other times. Seth carried on the debate with Galan acting as his support. The discussion went long into the afternoon with the council considering each point and counterpoint carefully.

Seth was never allowed to read from the scroll.

Chapter Fourteen:
A Lonely Path

Two days came and went, with Vilmos spending most of his time on the opposite side of a playing board from Edward. Although the break was enjoyable, Vilmos was growing increasingly anxious for Xith's return.

The inn was an unusually empty place, with Edward and Vilmos being the sole occupants. In the three days not a single visitor or traveler arrived. Vilmos would often glance out the window when he heard a noise hoping it was Xith, usually it was the wind rattling the shutters. Edward noticed this and often told Vilmos not to worry, his friend would find him soon enough. Vilmos fretted nonetheless.

Vilmos and Edward were in the middle of yet another game of King's Mate. So far Vilmos had lost three of his fools and his keeper. Edward had not lost a single piece. Vilmos did, however, have his king in the center raised square, which meant for a time he controlled the board.

Cleverly, Vilmos swung his second swordmaster onto an adjacent raised square, now it could not be taken. Edward thought long and hard and only after careful calculation did he move his priestess diagonally forward to endanger Vilmos' first swordmaster.

Vilmos rotated the swordmaster around the King, taking one of Edward's fools. This left Vilmos in a position to take a keeper or swordmaster the next turn.

Edward could not counter the move. He sought to gain by a loss. He moved his swordmaster, hoping Vilmos would claim the keeper.

Vilmos studied the board. The keeper was an easy piece to take, but the bold move was to take nothing and move his priest adjacent to Edward's king and swordmaster. Vilmos could not take the king while the swordmasters remained. He would wait until Edward tried to claim the priest. The priest was backed up by his own keeper, which in turn was further supported by a swordmaster, which could swing one space further to the left if necessary. The play was tight and tricky, but Vilmos attempted it.

Edward smiled at the move—it was amateurish. He quickly devoured Vilmos' swordmaster with his priestess. A broad smirk was evident on his face, until in a series of quick and calculated maneuvers Vilmos stripped four of Edward's pieces: the priestess with which Edward had taken his swordmaster, the swordmaster which had been backed by the priestess, the keeper Edward could do nothing to protect, and, lastly, Edward's only remaining swordmaster. Now Edward's king was without protection.

Edward could do nothing to prevent Vilmos from taking the pieces, only sit back and watch with amazement. Wide eyes replaced the smile. Edward couldn't maneuver his king out of the trap. In another move it was check. In one more, the game was over.

"Where were you hiding those moves? That was brilliant—your best playing!"

Vilmos held the black king in his hand. The ebony from which it was carved was cold, and, though the piece itself was smooth,

Vilmos felt as if the carved edges could slice into his fingers. "I just did as you said. I sacrificed the priest to gain the king."

Edward chuckled. "Do you know in all the years I've been playing that I've never been defeated? I've never lost until just now—and it was a grand loss at that! Brilliant play—you finally started to think like a King's Mate player and not like a boy playing Cross Rocks!"

"You are the one who told me to think five moves ahead. I tried that, honestly—but it took more than five moves to win. It was like I could see the board in my mind, how it would change with each option, and each option's option. Paths crisscrossed, the checked spaces of the board blurred and then everything become … became—"

"Real," said Edward. "Real, as if you were living the game rather than playing. Yes?" Vilmos held out the black king to Edward. Edward took the king and started setting his pieces on the board. "One more game and then we'll call it a night. Okay?"

***

Adrina had recounted every moment of the attack to Emel and the mere mention of Oshywon was enough to convince him that the attack was much more than it seemed. If there was anything a summer at High Road taught him, it was this: the lost kingdom did not exist and any dim-witted soul who said otherwise ended up at the wrong end of a blade. Gutted, usually, neatly—split down the middle like a ripe melon. He had no aspirations to end that way, but he would make inquiries all the same. It was an important tidbit, more so than anything else Adrina had said, too important to let go.

He paced back and forth, his movements erratic. The supply caravan was already a day's ride away. Ebony could catch them and they could easily make their way to the East—if he was smart, if he would let what was lost stay lost. A few seasons in the Territories, that's all it would take. He would return, the dark days, the dark desires, would be behind him.

Foolish. Foolish to be sure. Why couldn't he listen to reason?

He threw up his hands, batted his head against the wall. *Crazy. Crazy thoughts—not foolish.*

For good measure he batted his head against the wall again but this didn't bring reason. He picked up his rucksack and went down to the stables, making his way to Ebony. The stalls for the horses of lesser knights and other riders were at the far end.

Ebony was already saddled and bridled. His bedroll, sword and other belongings were in a pack on the ground nearby. The sack he carried now contained mostly food, the necessities of the road: hard bread, jerky, nuts and seed meal.

He checked Ebony's saddle and rubbed the stallion's mane. "Soon," he whispered, "I promise."

He put the packs in place. The sword went on top of everything, at the ready, and, as when riding the High Road, he tucked a half dozen throwing daggers into each side of the saddle. The dagger he tucked into his belt at the back made thirteen. Another thing a summer on the High Road had taught him was how to survive the wilds.

As he rode Ebony out of the stable he shook a fist at the early afternoon sun. He would ride hard, fast. With luck he would catch the caravan near Mellack or Ispeth.

"Chase the wind," Emel whispered to Ebony as they exited Imtal's gates, "Chase the wind." He looked back as he reached the low hills of the Braddabaggon, but by then his resolve was firm.

Ebony reared, turning as if in salute, then carried Emel down the long lonely road ahead.

***

"Is it or isn't it?" asked King Andrew. He and Chancellor Yi were the only ones in the council chambers. The others had been dismissed.

"Sire, a moment I beg of you."

"No more patience this day, Chancellor Yi. Guess if you must—a sensible guess—but a guess all the same! Is it or isn't it?"

Not one easily bothered, Chancellor Yi maintained his position, the eyepiece fixed in his hand as he studied the parchment paper. "In my opinion—"

"Opinions be damned!" shouted King Andrew, "Tell me!"

"It is. Yes, it is." Chancellor Yi sat bolt upright and looked directly at the king. He handed Andrew both scrolls, saying, "They are identical. Both penned by the same hand, with the same ink, signed in blood."

King Andrew handed the chancellor the lamp. "Burn them, burn them!"

"But sire the history, these have been—"

Andrew grabbed the scrolls, tossed them into the fire, threw the oil lamp in after to make sure the fire burned hot. "Let fire cleanse this away! We will have not another word of this! Keeper Martin must not know. The elves must not know. Understood?"

Chancellor Yi withstood the king's glare. "Surely the past cannot be lost forever. The truth of it will be heard. The Alder would not have—"

"The Alder doesn't have to live in the present. We cannot undo what has been done. Elves and Men must remain as they have remained. It is my will—it is also the will of the people. I can feel it, I know this."

"Their road is a lonely one is it not then? To have come all this way—to have failed."

King Andrew sighed. The weight of the world was on his shoulders. "It is what it is. No more, no less… Come now, tell me of the spring plans—that's a subject of less weight."

Chancellor Yi went back to the table. "The trust deeds for the lands from Heman to Klaive along River Opyl. Your quill, sire."

King Andrew nodded as he signed the trust deed. Chancellor Yi pressed the royal seal into the paper. "Any troubles with Family Heman?"

"Odwynne Heman took the offer well and gave her word to bide by the agreements. She's the family matriarch, I don't expect any dissent. She seemed pleased with the landholdings offered and of the fact that you may possibly hold her favor at court."

"Has the work begun? Adrina is…" King Andrew's voice trailed off.

"It will be a grand house—a grand house indeed by spring. Klaive masons are building a protective wall around a large courtyard and construction will start soon. The river trade is good, tree and fir. The coast trade abundant with fish and crab. A place to prosper."

"A place to prosper," said Andrew. "Imtal will truly be an empty place then, won't it?"

"It may be wise to call Valam home, sire. South Province has prospered. The people think him wise, generous—and the Battle of Quashan' has only further endeared him. His presence in Imtal would be a good thing. If he took charge of the councils and day ceremony, it would further prepare him for the crown. King Jarom will surely see this as a sign of strength—and certainty that the crown will go to Valam is a good thing. His daughter will be of age soon and their binding will be as a consummation of his desires."

"Indeed," said King Andrew.

***

Edward pored over every option. There was visible strain in the air.

Vilmos stretched out his arms and shifted frequently in his

chair. His backside was sore and numb. They had been sitting for hours. His weariness distracted his attention, but he would not yield.

In the first hours of the game not a piece had been taken or exchanged; the field was held in a careful ballet.

Outside the inn the gentle light of morning was forming on the horizon. Neither noticed. Nor did they take note when dawn gave way to the bright sunshine of a new day.

Edward wiped a dew-like perspiration from his brow without taking his eyes from the board or moving his other hand—the hand that rested on his king. He cursed under his breath, moved the king from the center square.

Waiting for Vilmos to make his next move, Edward watched the board, estimating which pieces Vilmos could move where and how he could counter. When Vilmos made the move Edward surmised he would, another offensive push toward center, Edward was ready for the counter. Before moving, Edward checked the alternatives.

A smile formed when Vilmos saw Edward's move. Suddenly weariness and fatigue were replaced by elation. He set in with a precise attack—a series of moves he had been saving for the right moment.

The intensity of the game built as Vilmos claimed his stake of Edward's pieces. On the run, Edward pulled his pieces back to defensive positions to prevent the capture of his king.

The wind outside picked up, though neither noticed; their attention was lost to the board, each carefully deducing the next move, the next counter. Vilmos was ready to make a claim for victory, soon he would push Edward into a corner from which he could not escape. He grinned, purposefully stalled as he sipped from a near-empty glass, brought his hand to the board, perhaps toying with the expectant expression on Edward's face. He would move the white priestess diagonally up the board to put the black king in check once more.

Vilmos eyed the dark king as he slowly brought the priestess across the board. He was lifting his fingers from the board and Edward was contemplating his next move when the wind outside surged, and in a sudden sweeping crash, the windows of the inn shattered.

Tattered shards still clattered to the floor as a voice rang out, a savage, eerie voice that slurred the words together into a fervent snarl. "Remain seated or you both die!"

Edward looked up from the board. "Can you not see we are in the middle of a game? And you'll pay for the windows, there was no need for any of that!"

Three hair-covered beasts stood inside the inn, one at the door, the speaker, with a henchman to either side of him. Edward glared at the intruders. Each was heavily armored in the typical banded mail of their kind, with weapons at the ready.

Edward knew these beasts well. He had seen them many times before, though he had never been a victim of their assault. They were the paid hunters of Under-Earth; the half-animal, half-human race disgusted him. He watched the leader, who was watching him back. Saliva dripping from the beast's upturned canine fangs as it licked its hair-covered face was a sign. The beast was on a hunt.

"What is it you seek?" asked Edward as he stood, trying both to gain time to think and to place the oddly familiar voice.

"We wish no harm. We seek out the boy. Give him to us," hissed the beast through its wolf-like mouth, saliva dripping with each word slapping the floor.

Edward turned to Vilmos. "Sorry about this, lad. It is as it must be."

The beast nodded to his fellows. "Leave the other. Take the boy."

Edward cleared his throat. "What good is this boy anyway? Not much of a meal. Not much of anything, really. You must be mistaken, maybe the one you seek is upstairs in the far room on the right?"

The beast sniffed at the air. "Upstairs on the right?"

"Came in yesterday from the road. Strange looking, an outrealmer for sure. Not like my servant boy here." Edward grabbed Vilmos by the scruff of the shirt. "Stole those clothes there didn't you?"

Vilmos didn't answer—couldn't answer. Words wouldn't come to his lips.

"Didn't you?" shouted Edward.

Chapter Fifteen:
The Final Game

Edward hesitated, carefully edging toward the hunter beasts, placing himself between them and Vilmos. "You are disturbing our game! I have nothing against the Hunter Clan, nor does my boy servant. Now if you will take your business upstairs and away, we will continue."

"Just do as ordered!" shouted the beast leader as he pointed his double-edged blade at Edward.

"You are making a mistake," said Edward. He gripped the chair beside him, eyeing closely the two crossbows of the henchmen. "Surely, you can lower your weapons. A mere boy and a fat troant can't hurt you. Go upstairs and find your bounty."

"Lies," screamed the beast. "Lies!"

Edward belted the closest beast with the chair, knocking it to the ground; its crossbow bolt triggered, flew harmlessly into the ceiling. The other beast shot Edward cleanly in the leg.

"Run, Vilmos run!" Edward shouted as he toppled the table.

Vilmos ran to the stairs. He shifted his gait to the right just in time—a bolt whizzed by his head. At the top of the stairs he stopped and peered over the rail. Only then did he consider his actions. How could he just leave Edward? He had to do something to help but what? Why did he run upstairs?

"Freeze!" shouted the beast leader, "Don't move!"

"Run Vilmos! Don't look back, go find the shaman!" shouted Edward.

Vilmos heard the desperation in Edward's voice. He didn't want to, but he was scared, so he ran.

Edward launched at the attackers. He took one step, a bolt pierced his chest. The pain was immediate and excruciating. Edward winced, determined. He had been in worse places before and survived. He had given the shaman his sacred word he would watch over and protect Vilmos.

"Up!" shouted the beast leader as he displayed his sword at the henchman sprawled on the floor. The beast scrambled to its feet and picked up its weapon. The second beast licked its furry mouth and reloaded its crossbow. "Quit while ahead and life in your veins," said the leader.

The pain was great but did not stop Edward. He shook a defiant fist and took another step. His wounded leg, slow to respond to his wishes, caused him to limp.

He snapped a leg off one of the chairs and bore it before him.

Two more bolts pierced Edward's body. He slumped harshly and suddenly to the floor. His eyes wandered to the stairs just as Vilmos disappeared down the hall. Life drained from his limbs.

***

Just like these Men, Seth directed to Galan—it was almost a curse. *They lied! The Kingdom is hardly returning to a state of peace… They fear their neighbor's every action. They greeted us with the same fear.*

Galan touched her hand to Seth's shoulder, whispering into his mind alone, *We have done our best; they will listen. It is fated…*

Adrina, unable to hear their private thoughts, said, "Today is not yesterday. You'll see. The waiting will be over soon. Do you want me to send for refreshments?" She was trying—in the only way she knew how—to be helpful.

Princess Adrina, we do not want any refreshments, shot back Seth, his thoughts angry.

He didn't mean that Adrina. Did you Seth? Galan directed the thoughts now, *Seth how could you? She didn't deserve that. She is not the one you are angry with. Are we so far away from our homeland that Queen Mother's love cannot find and fill our hearts?*

Seth was worried. He had perceived the many turnings in the conversation. The decision could go either way and waiting helped nothing, it only furthered his doubts.

Pretending she had not heard Seth's remark, Adrina tried again to spark a conversation. Galan tried to join in at first, but after a time she too became quiet.

The hours drifted by. Each falling into the next with slow persistence.

As her unease grew, Adrina had to restrain herself. She wanted to burst through the double doors. The antechamber doors had been open before. She had heard most of the discussion. She didn't understand the need to delay or why they were deliberating. And she understood Seth's bitterness. She had been so driven once.

Determined to break the silence, she did so. "Are you hungry? We can lunch here if so." Galan admitted she was hungry, as did Seth after Galan prodded him. Adrina found a servant and sent him to the kitchen to bring a light meal.

The servant had just returned when the great doors opened and Seth and Galan were beckoned to come back to the triangular council table. Even before he sat Seth read the thoughts of the council members. He knew the choice of everyone in the room. He could only sit and listen to the resolution as Chancellor Yi spoke it.

"Unanimous decision," said Chancellor Yi. "We understand the hardship of your journey and regret the decision, but we cannot support you in your endeavor. The meeting is concluded."

Seth hurled a wave of his will through the minds of the council, forcing tears. His anger was non-selective, so even Adrina, seated in the antechamber, felt it.

Seth, win through diplomacy, directed Galan to Seth's mind alone, *Use your knowledge; hope is not lost!*

Seth searched their minds, seeking the ones who understood what was at hand. "Keeper Martin, you know the ways of Aven and Riven—you must. Surely you of all people know the truth of what I speak. You know what must be done. How can you sit idle? I have given the scroll to Chancellor Yi surely you have read it?"

Keeper Martin raised an eyebrow as he turned to the chancellor and back to Seth.

You haven't, directed Seth to Keeper Martin. *They didn't tell you, did they?*

Seth turned to Father Jacob—the priest was another who should see truth. "Mother Earth cries out! The Father begs you listen! Can you not see this? Can you not feel the waters crest?"

Seth turned to Chancellor Yi. *The decision was not a unanimous one! You have tangled the truth with lies! You haven't told anyone of the scroll?*

Chancellor Yi stood, indignation on his face. "Brother Seth, we understand the way you feel—the decision was unanimous and final. We will hold no further discussion, please, no more outbursts!"

Galan held a restraining hand on Seth's leg. Seth glared and screamed into her mind, *Fear and anger are emotions these Men heed most often! Let them see anger and let them know fear!*

Seth wait, faith! returned Galan, *Look to Adrina...*

The council grew quiet. Galan squeezed her nails into Seth's leg as his emotions flared.

Chancellor Yi turned to King Andrew, "The resolution stands. I move to dismiss the council." King Andrew nodded. The chancellor said, "The meeting is at an end."

No, Seth, no! directed Galan to Seth, but her words of restraint could not stop him. Just as Adrina passed into the chamber from the anteroom, Seth jumped from his chair and began to lash out. The council cowered back from him, truly afraid, while those around King Andrew moved between their king and Seth.

Adrina stared openly at Seth and he stopped. Her eyes next fell on Father Jacob. She did not say a word, but her gaze forced words to Jacob's mouth. "Perhaps a review *is* in order, Your Majesty. There are some things that I have not stated, things that—"

King Andrew glared at the priest.

Keeper Martin said, "I believe Father Jacob has a point, perhaps we have been overly cautious. Our own concerns are centered on the affairs of the South. Perhaps our view is narrow. I would second the motion for a review. This decision is best not made hastily."

Chancellor Yi scoffed and held his ground.

King Andrew said, "A second has been put forth. Are there any who would object to a review tomorrow?"

Tomorrow? screamed Seth.

Seth! Galan directed the thoughts. *Faith!*

Adrina cast an angry glare around the chamber, then escorted Galan and Seth outside. Feelings of disappointment flowed through her mind as she walked alongside the two. "I'm sorry," she said, "I should have requested an audience with my father to discuss this yesterday. If he saw what I saw in Quashan', through my eyes, the decision might have been different."

No, said Seth, *It is the will of the Father. We will try again tomorrow and this time we will not fail. I am truly sorry about my behavior. There is no excuse for it. I hope you will be gracious enough to forgive me.*

"I know what it is to be so driven," whispered Adrina to herself, forgetting that the two could read minds.

Tomorrow then, said Seth.

"Then you have a plan?"

I will find one.

"Can you not show them your world? Perhaps then they will understand," said Adrina forgetting that Galan had been exhausted after the momentary image gifted to a single mind.

Show them my world, repeated Seth as he reached into Adrina's mind.

Galan's face showed fear. *No, you mustn't! We will find another way! Promise you won't?*

Seth tightened the seal on his mind and walked away.

***

Emel cursed. He should have been halfway to Mellack but he wasn't.

He waited, a bit claustrophobic in the small space behind the door. As the door swung open he stifled a breath. As the door swung closed he swept passed, clasping a hand firmly to the girl's mouth.

"Not a word," he whispered. "Be still and this will be over quickly."

She bit him. He removed his hand, started to say something. She spoke first. "Take what you want and be quick. You'll do nothing that hasn't been done before."

Emel swung Myrial around. "Well then. This will be quick, won't it?"

"I thought you had gone?" Myrial's heart raced. "You should have gone."

"Where is she?"

"Gone to council with the elves some hours ago. Why are you sneaking around?"

"Indeed why?" said another voice. Emel and Myrial turned as Adrina slipped into the room from the private entry door. "What are you doing here Emel? You should have been at Ispeth by now."

Emel was still holding Myrial's wrists. He let go as his eyes went from Myrial to Adrina. "Orders have changed, I'm to go to High Road instead."

"*High Road?*" Adrina said it like it was a dirty word. "That can't be."

"I've come back for the orb. I think I'll need it. Have you learned anything about it that will be useful?"

"Nothing." Adrina looked to Myrial then back to Emel. "You don't want it. It's nothing but a bauble, you said so yourself."

Emel went to Adrina's writing table. "Is it here?"

Adrina moved between Emel and the desk. "I think it's best left here. If you must go to High Road your thoughts should be on other things."

Myrial moved beside Adrina, reaching for the small leather pouch hidden away within the desk. Emel stopped her, grabbing her hand and the pouch. "Don't worry so. I'm thinking clearly Adrina. I know what I must do."

"Don't do this for me. I don't want you to—I'd rather you went to the Territories."

Realizing he was still holding Myrial's hand, which cupped the pouch, Emel snatched the pouch away and took a step back. "Tell me what you know about the orb. I will do my part in this. Not for you, but because I want to."

Myrial turned up Emel's hand, opened the drawstrings on the pouch, removed the orb. "Rub it in your hands," she said, "Squeeze and focus. The power flows."

Adrina was surprised and it showed.

"I have eyes," said Myrial, "I've seen you with it—I've tried it."

"Then you must know?"

"I know—I know very well the pull of it."

"Galan said I must find control or it would control me. She's teaching me how to breathe and focus. If you don't do this, the emotions—the anger—"

"I don't plan to use it Adrina. I'm not a believer. I think though that if I have it my task will be easier. When I've finished I'll return it to you if it's possible."

Adrina took the orb from Myrial. Emel tried to grab it away and for a few seconds both their hands touched the orb. Adrina's eyes grew wide. "Oshywon," she said, "What's lost should stay lost."

"How could you possibly know?"

Adrina put her hand over the top of Emel's. "Think any thought and—" Her face went red. "Well except *that!* Think something else—yes, you should've removed Ebony's bridle and saddle. It's going to be a long night."

Emel snatched back his hand as if the orb and Adrina's touch had burned him. "You couldn't possibly know—"

"You're not going anywhere this evening so forget that notion of sneaking away as well," said Adrina, "We have things to do—all of us!"

"I'd rather—"

"No," said Adrina smiling. "You're not going anywhere…" She turned to Myrial. "What him, watch him close. I've to see the elves, I'll be back shortly."

Chapter Sixteen:
Across the Distance

Seth leaned back onto the bed, staring up at the ceiling. He was lost in thought.

Galan attempted sleep but found none. Slowly her eyes found Seth. She stayed an urge to go to him but that didn't stop her from thinking about him. She owed him so much and it hurt to feel the pain that flowed from his thoughts. She wished she could do something—anything that could take away the pain.

The floor was cold against Galan's bare feet. Lost in his plight, Seth didn't notice her approach. A small voice told her not to go to him, yet a larger voice urged her on. She took the next step carefully and deliberately, knowing what it meant. Her conscious held her no more. There could be no turning back now.

She was about to lie beside Seth when a light knocked summoned at the door. Seth looked up, Galan started. She retied the strands she held, fixing her dress into place, moving directly to the door.

She touched a hand to the door, reaching out to the one who stood there. *Yes? What is it?*

She opened the door, pointed to Seth.

Father Jacob seemed disappointed to find Adrina absent, having wanted to speak to her as well as to the elves. "I wanted to speak to you about earlier. There are things that you don't—"

—*Save your words good Father Jacob. The fault rests on no one other than me. I should have seen this. I should have known...*

"Brother Seth, I must insist. Keeper Martin and I have been talking. We—"

Latching onto Jacob's hand, Galan led him from the chamber. *Go, we will manage.* She watched his retreating form until it mingled with the night shadows of the corridor. *Thank you,* she sent after him.

Seth returned to his thoughts, reviewing every word of the council, searching for where he had erred, already knowing what he must do.

Galan closed the door. For a time she stood quietly watching Seth. She would have turned away had the impulse not returned.

She crossed to Seth's bedside and touched delicate fingers to his hand, crouching down beside him and pressing her lips against his.

A circle of heat bathed the two forms pressed tightly one against the other. Galan redirected her will now, probing with emotion absent of thought. A single finger traced her curves and briefly Seth returned the passion that flowed to him.

Reality soon crept in. Seth reached deep within to find restraint. He touched a finger to Galan's lips. *No more, I cannot. We must not.*

Is this not what you have longed for? Galan asked, tears in her eyes. *Brother Liyan told me of your heart before we left Kapital. He told me to understand the desire even if those feelings did not find me. Such feelings are not lost on me. I need you beside me this night.*

Seth put his arm around her, closed his eyes. Before he drifted away to sleep he created a wall of thought around them to ensure the night would not be disturbed again.

***

Vilmos ran across a dusty plain without knowing how he had gotten there. The last thing he remembered was running up the stairs of the inn. Nervously, he glanced over his shoulder, catching glimpses of the inn and its surrounding structures. It seemed no one followed.

He didn't know where he could go. He didn't know anything about this area or Under-Earth. He could run, but to where he did not know. He did know that he must find Xith.

Find the shaman, run, that's what Edward told him—and he was running. He was running as fast as his legs could carry him, faster than he had ever run before.

There was a small rise behind the inn. He was running up it when he slipped, falling backward, twisting. He stood to find he was staring at the inn instead of up the hill. The world was still spinning so he couldn't be sure that he wasn't spinning with it.

He was about to turn back up the hill when his thoughts registered what he saw—horses, strange, abnormally large, but horses just the same. He had never seen such a wondrous sight, then he wondered if he could get to the horses before the hunter beasts found him.

Before he made a decision his feet were running toward the three black horses tethered at the back of the inn. The first horse screamed and reared up to the limit of its tether when he approached.

He backed away, keeping a wary distance, approaching a different horse, one that did not shy away.

Perhaps it was fear or the rush of adrenaline, but he had ridden for nearly an hour before he realized that he had escaped—or so it seemed. He also realized that he had never been on a horse before without someone alongside him to help him along. He felt suddenly alone and confused. *Where was he riding to? Was there anywhere he could go that would be safe? Where was Xith?*

He reigned in the horse. He could hear his heart beating in his ears. It was in that moment, when all the world seemed to echo the thump-thump-thump in his ears, that he could feel the wildness of the land. It was speaking to him, calling out, telling him to go.

Driven by the voice, Vilmos rode. It wasn't until much later after he calmed and his heart stopped pounding in his ears that he started to wonder why the hunter beasts never followed him. Images of the gnarl-faced beasts still chilled his thoughts. He wondered what had become of Edward, momentarily refusing to accept that Edward might be dead.

He thought maybe Edward killed the strange beasts and that was why they did not chase him. Yet the look on Edward's face as he fell was unmistakable—it was death that Vilmos had seen in those eyes. He also wondered if maybe the bastards followed him and were waiting for him to rest, and then they would pounce.

The horse of the beastmen was strangely resolute and powerful, galloping at speeds that amazed him. The animal seemed to be driven by the desires of its rider and was able to sustain high speeds for long periods without fatigue. If his sixth sense was urging the animal on, it was also guiding the animal along the trail back to a place he knew well. Soon he found himself at the magical gate he and Xith had used what seemed so long ago, his mind spinning so rapidly that he opened and triggered the gate without a second thought.

It could have been minutes, hours or days later that he found himself near the Trollbridge, the steady steed beneath him. The world faded to black until he found himself near a cave on an open valley floor. It was the cave where he and Xith had spent the night what seemed ages ago. Here he stopped. Both to rest the horse and to search the cave for signs—any sign that Xith had been there recently. He found nothing, only emptiness. The next day he continued on, driven on.

He soon perceived other agonies: hunger, thirst and weariness. He chanced on a small brook, the same brook where he and Xith had stopped many weeks previous, drinking from its cool clear waters until his thirst was quenched and his belly full. Seeing no signs of anyone near, he sat along the edge of the water and removed his shoes, bathing his sore feet in the cool, soothing waters.

Hours later as the sun sank low on the horizon, he was on the opposite side of a valley. A sudden peace swept over him as he made the long climb from the valley floor out onto a rocky precipice. He felt as if he had come home, and indeed he had.

Breathing deeply, he looked back across the valley, amazed at how much ground he had covered. It would have taken several days to cross the valley on foot.

The strange, powerful horse of the beastmen showed its first signs of fatigue now, and he was utterly exhausted as well. He let the horse cool down for a time, stroking its long, firm neck and mane.

Neither was able to stop for too long though, the compulsion that led him on seemed to flow to the horse and both were enthralled by it. He looked to the forest then, and to the trail that led into it and through it. He knew that on the other side of the forest lay the thing that pulled him on. He had to know, needed to know, what had happened there.

He rode into the forest, low branches and thick growth along the sides of the trail eventually causing him to reconsider. He cursed low under his breath as he dismounted, holding a grudge against the forest for forcing him to walk when he was so weary.

He led the horse then, walking along the tangled trail that was becoming increasingly treacherous in the ever-diminishing light. The only thing that kept him moving was the thought of his home just ahead somewhere. His face and hands were scratched from the branches that caught his skin, yet this was no more a distraction than the mosquitoes that bit at his hands and face.

The march along the now indiscernible trail seemed without end. But he was determined.

***

"Adrina?"

"Yes, it's me. Open the door."

"Well?"

"Well what? Why is the door locked?"

Emel looked to Myrial. Myrial looked to Emel.

Adrina sat next to them. "I didn't, I mean I couldn't. First it was Father Jacob and then—"

"What do you mean you didn't—couldn't? We've been waiting for hours." Emel balled his hands into fists. "Damn your foolishness, I have so much to do. Let me go do it!"

Adrina calmed Emel by putting her hand on his. "After Father Jacob visited the elves, there was no answer at the door. I knocked and knocked. Seth may be angry with me."

Emel stood. "It's time to sleep then. Tomorrow's another day."

"I don't know," said Adrina, "I've got a bad feeling about this. I must speak with Seth now. Before he does something."

"What do you mean?" asked Myrial.

"It was something he said, something about showing the council his world. He said it; Galan got really upset. I've been trying to understand and I think I do now." Myrial and Emel sat across from Adrina, their eyes telling her to go on. She told them of the image Galan had shown her—the palace with the beautiful, spiral towers reaching up into the heavens. "She was so tired afterward as if it drained all her strength. She went to sleep immediately, exhausted."

"And you think Seth will—"

Adrina didn't wait for Emel to finish. "Yes, I think Seth is planning something similar. Imagine how drained he'll be after sharing an image with the entire council, but I think there's more. I've never seen Galan so afraid. I think that that something more may kill him."

"And the orb? The orb is connected somehow to all this?"

"I think the orb is some kind of key that unlocks hidden truths. Seth should be able to use it."

"To unlock the truth about what is being hidden. He won't need to—"

"Exactly Myrial," said Adrina, "Exactly."

Emel held out the leather pouch containing the orb. "Then we'll go together—now!"

"Together," said Myrial standing.

Adrina took the pouch and led the way. They reached Seth and Galan's door quickly and knocked several times, but there was no answer. Emel looked to Adrina and smiled. "Private entrance," he said, "Is there a private entrance?"

Adrina's eyes widened. She led them around through the back halls until they were in the private corridors designed for the royal family.

"This one," said Adrina pointing to a barely visible outline in the wall. "You'll have to nudge it. It hasn't been used in some time."

Emel pressed his weight against the door and it popped open. Adrina, Myrial and Emel hurried into the room. As Adrina came around the door, she called out, "Seth? Galan?" Her heart stopped when she saw them lying in bed together, arm in arm.

Adrina put a hand to her mouth. Somehow she had never pictured Seth and Galan as a couple. Were they truly? Had she misunderstood their relationship?

Not understanding, Emel didn't know what to do. Should he do or say something? He didn't know.

Myrial did. She took Adrina's hand, pulling Emel behind her. Emel closed the door and the three walked off. "Tomorrow," Myrial said, "in the morning. It's late already."

***

With one hand held out in front of him for safety, Vilmos charged through the thick undergrowth, pulling the hesitant horse behind him. He knew that ahead lay his home, and with its finding, warmth and safety. It wasn't until a low branch appearing from out of the darkness nearly poked out his eye that he stopped; jaded, he slumped back against a nearby tree.

The world around him seemed a foreign place, not the place he had grown up in. He felt lost, completely lost, not knowing that where he stopped was just a few yards from the forest's edge. Still, even if he had known, sleep would have come. He was utterly exhausted.

Morning came as a rush of frenzied thoughts. He awoke waving a stick wildly, thwarting the attack of unseen hands. Perspiration dripped from his brow and into his eyes, blurring his already sleep-filled vision. He saw shapes looming before him and continued to wield the stick bravely.

"Who is it?" He shouted as he tried to wipe sleep and sweat from his eyes. "Go away, leave me alone!" He didn't know that he yelled into empty air and that his assailants were but images left over from a dream—a dream filled with dark images.

He shook his head from side to side, attempting to chase away the last of the night's chill as well as the dark spirits.

His senses returning, he looked around for the horse. The horse was nowhere to be found. He was saddened by its disappearance, later thinking that it was just as well, for he couldn't care for it or feed it. He couldn't even feed himself. He was starving, or at least he thought he was.

Bright sunlight from a clearing ahead caught his attention. He went to the light, slowly at first, then running, amazed when he came abruptly to the forest's edge. Across a grassy field stood the white brick house he remembered so fondly. Smoke rose from the chimney and everything seemed well.

Vilmos took off racing, wild thoughts spinning through his mind. He mounted the stairs, put his hand to the door, stopped. He didn't know what to expect. *What if his parents were lying on the floor, or what if they were there and nothing was wrong? What would he tell them? What questions would they ask? What questions would he answer?*

Still considering these thoughts, he opened the door and went inside. He ran through the kitchen, into the pantry. The pantry was full of fresh fruits, vegetables and bread. He ate.

Moments later he found his room much as he left it. "Was it a dream?" he asked himself, saying the words aloud to break the silence.

He ran into his parent's room. The bed was made, the room tidy, clean as his mother always left it.

A brief search revealed nothing out of the ordinary. The only thing wrong was that no one was home, but he was prepared to wait. Maybe they had gone into town? Maybe his father had a meeting in Olex or Two Falls, and Lillath went with him? If so, they would return soon and everything would be as it was.

Hours passed. He waited. Hungry again, he went to the pantry a second time. Afterward he went to his room, plopped onto the bed, patting his full stomach. The house was warm. His bed, comfortable.

Content, he lay still, staring up at the ceiling. A short while later he propped a pillow against the wall, removed his shoes and leaned against the pillow. His thoughts swept him away to the past. Everything had seemed so real. He could see Xith's face. He could see Edward and the hunter beasts. He could see Valam, Adrina, Seth and Galan.

A familiar place called him and so he went. He had not been there in what seemed ages. He stared down into the valley's depths, out into the world—the valley that had its mirror in the realm of the real as well as the imagined. He felt so soothed by the vision that he followed the mighty eagle into the sky. Lazily he swooped and turned, unaware of the danger, unaware of the other lurking nearby.

***

"Galan?" called out Myrial, "The sun rises and still you sleep. You must be ready for council within the hour."

Seth?

"He's not here. You were alone when I arrived."

Galan lurched up, moving so quickly out of bed that Myrial shivered—it wasn't natural for anyone to move like that. "Don't be frightened, it's just me Myrial. We must find Seth. I'm afraid for him. He's preparing to do something—something..."

"I know," said Myrial, "We're worried for you."

"You know? You can't know."

"Adrina was up all night pacing. She fell asleep a few hours ago. I'll take you to her. I think she can help."

No! Galan thrust out harder with her mind than she intended and she hadn't meant to slap away Myrial's hand either—it just happened.

Myrial was shivering uncontrollably. Her bones felt cold, her soul. "All this talk is frightening. I shouldn't be in the middle of this, I'm nobody. I'm better with the floors and a broom than this. My mother always told me never to try to rise above your station. Look what I've done now. It's—"

"You've done nothing." Galan touched her hand to Myrial's. The hand was cold. Galan could feel Myrial's chill reaching to her almost immediately. "What does anyone know of class and rank? I would be the first to tell you that anything is possible—your dream, the thing that frightens you is possible. You can rise above—you don't have to be frightened by what you have achieved. There is no devilry in it, you are not being punished, you did not bring bad luck."

"I brought this on as surely as I broke a mirror—I should've broken a mirror. Why can't I just keep to my own?"

"You are very brave Myrial. Your heart is true and you deserve whatever it is you desire. You can't wish something into existence any more than you can bring bad luck."

You're in my thoughts, aren't you? whispered Myrial to herself.

Yes, I am. I know it doesn't offend you as it does others. You have a gift Myrial, you have a pure heart. Now, do we sit and cry or do you help me find Seth?

Myrial led Galan to the dressing partition. "First you have to look presentable for council. Then we'll find Seth."

"Everything has its order, doesn't it?"

"It does," admitted Myrial as she handed Galan the clothes she had prepared.

Chapter Seventeen:
The Final Truth

The council was gathered and in full readiness as Seth, Galan and Adrina arrived. This day there was no way Adrina would not be present, she felt she had earned the right to sit beside the two and so she did.

When Father Jacob arrived, the proceedings began. Seth was not in a civil mood. From the moment he entered the council until the very instant he left he planned to seize the council's attention. A heavy burden of duty pulled down upon him—failure meant disgrace, a yoke around his neck that he shouldered silently.

He waited for the correct moment to seize the floor and when the time was right, he circled his voice around the room. *What I am about to do may take you by surprise, but when I am finished I am confident you will have no more doubts concerning your obligations.*

Chancellor Yi stood. "Elf Seth, you are breaking protocol. We are to begin with a review of yesterday."

Seth glared at the chancellor. "Your eyes betray you, chancellor. You have not slept well this past night and you are haunted by conscience. Tell King Andrew of your secret desire."

Murmurs swept through the council. Several council members

jumped to their feet. Chancellor Yi thumped his long staff against the floor. "Order!" he called out, "Order!" He turned to Seth. "No more outbursts or this proceeding will end, Elf Seth. I assure you."

Seth ignored the chancellor. He used the momentary disquiet to focus and gather his will. He closed his eyes and began a silent prayer. A glowing light, soft and pure began to enshroud his body. The rhythm of his chant reached out to all, though few understood the words.

With each word Galan felt stabbing pain in her heart. She burst into tears. *You promised you wouldn't!* she screamed into Seth's mind.

Seth ignored Galan, the chancellor's continued demands for order and the King's own command for silence. He launched his spirit upward, spiraling, soaring. His features changed and for an instant, it was as if another stood in his place.

His voice followed the changing flow of his body, shifting from unnatural to captivating and finally to a strange echoing rasp. Slowly his facial features changed, blended and melted away. Then a form, beautiful and feminine, filled the place where he had been. The distortion ended. A woman's face replaced Seth's. The voice enthralling, almost delicate.

I am Queen Mother of the Eastern Reaches, first to convey the will of the Mother and the Father. I have been long waiting for this day...

Shocked silence followed. Disbelief showed. Some of the council members started praying. "Witchcraft! Devilry! Wizardry!" they shouted. "Devil be gone!"

Chancellor Yi thumped his staff, attempting to restore order. Keeper Martin rose to his feet, waving his hands for calm. Father Jacob followed, saying "Please good councilors there is no devilry afoot! Listen and we may all find the answers we seek!"

The murmurs and disquiet continued.

"Do not disbelieve," said Queen Mother through Seth. "The

crossing of the minds is an ancient gift. Our council had discussed at length how we could prove our need to any doubters. We had faith in Brother Seth's resourcefulness and knew he would choose this method if the need was great. Please, I beg of you, listen. The link is taxing and cannot be maintained long."

Adrina gasped. She was so close to Seth that she could see his face beneath the mask of Queen Mother's—as she imagined Galan could as well. Huge tears welled up in her eyes. She could see the link feed off Seth's living soul. It was as if his life energy poured out of his body and into the image.

"Father bring order," Adrina called out, "Do this for me, I beg of you!"

Mesmerized by the images, King Andrew was slow to respond, but when he did instant silence followed.

Queen Mother said, "Join hands all to complete the link… Quickly now!"

Councilors returned to their seats, joined hands. Adrina grasped Seth's right hand, Galan his left, completing the circle and the link.

The completing of the link was as the turning of a switch. Suddenly they were in a different place, seeing through another's eyes. It was a strange and beautiful place wrapped in white. It was the royal palace seen through the eyes of a roaming hawk, soaring on puffs of air, zooming in through an open window, coming to rest just inside.

The hawk cried out, a high piercing cry that echoed in the ears long after it passed. It launched from its perch, bringing with it a light breeze that trickled around the room, blowing in a downward spiral—the same downward spiral that the hawk descended.

The hawk landed on a high-backed chair, calling out one final time before the vantagepoint changed. They saw through another's eyes now—a view from the throne, through the eyes of the Queen

Mother herself.

Her eyes drew up, up to the window on high, waiting until the free-spirited hawk passed without, then returning to the calm crystalline walls about her.

"High Council Hall of East Reach." Queen Mother paused, continuing in a soothing whisper, "Chambers are chosen for specific reasons… as I am sure you know."

As the queen's voice massaged their minds, the scene focused once more. High Council Hall at first seemed cluttered, designed without purpose. Then its purpose became clear, patterns in the walls told stories, depicted adventures, told the history of the Elves, ever growing, ever changing.

Keeper Martin held his breath as the focus turned to the oaken table that seemed a living thing, growing in the center of the hall.

"Great structures house tremendous power and it is this power that you must understand." Everyone in Kingdom Hall could feel Queen Mother's mood grow dark. "The business at hand is unpleasant, but it must be. Sathar has returned from the Dark Journey and the end of our age is at hand. Whether we succumb or survive is in your hands."

The hall shook as the image began to fade, not a flutter or a falter but an emotion-filled tremble.

Adrina screamed out even before the vision focused. A murmur rose, growing steadily loud and disquieted. Ripping winds swam across the chamber. Hands gripped a porous crag as eyes looked down from a mountaintop. The wind was cool, the touch of the rock cold. The mountain trembled and shook. A great mass of soldiers could be seen in the fields below, spread out like ants, tiny specks of black moving by the thousands. The earth shook to the beat of their march.

"Behold the great western plain! This mountain range marks the boundary between East and West Reach. The army on the western plain is the army of Sathar. Soon our mountain outposts will be overrun. They will pour through the mountain passes and not stop until our lands are his and then—"

"Queen Mother," said King Andrew, "Please, I beg of you, order. We have much else to discuss. We can see your need is great, but to send our people—"

Silence! Listen Man-Child, Queen Mother commanded. "Listen to what will happen, this will be your future! When the Cursed returns from the Dark Journey, all will flock to his banner or fall. Any who oppose his total domination, any who resist, will be enslaved or killed. During the time of the Gathering the earth shall be torn asunder and thus will the Coming begin. The tormented will cry out in anguish for their blindness. For at the very end of their existence they will discover their grave error, but it will be too late, their kind will be lost."

Thousands of marching soldiers and riders swarmed over the land, coming to rest before a great castle. The viewpoint was the same, a far-off rocky precipice, but the location was different. The rock was cold, as was the wind.

Behind the army came other armies, spreading across the horizon as a black wave. A city at the edge of the castle burned. Amid endless pillars of black smoke and red flames, fields burned. The dead lay scattered about the land and the living cried out.

Hands clutched bitterly the cold, cold rock, while eyes swept toward the castle that stood defiantly, resisting thunderous blows upon its walls. The hollow knocking on the walls resounded in their ears and chased their thoughts.

A valiant few protected the walls while the swarm gathered. The thrashing grew. Walls that had held secure fell away.

The great castle and the city were not unknown to the

Kingdomers. The castle and the city were Imtal, and the vision allowed much more than simple sight. The air about them filled with flames from the burning houses and land, dark smoke brought tears to their eyes and made breathing difficult. The anger and fear of the fleeing, the agony and pain of the dying, the putrid stench of scorched flesh, all flowed to them.

Queen Mother didn't hold back a single overwhelming emotion or sensation. Terror filled their hearts and minds, growing to the point where they just wanted it to stop so the pain would end. Almost believing that when it did end it would take them with it, and even this they would have welcomed.

Brought to the threshold of life and survival, then to the brink of what lay beyond, Queen Mother carried them swiftly back. Latched onto only the pain, making it linger as the scene dissolved. A face, a face of untainted beauty, filled their minds. One could not stare into a countenance of such magnitude, so powerful and yet so very exquisite, for very long.

Galan whispered, *Oh my Queen Mother, may they see your wisdom clearly.*

The Queen of the Elves shouted into their minds then, *I am sorry to be harsh, but it is the only way to bring resolve! You must understand, you must see. The path can only be changed now. If you delay there can be no hope. Time is everything—and we have little to spare.*

In an avalanche of silence the pain ended, leaving most beyond the capacity for words, even the most loquacious of the group. King Andrew regretted his earlier words, and now words were beyond him.

Father Jacob took the initiative, "I think I speak for the council Your Grace." He looked at each of the council members, and they each in turn nodded approval. And lastly he looked to the king, who also nodded approval.

"Your Grace," began Father Jacob as King Andrew touched his hand and with his eyes urged the priest to sit.

King Andrew found the courage of words in his heart. "We have heard your plea and we shall heed your warning. However you must also know that action will take time. We wish politics were a simple thing but they are not. Others will also be skeptical. The king's word is law but we must have the backing of the alliance and our people. Without this backing our kingdom would fall before our army returns. We are convinced of the sincerity of your words. We will do what we can."

I trust in your word and your honor King Andrew. Thanks to all of you gathered in council. I am afraid I must leave you now. The link has lasted overly long. My son's spirit yearns to journey to the Father.

***

Hours passed. Vilmos floated on the breezes churning up from the valley floor. The eagle's keen eyes scoured, expecting to find nothing, and found nothing. He was alone with his thoughts as he liked to be, alone and free.

He was about to land and change into human form when a voice rang out in his mind and he awoke. Propelled back to reality, he sprang to his feet. A muffled noise in the distance brought him through the kitchen to the porch. As he listened close, the noise sounded like hooves upon dry leaves.

He longed to see a single, horse-drawn coach approach with two occupants. The driver a stern-faced man with a whip in one hand and the reigns tucked in the other hand—that was how his father liked to ride. The other occupant would sit quietly beside him, her face would be gentle and kind, aged pleasantly with the years. A familiar figure did eventually approach, not from the road, but from the path that led to the forest, and not until hours later.

All delusion faded as the beckoning voice called out. "Vilmos come!" it commanded.

Vilmos walked to the path, saying, "I thought it was all a dream." Something along the path caught Vilmos' attention, but only for an instant. "How did you find me?"

The reply came in a voice that could only be Xith's but the figure was strange, as if Vilmos was trapped in a dream that warped the world around him, "You found me, but that is beside the point."

"Edward, is he...?"

"Edward is in a good place and would be happy to know you are safe."

After a lengthy walk the two came to an opening that led to a point overlooking the valley. The suspicion that his life was moving in circles and that no matter how far away he went he would always come back to the same place occurred to Vilmos, just as Xith said "We'll stop here to rest for a few moments."

Vilmos sat down on the ground with a thump. He was about to ask if there was anything to eat when Xith stopped him.

"Silence!" Vilmos had only seen Xith like this once before and he didn't like the expression he saw. He started to say something again, and again Xith cut him off.

Xith didn't make a sound after that or move. Vilmos knew better than to move or speak.

A moment later Xith yelled, "Duck!"

Vilmos fell to the ground on his belly. As he lay motionless, he had a strong feeling that he had been in this situation before. He looked to the shaman who nodded in agreement. Vilmos asked, "But why?"

The shaman turned his eyes heavenward, seeing things that Vilmos couldn't. He waited for a moment before responding, indicating as he did so that it was all right for Vilmos to sit back up.

"Vilmos, life can be complicated or simple, often times you take a step forward only to find that you have taken two steps backward. Do you understand?"

Vilmos wavered his head. He had no idea what Xith was talking about.

"That is good," said Xith, "don't try to understand. It is best just to accept it. Life is a series of circles that sometimes lead you back to the beginning, so instead of giving up you must keep your head high and start again. There will be times when you are not sure whether you are in the past or the present or whether perhaps you are without time and that you are never really far away from the place you are trying to reach. Do you understand?"

"I don't," admitted Vilmos honestly.

Sullenness fell over Xith's face and Vilmos could see dark circles under his companion's eyes. "You will, I promise. Edward would not have sacrificed himself for you otherwise. You see, he was the first, one that was taken from me before you. You are truly he, Vilmos, and the time will soon be upon us."

"You're real," said Vilmos, "That's all that matters!" Vilmos grabbed Xith in a great bear hug. He couldn't help himself. "It is good to see you, it is good to be with you again. Don't leave me alone anymore. Promise?"

The shaman raised his eyes to meet Vilmos' then and as he did so a glowing orb of brilliant white appeared in his outstretched hand. In the orb, Vilmos saw the visage of the Princess Adrina and there were tears streaming down her cheeks. As the image grew clearer he could see that she sat at a great table around which many were gathered. To her left was the elf Seth, and to Seth's left was Galan. Seth's skin was pale and his great round eyes stared up at the heavens.

***

Queen Mother's words hung in the air about the chamber. A tear, single and crystalline, shimmered down Seth's cheek. Tiny though it was, it conveyed a feeling of deepest sadness.

Galan clasped Seth's hand tightly; his will had nearly drained away. Her heart raced and her tears flowed without end.

Adrina gripped Seth's other hand, feeling it grow from warm, full of life, to cool and balmy. Her anguish matched the deep unbroken lines of tears cascading down her cheeks.

My son, you have done all that you could. You have done what you must, what you were meant to do. You shall be remembered, you shall not be forgotten, the sacrifice shall not go unaccounted for... and in a barely audible voice Queen Mother added, *... may Great Father grant you passage into his very house, so that you may sit by his side, my son.*

Queen Mother's voice faded away and the link was broken. All eyes remained in place, focusing now on Seth. A smile touched his lips at the gift of his mother, words of praise reserved only for the very great, said only at the passing of an elf king or queen.

As he breathed his last breath the smile broadened to the corners of his lips. He fancied he could smell the kingdom garden he had been in earlier and reveled in the flow of nature he had felt.

With that one last thought of peace, of life, and of nature, Seth collapsed to the table. No one doubted that he was indeed dead.

Galan whispered into their minds, *This is the holy light of the Great Father reclaiming his son, as are all at the last.* She let the faithful see the wondrous—but otherwise invisible—shimmering light surrounding Seth's fallen form. *Few are able to see the spirit pass thus, so if you can see it, you are truly blessed. You have found faith and sincerity in your heart.*

But faith and sincerity didn't fill Galan's heart —anger and rage did. She was angry with Seth for doing what he said he wouldn't. She was angry because in her mind this didn't have to be—and if it had to be, Seth shouldn't have been the one.

A pitiful wail, almost a plea, filled their minds as Galan

unleashed her sorrows. *No!* she cried out, *Please, no!*

Further words were broken by long sobs, followed by an unsettling calm. Galan held back the tears and the pain. She called out again, screaming to the heavens, speaking aloud. "As such is the way of my will, I cannot allow this to happen!"

A blast of icy air defiled the chamber. Galan reached her hands upward chasing after Seth in thought, forcing her will to take her to where the Father gathered up his son, knowing she had to hurry because the journey was almost complete.

She pursued the last shard of Seth's life, the tiny light hurtling upward into the heavens. Her own brilliant light, full of life, quickly caught and surpassed it.

Father I must, she begged. *Father hear me!*

Responding to a voice only she heard, she replied, "Yes, I understand." These words were spoken aloud and in thought.

The thread that guided Seth's way severed and his soul plummeted back earthward. His spirit collided with his body, taking with it the light of Galan's life and the place Galan occupied was suddenly empty.

The council hall was absolutely quiet. No one moved. No one said a word.

Many long minutes passed.

Adrina called to guards outside the door. With their help she led Seth from the room.

She turned back at the doorway, shouting, "You're all fools— you can't see! You can't act until it is too late! Open your eyes and see the world around you! This didn't have to be if only you had listened before!"

Chapter Eighteen:
Dreams of Tomorrow

Adrina rocked back and forth. She was quiet, angry—resolved to be angry forever. The darkness was a chasm that sought to swallow her, and if it did, nothing of the woman she was becoming would remain.

Everything she touched seemed to wither. Everything she cared about seemed to fade from the world. Why couldn't she wither and fade away as well? It would be so easy to slip into the night and be gone from the world.

A quiet voice behind her called out, "Adrina come down, let's talk about this. You can't control what other people do or think. You aren't responsible—we tried and that's all we could have done."

Adrina spun around, the narrow brickwork of the castle wall making it difficult to keep her footing. Her long black hair fluttered in the wind. Her slender body wobbled.

Emel turned to Myrial. "Talk some sense into her please."

"At times like this I would send Lady Isador to the wall. She would handle this, she'd know what to do."

"Lady Isador isn't here. It's just you and I."

Adrina stretched out her arms. She imagined she could float on the wind. "Come fly with me," she whispered. "We can steal away into the night and no one will know."

"Adrina you can't fly!" shouted Emel. "You're scaring me, please come down!"

Adrina turned away from Emel and stared out into the darkness. "Why can't I fly? If I can wish it, I can do it—and I wish to fly."

"You have no magical powers; you're no witch or devil," said Myrial. "You can't fly. Only birds can fly and you're no bird. Take my hand Adrina. Take my hand and come down from the wall."

Adrina started to wave her arms. In her mind she was a bird, a bird that could fly and soar away into the darkness. "I could have done much more. I could have. Seth would have seen the truth. He would have known. Galan would be here now."

Myrial took a few steps toward Adrina. "Galan is gone. Nothing you do will bring her back. Everything you do up there risks your life! You're no fool. Why would you want to end as a fool? Is that how you want to be remembered, as a fool? A girl who couldn't take the weight of the world.

"Let me tell you about the weight of the world, waking in dirt because there is no straw, eating food deemed unfit for the King's pigs, being ordered about as a house slave, and I may have been the housemaster's house slave, but he couldn't have my heart, stop my mind from thinking or my soul from crying out. Never in all that time did I really wish to go—I wanted to live. Oh how I wanted to live, to have the world see me as I saw the world. You gave me that chance Adrina, a chance to become much more than I was. You never asked anything in return. You gave freely.

"I would do the same for you if I could. I would take the weight of the world from your shoulders—I see you as you are Adrina. I love you for what you are. I would serve you to the ends of my days. I would give my life for yours. Take my hand. Will you take my hand?"

"Birds are free," said Adrina. "I want to be free."

"Take her hand Adrina—take my hand. We'll walk back to your room and talk. Tomorrow we'll visit Seth."

"It is already tomorrow." Adrina sank to her haunches. Below, High King's Square was coming to life. The early merchants were carrying lanterns, beginning to set up for the day ahead.

In her mind's eye she was in another time—that day she had dreamed of places far away: High Province, South Province and the Territories. Believing that she would never journey to any of them. But she had, and, just as the lady in the tower said, change came.

She wondered what else would come true and if she could bear the weight of it. She wondered what tomorrow would bring, knowing tomorrow was already at hand.

She stood, looked to Emel and Myrial. For a few heartbeats everything stopped. She lifted a foot from the brickwork of the wall, steadied herself as she stared down into the square. Birds could fly, so why couldn't she?

***

Xith closed his hand around the orb, ending the vision. Vilmos turned away, looking out over the valley.

"Do you see now why your training is so important?" Xith asked. "You've many more lessons to learn, but I think this latest lesson has been the most important."

"Is has?"

"Yes, it has. You've learned much more than I had hoped and you earned the trust of one who could have easily turned his back on you. He had the opportunity, the chance to do what he was recruited to do, yet he didn't. He saw in you what I see in you—he must have."

"Edward?"

Xith stretched out his hands, arcs of blue and white lightning moving between the outstretched fingers. "Forces in opposition. If the forces touched the explosion would tear down this hill, taking us with it, and sweep through the valley below.

"Those who don't understand see good and evil, light and dark, positive and negative. There is always a careful balance, always a cautious dance. Which dance would you dance if you could?"

"I don't know," said Vilmos, "I'm confused."

"Exactly, no one really knows what they'll do when the time comes, so how can anyone try to predict tomorrow's tomorrow with any accuracy. Sure there are those who can see the paths but the paths themselves are less important than the places they converge. In the places where the paths join, new paths can split off, creating new futures where once there were none. You and I, Vilmos, our job is to walk the paths, follow them to where they converge and make new possibilities possible. But you must believe. Do you believe?"

"I want to learn. I want to be a mage. I don't want you to go away again—"

"Oh but can you say that without knowing the fate of the last human magus? Did you read of Efryadde in the Great Book? Do you remember what happened?"

"The darkness took him and he was betrayed."

"Correct, both correct. I was there I should know. But the book doesn't tell you who betrayed Efryadde."

Vilmos closed his eyes, trying to remember the passage from the book. In the back of his mind her heard his mother telling him "Each tale, each bit of lore, tells a lesson. Relate the lesson through the lore; it is the way of the counselor. Choose the wrong tale, give the wrong advice."

"You're trying to teach—"

"No, you've already learned the lesson. I'm only trying to point out something you should remember when you wake from this dream—something important."

"Dream?"

"Dream. You were never really at your house, Vilmos, and you never rode through this valley. You wandered away from the inn and sprung the hunter beast's trap. You are caught in it now, but you and I are really here together—out of body."

"Corpeal stasis?"

Xith laughed. "Non-corporeal stasis, my boy, non-corporeal stasis."

"How do I return and wake from this dream?"

"Find the truth of Efryadde, it is within you."

"Will you be there then for real?"

"I will and then we will continue our travels, building the company that will change the converging paths."

"I want to—"

"I must be going now but I'll see you soon. It won't be long, I have every confidence in you. Be strong, believe, remember our talk."

***

"Take a chance, take my hand. You don't have to do this," Emel said, "Things can change, you'll see. How could you not believe that after Alderan and Quashan'?"

Adrina stared wild-eyed at Emel. "Change? What do you know about change?"

He started to reply, stopped, took in a deep breath. Profound awakening found him. The pilot light of the rage returned.

Suddenly he was back in the fields of Fraddylwicke, chasing

down the elves' attackers. He ran down three men, never stopping or looking back. They died screaming beneath Ebony's hooves. Four others he cut down as they fled.

Those that remained stopped running. They put up their hands, begged for mercy.

There was no mercy in his heart, only rage.

He was of their blood. He could sense it. He knew they could sense it too, but now it was too late.

Fire burned in his heart. It focused his fury, his need for vengeance. "Blood for blood," he whispered as he cut them down where they stood.

He sheathed his sword, raised a bloody fist in the air.

Ebony reared, then wheeled in a tight circle.

He raced away. One of the men he'd left for dead called out after him. The words were a blessing, not a curse. Emel didn't understand then and he didn't understand now as distant voices far below the wall brought him back to reality.

Adrina was staring down at him from atop the wall. Her eyes were wild. "I want to fly," she said, "I want to be free."

"You want to fly?" Emel shouted, "Fly then! Jump into the winds!"

Myrial's shouts of "No, no, no," weren't heeded. Adrina stood tall, stretched out her arms, closed her eyes. "I believe. Do you?" she said as she leapt from atop the wall.

***

Seth walked in dreams and in those dreams Galan walked with him. Together they had gone far and done things that would make such song—epic songs that he could hear elven children singing even now.

East Reach seemed so far away, so far that memories of Kapital could have been from another lifetime. Before setting sail for the lands of Man he had never been beyond the island city of Leklorall—at least not that he could recall—and now he was a world away.

Men weren't like elves. They didn't resolve to action unless action was the only recourse. They weren't inspired. They weren't driven to truth. They couldn't see—and at times refused to see. He had changed that. He had, but at what cost?

He saw Galan laughing, laughing as she had before they left Kapital. She was saying *You need to relax...You should join me.* He would, but he wouldn't see the world as she saw the world, each day new, each day fresh—alive.

Alive? he asked himself, his thoughts spinning away. Galan wasn't alive. She gave her soul for his life and her spirit would not rest in the next life now. Her spirit would never know an eternity of bliss and this was truly bitter.

Galan continued laughing. Her eyes danced and she reached out to him but as he reached out to her the dream ended and she faded away, leaving him with stark reality, leaving him with the knowledge that he was the one who didn't see, the one who moved through life with blinders.

"Tomorrow," he said. "Thank you, I can see it now. We'll make this right, I know it, and then I'll sail the waters of the Gildway to the ends of my days in your stead."

***

"Believe," Adrina whispered as she fell. If she believed hard enough Emel would catch her.

She lived between heartbeats, life racing before her eyes. She moved as through a tunnel and at the end was her mother, Queen Alexandria. Strange though it was, no matter how far she raced through the tunnel Adrina couldn't quite reach her mother—it was if unseen hands kept her away and these very same hands spun her around, shifting her until the tunnel faded from memory.

"Adrina?" called out Myrial.

Adrina opened her eyes, realizing then that her lungs burned. She sucked at the air, the first breath heavy as it traveled through her throat and into her lungs. She exhaled, breathed in again, waited.

"Talk to me," said Myrial. "Can you hear me?"

Adrina tried to sit up. Emel held her in place. "What happened?"

"You jumped, you fool," said Myrial. "Thank Great Father you had the good sense to jump to Emel and not to the square."

Adrina winced from Emel's firm grip. He seemed to suddenly realize he was squeezing her arms so hard there'd be bruises. He let go, squeezed his eyes together and shook his head as if warding off something, then said, "We tried to catch you. But all we could do was break your fall. You got the wind knocked out of you."

"And I'm not?"

"No you're not, most certainly not. Do you think we'd let you do something so stupid?" Myrial sat down as reality suddenly sank in. "You had us worried to death. I don't know what I would have done without you."

"I'd've missed you terribly," said Emel. "You great fool—idiot."

"Fool? Idiot? Hmm…" Adrina pouted.

"Now that's the temperamental Adrina I know!" said Emel.

Adrina bit back a laugh. "I did look a fool, didn't I?"

"A grand fool," said Myrial. "You won't do that again?"

Adrina tried to stand. Emel and Myrial helped her. She gave both a hug, wiping her sudden tears away. "I won't," she whispered.

"Promise?"

Adrina frowned, it was an honest response. "I won't."

So saying, Adrina took Emel's hand, Myrial's, then walked away. She led them to the watchtower which wasn't far away. The sun would be up soon. She wanted to see the brilliant blues, greens and reds that only an autumn sunrise could bring—and she wanted to share this splendor with Emel and Myrial.

Chapter Nineteen: Things Revealed

It was an odd-looking tree perched atop a rocky crag. The roots, stretching over rocks and gravel to the rich black earth a hundred yards away, seemed to have a stranglehold over the land and the trunk, all twisted and gnarled, spoke of the silent battle the tree was winning. Thick boughs stretched at odd angles to the heavens, seeming to taunt those that traveled below as their shadows lengthened with the waning of the day.

It was here at the base of the tree that the trail ended. Vilmos sank to his knees, studying the last of the tracks and catching his breath for the first time in what felt like days. The tracks didn't seem to lead anywhere else. He turned around carefully, his eyes scanning. He saw no sign of backtracking.

He wiped the sweat from his brow, his thoughts coming into focus once more on the tree. The cold nights of late had robbed the mighty oaks of most of their leaves. With the cold winds blowing steadily from the north, it wouldn't be long before the forest was blanketed in the thick snowy coat of winter.

Despite the panicked race through the forest, he knew exactly where he was. He had spent most of his days in this forest. He wasn't about to get lost now, or ever. Besides, the tree was a landmark of sorts. The rangers called it the Warden. It marked the easternmost edge of the forest and, some would say, the boundary between Sever and Vostok.

He stood momentarily as he looked up at the tree. The great oak had been through hard times and definitely showed its age. Seeing what appeared to be a fresh marking on the thick roots that ran down the rocky crag, he bent over to take a closer look. That was when he saw the prints clearly. The heel print of a woodsman's boot. The paw print of something he knew must be akin to a bear but just wasn't right.

Sudden silence hit him like a wall. In the forest silence often revealed more than sound. With sunset an hour away night sounds should have filled the air. The stillness told him something was wrong but he didn't know what.

A tiny whisper in his mind asked if the quiet was the last thing he would hear. He put his back to the tree, feeling that somehow it was. The whisper called out to him, tormenting with realizations just out of his reach. If only he could grasp them, he would know what to do.

For a moment he heard the chatter of a squirrel marking her territory. An instant later he saw a shadow move behind a tree not far off. He unsheathed his sword, stood his ground. Minutes passed. He chastised himself for letting his mind play tricks on him. He had followed the trail to its end, found nothing. He must accept it and return home.

Home? The word echoed in his mind. What did the word really mean? What was it like to have a home, to have a place where one felt safe and secure? Where *was* his home?

As he questioned his reality, the woods around him began to bend and warp as if he were in a pool of liquid steel and the steel was being poured and shaped by unseen hands. Ripples formed on the surface of the air. As if a curtain, Vilmos reached out and parted the veil of the world. He awoke. Discovering he was lying face down in a pile of wet leaves, he whirled around to sit upright and spit out the clumps of dirt and leaves in his mouth. His eyes were wild, arms raised, fists poised ready to fight.

He looked around. He was in the forest but everything was different. *But how?*

The horse—*where was it?*—his world spun. Images that were too real to be a dream raced through his mind and all the while Xith's voice foreshadowed his thoughts and filled his consciousness. The house, his house, his parent's house—Vilmos couldn't deny that the experience seemed real.

"How can I find you? Damn it!" he shouted in anger and frustration, though no one could hear.

He found the horse, galloped madly toward his home. He had to find out if someone, anyone, was there. He broke from the woods, pulling the reins sharply at the front porch. He didn't see danger, yet in the back of his mind he heard Xith's warning, "Don't return to the house." He didn't heed the warning. He couldn't stop his feet, which were in motion to the door.

He ran through the house, searching everywhere, but he found nothing and no one. He burst into his own room, collapsed onto his old bed. As he closed his eyes he thought he heard someone crying out "No! No, you mustn't—the fourth wind comes!"

He strained to listen to the voice. It faded in and out. "I warned you," the voice admonished, "I warned you."

His eyes flew open. He jumped out of bed, ran as fast as he could from the house. There was danger now. He sensed it, didn't know how. He only knew it was with him. He tripped, stumbled down the porch stairs. He ran into the forest alone along the tangled path. Never looked back.

***

In stop-start fashion, Princess Adrina recounted the story, meshing together Seth's words as best as she could recall. When she finished, Father Jacob didn't say anything; it was clear that he was beyond words. It seemed he could hear the warrior elf's unvoiced whisper repeating what Adrina had said. *She took my place. She thought she owed me her life for saving hers and for that she gave her soul for my life... Her spirit will never rest in the Father's house now. It will never rest... She gave up eternity for me.*

Heavy footfalls against the hard stone floor caused Father Jacob and Princess Adrina to turn. At first Adrina thought she heard the tapping of a staff muddled amidst the echoes of the footsteps. Martin or Emel, she thought, only Emel signified trouble. She had been avoiding him since the incident on the wall. Jumping had been foolish—yes—yet taking Emel and Myrial to the tower to watch the sunrise had been even more foolish. Some things just couldn't be undone and what happened that morning was one of them.

Snapping from her reverie she turned, saw the tall, broad-shouldered figure racing toward her. She stretched her arms out happily in greeting. "My Lord, Prince Valam!" she exclaimed, wrapping her arms around him, pushing her lips firmly against his cheek.

"Adrina!" shouted Prince Valam as he playfully kissed her and swept her off the ground, carrying her up in his arms to his towering height. He stared into the green of her eyes for a time, admiring the way the light reflected back. His mother Queen Alexandria had had the same eyes—eyes that seamed to beguile, eyes that others had told him were haunting.

Adrina pointed to the ground. She wanted to be put down. Valam's chainmail shirt was rough and cold and the hilt of his sword pressed into her side. "I didn't expect you home until the spring. Is something wrong?"

"Nothing like you may be thinking. It is just..." Valam paused. He turned to the open stone windows, stared down into the gardens in the inner courtyard. Creating the palace gardens had been a life's work—his mother's life's work. He was pleased to see that flowers still bloomed in great shades of blue, red, and yellow this late into the year. "I was lonesome. After Isador arrived I could do nothing but think of home and you. Later I received a message from father. I was worried. I needed time away as well. The city is restored, the garrison is at full company, all looks to be in order. Chancellor Van'te is perfectly capable of handling affairs for a time."

"How is the old scoundrel?" asked Father Jacob.

"As feisty as ever I'm afraid." Valam's response sparked a round of laughter. Before Yi, there had been Van'te. He had served their family for forty years. Valam and Adrina regarded the old chancellor as one of the family. When Valam had reached the proper age, Van'te had offered to help with South Province until the prince was ready to handle affairs on his own—grooming an heir to the throne was no easy task.

Adrina could still picture Valam setting off, his pride and hope showing in his expression and a far-off look in his deep brown eyes. He had been so worried. Adrina had been a girl then. She was a young woman now.

"Adrina," said Valam impatiently. He had so much to do. He had not even visited his father yet.

"Sorry, daydreaming. It seems a lifetime since I last saw you, yet it is mere weeks since the attacks on Quashan'." She eyed Valam, asked while brushing long strands of black hair behind her ear, "Did you really return because you were lonesome?"

"Yes and no. I came to learn more about Seth and Galan. The

pursuits of the Elves seem to be moving nowhere and I owe a debt that—"

Adrina pressed a finger to his lips. She considered telling him of Galan but didn't. Fortunately, Father Jacob was wise enough to know when to change the subject. "So tell us the other reason you returned," Jacob pried as he straightened the belt of his white-trimmed robe, the robe that was a symbol of his office as the king's First Minister, "obviously your thoughts are elsewhere."

Valam's eyes darted to the open window and the gardens. "Nothing gets passed you, does it?"

"Not much, young sire." Father Jacob thought to himself that the young prince looked more like his father each time he saw him, especially in the set of his face. He knew then as he had believed for some time that Valam would make a fine king when the time came.

Adrina followed Valam's eyes to the gardens below, though her attention was drawn away for a different reason. She was sure she had seen a handful of field commanders crossing the inner courtyard with King's Knight Captain Brodst. Unofficial word in the palace was that the armies of the bandit kings were on the move. The recent garrison activity certainly supported this notion.

"To tell the truth—" Valam stopped, looked at Adrina. "To tell the truth… It's about Chancellor Yi."

"Oh," stated Father Jacob knowingly, the wrinkles on his forehead suddenly becoming great deep lines of worry.

"Go on," prodded Adrina, displeasure in her tone.

"He sent me a personal communiqué… Nothing more…"

"And you came running all the way from the South?" snapped Adrina.

"Well," pleaded Valam.

"This is no laughing matter!" Adrina shouted as she stormed off down the hall.

"That's the Adrina I remember," Prince Valam said to Father Jacob, "What is she so upset about anyway?"

Father Jacob told Valam what Adrina had omitted. He told the prince of the prophecy and of Galan's death. As he spoke, he knew Valam experienced Great Kingdom's darkest hour just as he had. Valam saw the soldiers marching, the riders swarming over the land, the city burning. He heard the hollow knocking on the walls, saw the great black wave of the other armies that followed the first. He heard the despair, felt the flames, saw the smoke that clouded the air.

Valam took a deep breath. His first thought was to chase after Adrina and apologize but Father Jacob's hand on his shoulder told him to wait a moment. "What is it, Father Jacob? What is it that you aren't telling me?"

Father Jacob fixed the collar of his robe. He stared intently at the prince for a moment before speaking. "Things don't go well in council for the elves despite what was said to Queen Mother of East Reach. There is no popular support for this thing. It is only King Andrew's promise that keeps the matter moving forward. The divide in the council is growing."

"Divide? What do you mean?"

"Many go through the motions, acting is if in support, but they aren't. Your father, my king, once held popular support and there would be none to oppose him within Great Kingdom. But times have changed. The memories of Queen Alexandria's kindness are fading. Your father is not the man he once was."

Valam's eyes betrayed anger. "You speak treasonous words, dangerous words."

Father Jacob took a step back from the towering prince. "I speak the truth—and the growing will of the people. Quashan' and Alderan weren't the only cities attacked. The attack in the South was coordinated with an attack in the North. There is evidence of growing unrest, new alliances, dark alliances. King Jarom will not rest until he sits on Imtal's throne. He'll do whatever it takes. That makes the Bandit Kings bold."

"The Bandit Kings have ever been a thorn in our side. But I would not name them bold on the best of occasions."

"Bold enough to steal into Imtal Palace and try to kidnap Adrina."

"Kidnap? When did this ... What would you have me do?"

"For now you must act is if you know nothing. The time will come for action. You will know it." Father Jacob's face suddenly showed his age. "Promise me? Nothing."

Valam pressed his hands into Father Jacob's then hurried down the hall in the direction Adrina had gone.

***

Vilmos ran as fast and as long as he could until finally breathless he staggered, fell to the ground exhausted. The portent clung to his mind. He had to get away, as far away as he possibly could. Panting and weary he stood. His legs shook. His every thought told him to run.

Desperate to move on he crawled until he mustered the strength to run. His chest hurt. His legs ached. His head throbbed with pain.

"Xith!" he screamed desperately. His words echoed out over the valley. "Where are you? What is this journey of awakening?"

He shrieked until his voice was hoarse. He had long since lost the ability to reason. His words were gibberish. His cries grew, his voice barely audible as his strength and determination waned.

When he could no longer run, he collapsed, pounded his fists into the ground. "Think clearly, " he begged of himself. "Think clearly."

The throbbing pain of his bloodied knuckles brought clarity. He tried to calm himself, to push the nightmares of the world out of his mind. He tried to sort the real from the unreal.

Focus caused the world around him to coalesce and shimmer as if he stared out into a wading pool. Once more he could see the veil of the world. He reached out, parted the curtain between realities and found he was standing in a forest of ancient trees.

The odd-looking tree before him, perched atop a rocky crag, had roots that stretched over rocks and gravel to the rich black earth. The odd angles of the tree's branches taunted him. He stared up into the sky, catching a glimpse of scarlet fires in the heavens. He knew instantly where he was—and, just as important, where he wasn't.

The eerie glow from the tree spoke of its timeless power. A voice from far away in the past whispered to him, *"The land called Ril Akh Arr,"* and in that instant he knew that he had never left Under-Earth after Edward had died. Instead he had escaped from the hunter beast's trap into the forest, succumbed to the enchantment of the trees—*the* tree. The tree that was nearly as old as Under-Earth itself. The tree that had survived the millennia as men and beasts came and went around it.

The Ever Tree sang to Vilmos. The rhapsody of the song was one of movement not of words. The tree's branches twittered, leaves fluttered, as if blown by a breeze although the air was still. Vilmos listened, enchanted.

A face appeared within the bark of the ancient tree. As the face became clear the words of the song became clear. The song told of the masters of the three realms—titans, dragons, elves, dwarves, and men—and a time when they had lived as one. Lyrics of happy times were short lived. Soon the tree sang of a terrible, dark war and epic battles under blood red skies.

The song went on. The images in the song took shape. Vilmos

no longer heard but saw. He stood tall, staring out at the burning fields in the song. A strong southerly wind blew smoke from the fires into his eyes. He looked down the trench littered with the dead and dying. In either hand he held a great sword, downturned during a pause between attacks but ready for battle just the same.

In his line he was the only one that stood at the ready. The others around him were slumped and weary. It had been a long day; the night would be even longer. Odd though it was he knew a night in the trench wouldn't bother him. He was lineborn and linesworn. The darkness didn't frighten him as it did many of the others.

The dogs came. He swung up the great swords in unison, standing true.

Behind the dogs he saw the goblin servants of the elves. Their thick green skin, large muscular bodies, and upturned canines clear even at a distance. Mixed in with the goblin horde were human slaves wielding rusted swords and other hand-me-downs from the goblins and the elven lords.

The elven lords rode in great chariots, chariots pulled by wingless dragons and hastened by thick leather whips. The weapons of the elven lords glowed in the darkened sky. Some of the lords wielded maces with spikes as long as daggers. Others hefted swords as large and sometimes larger than those that Vilmos held.

The attack dogs set into the trenches. Vilmos closed his eyes just for an instant before he charged. The closing of his eyes was as the turning of a switch. It did not make the images stop. It made them swim faster in his mind. The tree called. Vilmos listened. He raced into the stream of images that danced before his mind's eye. It was the image of this past self wielding two great battle swords that Vilmos clung to and it was this image that would later walk in the shadow of his thoughts.

***

Valam paused, looking about the hall. He leaned close to the closed door and repeated, "If there was one who would understand, I thought it was you. Rudden Klaiveson attends to court every Seventh Day. Did you know that? I've found it hard not to like him. He is quick-witted, and at times funny."

Adrina slowly opened the door. Valam saw tears on her cheeks yet said nothing of them. Instead he asked, "Would you like to return to South Province with me? The winters are mild. It will do you good."

"And?" inquired Adrina, probing further with her unspoken expression and the great round circles of her eyes.

"All right, all right. It's Isador. She figures she's finished with you and now it's my turn. Are you conspiring against me too? My own sister…"

"Oh Valam!" Adrina cried out as she ran to embrace him. "Do you truly like Rudden?"

Valam didn't say a word. He held and comforted her. This reminded him of all those times she had come to him with her problems as a child. She was his favorite sister, though he would never tell her.

"It will be okay, just you wait and see," he whispered into her ear. He put her down, his hands still on her waist as he regarded her for a moment. She had turned into a very beautiful woman. Nothing like the messy-haired tomboy he had once known. "Come now. It's time I saw father. I can't have my escort looking such a mess."

Adrina smiled faintly, went to the mirror. She rang the bell beside the mirror. One of her attendants entered. After bowing to the prince, the attendant approached. "I must attend council. You must help me fix this mess," she said, fretting with her hair.

Myrial smiled but said nothing. She knew Adrina didn't know

that she had answered the bell. "Yes, my lady," she whispered quietly, firmly. The formal tone was due to the prince's presence. He made her nervous.

Adrina turned. She smiled, reached out her hand as Myrial came to stand behind her. "What of house duties?" she whispered.

"House duties can wait. I was on my way to talk to you so this is just as well."

"Emel?"

Myrial's eyes went to Valam, then back.

"Later then?"

Myrial nodded agreement.

Adrina and Myrial worked busily in front of the mirror. Valam waited impatiently until they were finished.

With her long black hair braided tightly and folded over her left shoulder, Adrina took Valam by the arm and led him down the hall to their father's council room. As they approached the closed council doors they could see by the presence of the guards and pages awaiting their tasks that the council was in session. Soon they could hear sounds of a heated conversation in the hall.

"Perhaps we should return later," Valam said quietly. He had a particular loathing of council sessions.

"Come, this should be interesting." Adrina had only to glare at the guards to get them to move out of the way. They did so expeditiously. Mostly because they recognized the crowned prince, partly because of her glare.

Valam started to say that he hated council sessions but Adrina wasn't listening. She linked her arm in his and led him into the council chamber.

Chancellor Yi was speaking when they entered. "This could lead to civil war," he said, "Is this what we want?" As the chancellor paused to take a sip of water, he saw Valam and Adrina enter unannounced.

"My Lord, Prince Valam," the chancellor announced, tossing in a wink as he spoke.

"Chancellor," returned Valam as he turned to his father, the king, and knelt appropriately. "Your Royal Majesty, father, you look well."

"Dispense pleasantries," King Andrew said, the thick lines of his jaw easing a bit. "It is good you are here, Valam, my son. We could use a fresh mind on this delicate subject."

The king nodded to Keeper Martin who started to recount the events of the past few days in detail. Prince Valam stopped him, saying, "Father Jacob and Adrina have already caught me up on all that."

"I can believe that... Is Father Jacob still attending to Seth?" Keeper Martin asked, the salt-and-pepper gray of his beard and hair marking him clearly as one of the elders in the room, yet there was no insignia on his lapel this day to speak of his office as Head of Lore Keepers. Instead, his rank of office was indicated by the arcane staff that he held in his right hand as he stood beside the long, triangular shaped table that filled the center of the great hall.

"Yes," Valam and Adrina answered at the same time.

"Good," returned the king. His heavy oaken chair was to the right of where Keeper Martin stood. Directly in front of him and across the table were the concentric rings of pews where the lower council members sat. "We could also use his help here at council. We were just discussing how best to bring aid to Queen Mother of East Reach. Go on, Chancellor Yi, finish what you were going to say."

The chancellor, seated to the king's right, turned to the king and asked, "Your Majesty, may I digress for a moment and ask Prince—"

King Andrew motioned with his hand before the chancellor could complete his request. The great green jewel on his ring finger glittered in the soft white light of the candelabras spread throughout the council hall. Its soft green matched the glow from the jewels in the crown he wore. There was great purpose in wearing the crown jewels this day. Both had been gifts from the elven people to the Alder, the first ruler of Great Kingdom. That time had been simpler, before the bloody wars in which the brother races turned against each other.

"Who is running South Province in your absence? Did my brother condone your departure?"

"Chancellor Yi, you worry unnecessarily. Chancellor Van'te is handling matters in my absence," replied Valam, understanding the direction the question was supposed to lead him in.

A silent message passed between the two that said, "Yes, I received your message." The reply was, "Good, good, very good."

Chancellor Yi smiled as he broke into a soliloquy. His thoughts were so evoking and precise in explaining his ideas on the probabilities of succeeding in a sustained campaign against King Mark of West Reach and his allies that there was no possibility of contention. Then surprisingly the chancellor reversed his premise and had all equally persuaded that dismal failure lay ahead. His intent was to open all sides of the discussion and lead the council in a positive direction, and on that he succeeded overwhelmingly.

"Very good points, Chancellor Yi," Keeper Martin said, "Still, I think convincing the populace is the key. We cannot do this thing alone"—Keeper Martin's eyes probed those of the council members as he talked, speaking as much to them as about the peoples and places they represented—"We need the support and resources of our allies. Without this support Great Kingdom will founder like a ship that takes on too much water in heavy seas."

King Andrew sat truer in his chair. He turned away from Adrina and Valam. His eyes betrayed his concern for his children and much more. "Yes, Keeper Martin, let us hope for popular support and plan a way to achieve it. A good reminding of the prophecies should aid the task."

"Agreed, sire," added Yi.

Prince Valam asked, "Chancellor Yi, have you received word from the Free Cities yet? Are they sending an emissary?"

"Good question, that reminds me…" answered the chancellor moving around one side of the enormous table so that he was standing in front of the lower council. "Yes, the governor of Solntse himself is coming as a representative for all the free cities. He should arrive within the week. Representatives from High Province and the Western Territories will arrive soon afterward, but no definite dates can be prescribed. No word from the Minor Kingdoms yet as there are no longer keepers there to contact."

Keeper Martin cleared his throat, quickly added, "Several are journeying there now. It shouldn't take long. Once they arrive I shall know of it. I will tell the council at once." What he did not say—what no one said—was what had happened to the other keepers.

"Chancellor Volnej, we have not heard from you. Usually you are brimming with clever solutions," said King Andrew sardonically. He was still incensed about the proceedings in the Territories and in the South.

"Forgive me, sire, this combined, upper and lower, council will take some getting used to. I just wish that Brother Seth were here today. We shall need maps and many tactical diagrams drawn up. Also, we must increase the production of ships, armor, and weapons. It is a logistical nightmare. I will attend to those details," Volnej said, grinning happily as he spoke the last few words. "I will keep you up to date. And, I believe it is a viable excuse..."

"Yes, it is double-edged is it not, good chancellor. See that it is carried out."

King Andrew dismissed the council with a wave of his hands but asked Chancellor Yi, Keeper Martin, and Prince Valam to remain. Adrina understood that she was being dismissed as well and went without protest. Andrew Alder stood then at the head of the great triangular meeting table. The three, Yi, Martin and Valam, sat on one side of the table close to the king.

"The Duardins and Braddabaggons are noble old kingdom families," Andrew said, speaking directly to Valam, of Yi Duardin and Martin Braddabaggon. "Their families have served the greater good for generations. In the dark times ahead you will need their counsel. I bind them to you, my son, and you to them. Trust their words, for there are none who have served so well."

Prince Valam tried to speak but King Andrew's glare silenced him. King Andrew turned to Keeper Martin and Chancellor Yi then, saying, "You know what it is that you must do. Do not hesitate or stray from course."

"And my special delivery?"

"In due course, my son, in due course."

Valam grinned, nodded agreement before turning away. Keeper Martin called after him as he exited the council chamber. Valam slowed down, waited for the elder to catch up.

"You do realize," Martin Braddabaggon said quietly, "Geoffrey of Solntse will never show. None of them will."

"Yi's response was for the benefit of the listeners, was it not?"

"It was. His brother has taught you well."

"He has." Valam clasped Martin's hand. "Geoffrey is the key. What will get his attention?"

"Yes, win him. The others will follow. ...Clever thinking," he mused.

"I am my father's son, we had the same mentor. What of these rumors? Who is spreading the lies?"

Martin started to respond, paused. "You and I and Chancellor Yi must find a way to deal with the whisperers. It is your father's unspoken wish. He has bound us to you because he fears his time is past."

"Tell me what to do, Keeper Martin, and I will."

Keeper Martin looked directly into Valam's eyes. "Back to Geoffrey, you bring interesting insight. Free peoples understand strength and deeds. Find a way to earn his respect through action."

"With steel?"

"Perhaps."

Chapter Twenty:
Messages & Shadows

Word of the elves returning spread throughout the kingdoms. Emissaries began to arrive regularly from the far lands. A messenger arrived this day from High Province dashed Adrina and Valam's hopes that they would see their sister, Calyin. Heavy rains were eroding the mountain paths and the only remaining route from the North would take many weeks.

When Adrina and Valam weren't busy with other affairs, they struggled to learn Seth's language and culture. It seemed important to learn as much about the elves as they could. Although the language of the elves was strange to them the words began to flow from their tongues with slow persistence.

The unofficial council sessions grew with the same slow persistence until they were a long and tedious daily occurrence. It appeared that no one wanted to be left out of the council proceedings.

The curious arrived in droves. King Andrew was on the verge of sealing the city gates and only allowing those with official business into the city. Several days previous he had ordered the palace gates closed to all save official visitors. To make matters worse a murderous riot between mercenaries from Veter and Territory free men caused the city and palace guards to be put on full alert.

King Andrew wasn't pleased with the dilemma at hand. The Kingdom seemed on the verge of eruption. The one thing he wanted most was out of his reach. In truth he didn't know if the other kingdoms were refusing to acknowledge his requests or if the messengers weren't getting through.

As a second week passed without word King Andrew watched delegates grow irritated at postponements and the council grow restless. Private sessions between his most trusted advisers were going nowhere. No one would speculate as to the cause of the delays. The last of the emissaries from the Western Territories had arrived yesterday and the distance they traveled was the greatest.

Keeper Martin could only lower his eyes in the presence of his failure, contributing no words of wisdom or excuses. Father Jacob's brief discourse turned the group's mood dismal when he offered the feelings he sensed from Great Father. To top it all it seemed as if Father Tenuus had fled the palace. He was nowhere to be found.

"King Andrew, father," Valam said, interrupting the sudden quiet of the council chamber, "I see no recourse other than sending a private party from Imtal to each of the Minors in turn. I believe the royal personage is what is necessary to solve the crisis at hand. No one, not even King Peter, will purposefully refuse a direct request sent from you that I personally deliver."

King Andrew didn't respond with words. He lowered his head and raised his hand as a sign of agreement, submission. Sadness was written in his tired features.

"Prince Valam speaks true, Your Majesty," said Chancellor Yi, "I believe that is the only option we have left."

"Then so be it," King Andrew said with regret.

The meeting continued at a somber pace with not much else being resolved. They did however, decide to keep things progressing. They could not turn back from the course they had set out on. All must be ready before the coming of winter or they would not be able to send aid to East Reach until long after the winter snows thawed.

***

Vilmos couldn't remember when the world that he knew returned and the world revealed by the tree went away. He only knew that he walked and walked, confused and dazed. His mind filled with colors, flashes of light, and images of things that he could hardly imagine. Yet the one who stood in the shadow of his mind understood and this shadow walker helped watch and guide him along River Efrusse and out of the forests of Ril Akh Arr.

The journey north lasted many days and took Vilmos through the swamp of Adrynne where the army of Stranth was defeated by the will of the Lady who guards Beyet Daren and her people. Nightfall found Vilmos curled beside a boulder hidden deep in a thicket. Huge tears rolled down his cheeks. He stared up at the insolent sky and cursed softly under his breath. Night in Under-Earth was unlike night anywhere else. The thorns on the bushes in the thicket would help protect him from the strange, dark creatures that roamed the night.

Night, Vilmos mused. He almost laughed then as he wiped the tears from his cheeks. Night in Under-Earth seemed indistinguishable from day. He only knew it arrived because the sound of life slowly disappeared until it was absolutely quiet—a quiet that was interrupted much later when the night creatures arrived and joined in their hunts.

To guard against the night Vilmos learned to sleep with his eyes open. If danger approached he knew the images would filter into his dreams and he would awake. What he didn't realize was that it was the other who watched while he slept and it was a voice from the shadows of his own mind that called out warnings to him.

This night was different from the others before it. Images filtered into his dreams and urged him to wake, to race through the darkened land. Vilmos followed the call, only the knowledge that something was close carried him on.

Many hours later Vilmos offered quiet thanks to the heavens. The outskirts of Beyet Daren, dark and shadowy, illuminated only by silvery red light filtering through a darkened sky, came into view. At first it seemed the city was a single mass of black stone, but as he approached the city walls he grew increasingly amazed at what he saw.

Every building in Beyet Daren was a veritable palace of stones. Stones that must have been carved from the mountains in the distance. The dark stone had a dull shine as if every surface was polished smooth. Indeed, as Vilmos passed quickly through a cavernous opening in the city walls that served as the entryway, he found the walls were polished smooth—smooth and cold to the touch.

Inside the strange city he found empty streets, and as he walked along them he imagined the city was deserted. Images flashed through his mind's eye as if in a dream. He delved deep into the heart of the city. He started to see signs of life. A light on. A voice in a back alleyway.

He found it strange that the streets remained empty. The voice in his mind told him to pull the hood of his cloak closer about his head as a precaution.

He walked on, unafraid of the growing whispers in darkened alleyways. He muttered a curse to the very air around him. His thoughts went to the shaman for a time. Xith had taken him away from everything: his home where he was cared for. His parents who loved him. His life in Tabborrath village.

He started to cry. As he cried he cursed the shaman for everything that had happened to him and all that would happen to him if he didn't find his way.

He maintained his curses as he walked, yet the more he cursed, the more harsh and wrong his words sounded. He didn't hate Xith. He was scared. Scared he would not find Xith. Scared of being alone. Scared about what the future would bring.

The streets grew from vaguely familiar to completely unfamiliar. He knew he was lost and this was made worse by the fact that he didn't even know where he was trying to go.

As he turned a corner and entered a shadowed street he heard footsteps behind him. Before he could react he felt the heavy tip of a cold blade against his back. The finely crafted steel sliced through his clothing and touched his skin. Steel met his spine. He screamed, tried to run, but it was too late.

***

By the time Seth and Adrina made their way downstairs the council had adjourned. Over the course of the next several days the council required Seth's presence only sporadically, mostly to push the skeptics back into their place. More often, the council was in heated debate without him—debates that didn't always pertain to the elves.

During the long days of waiting and listening Seth and Adrina continued to tell each other about their homelands. As it happened, if Seth wasn't with Adrina she could be sure that he was with Valam. A slow friendship was building between Seth and Valam. Adrina could see this and this pleased her as something more, something dangerous, was building between her and Seth.

Most mornings she paced the walkways of the garden. She was

often alone, left only with her thoughts, although eventually one of the two would find her. This morning it was Seth who found her first. She wasn't disappointed to see him but her thoughts went out to another for a few brief moments.

Beautiful day, imparted Seth wordlessly.

"Yes it is, isn't it," responded Adrina, adding, "No word from the Minor Kingdoms yet?"

No, Keeper Martin seems worried. He thinks something's wrong. The Seventh day session may not take place.

Adrina turned up her lip. Her expression became a frown. She knew Valam was planning something and that Seth was a part of those discussions. She wasn't allowed to know what was happening. It bothered her that they were keeping secrets, compounded by the fact that she had tried her best to learn about what they were planning but hadn't been able to. Valam knew her too well. He knew her tricks and blocked her every effort.

For a short time the two stood quietly, searching for anything to spark conversation. Adrina's thoughts continued to drift. She wished that she was still a girl and not the woman she was becoming. She didn't want to understand why it mattered so that she was coming of age. When Valam had come of age there had been a great celebration. Heralds throughout the lands proclaimed him as Lord of the South, Governor of South Province and King's Heir.

There would be none of this for her. She would not be granted titles or land. Those things would be granted to Rudden Klaiveson on their wedding day—a man she had promised herself to, yes, but not the man of her dreams. What did she know of dreams anyway? It seemed she had only recently started to live.

Turning to Seth, she asked, "You've said before that The Reaches are divided in two: East and West. A king in the West, a queen in the East. Why is that? Why are the peoples divided?"

Kapital was my home, yes, I know little of it in truth. Galan should have been the one to tell you about this, not me.

Remembering Galan's face as if in a dream, Adrina smiled. "She did. She told me some, and I am grateful but there is so much I don't understand."

I was chosen at birth, Adrina. I have no past memories to cling to. I know only that which the Brotherhood teaches and what I have seen with my own eyes.

"Surely you know why there is a king in the West and a queen in the East?" She said it like it was such a simple thing, knowing it wasn't.

Seth walked to the edge of the balcony. He gripped the stone railing, stared out over the gardens but did not reply.

"It is because of Queen Oread, is it not?" Prince Valam said as he joined them on the balcony.

Seth shot a quick response of, *Come to join the battle of wits and words?* and at the same time replied aloud to Adrina, "I know what I have been told and read."

Valam's timely laugh in response to Seth's words caused Adrina to bead her eyes and flip her long dark hair over her shoulder. At times it seemed she and Valam competed for Seth's attention. "Well then?"

Oread was but one of the fools in the game. To truly understand you must go back to the First Age. The time of Ky'el, the titan who led men, elves, and dwarves from the bonds of slavery. These histories I know as I studied many of the ancient texts regarding your kind.

"Did titans and dragons truly rule the skies?" Adrina asked excitedly.

It is said titans and dragons shared the skies of Over-Earth with the Eagle Clans of old, and together they ruled the sky kingdoms.

Valam said, "Back to Ky'el."

"Yes," agreed Adrina. "Our history of the great titans is very different."

Ky'el was a titan, but a very different sort. Dangerous to some, a genius to others...

Adrina saw movement out of the corner of her eye, turned, saw Myrial waving to her from the stairs. Valam saw Myrial as well and whispered, "Go," to Adrina.

She excused herself and turned away. "News from Emel?" she asked excitedly as she walked down the steps with Myrial. Myrial nodded and the two hurried off.

***

The nameless rogue prodded Vilmos along, turning him this way and that with careful pressure of the cold blade applied to the small of his back. Whenever Vilmos tried to resist, the rogue muttered under his breath, "Only Nyom strays," as if Vilmos understood what that meant.

Eventually the rogue led Vilmos to an alley where another waited, clad in dark leathers and a hooded mask with two slits in it for the eyes. The two rogues then guided Vilmos into the darkness, maneuvering him around unseen obstacles, finally coming to a place where a door of sorts stood. Vilmos couldn't see the door. He only heard the noise of its movement as it creaked open.

After entering a dimly lit room the rogue with the blade prodded Vilmos from behind to raise his arms while the second searched him. The hooded one stripped Vilmos of his cloak and, after a brief struggle, his boots.

"Human?" muttered a raspy voice, the voice of the figure with the blade.

Soon afterward strong hands pulled Vilmos' arms painfully behind his back. They bound his hands harshly with a thin rope that cut into his skin as he attempted to resist.

As shock settled in Vilmos froze. Void of thoughts, too awestruck to react, his only recourse was to wait. He didn't think they were going to kill him, or he thought—hoped—they would have already done the deed.

The one with the blade spoke again, "Human slave, from where did you come?"

He didn't say a word. He sensed a third figure watching—judging—from the shadows. An unconscious shiver built within him. His legs shook with nervous tremors. He bit his cheek against his jaw until he felt warm blood flow across his tongue and trickle down his throat.

"Slave, speak when spoken to!" The sharp blade sliced into his back.

Vilmos fell to his knees, stood, and remained silent. He understood the words though they were in a language different from his own. It was then that he realized the language spoken was that of the dark elves. He knew the rogues were not of that race for he could smell the stench of their fleshy hides, a stench that even their cloaks and masks could not hide. The rogues were goblins, servants of the dark elves.

"Check his tongue," said the second goblin. "His master may have removed it…"

Strong hands pried open Vilmos' mouth. He saw shiny eyes from within the slits of the goblin's mask. He thought about biting down but didn't.

"Tongue and no branding. He must be a rebel spy."

"Slave or spy?" the goblin behind Vilmos said, clear impatience in his voice.

The figure in the shadows of Vilmos' mind spoke. "Neither," he said in the language of those who held him.

"Neither," laughed the goblin standing in front of Vilmos.

"Human, you are one or the other. There is nothing else here. So which one are you? Off with it, don't try my patience. I haven't much to strain."

Vilmos winced as the blade sliced along the small of his back. He was afraid but the figure in his mind kept him standing tall—tall and nearly naked in the frigid night air.

"I'll bet he's a slave," the goblin standing behind him said, "or else we wouldn't have been able to sneak up on him."

"Yeah, that's it. I am a slave."

"I hate slaves… kill him," said the cloaked goblin behind him, turning to leave.

"Wait!" shouted Vilmos desperately, "Wait, I'm no slave. I'm a spy, honest."

The goblin, seemingly interested, asked, "Really?"

"Yes, yes, I am," Vilmos said with a laugh, half bemused, half about to cry. The shadow walker in his mind screamed out in alarm to silence him.

"I don't know," said the second goblin as he stood in front of Vilmos and pranced nervously back and forth. He lunged out. The blade ripped into Vilmos' side. "He doesn't look like a spy, doesn't bleed like one."

The shadow walker forced Vilmos to his feet but couldn't stop terror from gripping his thoughts. Hands tied behind his back, nearly naked with two dark figures poking and prodding him, he felt utterly helpless. A discharge of warm urine flowed down his leg yet he said firmly, "I am neither slave nor spy."

"Overstep your bounds and you shall finish as Stranth," the first goblin said. "I shall have the truth of it."

Vilmos swallowed his heart back down his throat as the second goblin pulled the long, slender dagger from its sheath again. He did not cringe away from the blade or the cold death he saw in the other's eyes.

The goblin held the dagger close against his throat, staring into his eyes, hesitating, seemingly, only for the sheer joy of the agony it caused. With one hand the goblin pulled his hair back and pressed the blade tighter with the other.

Vilmos never wavered the direction of his gaze. He held it fixed, wild, wide, glaring at the one who would kill him. An image, a flicker of something, in his eyes forced the would-be killer to back away. The goblin dropped the dagger as if it had stung him and backed away from Vilmos trembling, bumping into the wall behind him as he went, groping wildly until he found the adjacent corridor before running from the room shouting.

The hooded goblin behind Vilmos whispered to the other who stood in the shadows before he hurried after his companion. Only the final words carried to Vilmos' ears, "He's the one."

"It is you," the figure said stepping from the shadows, the voice not harsh but soft. He caught Vilmos, twisted him around, unsheathed his sword. Then he sliced through the air in a series of fluid motions that were almost too quick for the eye to follow.

Vilmos, his hands freed from the restraints, gulped and gasped at the air. He tried to speak, found no words.

"It is you but not you," the warrior said, "I knew you would come back."

Puzzled Vilmos stood quietly for a time. He stared incredulously at his mysterious benefactor. The large armored tower seemed hardly a man at all, more a hardened mountain of stone and metal than a man. He was hard pressed to gaze past the chained plate to see the face, yet as he did recognition came in an instant. The brankened collar, the iron bit, the face chiseled as if of solid rock— it was the warrior from Solntse. *But how and why?*

His thoughts raced. "Where's Xith? Can you take me to him?"

"I serve Shost and my masters," the other answered.

"Take me to him."

The warrior's puzzled look matched Vilmos' now. "I have been waiting for you. You are home. Shost awaits."

"*Home?*" He was even more confused. The one who walked in the shadows of his mind watched but didn't speak.

"Is it time?" the warrior asked.

"No," Vilmos said flippantly.

The warrior frowned, sheathed his weapon, then walked away. Vilmos followed the warrior into the dark hallway.

Chapter Twenty One:
Slipping Away

Seth stared at the prince. "I still don't understand why I should learn. I mean if I had ever needed to use such weapons, I am sure I would have been taught. Members of the Brotherhood rarely learn to use weapons, even then only for personal edification."

"Then you shall learn for personal edification and because I think it is a good idea. I need the practice as well," Valam said. "Besides we have an entire day to pass. We cannot leave for the South until the weather breaks."

Seth glanced out into the courtyard and at the heavy downpour. The timing of the storm couldn't have been worse. Long hours of heavy rains were flooding the trails, making them nearly impassable. He hoped tomorrow would be a clear day, a day to begin a journey. He even cast a prayer to the Mother to ensure it.

"Meet me on the western balcony overlooking the garden. The hall just beyond it is perfect, secluded and quiet. I'll see an old friend to procure weapons. It won't take long."

"You harbor hopes in these competitions?" Seth paused, continued in a voiceless whisper, *Tell me, will the winner of this competition gain your trust or true friendship?*

Valam bowed through an apology. "The competitions are hard to forget, even with all that is ahead. We won last year. After a decade of defeat, we won. Geoffrey of Solntse lost to Captain Brodst of the Kingdom in the final match. If only you could see the games, the competition fields, you would understand how much this means. Do you know how many disputes have been settled on a field with just two combatants instead of hundreds or thousands?"

Seth probed Valam's mind seeking understanding but didn't find anything that made sense of the matter. East Reach had no blood sport. He saw only futility in men facing each other and dying on bloody fields.

Seth stared out into the rain-filled courtyard. He was becoming disillusioned. The delays were aggravating and the ceaseless bantering of the kingdom council was frustrating. He longed for East Reach, to feel his will mixing in with Queen Mother's thoughts, all the things he might never see again.

***

"Emel?" asked Adrina excitedly as she followed Myrial down the stairs. "You must tell me everything."

Myrial didn't say a word; she only gripped Adrina's hand more tightly as she led the princess along the dark hallway.

"The orb?" Adrina asked when she could no longer endure the quiet.

Myrial faced Adrina. "Emel, the caravan. We must hurry or we'll be too late."

Myrial hurried along the hall, pulling Adrina behind her. Adrina followed close, partly because the twisting corridor was unknown to her and partly because the darkness frightened her.

Everything frightened her now, yet it seemed she had never been so alive or so free. The past was a terrible thing to drag with you wherever you went, she knew that now and it felt okay to let go. Jumping from the wall was her way of letting go, letting the past slip away from the present.

She didn't forget. She would never forget. But now she could accept that she was alive and her mother was gone. She no longer felt the guilt of every waking breath, the heavy sense that everything in the world around her was dead and dying, the desire to slip away from life.

"Adrina," repeated Myrial, holding out a hooded cloak. "Put this on."

Adrina saw that they were near a guarded doorway. Heavy bars and thick iron doors on either side of a small space created a secured antechamber. It was a guard post and on the other side of the guard post she saw the strong light of the day. This surprised her because she thought she knew every pathway in Imtal Palace.

She put on the cloak, fixed the hood about her shoulders. Its thick cowl partially hid her face.

Myrial moved out of the shadows, nodded to the guard inside the post. He unlocked and opened the heavy iron door. The grinding of rusty hinges as the door opened sent a chill down Adrina's back.

When they were inside the chamber the guard closed and locked the rear door. Moments later a different guard unlocked and opened the door to the square. As they passed through the outer door Adrina looked up. The bowmen at their posts high above looked down at her as she followed Myrial into the street.

The market was bustling with activity. As it was getting late in the day, bargain hunters were out and merchants were competing with song to attract them. A young girl stopped in front of her, looked up at her with wide eyes. She held out her hand, touched the top of the girl's head as she passed by. Myrial turned to look back, eyes filled with worry told Adrina to hasten her step.

Her heart beat faster now. She had thought that she was the impulsive one and not Emel. Why was he doing this? she asked herself, and to take the orb without asking... It didn't make sense. Why now? Why would he do this when she needed him the most?

One corner of High King's Square was reserved for caravans. It was to this place that Myrial hastened. As they approached Adrina could see the carts and the liners going about their work.

A large caravan train was assembling. The job of the carts, apprentice coachmen, was to prepare the coaches for passengers and care for the horses. The liners took care of the supply wagons, packing the goods that would be carted off to faraway markets, checking tents and other supplies needed on the open road, caring for the work horses, mules, and other pack animals. Every action of the carts and liners was watched by those who had endured their apprenticeship and become journeymen in their own right.

Adrina knew enough about caravan trains to understand what she saw. But such a large caravan train wasn't without its masters, so where were they? With a file forming and the train nearly ready to leave the city the caravanmaster and his coachmasters should have been mounted and watching. Their brightly-colored robes and matching turbans would be hard to miss, so it seemed that the masters weren't about.

She grabbed Myrial by the wrist. The girl stopped, turned. "Where is it bound for?"

"The Territories," Myrial said, her voice a half whisper. "We must hurry."

Myrial started walking. Adrina followed. They passed beyond the lines of wagons. Adrina saw an eye-catching tent near the far wall of the square. The tent, like the robes of the masters, was brightly colored and stood out from the others around it. "The carvanmaster's?" Adrina asked.

Myrial indicated agreement, continued. The only problem was that the area between them and the tent was filled with hired blades and guardsmen who busily practiced their trade despite the lateness of the day. Adrina heard clashes of steel on steel as blades and guardsmen paired off in mock combat. But that didn't bother her; it was the scraping of blades on whet stones that gave her goose bumps.

Clearly the caravan's protectors knew something that the rest of the caravan's crew didn't. Otherwise they'd be packing gear, preparing for the journey.

Myrial didn't slow her stride or veer off course. She made a straight line for the entrance to the master's tent—like she'd done this before, and somehow Adrina didn't doubt that the girl had. She knew Myrial wasn't as quiet and meek as she pretended. She was a real fighter. Her life had toughened her and little frightened her, truly.

***

Cold, tired, and barefoot, Vilmos collapsed into a stall of the tiny stable. For a time it would be a refuge from the harsh streets of Beyet Daren. He had only been a step behind the warrior but had found only an empty corridor when he had raced into the hall. A fading voice in his mind had told him to find Xith and he had tried, but he didn't know where to go or how to begin.

Exhausted, sleep quickly found him. Surreal images played in his dreams. He heard voices, saw masked faces. But the masks could not disguise what was underneath. He knew them.

The shirt and pants he had stolen did little to keep him warm during the cool night. At first he wriggled deep into the hay-like bedding on the floor of the stall to keep warm. As morning approached an acidic rain came, the rainwater pouring into the stable, bringing with it the stank smell of the city.

He awoke shivering, his eyes wild and unfocused. It took several long breaths before the vivid night dreams faded beyond the edges of his conscious thoughts. A noise followed by harsh voices startled him. He ran as fast as he could from the stable, slipping in the thick brown-red mud of the yard, nearly landing on his backside.

He escaped through an alleyway, wandered aimlessly through empty streets with a vision in the corner of his eye that he could not shake. It was the image of a warrior. The image brought memories yet the memories were not his own. They were another's.

Thoughts of the warrior and the lady swept him from conscious concerns. The lady's beauty created a spot of light in his mind that overcame the darkness and chased his inner demons away.

His bare feet covered in dried mud, his hair matted and wild, Vilmos aroused to the world around him. He stood in the middle of a thruway. Under-Earth denizens were all around him, single-mindedly going about their business.

As if through another's eyes he saw the dark elves. Their gray skin, dark hair, and pointed ears were unmistakable to the one that walked in the shadow of his mind. He saw the goblin servants of the elves. With thick green skin, large muscular bodies, and upturned canines, he suddenly understood why they were such fierce fighters.

Mixed in with the crowd were human slaves. Vilmos was surprised to see how many slaves the dark elves kept. The slaves, covered in dirt and reeking of disease, walked more like animals than men. Most were shackled and chained as they walked through the streets. A few like Vilmos, however, walked freely. These free humans were the ones Vilmos watched and followed.

The city seemed so large that he felt hopelessly lost. He shook the rain from his hair, wrung the moisture out of his pants and shirt, and emptied his pockets onto the ground as he walked. The last pocket had a stone in it, a small round pebble no bigger than his thumb.

Remembering the rock fight he and Xith had had during the magic shield lesson, he smiled. He tucked the stone into his palm, held it there as a good luck charm. He took to tossing it up into the air and catching it again every few steps as he went. Soon after he became lost in his thoughts.

A darkly robed figure passed in front of him. He let the stone drop to the ground. A sensation touched his mind, gnawed at him. He couldn't quite place what it was. Perhaps it was telling him to run but his mind was too disoriented to realize it.

He ran to catch up with the robed figure. The other looked like a priest. The shadow walker in his mind had seen their kind before. Vilmos had feared them once; he did not fear them now.

Vilmos followed the priest until it became obvious that he was doing so. The priest turned to face him. He shuddered as he glimpsed a hornmarked face seemingly etched from rough hewn alabaster within the dark recesses of the cowl.

"Boy, go away. I have no time for you…"

Vilmos withstood the glare, stared straight back at the priest with unmoving, unyielding eyes. "I wish to serve."

"The priesthood has no need of such. Return to your master." The dark figure spoke tersely but without anger.

"I am not a slave, I serve Shost," Vilmos said, the words coming to his tongue as if from another.

The priest grabbed Vilmos, hiding the boy's face in the recesses of his cloak as he slipped into an alleyway. The priest didn't say much more after that and neither did he release his iron grip. When they were several streets away the priest stopped, put Vilmos down. He pulled Vilmos by the scruff of the collar after him then, and through street after street they marched.

***

Valam walked rapidly, excitedly through the halls. The disappointment of the morning's downpour faded. His first stop would be the audience chambers to talk with his father and advise him that the plans for departure were completed, and then he would look up an old friend. He had been so wrapped up in affairs that he had not seen Timmer since his return. He wondered how the old swordmaster was getting along, and more importantly, how the years were affecting his sword arm.

As Valam was being admitted to his father's audience chamber he took note of outsiders in the room. Apparently Chancellor Yi saw and understood his confused expression. The chancellor hurriedly excused himself and escorted Valam into the hallway. "They are the delegation from the Minor Kingdoms."

"What? When did they arrive?"

"There is no time for that, young sire. You must find Brother Seth and send a runner for Captain Brodst."

"Captain Brodst?"

Chancellor Yi gripped Valam's sword arm with his outstretched hand. "Trust me on this, young sire. Do so quickly, tell him to come equipped." Chancellor Yi turned to return to the audience chambers.

The urgency sensed, Valam did not delay. He raced through the halls, found Seth, and sent a summons to Captain Brodst. Seth was not far from the place they were supposed to meet for practice. Valam did not have to tell Seth something was wrong. Seth could sense it. The two quickly made their way back to the audience chambers.

Captain Brodst arrived shortly after Valam and Seth. He replaced the guards who normally stood just outside the door with two of his personal sentinels, while he took a position just within the door. The captain's timing was smooth and the outsiders only noted the entrance of Valam and Seth. Seth wordlessly told Valam of the naked rage in the minds of the outsiders. He read their hatred and their hatred was not only for him as an elf, it was for King Andrew, Valam, and everything Great Kingdom represented.

Chancellor Yi made the customary introductions. Valam and Seth were seated near King Andrew. The tension in the air was clear. Something was about to happen.

The small-statured Chancellor de Vit stood in front of the emissaries from Vostok. He set his sullen eyes on Seth, then with unbroken stride returned to the point of the conversation he had been in before the interruption. "King Jarom will settle for nothing less than a full forum to discuss the issue at hand." So saying, he turned and spat at Seth. "Remove the elf from my sight at once. I will not be in the same room as one of these."

Outraged, Valam would have jumped from his seat and tackled the chancellor if it had not been for King Andrew's stern hand admonishing him. He clenched his fists and tightened his jaw, vowing that if the chancellor insulted his father, the king, he would kill the other where he sat.

King Andrew spoke openly, "By a full forum you mean a gathering as outlined in the Alliance Treaty?"

"King Jarom, East Warden of the Word, ruler of Vostok, will not concede otherwise."

King Andrew gripped Valam's left wrist as his face showed his anger. The king's grip, surprisingly firm for a man of his years, might have crushed the bones in a lesser man's arm, but Valam barely noticed. "How long will it take Jarom and the others to make the journey to Imtal?"

"It is King Jarom, and it will take at least another full month," snapped the chancellor.

Valam broke free of his father's grip, jumped from his seat and lunged across the table. Even Seth seemed surprised at the speed with which Valam crossed the eight foot stretch of oak. Valam's fist knocked the chancellor to the floor, and as the man fell Valam followed him to the ground. Unlike the chancellor, who didn't move after hitting the floor, Valam landed on his feet.

His fist poised to strike, Valam whirled around to face the remainder of the delegation from the Minor Kingdoms. "The next insult brings death, make no mistake, you will die by my hand."

Captain Brodst dragged the chancellor by the scruff of the collar out the door, telling the guards to shackle him and throw him into the courtyard. King Andrew almost reflexively said something, yet did not. A faint smile did touch the corners of his lips.

The other delegates babbled apologies. The head delegate from Yug was the first to speak above the others, "I am sorry, that is the word also from King Alexas." Valam cast angry eyes at the speaker. The man quickly modified his statement saying, "I mean, Your Majesty, King Alexas wishes a gathering to discuss the matter at hand."

"How long?"

Another delegate from Vostok moved into Chancellor de Vit's vacated place near King Andrew's high-backed audience chair and spoke, "I am afraid, Your Majesty, that we will require at least a month to make preparations. King Jarom wishes all the kings to make the journey together."

"A month?" said Valam angrily, "And you bow to Jarom like dogs?"

The man sank down in his chair, swallowed a lump that had just welled up in his throat. "That is what I was informed, Prince Valam, Your Royal Highness. I only relay the word. Do not judge the messenger by the words."

This is a counter, they know of your plan to journey to the South, imparted Seth to Valam.

How? thought Valam to himself, using the learned technique which allowed Seth to reach into his mind. *We only recently made those plans.*

Valam eyed the delegate from Vostok. It was clear now that Chancellor de Vit had been but the messenger and this man speaking now held the strings. The purple silk of the robe and the gold embroidery from his triangular hat to the tips of his curly toed boots spoke of the delegate's wealth and standing in the southern kingdom. The delegate was obviously of noble blood and perhaps even a royal cousin of Jarom.

They're planning something...

What? thought Valam.

Valam pointed a steady finger at the delegate, said coolly, "Action is required and requested, a month to prepare is not acceptable."

The audience chamber was still and silent. All eyes were fixed on Valam.

I see a city... A large city... A square with armed men...

An attack? thought Valam.

I'm not sure but I do know they don't want Kingdomers in the... Seth's thoughts trailed off. *This one, this man. He's the one, the one who saw to the murders of your envoys. I see it in his thoughts...*

Valam turned to face his father. "With your permission, sire?"

King Andrew nodded his head.

"Captain," charged Valam as he exited. "Kill the next man who dares insult any Kingdomer or elf."

He patted the captain knowingly on the shoulder. In a way it was an apology that he granted. In all the excitement and preparations, no one had enlightened the poor captain and now it really did seem that the whole of the kingdom had forgotten his deed. The celebrations had been cancelled and Imtal Proper was in turmoil. Valam lingered a moment, delving beneath the sullen eyes that stared back at him.

"Gladly, Prince Valam, gladly," said the captain as if to end the thing that passed between them unspoken.

Chapter Twenty Two:
Boundaries

Seth studied the training sword, holding it outstretched. The metal felt cold and awkward in his hand. He watched how Valam held the weapon, imitated the hold but the grip didn't feel right.

"On guard!" yelled Valam as he lunged with his blade. The blow knocked the weapon from Seth's hand.

Seth picked up the sword. Valam showed him the correct stance and grip, then took the offensive. He parried inward, striking full against Seth's blade, which held firm now.

Valam shuffled back along the floor, parrying in and out, giving Seth a feel for the balance and movement involved in swordplay. Seth was quick to adapt, to change with Valam's movements, but was still susceptible to harsh thrusts which stung and often ripped the hilt from his hands.

"Judge how tight you need to grasp. Remember, firm, don't strangle. Work with it, anticipate your opponent." Valam moved through the various steps, thrusting high and low. Valam's thoughts were only on the attack, thrust, parry and block.

Seth followed each movement. He watched the strategy, learned the timing involved. Tension eased from his thoughts as his mind opened. He waited only for Valam's next move, countered as necessary.

For the next phase of training, Valam took Seth to a two-handed stance. He showed Seth how much power could be gained in the attack as well as the defense, although at a cost to maneuverability.

My grip, can you show me again? asked Seth as he defended.

Valam paused to show Seth the proper two-handed grip, then executed a series of simple thrusts, demonstrating how one could use the tip of the blade to impale and rend. Afterward he switched to the defensive, allowing Seth to practice his thrusts.

"Watch your stance. The way you stand is as important as your attack. Place your feet wider apart so you have a good center of balance. It will allow you to move more easily and to react better in any direction necessary." Valam went through a series of fancy movements to the right, left, forward, and then back. "You see, balance is the key. If your balance is bad, your attack will be poor."

The two practiced for hours. The clash of metal on metal rang throughout the courtyard. Seth enjoyed the activity as did Valam.

Their thoughts became detached from everything around them. They had only the weapons in their hands.

"You see," Valam said, lunging forward, "I knew you would like it."

Yes, it is interesting. There is an art to it, replied Seth as he easily blocked, then swept in for an attack. *Would a lighter blade allow for more mobility?*

"Definitely, we train with these heavy blades for a reason." Valam countered with a low thrust, then a parry. "Seth, can I ask you something?"

You don't need to ask, groaned Seth, straining as the weight of

Valam's blade descended upon him. Seth pushed Valam away, forced the prince to parry against his thrust.

"When I first handed you the sword you acted as if you had never seen one before yet in the images from your homeland I saw numerous weapons."

Seth switched from thoughts to words. "It is the workmanship of the blade. It is so different from our own. The metal is different, dull and black. I remember ours as bright silver, and it is also the first time I had ever held a weapon."

"That is strange for me to conceive," Valam said through clenched teeth, "I have had a weapon of one sort or another in my hand ever since I was old enough to carry the weight."

Seth started to pass a thought on to Valam, paused to concentrate on his movements and steady his balance. "The Brotherhood doesn't use weapons. We rely on our skill of movement in weaponless combat. The techniques can be quite effective, as you've seen."

Valam's assaults grew quicker, harsher. "But how can one fight an enemy who uses a skill which we do not possess?"

"What do you mean?" asked Seth confused, reading mixed emotion in Valam's words.

"None of my people have your skill of hand. We cannot hope to match you on the field." Valam lunged at Seth with great vigor.

Seth's expression grew rigid. He stopped abruptly; luckily Valam pulled his thrust back at the last moment. Seth contemplated the question for a space, he understood Valam was agitated and he wanted to respond correctly. *Valam, it is not so. I have explained to you about the Brotherhood, only a select few are chosen, as it is with our enemy, and though the will of the land is in every living thing, few can harness those powers as we do. We would not have come if the need was not great. Queen Mother has seen the paths and she knows what will come without your aid.*

Seth chose swordplay as an alternative to further explanation, then changed the subject. *Are you going to tell me where you disappeared to?*

"Just probe my thoughts, you will anyway."

"That's not fair, what has happened? This is not like you, Valam. Has something happened in council that you're not telling me about?"

Valam slowed the attack to respond, shifting quietly while he spoke. He countered Seth's jab. "The delegates left Imtal immediately after speaking to my father."

"They withdrew the offer of support they had hinted of, did they not?"

Valam lowered his sword, took a step toward Seth, speaking in a hushed tone, "This must stay between you and I, not even Adrina must know of this."

"Agreed"

"King Jarom requested a gathering. It means he seeks the seat of power which Great Kingdom has always held."

"Or he has some other plan." Valam pushed for Seth to explain. Seth turned away. "Tell me, Prince Valam, what does the winner of this competition get?"

"Beyond respect?"

"Beyond respect."

"Is there anything beyond respect? Don't you see? Your cause needs popular support and there is no better way to gain such support. People from all corners of the land and beyond attend."

Then we practice for the competitions.

"No, we practice for ourselves," Valam said striking out with his sword. "I await my father's decision."

***

Vilmos' feet hurt from the rocks underfoot and because of the breakneck pace of his abductor. Several times he told the priest he wouldn't run but the priest, not listening, only told him to keep quiet or he would stuff a gag in his mouth—a thing Vilmos was starting to believe would happen.

Eventually they stopped while the priest gathered his bearings. Afterward, though, it was back to the double-time march through the streets, passing almost to the outskirts of the city. Vilmos wasn't sure which side of the city they were on. It was difficult for him to get his bearings in Under-Earth as there was no sun to mark direction. It did seem, though, that he was on the opposite side of the city from where he had entered.

The priest stopped, crossed the street, pulled Vilmos behind him. The building they stood in front of was different from those around it. It was built with white stones instead of black and had a single spire that rose into the sky hundreds of feet, making it the tallest building Vilmos had seen in the city.

The priest pushed Vilmos through the front door, sending him sprawling into a darkened antechamber. Vilmos lay still, unmoving. The antechamber's windows were coaled over and allowed no natural light to filter in. He prayed as his eyes adjusted to the darkness, wondering what the hand attached to his collar would do next.

The room swayed as he was raised from his haunches and thrust into another room, one lit by a conglomerate of lanterns whose dull, yellow spray scarcely touched the darkness. The room held a sense of foreboding. A group of darkly clad men sat at a table talking in hushed tones.

Afraid to move, Vilmos lay motionless as the group of men gathered around him, staring down at him. He knew that beneath the shadows of black the hooded robes afforded were eyes that held loathing. He could sense it.

"Can you believe it, Talem?" hissed his abductor, "All this way to find a mere boy."

"Are you sure?" answered Talem, lowering his hood to reveal his face as he did so.

Vilmos gasped. If there was one thing he knew for certain about the priests, it was that the hood was not to be removed. He had never seen so many of the priests in one place. At most he had seen two of the dark priests together and even that had been only on one occasion, an occasion that had sent his father into a hysterical frenzy.

"Yes, I'm sure. He was where you said he would be and he followed the lure."

"I don't know," said another, prodding Vilmos with sharp, stubby fingers. "I see nothing of the mystics, only a boy. Lord Boets will be displeased."

The priests started to debate over him as if he was some kind of prize. They decided to take a knife to him to see if that sparked a response.

He watched a priest withdraw a shiny blade from a black sheath. The priest's steady hand brought the blade closer and closer.

Terror gripped his mind, holding him while the blade's fine edge sliced into his arm. The icy sting of pain and the touch of his own warm blood came to him as through a vision. He did not flinch, whimper, or offer anything for them to gawk at. It was as if he looked in on another's dream.

"Go ahead, kill him," said one of the priests, disappointment in his voice.

Another objected, "Why? He's not the one."

"We can't just turn him to the streets. We have to kill him."

Vilmos was trembling. Only now that the threat of death loomed near did the happenings seem real. He tried to beg for his life, but his pleas only brought laughter. The priests enjoyed desperation; they fed on it.

"Stand as Gandrius and Gnoble," the shadow walker whispered in his mind. Suddenly he understood. Memories of old washed before his eyes. He could see the stone giants, Gandrius and Gnoble, standing tall as they defended Qerek from the Rhylle hordes—and it was then that his fear became anger.

He began to focus. A trickle of magic built within him. It circled outward.

The power overtook him; he could deny it no more. Like floodwaters racing along a stream bed, magic in its purest form raced to his fingertips, engulfing the outstretched fingers of his hands and arcing wildly. The deadly flames lashed out, engulfing the priests as though they stood within flaming waterfalls.

The dark priests began to writhe and scream. To Vilmos it seemed a horrendous sight, but he could do nothing to stop the flow of raw magic from within. He closed his eyes. He didn't want to see their agony, didn't want to hear their screams.

***

Adrina followed Myrial to the caravanmaster's tent. Anyone that stood in their way moved aside when Myrial raised her palace pass. "Being housemistress has its rewards," Myrial whispered as she hurried along.

Once inside the tent they made their way to the caravanmaster's table. The table strewn with charts and inventory scrolls looked in complete disarray but the caravanmaster seemed to know where everything he needed was as he passed out orders to those seated around him, often pointing to one of the items on the table.

Emel stood behind the caravanmaster, slightly to the right. It was a position of honor. The position reserved for the caravan's master at arms. A fresh cut along his left cheek told of a test of steel that Emel had won, if only barely.

Myrial and Adrina stopped in front of the table. The master looked up, spoke. "If you seek passage or wish us to convey goods, you are but late. Yemi will see to you at any rate, turn you away or not as he will." He nodded and pointed to a tall thin man seated at the far end of the table.

Adrina stood her ground, lowered the cowl of her cloak. She cleared her throat several times in an attempt to get the caravanmaster to look at her, thumped the table when he didn't. "Imagine I have your attention now, do I not good caravanmaster?"

The caravanmaster's aid bent over and whispered in the man's ear. "Yes, princess," the caravanmaster said, his far south accent only now clear to Adrina, "I did not know it was you. Is there something I can do for the Royal House of Alder?"

"You make for the Territories, do you not?" The caravanmaster nodded agreement. "Good," she said, smiling. "I would speak to this one." She pointed to Emel. "Dismiss him."

"As you wish your highness."

Emel glared at Adrina as he walked toward her. "My princess," he said, stopping in front of her. "What is your will?"

Adrina beaded her eyes and turned. The three exited the tent without a further word passing between them. Myrial took the lead as soon as they were outside. She walked to a secluded area where they could talk.

Adrina was near tears when they stopped. She turned to face Emel. "You were going to leave just like that? Without so much as a goodbye and taking what's mine with you?"

"It was for the best, Myrial knew."

Adrina turned to Myrial. Myrial said, "Yes, that's why I brought Adrina here."

"Why?" Adrina asked Emel. "Why are you doing this? You

don't need to, it serves no purpose."

"There was an opening, I've pledged my service."

Adrina grabbed Emel's chin, turned his face so she could see the long wound clearly. "I see, and you got this how?"

"I am told it will heal without scarring. The blades see and understand."

"They understand that if you slip up they can cut your throat and take your place. That's what they understand."

"That's not fair, Adrina. I'm needed here."

Adrina slammed her fists against his chest. "I need you. I can't do this without you."

Emel grabbed her wrists. "You are doing this without me." He stopped, looked at Myrial, seeming to judge her thoughts by her eyes. "Don't you understand? I can make a difference here. I've decided, I'm going."

"Going where?" Adrina glared.

"The Territories, surely you know that."

"What use to you is the orb then? Why did you take it?"

"It is for the best. I have seen what it can do to you. I will be its keeper and where better a place than the wilds of the Territories. It will be safe there and you will be safe from it."

Adrina played a hunch. "The southlands are a long way from the Territories."

"The caravan's to Krepost'."

"And you shall be there before the winter snows set in the forests?"

"Yes, before the snows set."

"Return in the spring?"

"Yes, in the spring."

"Yet I see no winter gear being packed, and your caravanmaster—"

"—Your point being?" Emel snapped. Myrial took a step closer, another step and she'd be standing in between them.

"I'm getting to that. I've eyes you know, and ears. I see, I hear."

Emel swept around Myrial, grabbed Adrina about the shoulders. His firm grip caused Adrina to wince in pain as he pushed her up against the wall behind her. He had been holding the orb in his hand and had dropped it just before taking action. Myrial picked up the orb. She attempted to wedge herself between them. She looked back for a moment to ensure that no one was watching or near.

"Forget what you think you know," Emel said, despite Myrial's attempt to put herself between them.

Myrial held the orb up for both of them to see.

"That's not fair," Adrina said, "You were using the orb. You know?"

"Yes, I do," Emel said.

"And I," said Myrial gripping the orb, smiling as she tried to remember to breathe and focus as she had learned from Galan.

"What then do we do with what we know?" Emel said, releasing Adrina.

"Nothing," Myrial said, pushing the two apart. "Nothing at all."

Adrina straightened her dress, glared. "You will remember to treat me like a lady, like the princess that I am. Do not touch my person again, I warn you."

Emel scrunched up his eyes, wondering at her sudden formalness. Then he followed her eyes, turning, understanding as he saw several palace guards approaching. Their look said they were on official business. Before the guards got too close, Emel snatched the orb from Myrial's hands and slipped it into the leather pouch around his neck.

None of them were really sure what the guardsmen had seen, if anything, so they waited.

"Your Royal Highness," the two men said as they came to stand before the trio. "We're minutes from sealing the city. You must come with us at once, by order of the king."

"My father?"

"Yes, you're to return to the palace."

"What's going on? I demand that you tell me."

The guardsmen looked at each other, unsure what to say for a moment. "Please, I beg of you. I've a family to think about, and I cannot—"

Adrina raised a hand as a sign for the guard to stop speaking and he did, midsentence. She turned back to Emel, touched his hand. "It won't be the same without you. Be well."

Emel put his free hand on top of hers. "And you," he said as he turned and walked away.

***

Swordmaster Timmer's presence near Valam and Seth was potent. Casually the swordmaster walked over to Seth and corrected his stance and grip, tossing a sharp glare at Valam, then sitting back down without saying a word. Thereafter Timmer conducted their movements with a point of his hand or a gesture, grunt or groan, never breaking their concentration.

Seth was gaining speed and agility dramatically—it was through Timmer that Seth had related his years of weaponless combat training with sword fighting. Indeed the movements were in many ways similar, and as soon as Seth realized this he was able to tap into his previous training and deliver attacks that increasingly put the young prince on the defensive.

As he planned movements in his mind's eye Seth focused on Valam. His thoughts fixed only on Valam's intentions. The thoughts that flowed into his mind helped him easily counter the prince's attacks and the expression on Valam's face became one of utter surprise.

Each time Valam attacked, Seth blocked. Valam found no openings and it seemed he was being pushed into a corner, making defense his only option. Only one other person could best him with such skill and that was the one who had trained him, Timmer. Out of breath from guarding, Valam yielded. He called a halt to the match.

"Are you two conspiring against me?"

"No," Seth said honestly.

"You weren't giving him *private* pointers, Timmer?"

Seth put the tip of the heavy training blade to the ground and leaned his weight against it. "Your mind is so open."

Valam thought about Seth's words before he replied, "By open, what do you mean?"

"Your thoughts flowed to me without effort. I used them to decide how to block and attack you."

Valam looked to Timmer who in turn stared back blankly. "How do I protect against that?"

In jest Valam plopped down beside Timmer, put a hand on Timmer's shoulder, and said through exhausted breaths, "Your turn, old friend."

I'll teach you. It is easy.

Teach me? I don't know how to use will, thought Valam, allowing Seth to read his mind.

"I only instruct now," replied Timmer softly, belatedly, "My sword arm isn't what it used to be."

You don't have to. Will is in everything—and besides, I'm not talking about reading minds. I'm talking about defending from a mind probe—a simple clouding of thoughts.

"You are still the best swordsman I have ever seen," Valam said replying to Timmer as he sheathed his weapon and waved for Seth to follow him.

"An unused dagger rusts," Timmer mumbled as the three walked through the entryway into the palace proper.

"Nonsense," added Valam as he turned toward the armory.

Chapter Twenty Three:
Stark Reality

Vilmos braced himself, clasped his hands to his ears. The screams, the screams. He couldn't take them anymore. Why didn't it end? Why did they still scream? Why couldn't it be quick—and over? Why? Why? Why?

He begged, pleaded with himself to let it end, to ebb the flow of magic. Then he realized that he wasn't hearing desperate cries of dying men. What should have been screams of pain had turned to raucous laughter and as he opened his eyes, he saw the dark priests standing within the flames, untouched by the fire.

The one who laughed the hardest was the one who had abducted Vilmos, but he was not a man like the others. His eyes were milk-white with blindness and yet he saw. He saw with the second sight of his kind. The sight that was inborn to those of his demon race.

The demon's scaly hands agilely stroked a medallion that was suspended on a thick, gold chain around his neck. His voice boomed with laughter as he spoke. "He is the one," the demon said. "He has the mystic power of the keeper to be certain, and perhaps more."

Vilmos turned in a tight circle. His eyes wild, wide.

"Did you honestly think that we were unprepared to fulfill our duties?" scoffed Talem, "I assure you, you are not the first. You will not be the last."

The priests pounced on Vilmos. Two held him while others bound his hands and feet, put a gag in his mouth. Then they slipped a large sack over him, propelling him into a sightless world of darkness.

For a time he relied on his sense of hearing. He listened to the fall of footsteps that were circling him and the muffled voices debating angrily. Then a smell, potent and sour, found its way to him. Afterward only darkness and unconsciousness.

**

Adrina paced in her room. It had been a long day. So much had happened. She was upset, but happy for Emel, because he had appeared to be happy. Everything seemed so wrong though. Why was the caravan train leaving Imtal now? Why was her father sealing the city? Why did Emel have to go?

The trail was muddy and wet from rain. The mud would make progress along the road slow. Wagons could get stuck. Pack mules could become reluctant or agitated. The rain could return. Passengers and crew wouldn't be happy.

The rain was only the beginning. It was late in the day. Caravans normally left early in the morning or at least by midday so they could make progress along the road before nightfall. So why was this caravan leaving the city when only a few hours of daylight remained? Did the caravanmaster know something she didn't? Was he planning on driving the caravan through the long night?

Myrial touched Adrina's arm, partly to remind the princess that she was there and partly to get her attention. Adrina turned to

Myrial and frowned. "You know what I'm thinking. Don't you?"

"Sealing the city against the night isn't that unusual, especially with all that has happened recently. Besides, I'm sure there is good reason."

"Then why does it all seem so wrong?"

"Go see your father. Talk to him."

"He told me nothing last time, only that he was pleased to see me. Like I was some prize toy that he had requested the guards to fetch."

Myrial touched a hand to Adrina's, then filled two cups with tea. "Sit, drink. It's one of your favorites. Strong spice and tropical fruit from the Southlands. The aroma is wonderful, soothing."

"And the biscuits?" Adrina asked with a soft laugh.

"Fresh-baked, with a hint of lemon. I spoke with the baker, just as you asked."

Adrina took a sip of tea, then bit into a biscuit that seemed to melt in her mouth. "You did, didn't you?"

Myrial didn't reply. She sipped her tea quietly, concentrated on the biscuits. She hadn't eaten much all day and was hungry.

Adrina watched Myrial eat as she nibbled on a biscuit and sipped her tea. "He shouldn't have dismissed me like that," she said, breaking the silence. "I'm not a child."

"It was for the benefit of the council I'm sure."

"For a bunch of old men that care nothing about anyone but themselves. They could care less if I were alive or dead."

"Exactly," Myrial said looking directly at Adrina. "I'm sure that's the truth of it. Your father couldn't act pleased or surprised to see you. He only wanted to see that you were well. Oh, don't you see? That's what it was about."

"You know something, don't you?" Adrina put down the tea cup, stared intently. "Tell me what you know, Myrial. Please, I beg of you."

Myrial said quietly, the tone of her voice so low Adrina had to lean forward to hear, "You don't want to know what they say in whispers Adrina, you don't want to know. The whispers are hurtful, they always are. You are better—"

"Whispers?" Adrina pushed, though she could see Myrial was frightened.

"The word in the hall, in the city, in the land. Things you shouldn't know or hear, Adrina."

"What do the whisperers say?"

Myrial turned away. She couldn't look at Adrina as she spoke, "If the whispers were even half true, I would tell you. The whispers don't have a spark of truth. Your father is a good and just king. Your family is strong and will rule for many generations to come. I know this as I know no other thing."

"Does my father know the things the whisperers say?"

"I'm sure he does," Myrial said quietly, turning back to her tea and acting as if it were the most interesting thing in the world.

Adrina knew then that Myrial was hiding from the truth of the whispers. Myrial didn't want to face painful truths anymore than she did and the truth *was* in Myrial's words. The whisperers must be saying that the House of Alder was weak and that it's time had come and gone.

Adrina didn't like the stark reality that she was faced with. She was frightened and hurt. If such whispers had spread throughout the land, very dangerous days were ahead. She knew her history, how monarchies were toppled, how kings were born, bled, and died.

The people rewarded good kings in word and deed. Good kings could rule with open hands, but that hand must be ready to clench into a fist, to strike, to defend, to keep land and people. A weak king was no king at all. He was a puppet on the throne who would bow to the will of the strong. Was her father weak?

***

Light filtering into the thick burlap bag caused Vilmos to wake. He could tell that he was outside. He couldn't tell where he was. Every now and then those carrying him would switch shoulders, jerking him around violently as they did so. He tried to struggle, to fight, to free his hands or at the very least find a comfortable position. His legs were cramped and he ached. His wrists stung where the ropes bit into them. His back hurt where bruised shoulders swelled.

Through it all, the shadow walker was there with him, whispering that he should calm himself and not worry, for they followed Stranth's trail back to Pakchek Daren where they would find safety. But Vilmos didn't want to listen to the voice in his mind. He wanted freedom and so he struggled.

Suddenly movement stopped. Vilmos was dumped onto the ground. He heard a creaking sound, perhaps that of a warped door being laboriously opened.

He was picked up again. Still in the burlap bag he was deposited in a box of sorts. He couldn't tell what kind of box, only that he heard the cover close over him and a lock being set in place, felt the walls about his shoulders.

Shrouded in total darkness now, Vilmos guessed the box was completely sealed. The air became stuffy and warm, hard to breathe. His listened, but the movement of those around him became the least of his worries. He fought to keep his eyes open. He was suddenly so tired. Sleep called out to him.

He beat against the box with his elbows, struggled to maintain consciousness. He knocked his head against the top of the box until it hurt. The last time he did so he saw a crack of light enter the box. A puff of air followed. It brought life to his burning lungs.

He pushed up with his head, fought to keep the top of the box open. The air. He needed it desperately.

Time slipped away. His neck became stiff and sore. He twisted his head from side to side but this didn't help. He began to wonder if air was more important than the need to relieve the pain? Or if the pain was the only thing keeping him here in this reality? Why were the priests being so cruel? Why didn't they just kill him and get it over with?

Then he thought that maybe it wasn't their intention to kill him. Maybe they wanted him to suffer.

The box jerked from side to side as it was picked up. Vilmos listened intently. He couldn't tell where he was going. The movement lasted only a few minutes, came to an abrupt end when the box was thrown onto a wooden floor or platform of sorts.

The sensation of movement returned though no one had picked up the box, or at least he hadn't felt them do so. He listened against the side of the box. He could hear a faint creaking. A rolling sound. He was in a wagon, he suddenly realized.

The road became rough and rocky. The box was thrown up with each bump, landing with a thud. He felt each and every movement. His body felt battered and bruised. He was so weary, felt he couldn't keep the top of the box open any more, but knew he had to. The constant swaying back and forth, up and down, gave him motion sickness. He started to gag, stomach acids burned the back of his throat but there nothing in his stomach to throw up. The dry heaves continued until he passed out.

***

A hooded bastion marked the entrance to the courtyard in which the central armory was housed. Seth had never been in this section of the castle-palace structure and it struck him as different from what he had seen. Out of place, old. The walls and gates. The columns of men practicing with swords, bows, and spears. All out of place with everything else he had seen in Imtal Palace.

"Seth?" asked Valam. "Do you really think you could teach me how to... *block*... my thoughts?"

"It would be a grand hope," Seth admitted. The grinding of the portcullis wheel drowned out further words. His thoughts grew distant. He looked to Swordmaster Timmer as he awaited his turn to pass through the protected entry.

Two gated stairwells led from the small, square chamber. Valam told him the stairwells worked their way gradually upward to the roof and were the only access to the upper battlements for this section of the palace—the innermost keep of the ancient castle from which the palace and the city had grown over hundreds of years.

Valam's face grew long and earnest. "Seriously, do you think you could teach them?" he asked, waving his hand, pointing to the columns of men training in the armory yards.

I never thought about it. Where I come from it is such a natural thing.

"In a land where the elite warriors speak with their mind, I guess it would be useful."

Very useful among the Brotherhood indeed. It helps to keep thoughts you want locked away private, and if you want someone to know your thoughts you allow them access to those thoughts... Children chosen to the Brotherhood are fast learners of this trick, or else they are always getting into trouble. The inner gate withdrew and the three entered the main armory yard. Soon after they came to the training grounds. Seth continued. *It is simple. In your mind you form a wall, a barrier, and inside that barrier you keep your thoughts.*

Valam stopped mid-stride and turned to Seth. "I don't understand."

Valam's sudden stop was what saved him from an arrow that ripped across the training yard. A second arrow followed but this time Seth was ready. He snatched the arrow from the air, turned quickly, catlike, in the direction that the arrow had come from.

Timmer's high-pitched whistle called out to his training masters. All eyes in the training yard were suddenly on him. "Halt!" shouted Timmer. "Cease training!" His training masters quickly relayed the order to the hundreds of men in the training yard. Weapons turned from the ready as many eyes turned to regard the prince and the elf.

Valam looked to Timmer then to Seth. Timmer was racing toward a huge mountain of a man who could only be the lead training master. Seth stood still, staring out into the training yard. *Was it an accident?* he wondered in his thoughts to Valam.

Moments later two burly training masters came from the corner of the yard. They dragged a smaller man between them. As they approached the prince one of the training master's grabbed the small man's hair, pulling the head back so that Prince Valam could see the face clearly. They forced the man to his knees. The man spat at Valam.

The training master drew a wide blade from his belt. He handed it to Valam with the hilt forward. Valam took the blade. He stared intently at the assailant.

Duty and honor required that he kill the man on the spot, letting his blood spill on the training field as a sign to all who watched. To serve and protect was a soldier's duty. To do otherwise, to bring harm to those you served, was to betray all that a soldier stood for.

The assailant's eyes became a window to his soul. It was in that moment—the moment when Valam was gripped by honor and duty—that Seth learned the deep love Valam had for his subjects. The love Valam had for life, all life. More importantly Seth learned something about himself, and was finally able to understand Valam the man. The fears and apathy that were carefully tucked away in the far reaches of his mind slipped away. Men in many ways were very much like elves.

"My life before your hands," whispered the attacker, accepting his fate and falling on Valam's outstretched blade.

The man did not move afterward. Valam withdrew the blade and handed it to the training master. His expression never betrayed his true feelings—the feelings that only Seth could read.

The training master wiped the bloody blade in the dirt. "My life before your hands," the training master whispered as he handed the blade back to Valam. "I have failed you. Let a rebel into our innermost sanction."

Valam took the blade that was thrust hilt first into his hand but he did not move for a few long heart beats. He made sure the blade was not accessible to the training master. He understood all too well the need for duty and honor among soldiers, especially when those soldiers were the King's Knights. The elite soldiers newly recruited to serve under King's Knight First Captain Brodst.

Valam knelt beside the training master. His eyes showed tears. His face betrayed a deep sadness. This emotion was reflected on the faces of those in the fields as surprise and veneration. "Training master, what is your name?" Valam asked.

The training master answered without looking up, "Dead men do not have names."

Valam put the long blade into the training master's hand, saying, "Then you shall be the walking dead but I will know your name and that blade shall not be stained with your blood. It is my wish."

"Redwalker Tae", whispered the training master, "Redcliff to those who knew me."

"If a dead man, my personal ghost on the training field, the executor of my will. Train these men. Train them to be loyal and true. Train them to be soldier's soldiers, to defend the House of

Alder against our enemies, to die in service if need be."

Redcliff raised his blade high and said, "To the High Prince!" Others on the field repeated his action, raising their weapons in salute. Redcliff and the men repeated the salute over and over as Valam, Timmer, and Seth walked away.

Valam grabbed Seth's shoulder as he walked and while the fingers of his right hand squeezed their way toward bone, he pointed to those about him with his left hand, those whose eyes regarded their prince and honored his deed. "Have you thought about what I said earlier?"

Seth nodded, admitted that he had.

The two left the training field, followed closely by Swordmaster Timmer who seemed to still be coming to terms with what he had just seen. The men on the field quietly chanted Valam's name as if his name alone now gave them strength and focus.

Seth knew in that moment when he turned to look back at the chanting soldiers that something miraculous had happened, and not because he had snatched an arrow from the air that might have ended the prince's life. But because the prince had shown compassion, mercy, and proven himself a man of honor. The so-called King's Knights, and not just Redwalker Tae, had just become the prince's men. They would do whatever the prince asked of them to the end of their days.

Chapter Twenty Four:
Guiding Fools

"Out with it!" hissed a feminine voice in a low, unsettling tone.

"Tomorrow, they leave tomorrow."

Adrina stifled a gasp and pressed up against the wall.

"Did you hear that?"

"Hear what? Never mind… Where are you going? Stand fast you fool!"

Adrina held her breath. Her heart raced. She watched the reflection offered by the torches that sparsely lined the near wall. The outline of the figure approached. A long glittering blade was drawn. Just when she was about to run, the figure turned and retreated.

"Are you sure?" hissed the feminine voice.

"Yes, I am sure. The plans are being finalized as we speak."

"Good, good. Will the prince be with them?"

"Yes, I think so."

"Don't think, you fool!"

"Did you hear that?" asked the other in a whisper, "Footsteps, someone approaches."

"Go, go!" the woman shouted.

Adrina ran from the rapidly approaching shadow. She was so shaken by the voices that she didn't stop running until she came to the council chambers where she knew her father and the others would be gathered. She nearly knocked down the outer guards as she bounded through the door.

King Andrew continued mid-sentence without even a pause to show his surprise at Adrina's hurried entrance, the skill of a practiced orator. "Brother Seth, about these mental powers that Prince Valam spoke of. All of the Brotherhood can read each others thoughts, intentions?"

"It is much as you have said, King Andrew. Only a few cannot."

"Can this really be learned as you suggest?" Father Jacob asked, earnestly intrigued.

Adrina sank into an empty chair beneath the towering glare of her father's stern eye.

"I think it can be learned, Father Jacob. More importantly, I think, we will need to mask open thoughts. What I discovered with Valam was quite by accident because his mind was so open. His thoughts radiated to my mind, more specifically his intentions. At first I think we should concentrate on masking open thought. It is like cluttering one's thoughts. You put your thoughts in disarray. Timmer's men seem to be adapting quickly. They are an intelligent group."

I can't continue, directed Seth to Valam.

"Won't the enemy discover this ploy, then force us to open our minds?" Valam asked despite Seth's statement.

"I don't think it will ever occur to them. It is so natural a talent. To force one's mind open takes very great concentration, so I don't believe they would bother trying. It is also a skill used mostly by the Brotherhood. I am afraid even my peoples' mind blocks would fall to the members of the Brotherhood."

Valam, you must speed this up, directed Seth.

"I believe you are right, Brother Seth." Valam feigned a smile while thinking, *It is the belief and not the deed that will give confidence on the field.*

A long pause followed. The council session had been underway since early morning and it was now late afternoon. Valam cast his eyes out to the mostly empty pews, then to the few clustered around the central table. Let the whisperers feed on that, he thought to himself.

"Father—" began Adrina, stopping under stern scrutiny.

"All our plans are set in motion. I move to adjourn," said Chancellor Yi after a doleful nod from the king.

Valam stood. "King Andrew, father, I have decided. I want to lead the first group. My skills will be greatly needed. It will improve the morale of the men to see their prince fighting beside them. I will also need to return immediately to South Province with Seth. I think together we can put speed to the—"

"Save your words, I know you too well, my son. I was afraid you would ask yet I knew eventually you would. Great Kingdom shall be empty without you, but you do have my blessing."

The king stopped and turned to the chancellor. "Is the team ready?" he asked.

"Yes, Your Majesty, it is set for tomorrow as you requested."

"Already?" Valam asked with what could have been surprise in his voice.

"You are my son. I knew you would ask. The time for action is at hand. Chancellor Van'te has sent me word that Isador eagerly awaits your return."

Valam swallowed a lump in his throat. The king smiled and turned his gaze to the others in the room.

Gripping his ancient staff Keeper Martin stood. "King Andrew, as head of the Council of Keepers I would also like to make this journey. I have selected a few others of the council who will go with me and will appoint Keeper Q'yer as Chief Lore Keeper in my absence. He is a good and able-bodied soul who will serve well."

King Andrew spoke for the benefit of those watching. "Agreed, Keeper Martin. It is a worthy notion. There will be much information to gather. So much lore that has not been passed down."

The king maintained his ardent gaze about the chamber. Soon afterward, Father Jacob took the floor, saying, "King Andrew, Chancellor Yi and I would also undertake the journey."

King Andrew's scowl grew long. "Father Jacob, will I lose all my trusted council this day?"

"I am sorry, Your Majesty," Father Jacob said. "It is a thing we must do."

"Yes of course, Father Jacob. Two of our most cunning minds are needed. I have great faith in all of you who are gathered in this room today, for if I did not you would not be here while we make this most conscious decision. Tomorrow will be a sad day, a sad day indeed, though perhaps a well intentioned start. I only wish that I were fit enough to make the sojourn southward. I long to have the wind in my hair and a saddle beneath me. Alas, it can not be so—"

"King Andrew, father," interrupted Adrina.

"You have my blessing as you go forth. The palace will hang in silence without you."

A wave of the king's hand brought the chancellor to a hurried dismissal.

"I move to close the meeting," the chancellor said.

"Father?" pleaded Adrina.

The timing of the chamber door bursting open couldn't have

been better. A royal page entered and while mumbling apologies, raced to the monarch.

"What is the meaning of this interruption?" demanded Yi, "Interruptions, interruptions, be damned! I would hope you have an excellent reason!"

Captain Brodst stepped into the room and made a gesture to King Andrew. The king motioned the page to proceed. The page eyed the chancellor closely and started toward the king once more. The page leaned close to Andrew's ear and whispered words which were meant for him alone to hear.

"What? When?" Andrew said, shock in his voice. The page continued in a low tone so that only the king heard his words. King Andrew looked to Captain Brodst. "Is this true, captain?"

"I am afraid so, sire."

"Poor Father Tenuus. He was a good and faithful servant."

"Yes, he was sire."

"The council is adjourned," King Andrew commanded as he hastily departed.

"Father Jacob? Chancellor Yi?" King Andrew called back as he entered the outer hall.

Father Jacob and Chancellor Yi rushed out of the room ahead of the others. Captain Brodst hesitantly approached the prince.

"I think you should go with him, Prince Valam," said Captain Brodst.

Valam seemed lost in his thoughts. "What has happened?"

"Father Tenuus has passed. He was found just a short time ago. It appears he has been dead for some time."

"Natural causes?"

"Nothing sinister, it would appear. Old age I would assume."

Seth probed the minds of the council. An ashen-faced Adrina rushed from the chamber. Seth knew she hadn't particularly cared for Father Tenuus and it was why she felt extraordinarily poor concerning his demise. She had wished a similar fate on him many times and most often during evening repast. A guilty conscious urged her to chase after her father.

"Captain, may I have a word as we walk?"

"Certainly, Prince Valam, anything you request."

"Dispense with the pleasantries…"

Captain Brodst started, looked around. He saw those milling about in the hall and understood.

"Settle down. What I meant to say was," began Valam, as he gestured for Seth to follow. "What I meant to say was that you needn't be so proper. I don't care for it. There is a time and a place for such formalities. Do you understand?"

"Yes, Your… Ah, yes, I do."

"No, do you understand?"

"Yes, yes, I do."

"Good." Prince Valam slapped Captain Brodst on the back to relax him. "Settle down, this is not an inquisition by any means—at least not yet."

Valam whispered to Seth, "Well?"

All seems to have gone well. I didn't sense anything out of the ordinary and Father Tenuus's passing was truly a surprise to everyone.

***

Occasionally as the wagon hit potholes along the path Vilmos would be thrown up into the top of the box, allowing air in, which often gave temporary consciousness. He was too weak to struggle with the box cover anymore though. It seemed that he spun in and out of consciousness and unconsciousness so rapidly that time was racing by. He just wanted to close his eyes—they felt so heavy—and sleep without disturbance.

Lost to a world of dreams filled with images mixed with the real and the unreal, Vilmos became utterly confused and out of sync with reality. A voice in his mind told him to be strong. Another told him to let go, drift away.

He saw faces in his dreams. Some were pale with cheek bones and brows lined with tiny horns like the demon that had taken him to the dark priests. Others were kind, inviting, and very human.

Then from somewhere within the darkness of his mind he heard screams of pain. Voices begged him to run and all the while blood ran bright and red around him.

"Find the strength of Uver," said a voice filtering into his dream. "In Zadridos you will find the key to the City of the Sky and there you can right the wrongs of the past."

Points of light entered into his eyes, spinning around in his consciousness, playing subtly in his subconscious. He saw bodies all around him, heard screams, then he saw black robes swaying back and forth, people running and the glimmer of a blade striking again and again.

Clearly now Vilmos saw swamp trolls and hill giants in the midst of it all. They were the ones attacking the human priests and their demon masters. For a moment he thought of Edward, Edward the troant who had died so that he could escape the hunter beasts, then something cold and heavy was thrust into his hands.

"Take this," said the warrior with the brankened collar and iron bit in his mouth. "You must go now. You are home, free."

Vilmos stared wild-eyed at the bloody scene. Was it real? Was this really happening? Or was he trapped in a horrible dream?

He closed his eyes, opened them. Nothing changed.

He bit down hard on his tongue. Blood and pain told him he was beyond dreams.

He started to run. The voice within told him strange things, gave him outlandish ideas. He could feel the wildness of the land play upon his mind.

Off in the distance he thought he saw movement. It was merely the wind rustling the leaves of a small stand of trees. Vilmos scrambled toward the trees. He felt safe as he lay down in their midst, as if he had reached an impenetrable sanctuary. The trees smelled fresh, not distinctive as pine or subdued as oak, thought Vilmos, perhaps hickory.

He propped his back up against a stout, stunted tree and gazed out into the darkness. His body was weary, so very tired. His struggle was almost at an end, or perhaps only at the beginning with the victor yet to be decided. As he closed his eyes a flood of visions came to him in the form of a dream. A dream that held a catching twist of realism.

Vilmos had not dreamed so fervently since Xith had been with him, but now there was no one to protect him or his soul. He was alone. The same dream had plagued his many sleepless nights in Tabborrath Village. Only now the dream seemed less strange, less frightening.

The dream carried him well into the night in what seemed an instant or an eternity depending on the moment. A shadow in his mind called out, *Wake... Move... move... hurry!* The bands of reality separated. The dream raced on. The wildness overtook him.

The voice cried out again. *Move, wake, hurry!* He lurched up. Just as he moved an arrow struck the tree where moments before his head had been.

He wasn't nervous or frightened. He had known that was going to happen. He had witnessed the attack in his dream as clearly as if he had lived through it once already. He knew what he must do and so he acted. With a casual thought he enacted his magical shield.

With another flicker of thought he lit the area around the knoll until everything around him glowed with a dim, yellow hue. He saw the creatures in the trees preparing to pounce. He knew what they were. They were called wood trolls, nothing but nuisances. He loathed such lowly creatures.

These were the same beasts that had attacked him and Xith what seemed ages ago. Only this time the trolls were in greater numbers and armored, perhaps they had remembered him or perhaps they were coming to kill the boy while he slept. They were going to get a lot more than they had bargained for.

He tossed a simple thought into their minds, saying, "Come unto me O' my children!"

The voice was not his own, but that of one with great power. It was this same strange power that gnawed away at Vilmos' consciousness. The same power the shaman wished to awaken. The same power that the shaman feared.

The wood trolls watched and waited. He struggled against the power growing within him. They made their attack, descending out of the trees in a pack.

In that instant Vilmos pitied them. In the next they were dead. Wiped out as one would swat bothersome bugs.

The power ate at his mind. It drove him to new heights of consciousness.

"I HAVE ARRIVED!" he cried out into the night, "GATHER UNTO ME O' MY CHILDREN. I AM THE FUTURE. I AM THE PAST. I AM THE PRESENT. I AM CREATED OUT OF THAT WHICH YOU FEAR MOST. I AM CREATED FROM YOURSELVES AND NOTHING SHALL STAND IN MY WAY!"

"No!" a voice cried out in his thoughts. "N-o-o!" the voice continued, filled with dread. "Control, you must find control!"

Control was a meaningless word. He did not care. The voice like the word was a meaningless echo in the corner of his mind. The strength of life eternal was within him. He bathed in it. It was magnificent.

"Stop!" the voice said.

A surge of pain ran through his head. His world went dark. The voices remained. They hovered all around him. They spoke words Vilmos couldn't understand in a sing-song ancient tongue.

All fell silent. Vilmos felt isolated, alone, or so he thought until a voice intruded upon his solitude again, *the* voice.

Vilmos, remember control! it said.

Something inside snapped. Recognition came and with it a moment of remembrance. The voice was Xith's. Yet there was something else that raked at the edges of his consciousness, gnawing, crying out to be released from the blackness that surrounded it. It demanded that Vilmos forget all else.

He could not stand it anymore. His head felt like it was about to explode. He had to get away, to escape, to get beyond anyone's grasp. He ran. He ran as far and as fast as he could. His path took him north to the hill country and it was the shadow walker who commented on the irony of his escape into the hills named after the once great bandit lord and oppressor of Oshio, especially since Vilmos' past self had been the one to plunge the blade into Lyudr's heart.

***

The caravan train was a moving city with a life of its own; wagons, horses, people, and pack animals made their way along the rough trail. Their movements were overseen by the masters, who in turn were watched by the caravanmaster himself.

As the master at arms Emel had his place in the moving city. Not only was he responsible for protecting the caravan from bandits, thieves, and things that went bump in the night, he was also the keeper of the peace. The kingdom guardsmen in his company spent as much of their time keeping order as they did seeing to the caravan's defense.

Quarrels and infighting were part of the daily routine. Men who didn't have anything to do as they rode along the trail would sometimes argue to pass the time. They'd argue over the ridiculous and everyone had something different to argue over. Hired blades would argue over who was the strongest, who could draw their blade the fastest, who could take the hardest punch and so on. Liners and carts would argue over who had set up or taken down the master's tent the fastest, who could pack the most on a single mule, who could ride the best.

As liners and carts were the last line of defense in the caravan, they'd also argue over issues of strength and combat with the hired blades and guardsmen. Those types of arguments didn't end well. One of the liners or carts usually ended up with a serious wound that made performing duties impossible, and that upset the caravanmaster. It was a tribute to Emel's diligence that no one had been killed yet—at least as a result of infighting.

They had lost a young cart on their second day. After failing to lead a pack mule out of mud hole by pulling, the youngster decided to go behind the animal and push. Stepping behind any beast of burden is a mistake, and trying to push the mule from behind cost the young cart his life. When the mule kicked it landed a blow on the side of the cart's head. The lethal blow knocked the young man back over ten feet. The spot where he fell, just off to the side of the main road, became his final resting place.

The coachman responsible for the young cart's apprenticeship received five lashes with the whip. At the time Emel had thought caravan justice harsh and indiscriminate. Coachmen couldn't watch their charges at all times—there were too many of them.

He came to realize that caravan justice sometimes wasn't harsh enough. The coachman had received five lashes. The youngster in his charge had received a death sentence. When a second young cart in the same coachman's care died beneath an overturned wagon, carts, liners, and blades joined together as a mob.

Emel faced this mob now. His hired blades were hesitant to come to his aid. Only the small band of guardsmen he hand picked in Imtal stood between him, the negligent coachman, and the angry mob.

Traveling with the caravan was a troupe of ridesmen. They were expert riders and tricksters all. As he watched the troupe turned in formation, coming straight toward the line of guardsman. As the closed the distance between them the ridesmen stood in their saddles, held their reins high as if giving a performance.

He breathed deeply, drew his long sword. The negligent coachman took a step back, ensuring that Emel was in front of him.

In his mind's eye Emel saw the gamble he must take. He must end this before things escalated—before the mob was allowed to draw blood. He didn't like the coachman he protected. He had learned the man was a drunkard and a fool.

But he wasn't going to let angry men have their way. The caravanmaster would mete out justice as needs be. Where *was* the caravanmaster? he wondered. The master wasn't within eyesight.

Emel waited for the riders to come at the line. Each time they closed ranks, the riders circled out and away as if they were taunting the guards.

He waited. As one, the riders put their hands to the saddles and did handstands. Some of the angry shouts for blood turned to cheers. It was then that Emel realized what the ridemaster was doing. He was putting on a show, the show of his life—or at least the show of the coachman's life.

He sheathed his sword, breathed a little easier. He turned back to take the coachman into custody but found the man was gone. He had slipped away and no one had seen him go—or so Emel thought.

As he looked around, he saw two men struggling near the tree line. One was trying to flee into the trees; the other trying to keep him from doing so. Emel walked over to them as the ridesmen continued their show. By now the angry shouts for blood had all but faded away.

"I'll take it from here," Emel called out to the huntsman.

Huntsman Faylin Gerowin grinned sheepishly as he replied, "I thought as much." He didn't release his grip on the coachman though. He waited for Emel to secure the man's hands, which Emel did with a thick rope. "Never trust one such as this, and never put your life in danger to save such. He'll not thank you. Isn't that so, Jossel?"

The coachman spit at Faylin.

Emel tripped the coachman, made sure the man fell on his backside. "Enough, or I'll turn you back to the mob."

Faylin said, "The masters aren't partisan."

"So you've said."

"Ridemaster Hindell didn't have to rouse his men to a diversion and I—"

Emel put a hand on Faylin's shoulder. "Forgive me, I know. You didn't have to help me save face and neither did the ridemaster. I am a great fool for thinking I could—"

"A man who guides fools is not himself a fool unless he lets himself become one. Do you think I achieved by luck and chance alone? Your father helped me no few times and I promised to look out for you as he looked out for me."

Emel with Faylin's help pulled Jossel to his feet. They started walking back to the road. "You know my father?"

"Most of the masters here are beholden to your father in one way or another. None more so than the caravanmaster."

Emel opened the hold wagon, pushed Jossel up and in. After he locked the thick door, he turned back to Faylin. He studied the huntsman as if seeing past the man's hawk-like eyes for the first time. "My father has his ghosts, does he not?"

"No more so than any man. You are very much like him, you know."

Emel's expression showed disagreement. The two were quiet for a time as they walked. The early afternoon sun came out from behind the clouds, bringing sudden, welcome warmth. "Does this business worry you?"

Faylin gestured at the air and the men returning to their duties as if to say don't let any of it bother you. Before the two said anything further the caravanmaster called an official halt. It was close enough to the midday meal to warrant the stop. With any luck the sun would dry the road and harden the last of the mud holes before they started up again.

"Not this," Emel said as he whistled to Ebony; the black stallion racing to him at his call.

"It is not my place to worry. Good advice to you, I think."

"But we waited two days at the crossing of the East-West road for nothing and there's been no explanation to any—"

"Nor will there be. Some things are best left unsaid. Our duty remains the same."

"Beyond the Stygian Palisade, to Zapad and beyond."

"Nothing's changed, Emel, of this I'm sure. We will go to the ends of the earth, see what few Kingdomers have ever seen, and with luck we will live to tell our children about the greatest adventure of our lives."

***

As they couldn't wait until the Seventh day as was customary, a service was scheduled for the morning following the grim discovery of Father Tenuus' death. Father Jacob conducted the service with a short remembrance spoken by Chancellor Yi at King Andrew's request. Then Father Tenuus was laid to rest. Tears streamed down Adrina's cheeks the entire time. She had never been kind to Father Tenuus. He annoyed her. She had always hated his invocations, regretted now that she had.

Accordingly, the departure was pushed back two days. Two of the longest days of Valam's life. Waiting seemed to play out hard on him. He was one to move, to act, not to wait. During those ensuing days Seth and Adrina spent much of their time together, much more time than they ever had previously.

When the long-awaited moment finally came it was wrapped in a grey dawn, and overcast skies mixed with a light monotonous drizzle. Only King Andrew and a few others watched as the group departed, saying nothing more than a few goodbyes.

Adrina watched from the balcony above the garden, her heart filled with despair. She sulked all that day, skipping the evening meal, which somehow wasn't the same without Father Tenuus to give the mealtime prayer. She spent that day wandering the garden or staring at it from the balcony, always alone, always wading through memories that ceaselessly flooded her thoughts.

Something had transpired between her and Seth those last few days. It seemed they were drawn together by an unseen force, and perhaps they were. The last remnants of the struggling girl in the young princess had ebbed. Odd feelings and unknown emotions had touched her mind. Thoughts she never would have had before.

Father Tenuus's untimely death played heavily on her mind. Suddenly the world had become a dark place with only one source of light.

She had been sitting on the edge of her bed, feeling desperately alone and crying when he had come to her. He had approached her without saying a word and embraced her. He had just held her and comforted her for a long, long time. She longed for him to be with her now even though she knew that it could not be. She wondered how he fared, knowing soon he would be leaving for East Reach. That he might never return.

The sounds of morning filtered in through a nearby window. The rains continued.

She went to the bath house, disrobed quickly. Myrial had just finished preparing her bath. The warm water felt so good as she descended into the bathing pool. Her thoughts slowed. For a brief time she slipped away from the cares of the world.

Some time later the call of a songbird roused her, but only for a moment. She took morning tea in the pool. Nibbled on toast as she soaked. Servants came and went. Myrial watched her from across the room.

She stood from the waters and wrapped a soft robe around her as Myrial handed it to her. The call of the songbird came again as she stepped out of the pool. Her eyes wandered up to the window. Her thoughts drifted. She thought of Emel, Valam, and Seth. Wondered why the men in her life always went away.

As she wrapped her hair in a towel she turned about, looking for Myrial. Myrial was gone. In the place she had occupied moments before stood another. Her eyes went wide. She took in the tall, broad shouldered figure. "How?" she asked.

Valam put a finger to his lips, hurriedly escorted her from the bathing pool. "Not a word," he whispered in her ear. Her heart skipped. He led her through her room, out through the secret door in the wall. Once in the back hallway, he stopped, threw his arms around her. "Speak in quiet tones," he said in her ear. "These halls should be clear. Better to be safe."

"Clear of what?" Adrina heard herself say. She was still trying to accept the fact that Valam was in Imtal, not on the road—and if he was in Imtal... "Seth? Is he—"

"Safe," Valam said, "Don't worry. Everything we've done these last few days has been for the benefit of the whisperers."

"Whisperers?"

Valam put a hand to her mouth, said softly in her ear. "Everything will be clear soon. They are close to revealing themselves. You must play along. Remember, you know nothing."

"Valam, you must tell me something more. I don't understand what's happening?"

"Revolution," Valam muttered under his breath. "Revolution. If you don't want our family to end as King Frederick II's, you'll do everything I say and ask no more questions."

"Impossible," Adrina replied, her voice becoming shrill.

"Possible, believe me."

"And the plight of the elves?"

Valam held her at arm's length. "How can you ask such a thing at a time like this? Seth has become like a brother to me. We will find a way to turn this around, to rally support, but first we must expose the chief whisperer. If we don't there will be no kingdom."

Chapter Twenty Five:
Blessed Sight

"Am I a toy, my prince?" she asked looking up at him, her eyes wide and clear like great blue jewels.

Valam turned back to her. He leaned over and kissed her. "You are not. I came back just as I said. Did I not?"

"And I am to forget the passing of the years without question? Am I to wait more years for your return, my prince?"

Valam kissed her as her nimble fingers fastened the buttons of his undertunic. "I did not ask that you wait."

"A prince does not have to ask, a lady does for him as must be done."

"And a fine lady you've become, my Soshi," he said, smiling, stepping into his trousers.

"You surprise me," said a voice from the shadows.

Soshi gasped, pulled the sheets up around her in bed.

Valam didn't turn, didn't act surprised. He wasn't. "You breathe loudly, I wonder if you—" he began as he turned and saw the milky white eyes.

"Pity is such an empty, wasteful emotion," the woman said as she stepped from the shadows. "I saw and heard nothing I haven't a thousand times in this life."

"You knew," Valam said, turning back to Soshi. It wasn't a question, it was a statement.

"I knew only that she would come, not that she would be here now," Soshi said rising from the bed. "I serve her as much as I do you, my lord prince."

"What does that mean?" Valam shouted, clear anger in his voice.

"Anger follows pity now," the woman said. "Understanding will come, this I promise you."

Soshi grabbed her belongings, raced from the room mumbling an apology. The blind woman touched a hand to Valam's face. Her fingers worked their way from his wide brow to his well-defined chin.

"Not always blind," the woman said, "A sacrifice for the greater good."

"Sacrifice?" Valam said, "You talk in riddles old woman. You are at once a stranger and yet I feel as if I've known you always."

"Familiar, yes," the woman said. Apparently satisfied with her survey of Valam's face, she led him to the window. "I once asked your sister to smell the wind. She didn't understand, but do you?"

"The winds of change," he said without hesitation, "Winter comes. The land grows weary. The old will pass; the new will come."

"You've had excellent tutors these many past years, haven't you my strong one?"

"It is you, isn't it?"

The old woman smiled. Valam could tell that it had been a long time since she had done so. "You have an excellent memory as well. Your sister, she didn't remember. To her, I was just an old woman who had something to tell her. Change comes, my boy, will you let it?"

"One cannot hold back the winds of change. Changes comes, you either accept it or you, you—"

"Fight it, yes, you fight it. But are you ready for such a fight, such a fight as you've never seen?"

"I will do what must be done, if action is needed."

"Will you? I wonder." The woman grabbed his chin, forced his gaze to the window just as she had done with Adrina those many months ago. "I was your nanny before Isador. I never forgot you. I know the ways of your heart. The hard decision isn't in you. You will be weak when the hour comes. You won't be able to do what must be done. I forgive you."

"Father doesn't believe in the old ways, the old gods. To him, there is but the Mother and the Father. He didn't want us to learn the old ways."

"As it should be. The old ways are all but forgotten now," the old woman said, redirecting his gaze. "The old gods were not gods at all, merely creatures of power, great power. I know that now. I see and understand."

"But your eyes?"

"Eyes can get in the way of true sight."

Valam turned back and stared at the milky white of her eyes. "True sight, you say that as if blindness were a gift?"

"It is a gift. My gift to you."

Valam started to say, "What do you mean?" but the old woman didn't let him speak. She hushed him, raised her hands and threw a white powder into his eyes. Valam's screams would have brought the guards if the old woman hadn't clamped her hand over his mouth with a viselike grip—a grip surprisingly strong.

"Hush, hush," she whispered as she stifled his screams. "The pain will pass. It will pass."

***

Vilmos leaned down to drink water from a crystal blue pool. The voices inside his mind had faded as he ran. Now they were completely gone.

The cool, clear water tasted pleasant against his palette, yet as he reached down to scoop up a second handful, he noticed something. It was the first time he had seen his reflection in what seemed ages. He saw a small boy, a boy not even ready to become a man, in that image. He didn't like what he saw.

He was not a boy—a mere boy—a scrawny little boy. His vanity wouldn't allow him to continue in the body of a mere boy. He decided he wanted to be older, bigger, stronger. It took only a moment to gather the required energy. He released the full force of those energies unto himself. Raw energy ripped through his body. Its wonder held and captivated him.

His legs collapsed under the strain. He fell to his knees. Voices in his head cried out in joy all around him and where a boy had fallen to the ground, a man rose in his place. He steadied himself, feeling awkward under the new weight, but good.

Gazing into the pool, he liked what he saw. He had accelerated his growth until he was at the edge of adolescence, on the verge of becoming a man, on the verge of coming into his own. The age when his mind was to awaken.

He eyed the reflection, liking the broad shouldered, muscular, young man that looked back at him. He stared fixedly at the image for a long time, then turned and walked northward once again. He walked all that morning. Something clung to the edge of his mind. The voices spurred him on, carrying him to a place only they knew.

He felt eyes upon him, all around him, though he saw no man or beast. He slowed to a wary, cautious pace.

Hours later, he spotted a pure white horse running at the head of a large herd. It was so beautiful, so perfect. He had to have it.

As if sensing him, the herd turned. He could see the white stallion's eyes as it came at him.

Unmoving, he waited. The ground shook. The thunder of hooves filled the air. He put his hands to his ears as the horses raced by.

The thunder faded. He turned, expecting to see a trail of dust. Instead, he found the white stallion waiting for him.

Vilmos approached the horse, staring with powerful, probing eyes. Temporarily, the horse's rampant spirit calmed. It could not run from him, though it wanted to.

Each time the horse attempted to flee Vilmos tightened the grip of his mind. He climbed onto the animal's back. It defiantly threw him. Its spirit was not entirely captivated.

He stood, wiped dust from his backside, made a second attempt. Again the horse threw him.

He persisted. His anger grew with each failed attempt. As it peaked he turned the anger on the poor creature whose only wish was to remain free. He raised a hand to focus, preparing to do his worst.

Pain, clear and precise, whipped through his mind, scattering his thoughts. It struck him down as he sought to strike down the horse. Try as he might, he couldn't kill the horse. Something wouldn't let him. In utter frustration he watched the animal run off.

He watched it go and it was then that he saw the tower far in the distance. The tower called to him. He went.

***

"I forgive you," the old woman said again and again as Valam screamed in pain. "I forgive what you will do, what you must do."

He was on his knees, pain sweeping through his body. He fought to maintain it but consciousness was slipping away.

# Kingdom Alliance

The old woman circled him, nodding in approval. "Pain is only the beginning. I promise you."

Through clenched teeth Valam shouted, "Why are you doing this to me?"

The old woman grabbed a handful of white powder from her pocket. As Valam sought to speak she threw the powder in his face. "You have great tolerance," she said, nodding to herself, "This is good. They will break you. I promise you. You will beg to die. I promise you this as well. I can't let that happen. You must do what must be done. I can't let you do otherwise."

Fighting for each breath, Valam collapsed to the floor. His lungs were on fire. "Why me?" he asked, his voice scarcely a whisper.

"With your sister I had luxury, time, with you I have no such luxury. You must see the world as it is, not as you believe it to be. You must do this now. You must know what is ahead."

She clapped her hands and shouted, "Soshi, enter!"

The olive-skinned girl entered, fought back a scream when she saw Valam on the floor writhing in pain. She turned away from the prince, shock clearly on her face, as she bowed before her mistress.

"Help me carry him to the bed," the old woman crooned. The two labored many long minutes. When the prince was finally in the bed the old woman said, "Bind feet and hands to the bedposts. Quickly now…"

Soshi did as asked without question. Binding the prince's feet and hands as he screamed and writhed in pain wasn't easy. Tomorrow she'd have deep purple bruises where his fists and feet smashed into her face and chest. Despite this and despite herself, she leaned over and kissed his cheek when she was done.

The old woman pushed her away, saying, "Leave us, go now."

Soshi paused at the doorway, turning back for a moment. Then she left, waiting outside as before. The door was slightly ajar, so she could see clearly into the room.

The old woman placed a blood mark on the prince's wrists and ankles. It could have been Soshi's imagination or the fact that the prince struggled violently against the bonds, but to Soshi it seemed tiny creatures moved within the red streams of blood. She could see their silver, black forms swirl within the red. Then they were burrowing into the prince's skin, spreading arcs of black silver along the blue of his veins.

She knew enough about the Cleansing to know that this was but the beginning. What came next, she didn't dare witness. She quietly closed the door, sank to her haunches.

She rocked back and forth, slowly at first but faster and faster as time passed. The fingers of her hands were clasped together in prayer, deep, reverent prayer. "Great Father," she begged, "hear me. Do not let him fail this test. Do no let him pass from this life. I do love him, I do, and if love is blind, let me take his blindness. Restore his sight so that he may see, so that he may see true."

***

"But fools in the game," she whispered, turning to the girl. She reached out. Her hands mapped the girl's face and checked the unfocussed gaze of the eyes.

A tear streamed down the girl's cheek, single and crystalline. The old woman wiped it away, saying, "No greater gift has there ever been." Her own cheeks were moist with tears, but they weren't tears of loss and sorrow as with Soshi. They were tears of joy. "My work here is done. I can do no more. You take my place now as I pass from this life."

"But I'm not ready," Soshi protested. "I'm but a girl. I don't know what I must do."

"You've given the greatest of gifts. Pure love in your heart will keep and guide you."

"But what of my prince?"

"What you choose to do is up to you, and while you could have the hearts and minds of a thousand such in your time, sight will come and you will see the truth of it all. You won't have questions then, only answers."

"I need you."

The old woman stumbled at the side of the bed, fell, fought to stand. A breeze which had been flowing gently through the open window behind her a moment before stopped, and as the sheer silk curtains in the window ceased to flutter, the old woman's heart gave way. She fell to the floor. Her last expression, a smile on her lips.

Her body turned to bone, then to ash before Soshi's eyes. Then just as suddenly as the breeze had stopped, it picked up, sweeping the old woman's ashes from the room and up into the heavens. Soshi raced to the window. In her mind's eye she could see the old woman flying in the clouds, soaring to heaven above.

She wasn't given time to enjoy the miracle or to grieve. The Sight hit her. She fell to the floor. She could see them coming. The palace was in a panic. Something dread was happening.

Soshi rose to her feet. She went to her dressing table, found the long knife in the bottom drawer. She hastened to the side of the bed, raised the blade high, slashed the bindings one by one until they all fell away.

She lay down beside the prince for what she knew in her heart would be the last time and waited. They were coming. Only a few fleeting moments remained. She sighed, kissed him one last time, put her arms around him.

The summons came. "Open the door in the name of the king!" they shouted.

Soshi didn't move. She feigned sleep. They tried to open the door. It was locked. They began to beat the door down, battering it over and over.

The lock gave way. The door crashed inward.

Soshi sat up. She pretended to be surprised and half asleep. The milk white of her eyes frightened the men who had crashed through the door. They raced to the prince, dragged him from the bed.

Chapter Twenty Six:
A Gentle Madness

Adrina screamed, knelt beside him. "Your eyes," she said at long last, "Your eyes."

Valam reached out a hand to her, groped until he found her face and cheeks. He wiped away the tears he found there. "It is my own fault for not seeing," he whispered.

Adrina dipped a thick cloth in the cold water of the basin, used the cloth to wipe away the strange white powder from his face and eyes. "What do you mean?"

Valam sighed, steadied her hand. The cool water took the sting from his eyes and at long last he was able to open them. "You've seen her too, haven't you?"

Adrina stared into the milky white of his eyes and started to shiver. "You're not making any sense? I don't understand."

Valam grabbed the cloth from her hand, stood, went to the wash basin. He stuck his face in the icy cold water and swished his head back and forth. The water in the basin turned to a milky white. He raised his head, water dripped from his face and hair.

Adrina put a clean cloth in his hand. He used it to dry himself.

"You can see," she whispered as she watched him.

"I see," Valam said as he dabbed his face.

"But how is that possible? Your eyes are the eyes of the blind and yet you see. What happened? You must tell me what happened?"

Valam touched a hand to her shoulder. He towered over her as she looked up at him. She shivered as the milky white that had covered his eyes a moment ago faded. She could tell Valam could feel it go. A transformation of sorts was taking place before her eyes. Soon all that remained of the blind eyes was a faint trace of white dulling the brown of his eyes.

"The old woman," Valam said after a long silence. "The old woman. You've seen her too, I know."

Adrina didn't understand at first. Valam explained. She told him about the encounters with the Lady of the Forest and the strange woman in the watch tower.

"The woman in the tower, that's her," Valam said. "Tell me more. Tell me everything."

"There isn't much to tell," Adrina said as she tried to remember the details of the encounter that seemed to have happened a lifetime ago. She told him more of what she remembered.

He stared blankly at the wall for a long time after she finished. For a time Adrina was afraid the blindness had returned. Then he turned to her, smiled. She didn't understand why he was grinning. "A gift, don't you see," he said, "We've been given a gift. A glimpse at what could be. We've been given a choice. Change comes."

"That's what she said," Adrina said excitedly, "That's what she said. 'Child, smell it. It comes, can you not tell?... Change, child. Sadness cannot hold forever the land.' Change comes."

Valam kissed her cheek and hugged her. "It is good not to be alone in this," he whispered in her ear.

"You are not alone," she whispered back.

"If I were I'd go mad."

***

Myrial touched a hand to the closed door, continued on her way. As she walked to the lower level of the palace her heart went out to them as never before. Valam had been her first love, a girlish crush really. He'd never had eyes for her, only her for him, and she'd been too young to even know what love really was. She still didn't know true love but she understood it better now.

What she felt for Valam now was more what a sister felt for a brother. It was the same way she felt about Adrina. Adrina was the sister she never had and Valam was the brother she never knew.

She hummed happily as she walked. She had a pretty voice when it was raised to song and cheer.

The day's tasks would seem mundane compared with the excitement of the last few days, but a household did not run itself. She would see to the stewards and the cooks first, even though it meant she would have to deal with the former housemaster directly to do so. Most of the stewards and cooks only listened to the old dog despite her best efforts. She didn't mind though, Sedrick Bever knew his place well enough, and through him she was learning to run the enormous household.

She was no fool. She knew better than to approach Sedrick alone. First she would stop by her chambers to freshen up and find an escort.

Garette Timmer waited outside her chamber door. He nodded to her as she passed by. She smiled. If there was anyone she was getting a crush on it was Garette Timmer. He was strong and true. He'd stand outside her door day and night without reprieve if she asked him too, which she never would. His day duty was enough of a reminder to those who needed such a reminder. She was housemistress now. There was no disputing it.

As she bathed she thought of Garette. He was cute with a wisp of his father the swordmaster in him. This gave him a sharp edge, a look of danger. Fresh clothes were laid out and waiting for her when she looked up from bubbles and steam.

It had been a long day already. She was tired, but reminded herself that for many the day was just beginning. There was so much to do, so very much to do. Keeping everything perfect, or as close to perfect as possible, meant that even in the wee hours of the night someone somewhere was working in support of the household.

When she began she vowed that she wouldn't forget the night workers as Sedrick Bever had done. Sure, the day cooks, stewards and workers were the ones whose labor most directly impacted the king, his family, honored guests, and the like, but the night staff had their place too.

One of her first official actions as housemistress had been to double their daily copper. She had gained important allies in doing so, but that had not been her intent. She saw no reason the night staff made half as much as their daytime counterparts. They were no less important. Their work no less meaningful.

She was dressing when the knock came on the door. She looked up, called out, "Enter, please." She blushed when she saw it was Princess Adrina, blurted out a quick apology. "What brings you to my door, Dri?"

Adrina smiled at the familiar childhood name. It always brought memories, even for Myrial. "Everything," she said, "Everything. I've never seen him so shaken. It was as if all the world fell away and he was left standing alone on a mountain top."

Myrial helped Adrina to a chair, pretended for Adrina's benefit that she knew nothing. She called out to Garette. He came running into the room. "Where's Anri?" she asked. Anri was the only member of the lavish personal staff of the former housemaster she had retained. "Send for him. Tell him we need food and drink."

Garette hurried away. She called after him, "Drink, first. Something warm, but not hot."

"We're alone now," Myrial whispered. "I'm here for you."

"I've never seen him like this. It's like… like…" her voice trailed off. She sat quietly until the refreshments arrived. Myrial didn't push for more information.

Myrial thanked Anri, nodded to the drink. She poured the deep black kindra-ale into two cups. One she handed to Adrina. As Adrina sipped the drink, the color returned to her face. "You've been walking the gardens," Myrial said, "You're likely to catch a chill that way. Winter's here. I can feel it. The snows will come early."

"I've lost him."

"Valam will recover. I know he will."

"Not Valam, Emel. He's really gone this time, isn't he? This isn't like High Road. There was no promise of return."

"I think he is," Myrial said solemnly, "I think he is."

"One man comes back into my life, another goes. Does it always have to be that way?"

Myrial didn't get a chance to respond. A loud alarm sounded throughout the palace. The two could hear the tinny gongs from the main level, followed by those spreading the alarm below. The clank clack of armored feet running down the halls followed.

Garette Timmer raced into the room. The open door provided a view into the hall. Adrina could see lines of guardsmen hurrying down the hall, weapons in hand.

Garette's face showed unease. To Adrina and Myrial the alarm meant little more than the rousing of the guards, but Timmer understood the signal within the alarm. The beats had a meaning.

Each series carried a message.

***

Adrina and Myrial looked at each other anxiously. They followed Garette down the crowded hall. He had enlisted four other guardsmen as their escort. Two of the guards cleared a path in front of them, two brought up the rear.

To onlookers it might have seemed that the palace was an ant hill suddenly come alive. In many ways this was true. The entire palace guard was on alert. The palace was sealed. No one allowed in. Only guards were allowed out. They poured out of the palace and into the streets of Imtal.

"The king has been attacked," went the whisper in the hall. This set Adrina's heart and mind on fire. Myrial tried to calm her, tried to remind her that she must find control, keep her composure, act like the princess she was.

Adrina couldn't. Her world was collapsing around her. Suddenly it seemed she was the one standing alone on a mountain top, the world in chaos all around her. It had taken years to come to terms with her mother's death. What would she do if something happened to her father? She couldn't cope with that pain. She didn't want to have to.

She stopped abruptly. Garette nearly collided with her. She started screaming hysterically. Everything and everyone around her stopped as if frozen in their places. Heads turned, eyes met hers.

Myrial grabbed Adrina's arms, smothered her in an embrace, all the while shouting, "Go on, go on! Get out of here!"

"Look at me, Adrina," Myrial said, "We can get through this. We can get through this."

"You don't understand," Adrina said through sobs. "Not again, I can't. I can't go through this again."

"You're strong, Adrina. Be strong now."

Alarms began to sound again. Myrial looked to Garette. "Assembly," he said.

"What does that mean?"

"Captain's muster, the Hall. We must hurry."

Myrial turned back to Adrina. "We can do this together, you and I."

Adrina nodded absently. They started walking. Within minutes they were standing outside the great hall.

"Are you ready to do this?" Myrial asked, knowing what Adrina knew. If the king sat on the throne, he lived; if Valam sat on the throne, the king was dead.

Adrina's heart pounded in her ears. The doors opened. Her worst fears were realized. She had a direct view of Valam. Their eyes met. It was all she could do to stand.

The weight of the world crushed her.

She couldn't breathe. Her face flushed. Her knees buckled. Only Myrial's arm locked in hers kept her from falling. Everything seemed surreal as if she looked in on another's nightmare.

For an instant the iris of Valam's eyes flashed white. It was as if Adrina had a window into his very soul. He stood beside their father's throne. His arm rested on top the thick dark wood on the mighty chair's back. He wore the crown jewels, and the great green jewel atop the crown glistened in the waning light of the day.

Beside Valam stood a woman Adrina had never seen before. She wore a circlet of gold. The color of the woman's thin silk dress was matched perfectly to the olive color of her skin. She looked like a queen, though Adrina knew she wasn't. It wasn't until the woman turned to look at her that Adrina saw, really saw.

She understood then, but she didn't want to. She started to scream. She wanted to scream.

A voice called out to her. The sound of it as if the person

speaking were far away, far away in another time and place. She gasped.

Feeling light-headed she put her hand to her face, closed her eyes. When she opened her eyes moments later she found she was still standing before the closed doors of the great hall. "Would you like to sit a moment?" a voice asked her. She nodded. She did need to sit.

Garette and Myrial helped Adrina to a chair near the hall's entrance. Adrina closed her eyes and breathed. All around her the palace was in an uproar. Alarms continued. Guards ran along the halls. Doors opened and closed. People shouted.

Someone handed her a cup, bade her drink. She put the cup to her lips and drank deeply. The bitter liquid went down poorly. She spit what she couldn't swallow back into the cup. "That's awful!"

"Stout," said a strong, clear voice. "The bitters clear the mind."

Adrina made face, looked up at Garette Timmer. "That's awful," she repeated.

Garette grinned. "Good to see you've regained your senses, princess. Trying times test a person's mettle. What kind of person are you?"

At first Adrina was taken aback by his directness, outrage followed. How dare he speak to her as if she were a commoner. How dare he speak to her in that tone. Her friends could speak candidly but Garette Timmer was a stranger to her. "Guard your tongue," she shot back, her face flushed with emotion.

"She's regained her senses, all right," Myrial said, winking at Garette. "We can sit here, or we can go in."

Adrina understood. She took Myrial's hand.

The three walked back to the doors of the great hall, their four-guard escort only a few steps behind. Adrina looked directly at the door guards, each in turn. Thy opened the doors in unison. Adrina led the way into the hall.

Her feet held steady when she saw Valam standing on the raised dais directly in front of the throne. He turned to look back at her, disquiet showing clearly in his eyes. She caught a breath in her throat. He took a step toward her, opening the view to the throne. It was empty.

Chapter Twenty Seven:
King's Decree

Valam saw Adrina enter with Myrial and the young guardsman, Garette Timmer. His heart beat faster and faster as he took a few quick steps toward her. His hands were raised as they met. "This isn't what you're thinking," he said matter of factly, "The city has been ordered sealed. The garrison and palace are on full alert. The king's decree."

"Father?" Adrina asked, "He's..."

"Of a mind to tell Lady Isador Froen d'Ga to return to Imtal."

Adrina turned, looked at the speaker. She smiled, found herself at a loss for words. Her father, King Andrew Alder, sat at a long table with Father Jacob and Keeper Martin. Across from him sat high-ranking palace and garrison commanders.

"Now then," King Andrew said turning back to the commanders, "the heir to the throne and my daughter stand before you. There is no foul play."

"The messenger," protested Chancellor Volnej, "He is without question a man of honor."

King Andrew stood. His eyes seemed to catch the last of the

sunlight streaming through the window as he spoke. "And yet my children stand before you. There's been no kidnapping, no murder, no attempt." His eyes had been fixed on the commanders, but now he turned and looked directly at the chancellor who stood at the far end of the table. "You are dismissed. Return to Council Hall, bring this message—those responsible for this folly will be dealt with. Judgment will be swift, retribution, final."

To Valam and other onlookers it was hard to tell whether the old chancellor collapsed or bowed so deeply that he got himself into a position that age simply wouldn't allow him to recover from. Either way, he had to be physically escorted out of the hall.

King Andrew turned to Adrina then. "My daughter, light of my life, listen carefully and speak truly. Has anyone made an attempt on your life or the life of your brother this day?"

Adrina didn't turn away from his piercing gaze. She answered directly and without hesitation. "No father. Who would say such a thing? I've been with Housemistress Myrial discussing matters of household, and to the market."

"Who indeed?" said the King, turning back to the commanders. "We must end this. The rabble rousers must be shown their place. We will have no more discord, no more dissent in council." A jeweled sword lay on the table in its sheath. He picked it up, drew the sword and raised it high, purposefully, so that the fine steel blade could catch the last of the sun's rays.

Valam knew what the sword signified. Commanders were warriors at heart, and warriors understood strength. The king wasn't as old and weak as the whispers. He could still wield the sovereign blade, play it in the air as if it were a toy.

But then the king did something that surprised everyone. In one swift motion, he lunged across the table and drove the blade into the chest of the man across from him. The blade easily sliced through the man's breastplate, finding his heart. Before he could draw a breath or scream, the man lay dead atop the king's blade.

Captain Imson Adylton who had been sitting to the left of the dead man, gulped at the air as if he were a fish out of water. Only the fact that he was the king's staunchest supporter brought quick words to his lips. He said, his voice a whisper at first, "For king and country... For king and country!"

Others joined the chant. Some hastily, others reluctantly.

As Valam watched there was a clear shift in the room. Some of the commanders who moments before had been haughty and arrogant now found themselves at a loss. Others who were loyal supporters of the king clearly felt vindicated. King Andrew wasn't weak. The reign of his line wasn't at an end.

The whispers were baseless. The king, who stood before them wielding a sword, slaying the chief whisperer, wasn't weak. He was strong and true, unafraid to confront those who were afraid to confront him. His justice was as true as his sword arm.

Valam and Imson pulled Captain Atford from the table, dumped him on the floor near the exit doors. As Valam passed Adrina on the return, he squeezed her arm, whispered, "Be strong, if ever, now."

Adrina took a deep breath, checked her demeanor, whispered to herself, "Be strong, if ever, now."

King Andrew pounded his fists on the table. "Let the word go forth from this hall with your own lips. The House of Alder stands. All who oppose it will find death at the hands of a just king."

It was a dismissal. The commanders knew it. They fled the room as though their feet had wings. Only Imson Adylton lingered. He had been there in Quashan'. He understood the treachery that had been at hand then and he understood what was happening now. He put a hand on Valam's shoulder, spoke clearly, "There is nothing you can't ask of me. Ask and it shall be done so long as I live and breathe."

***

Adrina followed her father as he called out to her and Valam. They went out the rear doors of the great hall and made a direct path for the council. Keeper Martin and Father Jacob flanked her father and behind them were a dozen of the King's Knights. Myrial and Garette followed the others out the front doors of the hall.

The Battle of Quashan' had hardened Adrina and, to be sure, the death and madness all around her had changed her forever. Wars changed people. There was no going back. No finding the person that had been there before. She had a new and profound understanding of life and death. The value of life, the finality of death. But a battle and a war hadn't taken away her pain, she had. She had found a way to look inside herself and find a way past the pain.

None of that had prepared her for what she had just seen. Her father had killed man before her eyes, in a room full of people who had simply accepted his meting out justice.

She loved her father beyond doubt. She could sense the danger. She understood Valam's warning. Still, that didn't mean she had to accept everything that was happening. If she couldn't understand what was happening, how could she accept it?

The palace was in chaos. It seemed the madness of the last few days was spreading to everyone and everything. She was scared, trembling.

She fought to find control. She couldn't show fear in front of the council. She was an Alder.

Her private thoughts ended when they reached Council Hall. The doors opened. The king and the entourage that she was a part of swept into the crowded room. She could see that both houses of the council were assembled as well as representatives from the noble houses.

The king took his place at the far side of the triangular table that dominated the room. Father Jacob and Keeper Martin followed, each taking their place at the table. Chancellor Yi indicated that she should stand behind her father, next to Valam. She did.

Voices that had been raised in anger and outrage as the doors opened fell away to quiet whispers. Eventually the whispers fell away as well.

It was when the hall was absolutely quiet that King Andrew stood, surveyed the hall. "So you've come," he said after many long minutes of uncomfortable silence. "Word goes out. Whispers spread through the realm. You come as buzzards to the kill."

One of the council members jumped from his chair. "You misunderstand, majesty. You don't—"

"I don't what?" interrupted King Andrew, "Speak quickly now."

The councilor sat back down without another word.

One of the noblemen seated in the high seats to the right of the table stood. "I am Peter Eragol, the seventeenth Peter of my line, Baron of Eragol, of Family Eragol."

"I know who you are," said the king.

Peter Eragol turned his eyes about the room, then stared directly at the king, his gaze unwavering as he spoke. "There are some who say the House of Alder has lost touch with the people, forfeited its power and the right to rule." Gasps crisscrossed the hall—Peter Eragol spoke treasonous words.

Adrina did more than gasp. She nearly lost control. The Eragol's were one of the most powerful families. They were the Wardens of the Mouth of the World. Their fleet in Eragol Bay was the largest in the Kingdom. They controlled shipping along the Krasnyj River, shipping lines that brought the majority of supplies to Solntse and

Imtal.

Valam reached his arm around Adrina to steady her. His movements were subtle, making it look to any who had their eyes on them that he was simply reaching out to his sister. Adrina recovered nicely, the evident dismay in her expression fading as she regained her composure.

Chancellor Yi was the first to speak when the murmurs quieted. "I wonder, Peter," he said walking toward the baron, "May I call you, Peter?" The baron was obviously taken aback by the familiar greeting and mocking tone, but said nothing, so the chancellor continued. "I wonder if you'd be so bold if you knew what I know."

"And just what is that?" snapped the baron, his tone showing irritation. He didn't like being addressed by the king's underling. Clearly he wanted the king to respond—no doubt he had planned the clever rebuffs that would help drive home his point.

On the chancellor's signal two guards dragged in the body of the dead commander. The baron's hauteur quickly fell away. He stumbled back into the chair behind him—there was no one to catch him. Any supporters he may have had were probably busy thinking up clever denials.

That her father was wise and had excellent advisors, Adrina had no doubts. He had defied tradition, held a meeting with his commanders before speaking to the council. Any plans for seizing power should have been crushed right there, she knew, but didn't dare to hope.

There was clear tension in the air. She wondered if her father or one of his men would kill the baron right then in front of everyone.

She closed her eyes for a few heartbeats. It didn't help. When she opened her eyes, everything was the same.

She waited, remembered her poise. She must stand tall and true. She was a princess, an Alder.

"I am Peter Eragol," the baron said, "the seventeenth Peter of my line, Baron of Eragol, of Family Eragol. I have a voice. I will be heard."

Someone started to snicker. The situation wasn't funny, but the snickering spread. The Baron of Eragol was quickly reduced to a babbling fool. He continued to babble though no one listened.

The king turned to the council and spoke. Adrina heard the words, but didn't really listen. To her, it seemed they were just starting to unravel the treachery that had led to the attacks on Great Kingdom. She was certain they hadn't heard the last of the East Warden of the Word. That King Jarom could reach into the highest circles of power in the Kingdom, there wasn't any question. That he could do it and get away with it, terrified her.

***

When the meeting ended Valam took Adrina by the arm and led her from the hall. They didn't speak until they reached her quarters. "Was this your doing?" she asked, "Some message from the old woman that you didn't tell me of?"

Valam secured the door, walked across the room before responding. "Not mine," he said quietly. "When I first arrived from Quashan' Father Jacob told me of a divide growing in the council. But it was later when I spoke to father with Chancellor Yi and Keeper Martin that I..." His voice trailed off.

Adrina grabbed his hand. "And?"

The look in Valam's eyes silenced her. He turned about on his heel quickly, catlike. He was much faster than his size suggested he could be, as if he could defy the laws of nature—perhaps he was learning as much from Seth as Seth was learning from him.

He raced across the room to the window beside Adrina's bed, threw back the drapes. Adrina started to scream, "Stop, stop!" but it was too late. Valam grabbed the girl hiding behind the curtain and the next moment she was flying through the air, landing with a dull thud on Adrina's bed.

"It's Myrial, Valam," Adrina screamed. "Myrial."

"I know who it is," Valam said through clenched teeth. "King Jarom's spies are everywhere, don't you know that? And it's just a little too much, okay?"

Valam's arm was raised, his fist poised ready to strike as if his fingers were a cobra's fangs. Adrina grabbed his arm with both hands, begged him not to hit Myrial. She grabbed his waist and hugged him then. "Don't, don't," she whispered. "Myrial would never betray our family."

"Everyone is suspect," Valam said.

Myrial crawled backward across the bed, straightened her dress. She didn't look at Valam. Her eyes were on Adrina. "I don't know what happened after I left," she said, "But I assure you that I've never done anything to harm you, Adrina. And I would never do anything to harm anyone in your family. You've got to believe me."

Adrina helped Myrial stand, saying, "I believe you, I do." She paused for a moment, hugged Myrial. "It has been a very trying day. We're all a little frayed on the edges. Isn't that right, Valam?"

Valam glared, started to leave.

Adrina ran after him. "If there was ever a time, ever a time for friends, it is now. You can't turn away. Not now, not ever. Don't you see?"

The weight of the day was on Valam's shoulders as he turned back to Adrina. "You don't understand. I trusted her. She betrayed me."

Adrina furrowed her brow, crinkled her nose as she did sometimes when confused or upset. "We aren't talking about Myrial, are we?"

Valam shook his head. "We're not."

"Who then?"

Valam didn't say anything, Myrial did. "Soshi," she said.

"Soshi?" Adrina asked.

Valam turned to Myrial. "Do you know everything that goes on?"

"No," Myrial admitted. "But I do make it a point to know certain things." She added after a moment of silence, "Your secrets are safe with me. I would never reveal them to anyone."

"Words," Valam said, the anger growing in his voice. "Easy enough to say. Actions reveal truths."

"Enough," snapped Adrina, "You have my word, Valam. Myrial can be trusted. What more do you want?"

"Proof," Valam whispered.

"What would it take?" Myrial shot back.

"You take such familiar tone with my family. Have you no respect?"

Myrial's eyes told Adrina not to come to her defense. "What would you have me do?"

"Actions speak louder than words. Prove to me that I shouldn't run you through." Valam pulled a long dagger from a sheath at his side. Adrina saw this, tried to grab his arm. "Stay out of this, Adrina. King Jarom's spies are everywhere, and this one is a little too clever for her own good."

Myrial went to the window, jumped up to the wide ledge at its base. "If it is your wish, I will jump. Do you wish it? Would that be proof enough?"

Adrina felt like she was experiencing déjà vu. In her mind she saw herself standing on the ledge. She started screaming but Valam and Myrial weren't listening to her.

Valam provoked Myrial. "It would—it would prove beyond doubt that you were King's Jarom's agent. Bought and paid for with the blood of many. Anyone with a bit of mettle would put an end to it after they've been exposed. That haughty Baron of Eragol will surely be found that way by morning, one way or the other, so go on, join him."

Myrial surprised Adrina. She jumped at Valam, grabbing the blade he held out in both hands. The sharp blade sliced into her palms. Her blood ran pure and crimson down the blade, bathing Valam's hands.

Myrial looked into Valam's eyes, unwavering, unflinching while she held the blade. "The blood of one," she said. "The only way it will ever be."

"Are you satisfied now?" Adrina shouted. She tried to pull Myrial away from Valam but Myrial wouldn't relinquish her grip on the blade.

Valam dropped the dagger, stared in dismay at the blood on his hands. "It is in dark times such as these that one must know who they can truly trust. The only way to know for sure is to test. Do you understand?"

"I do," Myrial admitted, her eyes fixed on the prince.

"You've earned my trust, Myrial. I can only hope that I still have your respect as well."

Myrial nodded, broke into tears as pain overcame her nerve. Her knees buckled. Valam was there to catch her as he had been there for Adrina. Forgetting that he had secured the door he called to the guards. They came at the call, broke down the door before Adrina had a chance to unlock it.

"A priest, find a priest," Valam told one of the guards.

"Seth," Adrina said, "Seth is closest. He can heal Myrial. His kind have the gift."

Adrina ran back to her dressing mirror, pulled a cloth from the table top, used it to wrap Myrial's hands. She led Valam through the palace as he carried Myrial. Soon they found themselves at the door to Seth's chambers.

Adrina knocked, prayed there would be an answer, and there was. Seth answered the door. Candles spread on the floor said he had been meditating.

***

Seeing the girl and the blood-soaked cloth, Seth acted without hesitation. He reached back, and, with a touch of his will, extinguished the candles spread out on the floor, then prepared to do what must be done.

"Place her on the floor, there." He pointed. He spoke aloud so as not to upset anyone. Myrial's face was pale from blood loss and he was suddenly worried for her.

"How did this happen?" he asked as he studied the wounds. Adrina looked to Valam, Valam to Adrina. "No need to explain then," Seth continued, "I've heard the alarms. I know something is afoot though no one has told me what."

What he didn't say is that he had ventured to the winds. He had seen the chaos from on high: the guards sealing the palace, the city watch closing the gates, the soldiers searching house to house.

Reading their emotions he could sense that something terrible had happened these past few hours. He wondered if they knew what had gone on beyond the palace walls: the fires, the looting, the arrests. He doubted that they knew of these things. These weren't things kings and princes spoke of proudly, and probably not even in quiet whispers.

Myrial's moans of pain told him to hurry. He closed his eyes, drew the will of the land within. As he cleared his thoughts, he reached out, took Myrial's hands in his.

A soft white glow, a simple, pure radiance, spread from his palms to Myrial hands. He whispered words, ancient words, concentrated as he took Myrial's pain away. Myrial slipped from consciousness. He began the healing chant. The strength of his will was at once reflected in the light that bathed the room and swept it of shadows.

He smiled when he finished and sighed. *My task is done,* he whispered to their minds. *She will sleep.*

Chapter Twenty Eight:
Hidden Doorways

Something fought to free itself from within his mind, but as it was not able to or not allowed to, it levied pain. Pain that wrenched its way through his body, twisting away at his innards and his soul. His vision grew dim. He fell to the ground at the foot of the tower.

Thoughts filled his mind like a dream, reality bound by dreams. It was a strange and frightening dream. He dreamed of the boy he had once been. He dreamed of home, of his father and mother. He tried to force the thoughts away.

"Vilmos, control!" a friendly voice said to him.

He fought the pain, tried to listen to the voice. "I am me!" He cried out between clenched teeth, "I am in control!"

The pain grew. It was in brief moments of consciousness that the voice spoke to him, telling him to find control, to find a way beyond the pain. "The pain is their leash. Break the leash, become free."

Other voices cried out. He gulped for air as if he had just returned from the dead. White-hot pain followed. It felt as if he were being burned alive. He wanted to tear off his skin to be rid of the pain. But he wouldn't allow the pain to sweep him away again. He didn't want to die. He wanted to live.

His struggle was brief. Darkness enveloped his thoughts. The voices cried out telling him to come back to endure the test, yet he would not.

"Xith!" he cried out.

"I am here," came the answer from beyond the darkness.

"Is it night already?" Vilmos asked as he sat up and looked at the night sky.

"If you say it is, it is."

Vilmos started to reply. Xith cut him off. "We haven't much time, Vilmos. We must hurry. Your struggle is not over. The real fight has only begun."

"Struggle? Fight?"

"You have learned to get around their controls. They must never learn this. If they do, they will ensure you fail this test."

"What if I fail?"

"If you fail, we won't be able to let you live in this place. We will be forced to kill you here, once and for all eternity."

"We?" Vilmos asked, "Kill me?"

"It would be necessary to try."

"Try?"

"Silence, listen. Our time is growing short. I have things of great import to explain, things you must accept." Xith moved out of the darkness. He sat on the ground beside Vilmos and stared into his eyes. Another approached out of the darkness but did not move fully from the shadows.

"Who is that?"

"All in good time," Xith said, quickly re-directing Vilmos' attention. "This is a dangerous business, this thing between you and I. Do you understand?"

Vilmos nodded.

"I knew what you were and yet I helped you into the world. Kept you safe. Have I made the right decision?"

Vilmos didn't respond.

"Don't struggle with the truth. You know. A part of you has known ever since I first came to you."

"What have you let me become? What gave you the right to let this thing come to pass?"

"Even if I had wanted to I couldn't have done what needed to be done until I was sure, so I waited and watched. When the time came near I felt the presence. It was then that I left. I watched you in the shadows of your thoughts, offering guidance as I could.

"If you refused my guidance I knew I would then have to do what must be done. The magic in you is great but your past does not have to be your future. Control it, without letting it control you. At times it will be difficult. You will feel it. This is when you must seize the moment. Focus. You are the key to the wild magic.

"The wild magic of the beginning when all was chaos. In life or death all things have a beginning and an ending. When one era comes to an end, a new one starts. It is an endless cycle. In the end all things revert back to the beginning. Out of the chaos comes order, but only at the very end, and at a cost that cannot be known.

"Long have I troubled over my decision. The great burden I have placed on everything and everyone you will ever touch. It may have been pity for a child that spared you. That pity may also be what changes the course of the path."

Vilmos waved his arms, a caged bird trying to fly. "You talk as if you are leaving."

"Of course I am, don't be foolish. Our time is spent. Fight, Vilmos. Don't give in. I will find you again."

Darkness swept in from the corners of his mind. Vision

returned. Reality spilled upon dream, dream upon reality. The robed figures around him started running as they realized what had returned from the darkness. Their rhythmic chants faded to a cacophony of muddled screams.

"Fools, don't stop! You must maintain the rhythm!" cried out a strangely compelling voice, "Now we must begin again..."

"Begin again... begin again," the words echoed in Vilmos' mind.

A voice cried out to him in one last attempt to put reason into his mind, "Find, control... Remember, you are the sleeping dragon."

***

Adrina collapsed onto her bed. She was exhausted, but pleased that Seth had been able to help Myrial. Friends, true friends like Myrial, were hard to find.

She tried to sleep. Her body was weary, but her mind wasn't. She had so many questions, needed so many answers. She was struggling with her thoughts and deep in concentration when a hand clasped suddenly, unexpectedly to her mouth. Eyes round and wild, she resisted, fighting with all the strength she had.

She broke the grip, slipped to the side of the bed.

Strong hands grabbed and groped. She bit down in the fingers of the hand at her mouth, tasted the leather of the gloves on the attackers hands.

Her muffled screams were barely audible. The attacker was strong, wouldn't let go. She stomped down, winced in pain as her bare foot met rock-hard boots.

"Dear Father, help me," she prayed as she struggled. All she could think about were the events of the last few days. The turmoil in the palace. The whisperers who wanted to kill her father and everyone else who stood in the way of claiming the throne.

"Revolution," Valam had told her. "You don't want our family to end as King Frederick II's." She didn't. King Frederick, his wife, and most of his family were murdered in their sleep. Two sons and a daughter escaped the slaughter, but they were hunted down by the new, self-proclaimed ruler.

A flicker in the mirror caught her attention. She could see the dark robes of the figure that was holding her.

She looked back to the mirror. It took a long, extended second to understand what she saw.

The attacker was a woman, just like the whisperer in the hall. Could it be the same person? Had she returned to finish what she started? Where was her accomplice? Adrina had heard two speakers—both feminine.

"Do not scream," an ominous voice whispered, "I will lower the hand, but do not scream."

The voice was feminine. Adrina recognized it as if from a dream.

Strong, steady hands twisted her around. She looked up into the dark eyes, saw the long flowing black hair. Momentarily her despair edged toward panic.

Then the hand was removed from her mouth. Adrina considered screaming. She could have, easily, and aid probably would have arrived within moments, but she did not scream. Instead she regarded the figure that stood over her.

"Must we always meet like this, sister?" she asked, "Can you not knock and announce yourself like a normal person?"

"Silence," Midori said, touching a finger to Adrina's lips.

Adrina would not be silenced so easily. "Not again, and not like this. Father has forgiven you in his heart. I know he has."

"Dear sister, I am as an enemy to the crown and people, only the robes of my office will protect me if I am discovered." Midori passed warding hands about the air. "It is time I told you the truth of it."

"Truth of what?"

Another figure stepped out of the shadows. Adrina recognized the face of the burly captain immediately. "Captain Brodst?"

Midori understood the expression in Adrina's eyes. She took Adrina's hand and coaxed her into a chair. "Ansh and I are more than we seem."

Adrina didn't understand. She felt uncomfortable and suddenly underdressed in front of Captain Ansh Brodst.

"I know the ways of your heart and mind, sister. You think that King Jarom's bitter harvest would not be so wrought if I had wed him as father commanded. Father thinks it and so do the members of the council."

Midori paused, looked at the captain. He nodded. She continued. "I told you once that I remembered it all. That I lived with the pain and paid and paid and am still paying a debt that I never owed. You told me that you could not forgive me and that I was dead to father—that he had buried me and there was a grave marker to prove it. It is true, Adrina. No matter what I do, I am dead to father, but I am not dead to you."

Adrina stared coolly at her sister. She started to speak. The captain cut her off. "Let her finish," he said.

"I am not responsible for Quashan' or the attacks on Imtal. Even if I had wed Jarom, it wouldn't have changed the path. To the contrary, it would have hastened the path—Jarom's path to power. He wants to sit upon Imtal's throne and from there rule all the known lands of our realm."

Adrina turned to Captain Brodst. "How can you know this with such certainty?"

"The shaman, Xith," whispered the captain reverently.

Midori continued, "Xith showed me the path. With my own

eyes I saw what the future would bring if I wed Jarom and birthed the child from my womb. The child that was..." She took Captain Brodst's hand. "Not Jarom's, but ours."

Adrina looked from her sister to the captain, for the truth of it only their eyes could tell her. "Is the captain? Is the—"

"I am," said Captain Brodst.

"Is that child Emel?"

Midori turned away to look out the window. A sound in the night caught her cautioned ear. "We have told you this, our deepest secret, so that you may know that you can trust us above all others. Knowing who you can trust will save your life in the days and weeks ahead."

"Save my life?"

Midori's eyes were drawn to movement few others could have seen. "I must go. The captain will tell you soon what we require of you in return. For now, I ask only silence and I give you this."

Midori thrust a scroll into Adrina's hands. Adrina unrolled the scroll.

"Read it now," Midori commanded. "Hurry, we haven't much time."

Adrina regarded Midori quizzically. She started to read, felt the urge to turn back to her sister, but found that she couldn't.

The words printed on the scroll began to move about the parchment as if they were marionettes controlled by unseen hands. The words stopped moving when they formed a dark ring. In the center of the ring these words appeared:

> *Dragon's Keep*
> *Kingdom of the Sky*
> *Through danger deep*
> *Death's door does lie*

ഇൻഇ Kingdom Alliance ഇൻഇ

As Adrina read the words the world around her began to bend and shift. She could see ripples in the air. The center ring of the scroll no longer contained words but a picture—a picture painted in vivid colors, portraying a scene that seemed utterly real. She could see a stairs, twisting and winding into the heavens. At the very top of the stairs was a door.

Midori's eyes darted to the window. She pushed Captain Brodst to the door as it started to open. "Forgive me, sister," she said, plunging Adrina's hand into the image.

Adrina's hand disappeared into the other realm the scroll revealed. A glowing white aura raced up her arm, across her chest, then down to her feet until only her head remained outside the searing white glow.

Midori stared directly into Adrina's eyes—the last bit of Adrina that remained in the Kingdom realm. "Don't give in to the fear," she said, "Remember, two as one."

***

Vilmos remembered and something inside of him cracked. He recognized the voice. It was Xith's voice but something else raked at the edges of his consciousness. It cried out to be released from the blackness that surrounded it. It demanded to be freed from its prison.

The pleas were heart-wrenching. Each ripped further and further into his heart. He had to get away. He had to escape. He began to run, running until he was breathless.

He ran north out of instinct, finally stood heaving by the side of a small wading pool. The voices in his mind seemed to fade as he ran and now they were gone. He was alone.

He leaned toward the quiet waters of the pool, following the beckoning call of the cool, refreshing water. As he leaned down, the strange fiery radiance of the heavens cast his image onto the pool and this was the first time he had seen his reflection, in what seemed ages to him.

He saw a small boy, a boy not even close to being a man in that image. He didn't like what he saw. He knew he was not a boy. His vanity would not allow him to continue in this form. He decided he wanted to be older, to be more mature looking. It took the flickering of an eye to gather the energy required and then release the full force onto himself. The power exploded throughout his body, knocking him to the ground and where a small boy fell to the ground, a man rose in his place.

Vilmos steadied himself. He looked into the pool and smiled. He liked the broad-shouldered, muscular young man staring back at him. He stared at the image for a very long time, then turned around and walked away.

He walked all morning. Something clung to the edge of his thoughts and drove him on. There were eyes on his back. He felt them.

Off in the distance he spotted a pure black horse. It looked so pristine and powerful. It called out to him to take it. He walked toward it, climbed onto its back, and with the heels of his boots, he spurred it on.

The wind flowing through his hair and blowing on his face felt so wonderful. It was then that a troubling notion came, sending his thoughts spinning into turmoil. Pain ripped through his body. Darkness enveloped him. An instant of coherent thought came and in that brief twinkling he saw the forces in his mind fighting to gain control.

A familiar voice called out to him. Against the wishes of the other, Vilmos went to it.

"Welcome, Vilmos, keeper of the new age. Stay with us. Do not flee."

"Who are you?"

"I am he who is you. Stay with us. Let us preserve this time forever."

Vilmos backed away warily. "No. You are not me. I am me."

The voices grew distant. A light sparked in the darkness. Vilmos followed it. He saw Xith. Behind him was another, a stranger who seemed to loom up suddenly from the darkness.

This stranger wore a costume of feathers. Xith held out his hand and the orb of light which had drawn Vilmos blossomed. It beguiled him as it wandered through the colors of the spectrum— red, orange, yellow, green, blue, indigo, violet. It revealed the newcomer as he truly was. Vilmos stared at the clawed hands and feet, the beaked mouth, the great wings.

"I am Ayrian of the Eagle Lords," said the stranger. The words seemed to drift through the air into Vilmos' ears, for surely the sound didn't come from the throat as it did from other beasts. "Sole survivor of my kind."

"We are the same," came a voice out of Vilmos that was not his own.

As Vilmos stared at Ayrian, thoughts flooded his mind. Memories from the past. He remembered seeing the Eagle Clan flying over their domain. They had been a beautiful, proud race. He remembered the leader of the Gray Clan. He had also been powerful and proud. Ayrian didn't look so powerful or proud anymore. With sudden acuity, he knew the sadness of Ayrian's soul.

"Do not mourn for times past. We live in the present," said Ayrian almost coldly.

Vilmos suddenly felt the bitterness that had replaced Ayrian's pride. "Where do we go now? Is the test at an end?"

"You shall continue north, that is the direction you have chosen.

Find the tower and the key. We need the key to reach Over-Earth."

Vilmos didn't recall choosing any particular direction.

"Well at least we won't have to walk anymore. A quick jump and we'll..."

"Still so impatient. You forget where we are. Soon your memory will clear. They can't control forever, although they try. You will know how to do many things. You will know the names of places, peoples, things from ages past. It will take time."

Vilmos sulked. Without being asked he went to get wood for the fire. It would be a long night. The air was growing cool. He walked away into the darkness. When he returned Xith and Ayrian were gone.

"Xith?" he called out, "Where are you?" His voice echoed in empty air for an instant, then the world around him became clear once more.

"We are here," said Xith. "You must not walk away again. Promise me?"

"Yes," returned Vilmos.

"Listen very carefully for we haven't much time. They come. There are those who wish this time to end. We must not let that happen. Do you understand? We must kill them or chase them from our lands. We must burn their houses and their fields so that they have nothing to return to. We must do this to ensure our survival."

"Hurry, he comes," said a voice.

"Vilmos, you are evil. You were spawned from evil and you will always be evil. You must help me end all that is good. The people of this land have no right to dwell here. You should rule over them. Let the power take control. Let it devour you. Can you feel it? Can you truly feel it?"

"Yes," whispered Vilmos, enticed by the luring voice.

"Drink it in. Bath in it... You are he. Let go, follow the power!

Release those that have served you faithfully through these many dread years."

"Yes!" Vilmos shouted. A surge of power jolted through him. A part of him cried out in release. Another part of him knew something was terribly wrong. Suddenly he felt cheated and empty.

"You are not Xith! You are not Xith!"

The chanting became louder and more frantic. Vilmos fought the control. Agony found its way back into his mind, yet he was beyond pain. He had found truth.

The priests struggled to regain control. Their rhythmic cries echoed into the night sky, but it was too late. The warrior was upon them.

The warrior's eyes blazed with hate. The muscles of his arms bulged as he gripped his long blade. He let out a guttural rasp, a blood cry, as he set upon the priests, "In the name of the Great Father, I banish you to the pits of hell!"

Pure shock and reflex made Vilmos turn away, cover his ears.

Turning away only made things worse. He could see the warrior's movements reflected in the shadows of the campfires. He saw the warrior's great blade lash out over and over.

Screams echoed in the night.

He fell forward. Someone wretched his arm out of the socket. He screamed, a long wailing sound. He didn't fight back. He couldn't move and whether frozen from fear or something supernatural he didn't know.

Shooting pains went through his arm and shoulder. The wind went out as he took a powerful blow to the stomach. He feared this might be the end.

He was aware of everything. He wouldn't let himself black out. If this was the end, he wanted to face it.

Strong hands levered him up. *This is it*, he thought, *oh please, oh please, not like this.*

Suddenly his hands were free, then his legs. He got to his knees, only to be knocked down. He hit the ground hard. Lancing pain radiated from a blow to the side of his head.

"Help! Somebody please help," he heard himself saying.

"I know the truth about you," the one holding him said, "I know your secrets."

He saw a long double-edged knife coming toward him. He braced for the pain that he knew would shoot up his side. There was no escape.

He heard a loud crack, a sound like thunder. Blood sheeted from the man's neck. The man's face was frozen in disbelief. Then the man fell over like a stone on top of Vilmos.

Everything was quiet.

Vilmos twisted and turned, trying to get out from under the heavy man. The weight was lifted off. He spun around, fearing another attack.

He waited.

"Run, you are free," whispered a voice into his mind.

Other voices followed in a flood like voracious fiends. He huddled in the darkness, clutched the golden medallion of the man who had fallen on top of him. He wondered if this was a trick, some kind of new torture.

"You are home, you are free," the voice said.

Vilmos stood on weak legs, saw an ancient tower with its twin spires in the distance. With a jolt of unwelcome recognition he knew the tower represented two serpents. The twin spires were tails. The base of the tower, the heads. Where the serpents faced each other was a great doorway.

He listened to the sound of a bell tolling.

But something about the toll was wrong.

The toll came again. A piercing ring that seemed to come from everywhere and nowhere. It increased in intensity until he couldn't bear it, then it was gone.

He stared in awe.

The tower beckoned.

He went.

Chapter Twenty Nine:
Destinations Reached

Four men entered a dark room. One tossed a leather pouch onto a small wooden table. The pouch landed with a heavy thunk.

The man seated at the table emptied the pouch absently, obviously displeased at the interruption. His eyes were fixed on an open window. The sounds of clanging steel could be heard clearly from outside. "There are entry fees for four, but no burial fees."

"We do not intend to be buried," grunted the man who had thrown the pouch.

"Burial fees are standard. The carts were full of the dead every day last year."

A second coin purse was thrown onto the table.

"Late arrivals are not normally accepted, but this year we do lack for the sparring rounds. Names?" The attendant readied quill and ink.

"The sparring rounds," objected one of the men. The original speaker put a heavy hand on the man's shoulder.

"Sparring rounds all I got open. Should've come earlier. You still have a chance."

"A slim one... I had hoped for the secondary rounds."

"Secondary rounds," scoffed the attendant, "for newcomers without announcement? Who do you think you are? I ought to..."

The man raised his hand with an open palm. "We accept."

"Names?"

"My associates and I prefer to—"

"Names?" repeated the attendant.

"Name's Greer. My companions here are... Tenman, Viller, and—"

"Seth," completed the last man.

"Not from these parts are you?"

"He's from the Far North," said the original speaker. The man who had identified himself as Greer.

"Origin?" asked the attendant.

"Origin?"

"For the marker. Do you know nothing?"

"We won't need markers."

"Look friends, I've got things to attend to. If you don't mind, let's speed this along." The attendant gave a longing glance to the window.

"Great Kingdom."

"Kingdom's got no participants this year."

"Well, it does now. And enter us in the trios as well."

"You won't make it that far," the attendant replied offhandedly.

"Just do it," grunted Greer angrily.

"All right, all right, if you'll let me return to my business, I'll do it, but you aren't going to make it that far."

***

The caravan train lumbered toward the city with slow persistence. Emel rode with the advance party. It seemed Ebony Lightning was excited as he was. Soon they would be within the shadow cast by the city walls—walls that towered over everything, seeming to dwarf even the mountains in the distance.

Emel wondered at the expert workmanship of the wall. It had three levels, each with its own parapets. Men and beasts moving along the upper ramparts looked like ants. And, like ants, they marched in fixed lines, moving back and forth along the top of the wall.

Emel knew this show of force was meant to send a not-so-subtle message to the thousands of men in the caravan train that approached: Gregortonn is the mightiest city in the land, remember your place.

Emel rode quietly, sure that even without the show of force the men of the caravan understood that they were no longer in Great Kingdom. For some this was good as it meant they were getting close to home after many months or years away. For others, most of the Kingdomers included, it meant they had arrived in a foreign land where everything they knew and everything they represented would be questioned and put to the test.

The true Kingdomers in the caravan had planned for this day, wished for it. They were in the Southlands. Now they could begin to do what they had set out to do. Emel had his part as well, though his task would have been far easier if the prince and the elf had joined the caravan. He didn't know what had kept them away, but knew that whatever it was, it was equally as important as what he had to do.

He rode under the great wall of Gregortonn. He clutched the orb in its leather pouch, thinking it odd that he sought answers to things he didn't understand in a place he knew little about. He did know one thing: Dnyarr, Elf King of Greye was a genius. No other could build such a city as Gregortonn was.

Designed to withstand full assaults by giants, titans, and

dragon's kin, the city's fortified towers were dense along the walls. The towers could house armies and store everything needed to sustain those armies during campaigns and sieges—something Dnyarr had proved over and over. Right then, Emel knew he had been right to confide in Keeper Martin, and that the keeper spoke the truth. If Dnyarr's secrets were to be found it would be here in these lands.

Ebony snorted excitedly as they entered the city. Emel leaned forward, stroked the stallion's mane.

Smelling something strange, he turned. He caught sight of a king cat and its rider. Ebony reared as the king cat approached, nearly throwing Emel.

"Rein in that beast!" the kingcat rider shouted out.

Emel was thinking the same thing, but held his tongue. The rider appeared to be wearing an official uniform and she carried a long-bladed javelin openly. As a king's messenger, he had been to the far corners of the kingdom, seen strange and wondrous things, but he had never been beyond Great Kingdom's borders. He had never seen a city such as Gregortonn, and he had never seen a king cat. He had heard stories about them yes, how they could take down a horse and rider with their powerful jaws and claws, how the cat would continue a fight even if its rider died, how the cat would sometimes turn on its rider.

"The caravan?" the rider asked when she saw the strange look in his eyes. She didn't give him time to respond before adding, "Untrained beasts are not allowed in the city."

Faylin Gerowin reined in his mount next to Emel. "The cat," he said, steadying his horse as he talked, "Most of our animals have never seen a king cat before."

"Kingdomers?" the rider asked, spitting out the word as if it were a curse.

Faylin nodded.

The rider turned to Emel. "You'll do well then to remember that the king cat patrol has the wall. Stick to the central market area." The rider turned, moved off without waiting for a response.

"Nothing like a warm welcome," Faylin said sarcastically.

Emel stroked Ebony's mane, soothing away the last of the unease from himself and the horse. He couldn't, however, sweep away the fact that he felt humiliated. Ebony Lightning was a champion. His pride and joy. How could anyone call such a magnificent horse a beast and treat it like it was nothing?

"I know what you're thinking," Faylin said, "Don't do that to yourself. We're in the Old World, different rules apply."

Emel beaded his eyes. "What, they don't teach manners?"

"Cat Patrollers are elitists. You would have got the same treatment if your skin was a golden bronze. Trust me on that."

"I didn't think there were any king cats this far north."

"Gregortonn is an exception. The cats are born and bred here, domesticated. Well, as domesticated as they'll ever be."

Emel decided to broach a more dangerous subject than the king cats. "Do you think King William will listen?"

Faylin was silent for a time, then said quietly, "William Riven, King of Sever, is no fool. He has come a long way since his father's death, since the coronation."

"You say that as if you know King William personally. Do you?"

Faylin turned to Emel, his eyes unwavering, focused. "Emel, my friend, I am King William." So saying, he spurred his mount and raced off, leaving Emel to wonder whether he was joking or telling the truth.

***

Bladesman S'tryil had a shallow wound stemming from navel to shoulder. In a day or two he would be able to compete again. Valam had a gash above his right eye and several other superficial wounds. Seth and Ansh Brodst were weary, but otherwise fine. Two sparring rounds remained and thus far the four had managed to keep their identities secret. A remarkable feat that wouldn't have been successful without Seth's help.

"Two rounds," whispered Valam, "we've gone far enough to skip the individuals. We don't have to compete tomorrow."

Ansh, who had matched last, was still breathing hard as he spoke, "If we skip the individuals, take these last two rounds, we advance to the trios. If we lose a round, we have nothing to fall back on, no way to get to the championship round." He emptied a pitcher of cool water over his head.

"S'tryil is wounded," Valam said, "there is no way we can hope to win if another of us gets wounded. Two against three isn't much of a match. I say we wait. In two days we will be strong, ready."

"I side with Captain Brodst," Seth said.

"And if you hold back tomorrow and one of us gets hurt, what then?" Valam asked. Seth didn't have the heart for the barbarism of the rounds. He matched not for the kill, as did others, but to subdue. Valam knew this. He had said nothing of the matter until now.

"That's unfair, Seth is better than both of us," remarked Ansh. He was gaining respect for the elf with each day. "Do you really think the whisperers haven't already relayed that we never arrived in South Province?"

"One thing is sure: They don't know we are here. So let them guess," replied S'tryil, wincing as he spoke. The wound looked worse than it actually was and it was only the salve Seth applied that stung.

Valam, imparted Seth, *I once remarked that Man's fear was his greatest enemy. I think I was wrong about that. I also asked myself once whether the winner of these competitions would win your trust.*

"You have already earned my trust, Seth."

Have I truly? If I do not hold back out there tomorrow or the next day and I kill a man, what will it mean? Will it be for something?

"My remark was uncalled for... I do not take oaths lightly. My father made an oath to your queen and I have signed on too..."

Seth spoke aloud. "But do you believe, Valam? This is what matters. Nothing else matters. Do you believe?"

"Footsteps!" Brodst called out. The room quieted, then darkened as candles were snuffed out.

A knock came on the door. The four held still. "I was told I could find a man called Greer here," said an unfamiliar voice.

S'tryil opened the door a crack, looked into the dim hall. "Yes?"

"Do you always greet friends so?" asked the other moving into the doorway.

"By the Father!" exclaimed S'tryil, "Come in quickly, quickly. Were you followed?"

"I don't think so, but I'm afraid your charade hasn't fooled everyone."

S'tryil closed the door quickly, and ushered the speaker into a chair. "Go on," he urged.

"I have grave news." The man stopped, looked about the room as candles were re-lit. He went on to speak of a plot to kill the heir to the throne, Prince Valam.

"This is old news," S'tryil said.

"They've tried, and failed," Valam added.

"This news is fresh," the man said, looking directly at Valam. "You must not continue. They plan to poison the blades. Dragon's milk. One scratch is all it takes. You are all doomed. The prince especially so."

We must go on, Valam, directed Seth.

Valam said, "Thank you, friend. We will be on our guard, but we have come too far to turn back. Death awaits us all, does it not?"

The man stood, looking indignant.

"Go," whispered S'tryil. "I am grateful for the warning, old friend. Do not fear. We will be ready." S'tryil ushered the man into the hall, staying with him a moment. When he returned, his face was visibly pale.

"What do you make of it?" asked Valam, "Does he speak the truth?"

S'tryil fidgeted with something in his hands. "He is an old friend. He handed me this to give to you, says it is proof."

Chapter Thirty:
Finding Truth

Emel walked stiffly beside the king, his eyes taking in the grandeur of the ancient palace. The aide that walked with them talked about the history of the rooms and halls they passed. Emel listened absently, nodded cordially from time to time. His thoughts were uneasy; a chill ran the length of his spine. It was as if he could hear the wailing of the slaves who had died building the palace stone by stone.

He had never been to a place where every room, every hall, had a history all its own. That's the difference between the Old World and the New, he told himself. Great Kingdom's history went back to the time of the Alder King. The history of Vostok and the southern kingdoms seemingly went back to the beginning of time itself.

In a way, that rich history was the reason he had set out from Imtal. If there was ever a place he would learn about Dnyarr the Greye, the orbs, and everything that finding the orbs meant, it would be here in the Southlands. There was no better place to start than in Gregortonn—the city built by Dnyarr the Greye himself.

"You feel it don't you?" King William asked, turning to Emel. "The ghosts of the past haunt the Old World." The king laughed softly, added, "You're going to have to get used to that or it will drive you to madness. Choose now, you either listen to the voices or you ignore them."

Emel frowned, started to reply when the heralds standing outside the throne room sounded off in greeting. Emel watched awestruck as the golden doors to the throne room were opened. He had heard stories of the great doors banded in gold, but never thought he'd see them with his own eyes.

To say that the throne room was opulent was to understate the marvelous architectural achievement it represented. Its every feature was an extravagance, a flaunting of luxury, from the lavish chairs that formed an aisle, to the throne, to the three-domed cathedral ceiling, to the great bejeweled throne itself.

The aide told Emel about the history of the throne room, how it was created, what the chairs symbolized, why there were three domes instead of one, and how it was said that the jewels of the throne were used by the Elf King Dnyarr to focus his elvish powers in a most unnatural way. What the aide never said, what no one said, was the one thing Emel wanted to know the most: was King William related to Dnyarr the Greye, as some said in quiet whispers.

Kingdom lore said that Alexia D'Ardynne, a human slave, seduced Dnyarr the Greye and later gave birth to bastard twins, Aven and Riven. The two brothers would later be credited with liberating the kingdoms from Dnyarr's tyranny. While the current Riven line surely had little connection to the elvish blood that coursed through the veins of King Etry Riven I, Emel couldn't help but wonder if King William somehow felt connected to Seth and Galan, and to the plight of East Reach.

King William turned about at the throne, dismissed the aide with a nod, but didn't sit in the grand chair as Emel thought he would. He smiled regally. The last trace of the cordial mannerisms of Faylin Gerowin, the man the king had pretended to be, faded away. "You want to know why?" the king asked, his voice steady.

"I do," Emel admitted.

King William snapped his fingers, gestured. Two men from his entourage ran forward, kneeled before him. William whispered something Emel couldn't hear. The two hurriedly departed. "You are the only one who knows, except for the caravanmaster, my men, and perhaps Etri Hindell if he's as clever as I surmise. My disguise was quite complete, wouldn't you say?"

Emel nodded agreement; indeed he had found the king's sudden transformation unnerving. It was as if one moment he had been talking to Faylin Gerowin and the next he had turned and saw another. It was hard to miss the trademark blue eyes of the king, a blue so deep it seemed unnatural. So how did brown eyes suddenly become blue?

"I traveled to the North with Prince Valam of Great Kingdom. My journey was a secret one. I needed to speak directly to King Andrew, and I did. Few, except my most trusted, knew of it. Everyone else believed I was closed away in the palace, still mourning my father's passing and catching up with affairs of state."

"Why did you reveal yourself to me?" Emel asked, suddenly nervous, his voice unsteady.

"Keeper Martin approached me before I left Imtal. He asked me something, and Prince Valam said you could be trusted. I thought it most unusual at the..." The king's voice trailed off as trumpets sounded in greeting from the hall. He waited, watched as the doors opened and the expected guest was admitted.

"Keeper Martin?" Emel asked.

King William smiled regally, his gaze fixed on the distant figure. "Captain Galia," he spoke tersely, "so nice of you to join us."

"Cousin," Galia said, her voice held a fine edge that was almost contempt.

Emel turned, surprised to see the haughty kingcat rider that had snubbed him in the streets of Gregortonn. "You?" Emel and Galia said at the same time.

King William maintained his regal smile. "So pleased to see you remember Captain Emel Brodstson of Great Kingdom." He turned back to Emel, said "Emel Brodstson, Galia Tyr'anth."

Emel's expression broadened, and suddenly he was glad he had kept up with the reading Keeper Martin suggested would prepare him for the journey. If he remembered correctly, Gregor Tyr'anth was the namesake of Gregortonn and the brother of King Etry Riven II.

"Yes, *that* Tyr'anth," Galia said before Emel could respond. "But if you must know, the Tyr'anths have no claim to the throne and you need not address me as a royal."

Emel found himself at a loss for words. King William spoke first, saying, "She has a mind as sharp as her tongue, I assure you, which is why I wish her to accompany you..." Galia was about to say something. William silenced her with his eyes, continued, "No one knows the kingdoms of the South better. She will be your guide. Go well."

It was a dismissal. Emel stood his ground. "The alliance," he said. "Is it broken?"

King William glared, his eyes seemingly probing Emel's heart and mind. "I will not let the past repeat itself, know that."

"And the elves?"

"The book?" Galia interrupted.

"Yes, the book," the king said, moving to the throne. William's gaze grew distant.

To Emel it seemed he was seeing a thing no one else had ever seen. He could tell Galia saw it as well. It was as if William was coming to terms with something that haunted from within.

"You can listen or not," William said at long last. "I choose to listen, will you?"

***

They skipped the individual rounds. Their final two sparring rounds were victories, and now they waited for the trios to begin. Their identities were still a secret, at least to those who observed, and to those who weren't out to assassinate the prince. The hope was that they would get through, and that Prince Valam, Captain Brodst, and Bladesman S'tryil would match up against the trio from the Free City of Solntse for the championship match. On that day, the kingdomers would use no guises. Seth's identity was to remain secret, however, as long as was possible.

They were quartered in old barracks opposite the competition square. This made their daily walk back and forth to the matches a short one. This day especially so.

The morning bouts were already underway. The day's highlights were the trio matches. Those would come later, after the final individual rounds.

A large crowd gathered, filling the square save for the large outlined circle where a pair of singles matched up. Even the many levels of balconies of the four great structures surrounding the square were full this day. The one exception was the top level of the five-storied building that was City Garrison Central Post.

As he watched the two combatants struggle S'tryil remembered a conversation he had had with a young boy near the edge of the same circle he bordered now. "You see that circle there," he had said, "good, don't break it... And if someone comes lunging at you, in the name of the Great-Father, jump out of the way..." He chuckled to himself.

The four had come down to size up potential opponents, since winners of the individual finals could join the trio teams of their countrymen if they so chose.

Ansh and Valam had taken positions on one side of the circle. S'tryil and Seth, the other. A match was underway. The chosen weapon was the great axe.

"I'm concerned about the trios, my friend," whispered S'tryil, wincing at the sound of the great axes clashing together. He had a particular dislike of axes, having nearly lost a hand to one.

"Me too," Seth said honestly.

The combatants matched up again. One brought a knee up to the other's groin. "Is that legal?" whispered Seth. He hadn't seen that before.

"That's something you don't see in the trios. There's no time for it."

"So it is legal?"

"Anything's legal," S'tryil replied, smiling, "except of course poisoned blades..." He quickly appended his statement, adding, "And throwing dirt, like that man just did. He'll be thrown out if others saw it."

"Does the crowd always cry for blood in the finals?"

Seth stepped back. S'tryil did likewise, saying, "Sometimes, sometimes not."

The two watched as the bout progressed. A short while later a new match was called, with single long blades chosen as the weapon. Seth's eyes went to the fifth floor balcony of the garrison building. "None of them were there yesterday."

"That's because yesterday didn't matter. The man seated up on the high balcony... He is Lord Geoffrey... He was the best throughout the land until last year, when our good friend Captain Brodst defeated him."

The clanging of steel on steel rose to a powerful din. Seth nodded. He probed further with his eyes. "The others?"

"The three to the right I don't recognize, but the three to the left I know. They likely be who we'll be up against if we make it to the trio championship match. Shalimar is the first man. I've seen him win five matches in one day. He is good, really good. The man in the middle is the Lord's son, Nijal—the test of steel lasted six days for that one, a record. He teaches the meaning of the word defeat. The one on the end is Shchander, quick and sharp. His attack is his best skill, not very good on the defense. He'll get at least two extra thrusts against any opponent, myself included, though perhaps not against you. Would be an interesting pairing, you and he."

"You know your foe well."

"Valam did not mean to slight you."

I know this, directed Seth.

"No, let me finish. The championship match is different from the others. It allows for one replacement should one of us get seriously injured. Valam figures one of us will get injured…"

"It is all right, friend," Seth replied reassuringly, "I truly understand." He understood the concept now of winner take all and he really did understand how much these competitions meant to everyone involved. He had seen riots break out when a favored competitor lost. He had seen carts of the dead piled high. Valam had been right about other things as well. The spectators were fanatical followers. Gossip did spread like wildfire—and there was hope.

Hope for him and his people. If they could win. If Seth could reveal himself. If men could accept that he wasn't of the same darkness as those before him. If, if, if. So many if's, but oh so great a hope.

***

Majestic mountains loomed before them. Emel paused, took survey of the wagons and men weaving their way up the trail to Fool's Pass. The stones of the mountains, rich with ore, glistened purple in the early light of the day. A purple that was as deep and striking as the mountains themselves.

Ridemaster Etri Hindell was mounted to Emel's left. The great gray charger he rode was very different from the show horses his men rode, and the difference said more about him than Emel had learned from their idle conversations.

Etri was surveying the path, and, like Emel, was not pleased about the prospect of spending days in the mountains. The caravan would reach Fool's Pass after two days of climbing, up, up the steep trail. As the name implied Fool's Pass wasn't the wisest of choices for travel—a fact not lost of Etri or Emel, or anyone else for that matter—but it was the most direct route into the Kingdom of Zapad and the lands beyond.

Emel stroked Ebony's mane as Galia approached, riding her king cat. Days of traveling together had taken away some of the unease when the big cat was around, but Ebony would still snort and rear sometimes. "Going to be a long climb," he said quietly.

"The snows will come to the mountains soon," she said, "No turning back once we hit the pass. Understood?"

Emel said that he did, but he knew she was talking about more than she said. She resented him, disliked him because he was a Kingdomer and because she'd been commanded to be his guide. She was telling him in her way that he was taking her away from those she loved and things she knew. She wanted him to understand that and bear the weight of the burden. She couldn't have known that he already had the weight of many burdens on his shoulders. "The book?" he asked her before she turned away.

"The Book of the Peoples?"

It was one of the books Keeper Martin had shown him. Emel nodded as if he understood. He had assumed it was a book of Kingdom lore, now he wasn't so sure—and if the book wasn't penned by Kingdomers, then what about the things he had read? What did they mean then? Were they lies? Was it true they were secrets kept from commoners to guard the past?

She continued, "It holds truths no few wish to know."

"Or lies," Emel shot back.

"Subject to interpretation yes."

"Whose interpretation?" Emel waited. Galia smiled, didn't reply. He could tell she liked this verbal sparring. He pushed. "Do you know of the elves too?"

"There is little I don't know," Galia said proudly.

Emel couldn't tell if she was bragging or lying. "What is King William to you?"

"What is he to you?"

Emel didn't have to think about his answer. He said immediately, "A friend."

Galia was agitated with the turn of the conversation. Her mount apparently felt this too, and reared. A king cat on its hind legs with front paws outstretched was more than enough to spook Emel's Ebony.

To regain control Emel charged up the trail. He didn't look back, though in that moment he knew he may never see what he was leaving behind again. As he climbed the mountain trail he thought of Galia and the book. Soon after his thoughts went to Adrina and Myrial.

He loved them both in his own way. Adrina was the princess

he'd always dreamed of marrying as a boy, but knew from experience, his father's condemnation of their friendship in particular, that someone of his station could never marry a princess. Myrial was the loyal friend who had endured hardship and stayed true. She had a simple beauty, a purity of heart that attracted him.

"Goodbye," he whispered to the wind and to them, gripping the orb in its leather pouch, "Goodbye."

Chapter Thirty One:
Losing Touch

Myrial started, bolted upright in bed. Sometimes it seemed she had a preternatural connection to Adrina. This was one of those times. Adrina was in trouble. She knew this somehow. She grabbed a robe from the corner bed stand, ran from the room.

As she ran into the hall, she wasn't surprised by Garette's absence. She had been the one to send him away. "Sleep," she had told him, "No need to send the night watchman." Suddenly she regretted the decision. Something was wrong. She didn't know what. A thousand panicked thoughts raced through her mind.

The lower level of the palace was strangely quiet. It was early morning. The change of the guard couldn't have been more than an hour away. So where was everyone?

She raced up the stairs to the main level of the palace. The strange quiet continued. She found guard posts vacant, hallways empty. She cut through the kitchens, hoping to find the usual early morning frenzy as the cooks prepared the morning meal. Her panic became terror when she found the kitchens were empty as well.

She reached the door to Adrina's chambers, nearly out of

breath. The door was open. There were no guards posted within or without. She screamed as she ran into the bedroom, "Adrina? Adrina?"

Finding she couldn't breathe, she gulped at the air. But there was no air. "Help me," she cried, her voice a muffled whisper, "help me..."

She opened her eyes. The screams and the dream fell away. She was left with stark reality—the stark reality that she couldn't breathe—and the person pressing the hand over her nose and mouth had every intention of not letting her screams escape her lips, not letting her lungs find air.

She struggled against the weight on her chest and shoulders, stared up into the intent, wild eyes of Sedrick Bever. "Dogs should know their place," he hissed at her. "Bark for me little doggie?"

Myrial blinked, attempted to nod her head. She'd do anything to be able to breathe, to end the fire in her lungs. The fat former housemaster outweighed her several times. He was kneeling on her, pinning her to the bed.

He removed the hand. She gulped at the air, started to scream but before the scream escaped her lips, the hand was back over her nose and mouth. He slapped her with his free hand.

"Bad dog," he said, "Don't know your place." He pushed her to the floor, grabbed her by the back of the head, pulled so hard she thought her hair would come out by the roots, and all the while he maintained the viselike clamp over her nose and mouth with his other hand.

The fire in her lungs grew so intense that the rest of her body seemed numb. This was perhaps a good thing, as Sedrick pounded her head into the floor.

"Not so fast, not so easy," he whispered to her as he removed the hand from her nose and mouth.

Myrial sucked at the air, struggled to say, "Why?"

Sedrick laughed. She felt his hot heavy breath on her cheek, smelled the heavy scent of wine. She started to gag.

Sedrick clamped a hand over her mouth, made her swallow the vomit. Her throat burned as the sour liquid slid back down.

She threw up again. The vomit wasn't allowed out of her mouth. He seemed to enjoy the moment.

His left hand groped along the floor.

All Myrial could think of was that he was trying to find something to club her with. Tears rolled down her cheeks. She couldn't hold them back anymore. She was terrified, had never been so terrified in all her life.

He was going to kill her; she knew this. It didn't seem fair. All she wanted was a better life—the life that should have been hers.

Surety of death brought clarity. Briefly she thought of Adrina. Adrina needed her but she couldn't get there—wouldn't get there in this lifetime.

Sedrick found what he had been looking for, doused Myrial with wine. "Drink, "he said laughing. "drink."

Myrial blinked up at the blood red liquid pouring over her face, running down her chest and back, pooling on the floor all around her. She tried to shield herself with her hands, but Sedrick was kneeling on one hand, his weight crushing her fingers, and holding the other hand at bay. It was a game to him; she knew it. Everything was a game to the former housemaster.

"Kill me," she begged.

"In time," Sedrick whispered. "You don't want it bad enough yet. You will, trust me."

She nodded at the large, horrifying face staring down at her. She spoke in a tiny whisper, "I'm dead already." She knew she was. That was the scariest thing of all.

ೞಣ Kingdom Alliance ೞಣ

***

The final trio match had been underway for two full hours. The square was darkening as evening approached, and ever more onlookers pressed into the square to get a look at the competitors. Once word spread that Prince Valam and Captain Brodst were participants the square erupted. The city garrison was called in to clear the circle, and now they protected it with their lives—for the press of the masses pushed ever inward.

Bladesman S'tryil continued despite the re-opening of his earlier wound. Valam was drenched in sweat and judiciously matched his opponent. He had taken Shchander despite the warnings otherwise. He was nearly exhausted. His opponent on the other hand seemed to have boundless energy.

Ansh Brodst circled Nijal, catlike. His blade danced back and forth between his hands. Mid-length blades had been chosen, which meant that a combination of defensive and offensive styles was called for, and the use of the body, legs, and fists, mandatory.

Switching tactics S'tryil, Valam, and Brodst circled along the inside. Their opponents on the outside. Neither side attacked.

Torches were raised around the square and mounted in iron racks along the balconies as dusk shadows deepened. Shchander lunged at S'tryil while Shalimar took him from the side. It was a lightning attack and neither Valam nor S'tryil was able to move fast enough to counter.

S'tryil was hit and went down. The two retreated from the three, Valam jumped over S'tryil as the other fell almost taking them both down.

"Call it, damn it!" Valam cursed as he waited for the call to relief, defending heroically.

Brodst kicked out laterally and hit Shchander in the side as the other spun around to face Valam. Valam rotated to the right. He knew they were stalling on purpose. Three-two wasn't much of a match. He lunged recklessly at Shchander who was already off balance.

He scored a direct. The fine edge sank deep into Shchander's chest. Relief was called then, but it was too late. Valam grinned.

Geoffrey of Solntse replaced Shchander. Seth stepped in for S'tryil. The crowd erupted in cheers. "Geoffrey is matching!" went the chant that started out singly and then was joined by many, many others who carried along the growing echo. "Geoffrey is matching!"

As Prince Valam had done, Seth removed his mask after stepping into the circle. It only took one person who recognized Seth as an elf of legend—Seth without the usual hood and guise—to bring the crowd near riot. Trumpets blared. Garrison reinforcements stormed into the square. Hundreds fell in the ensuing clash. Cries of "Kill him! Kill the elf!" were everywhere. Everyone wanted to catch of glimpse of the elusive figure. And everyone tried.

A hush came when Valam raised Seth's sword arm, saying "He fights for Great Kingdom. Any man that wants to kill him must come through me first."

The crowd was agitated. The day had been long. More than a few were drunk; as many, perhaps more, were brave—or foolish—enough to try to get past Prince Valam. The crowd wanted blood. Would settle for nothing less.

Valam, Captain Brodst, Nijal, Geoffrey, and Shalimar worked together to fend off the attackers—all of whom were intent on getting to Seth. Seth watched the five men circle him, surprised that three strangers would put their lives at risk to defend him.

"What have you started here?" Geoffrey screamed at Valam through the din of the attack.

"Only what I must," Valam replied. "The Elves of the Light, of the Reach, are not our enemies of old. Our peoples were once united in the fight against the dark elves of Under-Earth."

Geoffrey scoffed, blocked with his blade, used the flat edge of the sword to bash one of the attackers as Valam had done a moment before. "What proof?"

"For now only my word." Valam looked directly as Geoffrey as he spoke.

"Blasphemy, you have no respect for this circle."

"And yet you defend alongside us?"

"I have the deepest respect for your father. If you were to die in the match, then so be it. But to die at the hands of this mob is not fitting."

"Then accept my word."

Geoffrey sidestepped an assailant, regarded Valam meaningfully. "I'll accept that you are bewitched, enthralled as may be the case."

"I'm in full count of my faculties, I assure you."

***

It was the thought of Adrina in danger that Myrial clung to. It was what kept her sane as Sedrick did what he did. She was shaking, covered in sweat and wine as he backed away from her for a moment.

Her voice was hoarse from screaming and her throat hurt. She thought she had won when Sedrick finally allowed her to scream. She hadn't won, and he relished every moment as terror sank deep into her mind.

She didn't know why no one answered her screams, but she could guess why. Sedrick had always been good at bribing the guards to get what he wanted. Those who couldn't be bribed could be coerced in other ways. She doubted that anyone knew what was really going on. Still, the fact that they had turned a blind eye in the first place made her angry enough to want revenge, and the need for payback ran deep in her mind. She'd repay them all. Every last one.

Sedrick stared at her. His eyes seemed like dark holes. Her heart raced. He was going to kill her now. She knew it, was too full of rage to let it happen.

He stamped a black-booted foot down hard. Bones broke. Myrial didn't feel pain, only rage. The rage was a shield.

He flared at her again. "Don't you dare try anything! Don't you dare."

"I wouldn't," she said, her voice barely a whisper as she crawled backward using her hands.

He chased after her. "I have to do this… It's the only way. You understand, don't you?"

She sensed what was coming. She knew she had to do something. She prayed for strength, wasn't sure if the jumbled words escaped her lips or if she only imagined they did.

"You trying to trick me? Is this some sort of trick?" he asked. "That why you're backing away from me?"

She started laughing, didn't know why. There was nothing else, nothing else for him to take. Death was a good thing for her, she was sure of it. She was prepared for it.

"Mocking me?" he shouted, kicking her in the side. He grinned. He had such a fiendish, mad look.

She spoke quietly, mimicking him. Her instincts could be as sharp and cruel as his. It scared her to think that. It scared him too; she could see it in his eyes. The girl he had taken everything from had something left that he couldn't take.

She realized she wasn't afraid anymore. He had taken away everything, even her fear. There was nothing left to be afraid of. What could he do to her that hadn't already been done?

She pulled herself toward him. "Do it," she whispered.

"Shut up!" he yelled. "I'll do it when I'm ready." He lifted his boot. He was an instant away from breaking her right arm like he had broken her right leg. "When I say something I mean it."

She knew she couldn't block the blow, couldn't move away in time. She waited, rage flooding her thoughts and giving her strength she wouldn't have had otherwise. She had to try something, make a move immediately.

She watched his eyes, concentrating on what she saw there. She was fearless, trying to gauge his weaknesses. He had them. Everyone did.

"Your beloved princess isn't going to save you this time," he said with a wicked smile. "I have seen to that. She's gone. I watched her go."

Myrial sprang at him like a wounded wolf, attacking rabidly while dragging her leg. "You are one of the whisperers. What have you done?...What have you done?"

Sedrick dodged, cackled madly. "Nothing I shouldn't have done long ago."

***

Night arrived fully before the square calmed. A half-moon rose in a star-filled sky. The two trio teams were allowed the privilege of a much needed reprieve. Water was passed out, returned.

As quiet returned the six faced off. At first, Valam sided against Geoffrey, Brodst against Shalimar, and Seth against Nijal. Each side intentionally splitting up the more protective ring of three.

The three crossed pairs circled slowly. Valam thought it peculiar that Geoffrey had joined in now. But he knew Geoffrey must have also understood that whoever took this trio match would take it all. There was no doubt. Neither had ever seen the crowd this excited, ever. Not even after last year's upset.

Ansh Brodst circled catlike, counterclockwise. Valam and Seth, clockwise. Then on Valam's signal, they changed opponents. Valam took Shalimar. Seth, Geoffrey. Brodst, Nijal. The maneuver got the momentary confusion they had been hoping for—they had not used the move until now.

Seth was excellent with his hands, and thus the reason Valam had agreed to the mid-length blades. Geoffrey was slower on the defense. Seth moved in, a kick to the groin as he hacked across. He wondered at the effectiveness of the recently learned trick. Geoffrey faltered.

Ansh Brodst lunged inward at Geoffrey. Seth launched at Nijal. Both targets were caught. They fell, jumped to their feet.

The men of the Free City had their own well practiced moves. They knew how to feint from a blade even if it meant going down.

The three formed a protective trio. A momentary lull ensued while Seth, Brodst, and Valam circled on the outside.

Valam grimaced and Brodst's compulsory scowl deepened. They needed to split the trio up—on the outside, they were more vulnerable.

Valam, Lord Geoffrey will take you… warned Seth, just as the other attacked. Valam countered and rotated to separate the trio.

While it seemed an unfair advantage to use his powers, it wasn't. Seth was not as skilled in defensive plays as the others and they needed anything that could give them a slight advantage. He found it increasingly difficult to keep focused on a single opponent as he tired, let alone three. He found it easier to follow the flow of his reactions and reach out with his will only during moments such as the previous lull.

Valam played at a jab while bringing a fist across to connect with Geoffrey's chin. The free man countered. His blade ripped into Valam's arm. New blood to join the reddened dirt of the circle.

Valam sighed and then strangely, smiled. It wasn't his sword arm.

Kingdom Alliance

He wasn't expecting an immediate follow through or the simultaneous side attack from another. The momentary frenzy of two on one was enough to throw him off. Geoffrey's next blow hit Valam full in the chest. He went down, couldn't get up.

Three circled two while Valam was carried out.

Valam? called out Seth in alarm.

"I'll live damn it! Worry about the match! Don't hold back. No more holding back!" screamed Valam in his thoughts.

The crowd erupted violently. It seemed a rather large contingent of Kingdomers had pushed into the square.

As Valam was carried out he could have sworn that he saw a young girl with long black hair staring at him with worried eyes. He turned back quickly, but by that time she was lost in the crowd.

He was being carried to the death house. "I'm not going to die, damn it!" he barked.

"It's either in here or out there where that mob'll tear you apart. I'd be quiet if I were you, Prince Valam."

Valam recognized the voice. He stared in wonder at the two who had carried him from the field. "Father Jacob? Keeper Martin?"

325

Chapter Thirty Two:
Dragon King

The heavy gold medallion slipped from his hands. It seemed as though his life was held frozen while the rest of the world raced to catch up to the point where he was suspended in time.

A great toll sounded, reverberating in his mind. The paralysis lifted. The haze in his mind fell away. He gulped, taken aback as he was left staring into the eyes of another. He bit his hand to make sure he was truly awake. He yelped in pain. Real pain, not imagined. He was awake, alive, beyond the unseen hands that tried to control him.

"Xith?" Vilmos asked, disbelief in his voice.

"Vilmos!" exclaimed Xith happily.

"Xith, is it really you?" Vilmos prodded the shaman with an outstretched hand. "Are you truly flesh and bone?"

Xith paused a moment. He hugged Vilmos. "What is this thing that I have done?" he muttered to himself, "Such a heavy burden for one so small and new to the world."

"Where am I and what of—"

"Don't worry about that now. Rest, save your strength."

"There was darkness. I heard voices and... and..."

"The darkness has nearly run its course. You will be free soon and this business will be behind us for a time. Be thankful."

"I can't take any more, make it end. Please, make it end. I'm losing myself."

"Yes, soon. Soon it will all be over."

"How long have you been here with me?"

A prolonged pause followed. "Why do you ask?"

"How long?"

"A long time, a very long time. Days"

"Who is tha-at?" began Vilmos, finishing his own sentence before the other could reply. "You are Ayrian, Eagle Lord of the Gray Clan."

"Yes, I am," replied Ayrian, emerging from the shadows. He carried a large bundle of firewood. As he piled the wood next to the low fire, the once proud eagle lord stared into Vilmos' eyes. He stroked his beak with a clawed hand, then spread his arms in a wide arc which revealed the shadowed bulk of his great wings as though they were the folds of a great gray cloak.

Ayrian spoke then in the pitched calls of his people, "He knew who I was. He didn't have to even think about it. I didn't see a stirring of the old memories as we had expected."

Xith replied in the same language, "Yes, I saw. They took him farther than we had anticipated. What's done is done. We must undo it that is all. What they have altered we must continue, yet I think in time the remembrance will diminish."

Vilmos stared at the shaman and the eagle lord, hearing only the strange calls and not the words, but understanding what was said just the same.

"Save your strength, Vilmos. Eat this, then sleep," Xith said.

"No, please," begged Vilmos. "I don't want to sleep. No more sleep. Anything but that!"

Vilmos sat up, his eyes wide. Yet as Xith spooned hot broth into his mouth and it slipped down his throat to settle in his empty stomach the growing warmth began to lull him to sleep. Sagging eyes that sought to look out upon the world didn't resist long.

Vilmos blinked, blinked again. The great doorway of the tower beckoned. He strained to move the huge door as it ground upon its hinges. He entered the tower without hesitation. A stair twisted and wound its way to the top of the tower. Odd though it was, he saw a single stair but knew that the serpentine tower had two spires.

The same beckoning call that led him to the tower door led him to the stairs. He could not resist the pull of the lure and did not try. As he started up and rounded the twisted staircase, he saw a girl with long black hair. She wore a flowing white robe that seemed out of place. He watched her climb as he climbed. He saw the stairs bend and shift around her, leading her in a constant circle. To her he knew it must seem that she climbed and was making progress toward the door at the top of the stairs. It was the same for him. He seemed to be making progress but neither was getting any closer to the top of the stairs.

He called out to her. She turned. He immediately recognized the green jewels of the eyes, the high noble cheek bones and the gentle curves of her chin. "Princess Adrina?" he shouted.

***

Adrina stopped climbing. She turned to look at the boy who called her name. Recognition didn't come immediately, but the short black hair and brown eyes were not completely unfamiliar to her. "Vilmos?" she called back.

"What are you doing in my dream?"

"Dream?" Adrina asked, "This is no dream to me, more like a waking nightmare."

"Exactly," Vilmos said, "One from which I can never escape no matter how hard I try, and I have tried, believe me."

Adrina sat on a step, still looking at Vilmos. "I've been climbing for hours. I still haven't reached the door. It's the strangest thing. One minute I was in Imtal reading from a scroll. The next, I was here. I have been stuck here ever since."

"It's an illusion—it's all a damned illusion." Vilmos kicked out at the wall. "The stairs aren't letting you go anywhere. You have been walking in a great circle."

"Impossible. I climbed and climbed. How can you be certain?"

"The stairs move around you." Vilmos prepared to jump to Adrina.

"Stop! If you can see the stairs move, perhaps you can guide me."

Vilmos agreed to try and though he did try, they did not succeed. The stairs continued to lead Adrina in a great circle. When Vilmos tried to reach Adrina, the stairs took him on a different path. He tried jumping to her. He went up the stairs until he was even with her, then tried to reach out to her. But he couldn't reach her. He was soon locked in a never ending circle of his own. Frustrated, he sat down and pounded his fist into the stones.

"How did you get here again?" he asked.

She could see him seated on the step, almost as if he was next to her. She knew he wasn't. It was an illusion, because try as she might she couldn't reach him either. It was as if they were separated by an unseen shadow world.

He shrugged his shoulders, waved his arms, waiting for a response.

Adrina shouted, "I was reading a scroll."

"You don't have to shout. I can hear you clearly enough. What did it say?"

"The scroll?... I never got to read what it said at first, as soon as

I laid eyes on it the words started moving. Then there was this ring of words… Something about a castle." Adrina pulled nervously at her hair. "No, a dragon's keep."

Vilmos stood, reached out into the gray world as he spoke. His hands passed right through the image of Adrina as if she wasn't there, but he knew she was. "Dragon's keep?" he asked.

She paced back and forth, muttered to herself, "Dragon's keep, dragon's keep." She stopped pacing suddenly as a dark ring of words formed before her eyes. "Dragon's Keep. Kingdom of the Sky. Through danger deep. Death's door does lie," she whispered to herself and then repeated louder for Vilmos' sake.

"Kingdom of the Sky?" repeated Vilmos, then he whispered in a strange voice, "Find the strength of Uver. In Zadridos, you will find the key to the City of the Sky and there you can right the wrongs of the past." His eyes flashed. He said aloud, "I am in Zadridos in Under-Earth, and if I am, why is Adrina here?

Adrina glared at him, confused. He spoke in strange voices. "Under-Earth is but a myth."

He laughed. "A myth? Not to me, not to you. You're standing…" His eyes went wide. "Dragon's Keep, this tower has two spires. They are the tails of two great serpents, and where the serpents meet is the door I used."

"Two spires, two stairs, two people," Adrina said, looking at the stairs around her and above her and then to Vilmos. She heard her sister's words. "Do not fear. Remember, two as one."

"Climb!" she shouted, "Climb with me!"

Vilmos didn't move. He was puzzled.

"Don't you see," Adrina said, "The tower gives the illusion of one yet there are two—and there are two of us. If we act as one, maybe we can break the illusion, reach the door. Follow my lead."

***

Vilmos turned eyes filled with astonishment away from the princess and concentrated on climbing as she called out to him. Before long he was at the top of the stairs and Adrina was just in front of him.

She smiled at him. He ran to hug her, but his hands passed through her instead of touching her. The surprise caused him to falter and loose his balance. He tumbled to the stone floor.

Vilmos stood on uneasy feet, then turned to the door and opened it before Adrina's scream of "No!" registered.

A great clawed hand came out of the darkness behind the door. It snatched Vilmos up from the ground. Vilmos struggled against what felt like a great clamp squeezing the life from him. He had no weapon and used the only resource he had. He clamped down with his teeth on the fleshy part of the hand. For an instant the claws and the hand relaxed.

It was enough for Vilmos to break free. Adrina shouted, "Close the door, Vilmos! You must!"

Vilmos scrambled to close the door. The great hand sought to grab him again. He pushed and pushed with all his might, working the door against the hand. The hand lashed out, swept him off his feet.

The creature must have assumed it had a moment to snatch him up. But as the claws of the hand opened, Vilmos kicked at the door with all his strength. From behind the door he heard a terrible roar. The creature pulled back the hand.

He slammed the door shut, pushed his weight against it.

"The key, Vilmos," a voice whispered in his mind. "We need the key to reach Over-Earth. You must get it."

"Are you okay?" Adrina asked, adding almost to herself, "We must do this, two as one."

Vilmos watched as Adrina turned to the door in her part of the shadow world. He was hesitant to follow her actions and it showed clearly in his eyes.

"Two as one," Adrina said, asking, "Are you ready?"

Vilmos nodded. Adrina signaled to open the door. She started to open it. He hesitated, screamed, "Stop! Stop! Stop! What if the creature is still there? What if it attacks us both? What—"

"Trust me," she said, "I don't know how I know, but I know. If we open the door together." She coaxed him back to the door.

He grabbed the door handle, but not because he was optimistic about what was behind the door, rather because he didn't want Adrina to have to face whatever it was alone. He nodded that he was ready, took a deep breath, braced for what surely must follow.

As one, they opened. As one, they breathed a sigh of relief. As one, they entered the room at the top of the tower, stepping into total darkness and a complete unknown beyond.

The darkness was fleeting. Hundreds of torches lining the walls from floor to ceiling sprang to life. Vilmos turned to Adrina, Adrina to Vilmos. She nodded; he acknowledged. They prepared to continue.

It was in that moment when it seemed nothing dark and sinister was in the room that they both realized the flames were not those of torches but of creatures—hundreds of tiny creatures that breathed fire. Soon the creatures, no bigger than a man's finger, were swarming about the room, moving on wispy wings that were almost evanescent.

Vilmos reached a hand up to ward off the tiny flyers. One of the creatures set upon him, locked its jaws around his hand. The instant the teeth plunged into his flesh he could feel the slow crawl of something up his arm. He looked at his arm in horror, saw the flesh turning to stone.

Adrina put her hands to her face in shock. She slumped to her knees, rocked back and forth. She muttered to herself, "Don't give in to the fear. Don't give in to the fear."

"Two as one," Vilmos said, his voice firm. "You must reach out your hand. Succumb to death. It is the only way to see what I see."

***

Adrina rocked back and forth, whispering to herself. She saw tiny flashes of fire all around her. She saw the creature latched onto Vilmos' hand. She watched as his body turned to stone.

She started to second guess herself. She didn't want to do what must be done. Was it the right choice? Was there something else she should do? What if she did nothing? And then she took her right hand and gripped the forearm of her left, forcing the hand into the air and holding it steady. She braced for the pain.

One of the creatures latched onto her hand almost immediately and just as suddenly her fate was locked with that of Vilmos. The petrification was quick. The stone spread up her left arm and to her torso in a few heartbeats. It then moved down her right arm and both her legs until only her neck and head were outside its bounds.

It was then that the great clutter of tiny creatures flying through the air became one, and then that the thin veil between her and Vilmos lifted. The creature that stood before her had the great wings and body of a winged serpent, the torso of a man.

Adrina couldn't turn to see Vilmos, but she knew he was solid stone, and that like her only his face remained outside the petrification. She could feel the mortification of the flesh of her face. She could no longer breathe. Her eyes were the only part of her that she could move.

The Dragon King's great clawed hands rushed toward them. She thought he would crush the stone of their bodies. He didn't. Instead his touch restored their flesh.

"You seek answers and a key," the Dragon King said, "Which shall it be?"

Adrina and Vilmos didn't speak. They turned, looked at each other, said, "Two as one."

"So shall it be," said the Dragon King.

The room started to crumble around them. Vilmos ran. Adrina ran. They ran as fast as they could back to the stairs. They ran and ran, but they seemed to go nowhere.

Vilmos panicked, started screaming. Adrina held him in place. "It's an illusion. A test," she said, surprised she could still touch him.

She watched pieces of the stairs fall away around them. Vilmos did too. A nervous tremor came to his lip. "How can you know?"

"Don't give in to the fear," she whispered to herself and to him. She closed her eyes, concentrated. She heard him turn away from her. Before he could step away, she grabbed his arm. "The answers are here."

"Let me go!" he shouted as he struggled to break free.

"Knowing who you can trust can save your life," she said. They were borrowed words, the words of her sister, Midori. Other words came to her as through a dream. She remembered the scroll.

For a moment she saw the milk-white eyes of a blind woman. She breathed deeply, concentrated. "Nothing to fear," she told herself.

She saw, understood. She knew why Midori had given her the scroll and why the old woman appeared now in her mind's eye. Everything was linked. Everything was a part of the circle.

She opened her eyes, released the iron grip on Vilmos' arm. The great clutter of tiny creatures flying about the air once again became a single being—the Dragon King.

She stared up at the Dragon King unafraid. "There are no answers. No keys. We're here because we have something you need."

The Dragon King nodded. "You are the key."

"It's why you've been helping us. Why the Mistress of the Night and Lady of the Forest appear." She grabbed Vilmos' hand, took a step toward the Dragon King. "You want our help as much as we require yours. You help us to help yourself."

"Find the door," the Dragon King said. "Open it. You are the children of the light and of the dark. You must do what must be done."

"What of the elves?"

"What of the elves," scoffed the Dragon King.

"You are honor-bound to their service."

"As you shall be to me."

"You wish return from exile, to power."

"As would any."

Adrina and Vilmos took another step toward the Dragon King. "You released the Dark Lord the Elf Queen warned of," Adrina said.

"It is the game. I am the keeper of the Fourth Wind."

Vilmos remained uncharacteristically quiet. Adrina made a fist as if she was going to strike the Dragon King. "What do you want from us?" She didn't wait for an answer. She drove her fist into the Dragon King's serpent-like body. Her fist cut through the outer scales. Her arm sank up to the elbow in the wet flesh. She grabbed at the fleshy meat within and, gripping it, withdrew her arm. In her hand she held one of the tiny dragons. "You are going to tell us now why we are here?"

"I cry for the children who at the end of the journey will never be the same." The Dragon King changed forms as he spoke, taking on the form of the old blind woman. "Child, I cry for you. I cry because I see you standing in the middle of a killing field. I cry for the thousands dead at your feet…"

"Who are you?" Vilmos and Adrina shouted at the same time.

"Why us?"

The Dragon King changed forms as he spoke again. "Speak not words in haste, oft you may regret the reply. Yet if this is what you truly wish to know, I will tell you."

Adrina stared into the eyes of the Lady of the Forest. "It is not true. It can't be true. I won't let it be true."

"As it is," the Dragon King said readily. "I am what I choose to be, what you need me to be."

"Lies, lies, lies!" Adrina shouted.

"One truth," the Dragon King said, offering the words like candy.

"Truth. What would you know of truth?" The tiny dragon she held in her hand opened its wings as if in response.

"Your brother dies just after moonrise and with him the hope that the peoples will ever be united."

"Leave Valam out of this!" Adrina flew into a rage, started kicking, punching, screaming.

"Let him finish," Vilmos pleaded. "I want to know."

"Yes, indeed," the Dragon King said. "You'd like to know wouldn't you little one? Why? Why? Why?"

Vilmos held Adrina back. They both took a step away from the menacing figure who suddenly seemed more like a creature of the underworld than one of the great dragons. "One truth," Vilmos said, "You offered."

"One truth was given. Heed it as you would."

Vilmos stepped in front of Adrina. "And if we open this door you spoke of?"

"No if's. You must. The prince dies. The prince lives. You choose." The Dragon King waved his hands, transporting them out of the tower, taking them to a plateau where they could look down into Great Kingdom from the heavens. He pointed to the tiny dragon Adrina held in her hand.

The creature threw back its head; fire came out of its mouth. Adrina was compelled to look into the flames.

Her heart beat faster and faster.

She saw images within the flames. Valam lying wounded in a bed. Father Jacob and Keeper Martin were beside him. Dead men piled behind them.

The Dragon King spoke, "The wounds aren't fatal. Dragon's milk is, however."

"Dragon's milk?" Adrina asked.

"Only one cure, only those in the service of the Dragon survive. Will you choose life for your brother or death?"

"To what end?"

"Choose."

"I will not."

The Dragon King lashed out with his tail. They jumped to avoid tripping and falling. "My dears, one way or the other." He waved his hands. Four doors appeared. Two to the left of Vilmos. Two to the right of Adrina. "One of you will always be mine. Act now to save him, or not. If you save him, he's mine and you are both free."

"If we don't choose?" Adrina asked. Vilmos added, "What then?"

"White brings the hope of life. Black brings death. Two as one. Choose or stay. I don't care."

The tiny dragon in Adrina's hand squawked. Adrina looked down, saw it was looking at her. Behind the iris of its tiny eyes she could see flames—the same flames that were in the Dragon King's eyes. "Mine," she said boldly. "I will take this with me."

The Dragon King mocked her, saying, "As if you had a choice. Remember, one of you will be mine regardless."

There was a flash of lighting, but the lightning went from the ground to the sky. A torrent of smoke and debris exploded outward. Adrina jumped out of the way. When she turned back, it seemed she was alone.

"Vilmos, Vilmos?" she called out through the smoke. She coughed and sputtered.

Vilmos groaned, said, "Here, I'm here."

When the smoke cleared they found the doors remained. Two white and two black.

"Doorways to nowhere," Vilmos grumbled.

"No," Adrina said, "It's a puzzle. White is life. Black is death. One of you is mine regardless. Two as one. Don't you see?"

"If you only knew." Vilmos put his hands to his head. "We choose white then?"

Adrina stopped Vilmos from going to the door. "Not so fast, I don't think so."

"Black then?"

"Too easy," she said, turning about in a close circle. "One of you is mine," she said to herself as much as Vilmos. "Two as one."

"We choose white. We have to. He said so. White is life."

"For us, but what about my brother? Is that death for him then?" The tiny dragon she held squawked as if in response.

"Black then?" she asked, speaking not to Vilmos but to the dragon. The dragon made no response.

"Black and white," she said, "We choose both." The dragon squawked and flapped its wings as if to say yes, yes. Adrina was sure that was the right choice.

Vilmos gulped, asked. "Which of us chooses black and dies if you are wrong?"

"I do," Adrina said stepping up to the black door to her right, grabbing the door handle. "Are you ready?"

Vilmos moved to the white door to his left. He nodded, asked,

"You're sure about this?"

"On the count of three," Adrina said, closing her eyes, preparing herself for whatever might come. She turned to Vilmos, made sure he was ready. "Three," she said without counting one and two. She opened the door, stepped into darkness.

Chapter Thirty Three:
Endgame

People crowded onto rooftops. It seemed everyone carried a torch, lighting up the night sky. The balconies had people hanging over the rail, clinging desperately to their bit of space and vantage point.

Seth and Captain Brodst circled, back to back. The opposing trio pressed from the outside. Seth had finally gone beyond restraint, vowing he would not hold back anymore.

The dark orange flames on the rooftops reminded him of the battle at sea. The hungry black flames rising from the sinking ships. The battle that only four had survived.

Seth lashed out at laterally at Geoffrey, eyeing Shalimar as he moved. He thumped Brodst's right side, indicating a change.

The captain turned, lunged at Geoffrey.

Seth swept around the captain, arcing with his blade. He jumped into the air, kicked out at Shalimar with his left foot. His foot made a clean blow to the side of Shalimar's head. Shalimar went down.

Captain Brodst took a step back, hit Shalimar's head with the butt end of his sword. Shalimar's head slapped the dirt. He didn't move.

Men rushed into the circle to carry him out.

It was a two on two match. Father and son against the captain and the warrior elf.

Geoffrey and Nijal squared off against Seth and Ansh. Geoffrey made a quick move to separate the pair.

The crowd roared.

Both pairs were visibly fatigued. It became a struggle to make simple attacks and counters.

Then, as swiftly as it all began, it nearly ended. Brodst fell, taking Nijal with him.

Seth and Geoffrey had to sidestep to avoid going down as well.

The two circled.

Seth took measure of the Lord of Solntse. His movements were catlike and precise. He used the momentary lull to gather his strength, focus.

The Lord of Solntse's moves were sluggish. He bled from a wound in his side. He held the mid-length blade like a club.

Seth studied his eyes, trying to see if it was some sort of trick. He jabbed with his sword, whipped around, turned back, intending on elbowing Geoffrey, only to find the man wasn't there.

The lord had ducked out of the way. His blade was coming up to gut Seth from navel to sternum.

Seth saw the blade, had only an instant to react. He feinted, shifting too far back to support his weight.

He went down. Geoffrey pounced on him, pummeling him with the side of the blade.

The crowd grew quiet. The silence was apparent to Seth even as he struggled to break Geoffrey's grip.

He stared into Geoffrey's eyes. Geoffrey clearly wasn't afraid. He surely thought he held the strongest position, that he was moments from victory. Seth knew, however, that he could reach up and snap Geoffrey's neck in an instant. The lord would never have suspected Seth capable. He wouldn't even know what happened to him as his life ended.

Seth broke Geoffrey's grip, brought his hands up to the man's neck. He knew the next heartbeat would change everything. He promised Prince Valam he wouldn't hold back. But would Geoffrey's death bring the thing he sought?

He brought his fists down.

Geoffrey collapsed.

Seth pushed the other off, spun around, found his sword. He got to his feet, watched Geoffrey struggle to his knees.

Seth gripped the sword. He could end this with a single blow. Geoffrey expected it. Seth could tell.

When Seth didn't move, Geoffrey struggled to his feet. Geoffrey looked at Seth, his eyes seeming to ask "What are you waiting for? Strike, end this."

The image of Redwalker Tae flashed through Seth's mind. Loyalty to his cause is what he needed, not a dead lord. Geoffrey dead at his feet would solve nothing.

Seth tossed his sword to the ground at Geoffrey's feet. Geoffrey stared at Seth, awe written in his expression.

Geoffrey stumbled, fell forward, clinging at Seth's waist as his legs collapsed. Seth held him up.

The two walked from the circle.

At first the crowd did not roar or cheer. They simply parted. The viewers were as awestruck as Geoffrey had been. Men and women reached out to touch Seth as he passed.

Chanting began. In the hearts and minds of those who had seen the match the victors were clear. The Kingdom trio had won. They had won in grand style.

Seth assisted Geoffrey. The two went to the place Valam had been taken. A girl with long black hair followed in the shadows. Seth saw her out of the corner of his eye.

***

Seth helped Geoffrey to a bench just inside the door.

Valam lay near death. Keeper Martin and Father Jacob were gathered around him.

Valam motioned Seth to come closer. "They told me what you did," he whispered, "I believe. Word will spread. You will have your army."

"Save your strength. Rest," Seth said wearily.

The door opened and closed. Seth turned to see Princess Adrina enter. He had felt her presence in the shadows. There had been sadness in her mind and tears in her eyes then too.

"He dies," whispered Jacob to Seth, hardly looking up "I pray, but there are no answers."

"Oh, there are answers," Adrina said wiping tears from her eyes as she found sudden resolve. "There is poison in his veins."

"Poison?" asked Jacob.

"That's impossible," Geoffrey said, "Weapons are all checked and cleaned before each use."

"Trust me," Adrina said. "Anything is possible." She unshouldered the bag she was carrying and knelt beside her brother. She reached into the bag carefully, making sure to grab the tiny beast it held just behind the head. "Give me your hand, brother," she said. She took Valam's left hand in her free hand as he offered it. "Don't give in to the fear," she whispered. "It will be all right, I promise."

Geoffrey turned to Seth. "Know this," he said. "You've earned my respect and that of the Free Peoples."

Chapter Thirty Four:
Return to Imtal

Celebrations followed the competitions as they did every year. It was during the celebrations that the Kingdomers stole away from the great city of Solntse. The return journey to Imtal was brief and uneventful.

Upon her return Adrina held council with her father, Keeper Martin and Father Jacob. Her father was pleased to learn of the victory, overjoyed to know that Valam would recover from his wounds. No one spoke of the poison lest the whisperers know they had almost succeeded. King Andrew understood. He didn't need to be told that something grave had almost happened.

Adrina left the council, speaking not a word about how she had came to be in Solntse. For hours afterward she paced in her room. She was upset, agitated.

After the ordeal in Solntse she had not been able to vent. Keeper Martin, Father Jacob, and everyone else were always around. She had had no private time, no time alone to come to terms with what she had done.

A servant had delivered her dinner some hours ago. The food

sat on the tray untouched.

She was shivering, she realized. The air was cold. The thin dress she wore wasn't helping. She didn't care. A part of her wanted to catch her death of a cold.

She had sentenced Vilmos to death, so why shouldn't she suffer.

She saw herself in the long dressing mirror as she paced. She almost didn't recognize the pale, thin girl staring back at her. She hadn't been eating, couldn't find the will to eat.

Spotting the tray of food, she picked it up and hurled it at the mirror. The shattering brought the guards running.

"Get out! Get out!" she screamed at them.

They backed out of the room, eyes down turned.

"Treat people as you want to be treated," a voice said quietly from the corner of the room.

Adrina's eyes lit up. "Myrial? Myrial?" She turned. "Where are you?"

"First agree that you won't scream, no matter what."

Adrina walked in the direction of the voice. "Why are you speaking such nonsense?"

"Agree?"

"Yes, whatever you say. Oh Myrial, it is so good—" Adrina put a hand to her mouth, held back a scream. She sucked at the air until she could speak calmly. "Who? Who did this to you?"

"It is my own fault, my own fault for wanting it all. I should have seen—"

Adrina hushed Myrial by putting her arms around her. "I missed you. How could I have ever let this happen to you?"

"You didn't," Myrial said sternly.

Adrina helped Myrial to a chair. "You warned me not to meddle. Housemaster Bever did this to you, didn't he?" Myrial didn't say a word. Adrina continued, "We'll pay him back. Every bruise, every pain, accounted for."

Myrial turned quiet eyes to Adrina. "He has already paid," she said, "I killed him."

"He's dead?"

"Dead as can be. He said he made sure you were gone. He was going to kill me. I thought he was going after you next. I couldn't—"

"Don't," Adrina said. "No need to explain. I don't want to know. I trust you did what you had to do as I did what I had to do?"

"Valam?" Myrial asked, "I heard that he—"

"He will live. I have seen to that, but at what price?" Adrina said under her breath. She was asking herself, trying to come to terms with what she had done. She spoke loud enough for Myrial to hear as well. She couldn't bare the burden alone.

"The dragon mark?"

Adrina kneeled, looked up at Myrial. "Who told you of the dragon mark?"

"I hear things," Myrial said.

Adrina's face was screwed up, livid, her eyes filled with pain and rage. The fingers of her hands tensed while the nails dug into her palms. "I did what I had to do." She cried, her sobs echoed off the walls of the room. "I did what I had to do."

"No need to explain," Myrial said, turning Adrina's own words back on her. "I don't want to know. I trust you did what you had to do."

Adrina put her head in Myrial's lap. "Valam will live."

Myrial combed Adrina's hair with her fingers. "Yes, he will. You did what you had to do."

"And the elves, have I damned them too?"

"You have damned no one. Lord Geoffrey brings word of

renewed commitment to the Alliance from the leaders of the Free Peoples. Representatives arrive within the week. True, earnest discussions will begin."

Adrina looked up at Myrial. "How do you know such things?"

Myrial said coolly, "Bever's whisperers are now mine."

"He was a spy?"

"So it would seem."

The story continues with:

Mark of the Dragon

About the Author

Robert Stanek is the author of many previously published books, including several bestsellers. Currently, he lives in the Pacific Northwest with his wife and children. Robert is proud to have served in the Persian Gulf War as a combat crewmember on an electronic warfare aircraft. During the war, he flew numerous combat and combat support missions, logging over two hundred combat flight hours.

His distinguished accomplishments during the Persian Gulf War earned him nine medals, including the United States of America's highest flying honor, the Air Force Distinguished Flying Cross. His career total was 17 medals in only 11 years of military service, making him one of the most highly decorated veterans of the Persian Gulf War.

Overwhelmingly, readers agree that Robert's books are among the best they've ever read. His books have very vocal supporters who aren't afraid to voice their opinion, and they frequently do so in online communities and lists, such as at Amazon.com, where you'll find that his books are consistently listed at the top of their class. Strong reader support has led to strong sales.

About Reagent Press

Reagent Press is a small press that publishes both fiction and non-fiction titles. Current fiction titles include *Keeper Martin's Tale* and *Elf Queen's Quest* from the Ruin Mist Chronicles, *The Kingdoms & The Elves of the Reaches Book I* and *Book II* from Keeper Martin's Tales, and *The Elf Queen & The King Book I* and *Book II* from Ruin Mist Tales. Current non-fiction titles include: *Effective Writing for Business, College & Life*, *Essential Windows 2000 Commands Reference*, and *Essential Windows XP Commands Reference*.

Thank you for your continued support! Without the help of you, the reader, we will not be able to produce future works. If you liked this book, please tell your friends!

Edited by nSight, Inc.

Editor: Erin Connaughton
Special thanks to Sarah Hains for acting as the project coordinator!

Keeper Martin's Tale

The first book in the light path through Ruin Mist's history. Three heroes set out on an epic journey of discovery only to find that nothing is what they thought it was and that their world is undergoing a transformation that will change everything. Survival in a changing world depends on their ability to adapt and if they fail, their world and everything they believe in will perish.

Elf Queen's Quest

The first book in the dark path through Ruin Mist's history. After the Great War that divided the peoples, the kingdoms of men plunged into a Dark Age that lasted 500 hundred years. To heal the lands and restore the light, the great kings decreed that magic and all that is magical, be it creature, man or device, shall be cleansed to dust. Creatures born of magic were hunted to extinction. Any who dared call magic to their hands were butchered in the streets and afterward their kin were cast out of the known lands or hunted in the blood sport. The cleansing raged for so long that no human could recall a time without it and it is in this time that the Dark Lord Sathar returned from the dark beyond. The one hope of the peoples of Ruin Mist was Queen Mother, the elf queen of old. She saw a way out of everlasting darkness, a path that required the union of the divided peoples.

Ruin Mist Heroes, Legends & Beyond

Just about everyone that has read about Ruin Mist has wondered about the back story, where it all began, how the story all fits together, and now you can find answers in *Ruin Mist Heroes, Legends & Beyond*, a companion volume to the top-selling Ruin Mist books. *Ruin Mist Heroes, Legends & Beyond* allows you to learn about the dark elves of Under-Earth, common trades in the kingdoms, and beasts that go bump in the night. You can read the complete rules for King's Mate: the game, explore dozens of maps detailing the known realms, learn about the author, and more. In short, this is one book you shouldn't be without.

Sovereign Rule

A tautly told and suspenseful thriller from a hell of a storyteller!

Between fear and freedom lies the shadowed reality through which Scott Evers must go. If he lets them know that he's afraid for, and therefore cares about, those around him, the powerbrokers will take them away one by one until Scott's the only one left between us and those that want to control us. He's desperate to keep his wife and unborn child alive but as Scott's about to find out, the rules of the game have changed and those that control the rules, control the game. The weak and rash take power using bombs and terror; the strong and resolute by sovereign rule. Only one man is in a position to take back control, but can Scott Evers unravel the secrets and lies before it's too late?

Printed in the United States
22528LVS00002B/129